The Name
of the Beast

The Chain of Living Fire: Book 2

Phillip M. Locey

Elisahd Books

DURHAM, NORTH CAROLINA

Phillip M. Locey/Elisahd Books
5 Waterview Ct
Durham, North Carolina 27703
www.elisahdbooks.com

Publisher's Note: This is a work of fiction. Names, characters, places, and incidents are a product of the author's imagination. Locales and public names are sometimes used for atmospheric purposes. Any resemblance to actual people, living or dead, or to businesses, companies, events, institutions, or locales is completely coincidental.

Book Layout © 2017 BookDesignTemplates.com
Cover Art by Soheil Toosi

The Name of the Beast / Phillip M. Locey. -- 1st ed.
ISBN 978-1-947579-09-5

This book is dedicated to my wonderfully diverse friends,
without whom life would be much too bland.

*"The Beast has a name; it can be known
through the disorder that follows in its wake."*

–SIRRAN, OF THE CIRCLE OF TWELVE

ÍFELIAN

SEPATHIA'S LAIR

RINN-RHULIAN

NIGHTWING CASTLE

SKYWATCH HAVEN

BLACKFEATHER PERCH

GILSAGE

PASAXTREE

N
W   E
S

Contents

Chapter 1

An Irregular Audience

Annoxoria Nefzen pushed the toe of her black leather boot into the cheek of the slave held prostrate before her. Her too-human blood rushed through her veins, burning to be more – but as long as her designs faced this level of incompetence and disobedience, she doubted whether she might ever reach her potential. "Have you ever imagined there might be something greater than yourself?" she asked, the corner of her lip curled in a half-snarl.

The slave was not in a position to say much of anything, but it mattered little. His fate was already sealed. She spoke now for the benefit of the others, lined up on their knees, iron chains connecting them. Perhaps they were fellow conspirators or

perhaps they were simply bound to the single perpetrator –
another occurrence in a series of random misfortunes.

"Well, I can assure you there is …" Annoxoria answered
herself as her mind wandered to earlier that morning when the
cool and supple, scale-covered skin of her half-Nightwing lover
had pressed against her naked body from behind, pinning her to
their bed. Thuvian was so strong, and she'd gasped as his coal-
black hand caught underneath her hip and raised her back onto
him.

The rattle of chains brought her back to the throne room, and
she smashed the slave's face into the dusty floor of the oft-
neglected chamber. "You are all here for a purpose – to serve
me. If you cannot fulfill that purpose, or do so in an
unsatisfactory way, you force me to make you suffer."

Annoxoria nodded to her ogre guardsman, her tight black
curls bobbing softly with the movement. Thuvian complimented
her beauty regularly – how her intense, mahogany eyes dazzled
against her cherrywood complexion, or her equally intense
curves offset her lithe, muscular frame. Yet her slaves needed to
know better than to confuse such beauty with weakness.

The ogre, over seven feet tall and thick as a rhinoceros, had
no problem lifting the half-starved, human slave by the neck
with one strong hand.

"No, no please!" the man screamed in desperation as the
guard carried him toward the room's front wall, where a number
of long, iron spikes protruded. The other slaves tried to distance
themselves but were inexorably dragged along by the chain
running through the manacles around their ankles.

"You are all new here," Annoxoria addressed the pathetic
train before her, "so let this serve as your one and only free

lesson." She nodded again to the ogre, whose mouth spread in a nasty grin before he slammed the slave's body into the wall, its spikes piercing him in four places. Luckily for the man, one of those spikes found his heart – Annoxoria had seen one last for two agonizing days before expiring.

Her voice rose suddenly like a terrible storm. "You will go only where your whip-marshal tells you to. You will work until he releases you from your shift, and you will leave *all* the rubies you find during your shift in the buckets."

She looked over the faces of the half-dozen remaining slaves, several of whom desperately tried to stifle their whimpering. Man or woman, they all lowered their eyes as her gaze reached them, unwilling to risk challenging their new mistress. That was good; they wouldn't soon forget this demonstration, and hopefully stories of it would also help the dozens – or was it hundreds, now? – of other slaves working the mines to remember their place.

One more nod to the ogre spurred him to unlock the manacle from the ankle of the man embedded on the wall, then lead the others out of the room by the end of the chain. Annoxoria relaxed onto Thuvian's throne and crossed her legs as if the undignified business had never even happened. Duty demanded she meet the needs of court while her lover was away from the castle, though she relished these moments when they came. She felt so small, so fragile in Thuvian's presence, and needed these opportunities to remember and show her strength, to maintain balance, to not disappear beside his blinding perfection.

"What's next, chamberlain?" she asked, wiping a bit of dust from her eyelashes.

A gaunt man, wrapped tightly in a vermillion cloak with a sword sheathed at his waist, stepped into view from the antechamber. "Visitors, Lady Nefzen."

"Visitors?" she replied. She had not been apprised of hosting any ambassadors so soon and had little patience for commoners. "What manner of visitors, and what is their business?" She made no attempt to mask her contempt.

"They said they would state their business to you alone—"

"But you will want to hear it, my Lady."

Annoxoria sat up straighter. She heard the response, but not with her ears. The words, spoken in a deep, calm tone, were projected directly to her mind. Her eyes flickered around the room, searching for the speaker.

Two creatures stepped into view behind her chamberlain, both clearly *more* than human. The one in front was only slightly taller than an average man. She spied hints of a leather breastplate beneath his black cloak as he strode forward. The skin of his hands and face were a dark, ruddy color, like unchecked rust on exposed iron. His eyes were a bright shade of solid crimson with no distinction between iris and sclera, and twin, serrated horns curved upward from above long, pointed ears. He smiled at her, perhaps to show off the row of pointed teeth previously obscured by his lips.

The second creature was a stark contrast to the first. He towered at least a head-and-a-half over her chamberlain and wore only a draped loincloth for modesty. His skin was a luminescent pearl-white, flawless and stretched over the rippling muscles of a near-perfect physique. More striking, though, were the ample, feathered wings folded behind his shoulders. They were almost completely snowy white, but she caught flashes of scarlet at their tips, which matched the bright, wavy hair upon his head.

Annoxoria had the feeling this might turn into the most interesting day she'd had in a while. She wished Thuvian was here to share it with her. "You certainly are an odd-looking pair. What brings you to Nightwing Castle and the Court of Lord Thuvian Skullreaver?"

"*It is not Lord Skullreaver we have come to see.*" The darkly cloaked figure stepped closer, and she surmised he was the one speaking telepathically. "*We have come to bargain with the incomparable Lady Annoxoria Nefzen, Sorceress of Drachenmark.*" He bowed, at least able to show appropriate deference.

"Bargain, is it? What do you seek, and what have you to offer that would interest me?"

"*Surely it has not gone unobserved by one so skilled in the Craft that your mines possess a treasure even more valuable than the rubies you ship to Renramore?*"

Annoxoria's eyes narrowed. "From whence comes your knowledge, and what is your heritage? I would have it known if a fiendling is despoiling Thuvian's Court." She'd heard rumors from Thuvian's spymaster of an Abyssal creature operating in the Ifelian Corridor.

Despite her challenge, the visitor's voice remained steady. "*I did not intend to upset you, Lady Nefzen. In fact, I hold you and your Lord in the highest regard. I represent a cause, greater than myself, known as The Name of the Beast. But if you must call me something, Izefet will suffice.*" Izefet took a long look at the man recently mounted to the wall on spikes. Was that admiration she saw on his face?

"Well, Izefet, you still have questions left to answer." Annoxoria wasn't letting him off easily, fiend or not.

"*You of all people should know there are numerous ways to obtain information.*" Izefet extended an upward palm toward the impaled man. "*Some of them less subtle than others.*" He walked several steps closer until near enough to the throne that one of Annoxoria's ogre guards took a lumbering step forward, making sure his spiked club was visible. Izefet stopped and glared at the hulking creature but maintained his current distance.

"*It is not the* how *that concerns individuals like ourselves, Lady Nefzen. We really want to know the* what. What *it is I want from you, and* what *I can give you in return.*" He provided a moment for the thought to sink in before continuing. "*Your mines hold within them the most precious of jewels – the Living Fire. The Aasimar,*" Izefet glanced back at the winged creature who accompanied him, "*can feel their presence, and I know you're already aware of it, too. The Name of the Beast requires that I procure some.*"

Annoxoria laughed and leaned forward. "I see you are a court jester, how marvelous!" When Izefet's demeanor remained unchanged, she snorted. "And why on the Great Isle of Elisahd would I give you these Seeds of the Avatars, if I had any? Don't you imagine I have my own designs for their power?" She looked defiantly into the fiendish, crimson eyes of her petitioner, but without pupils, Annoxoria found them impossible to read.

Izefet languidly stroked his barbed chin. "*I mean no offense, for I am aware of your ... reputation. However, the Living Fire's true potential can only be harnessed by a few entities, for unfortunately their power is tied to this world. Potent as I am sure you are, Lady Nefzen, you are still an adolescent of the* arcane. I have access to those who could accomplish truly magnificent feats with these foci."

Annoxoria's brow furrowed and her cheeks grew hot. She stood and unfurled the cape from her shoulders. "Do you wish to see, Izefet the Damned, just how potent a sorceress I am?"

"I was not casting an insult, I assure you." Somehow, the Abyssal ambassador remained stationary. "I merely meant to illustrate that greater things could be accomplished with the Living Fire, even for your benefit, if you were to hand it over to me." Izefet took a few steps toward the hanging body of the impaled slave and extended a finger to test the point of a blood-stained spike protruding from it. "What would you do with the gems if I were not here to offer an alternative?"

He was testing her – Annoxoria could see that much. This Izefet thought he was clever, trying to lull her into revealing her designs in casual conversation, but there was no chance of that. "Perhaps your sources don't know me as well as they think. There is nothing you could give me that Lord Skullreaver and I cannot simply take for ourselves, given time. Sometimes, desires need to be tempered by patience."

The truth was, Annoxoria had been born into the wrong body. She'd always felt like a stranger in the one she owned, and when she saw her cruel parents melting away from the deadly spittle of a Nightwing when she was seven, it came with a dose of clarity. That power, that justice – and the form that embodied it – was the one her soul had been intended for. Perhaps others whose veins coursed with sorcerer's blood harbored similar desires, but Annoxoria's were fueled by a yearning to be her true self, not merely a craving for power. These desires carried over into her waking appearance.

Since becoming the consort of Lord Thuvian Skullreaver, all the outfits made for her were meticulously covered by tiny scales of cloth or leather, sewn over the base garment. She wore dark coloring around her eyes, giving the impression they were sunken cauldrons of seething power. The tight curls on her head were held back with a band adorned by rimmed, draconic horns.

"Come now," Izefet smiled, *"there must be something you want the Living Fire for? I do not think it coincidence that you managed to become the consort of a half-Nightwing. Being of mixed heritage myself, I certainly understand the appeal, but I also understand that most humans find half-breeds ... off-putting, to say the least.*

"I have to wonder if your affection for Lord Skullreaver – charming name, I should mention – might have deeper implications. After all," he gestured toward her personage, *"you have taken measures to appear not unlike a half-Nightwing yourself."*

Annoxoria let out a nervous laugh. "Have you ever seen Thuvian? I assure you, my visage doesn't compare."

"But it could, my Lady." For once, Izefet's tone betrayed emotion: excitement. *"Join the Name of the Beast, share the Living Fire with us, and I will help you transform into a glorious Nightwing dragon!"*

"Horse-dung." Perhaps her secret was discovered, but that didn't mean Annoxoria was going to allow herself to believe this charlatan. "Why should I trust that you can deliver on such a promise?" Of course, she had hoped to use the Living Fire for just that purpose, though she had no idea yet as to how. Like it or not, Izefet was right. Her focus until now had been on magic that mimicked the terrible force of the Nightwing: magic that would intimidate, that would scar those who defied her. Transmutation was a different matter entirely, and her research in the field was in its infancy.

"Because I only said I would help *you transform. The dweomercraft would be left to none other than Hadrian No More."*

The name hung in her mind, shocking her into silence. For two deep breaths, Annoxoria could hear nothing else. "Horse-dung," she repeated in a whisper. She looked from Izefet to the winged creature standing just inside the throne room. Gods if they weren't an odd pair. Was it really possible that this 'Name of the Beast' Izefet claimed to belong to had ties with the Dread Lich as well?

"Why in the Nine Hells would Hadrian No More take an interest in turning me into a Nightwing?" Her lips quivered just mentioning the name aloud.

Izefet shrugged. *"He is a peculiar one, who keeps his own reasons. But I shall give you proof, Lady Nefzen."* He walked back toward the antechamber and placed a russet hand on the shoulder of his winged companion, who stared silently at the hand with a distasteful look.

"Let my Aasimar friend stay here and help you search for the Fire. His kind are drawn to it, and it should quicken the task considerably. He will let me know when some is found. I have other business that requires my attention, but I shall return with a messenger who will leave no doubt he speaks for Hadrian No More, and he shall take possession of the imbued rubies. Do we have an agreement?"

Annoxoria licked her lips. Of course, something was wrong; she could feel it crawl along her skin. Just looking at Izefet, she knew better than to trust him. Still, if he could hasten her dream to become what she was born to be, she couldn't dismiss the opportunity out-of-hand. There would still be time to investigate the background of her visitors further, before any exchange was made.

"Return with your messenger, then. If he truly speaks for Hadrian No More, and can guarantee delivery on your promise, then we have an agreement."

"Excellent, my Lady."

"Now, leave me. My chamberlain will show you out." Annoxoria sank back onto the throne, already pondering her next move. She would have to include Thuvian, of course, but didn't want to tell him everything until she was certain she wasn't simply being played.

Chapter 2

The Golden Crucible

S affron shifted in her saddle to stretch her back. Her fourth straight day of riding alongside a merchant train on the way to Pasaxtree brought its fair share of soreness. The trading guild had been glad to exchange meals and transport of her luggage for the extra protection she offered, for the lands between Crioc and Ifelian were wild and untended. Calls making their way back from the forward wagons suggested they might end up needing it.

She snapped to attention atop Sheen and spurred her mare forward to the front of the nearest covered cart. "What is it?" she asked the driver.

"Banner-men," the man answered, stretching his neck to see around the wagon in front of them.

"Whose?" Saffron wondered aloud, but the driver had no answer. She strapped the shield from her back onto her arm, then urged Sheen to pick up speed. Weaving in front of the draft horses, she crossed to the far side of the worn path.

A squadron of riders approached from the west, riding in loose formation. Though not in uniform, they wore crude armor, and the lead horseman carried a banner that reminded her of something she'd seen but couldn't place: a clawed hand scratching the black field behind it, with runes of an unrecognizable script on either side.

Brigands didn't tend to make such displays. Were they soldiers of some army, travelling abroad? Could they be heading for Talon Barge, or did they intend on pillaging this very caravan? Saffron began humming a war-song, just in case.

She'd learned from Palomar how to summon fire, but as she cycled through the ways she knew how to manifest it, nothing seemed to fit her current situation. She didn't want to instigate an attack if the travelers weren't hostile, and if she needed to fend off a large group, she didn't want to scorch the entire caravan in the process. She needed something defensive, or at least a display to discourage violence, but couldn't think of anything in her repertoire.

The seed of melody died on her lips as the riders slowed to stare at the merchants, and as they grew closer, Saffron. One near the front clearly had orc-blood in him, displaying tusk-like incisors that protruded past his lower lip. Saffron gripped her spear tighter, keeping her posture rigid as she returned the dour looks of the passing company. Even if she couldn't think of a useful spell, they would find her weapon and shield a hard test should they turn aggressive.

In the end, the squadron continued south without conflict, though Saffron found it difficult to relax over the next hour, thinking back on her moment of magical impotence – all the more reason she needed a new teacher.

Only another day or two, she told herself, before the caravan reached its next destination and she earned a break from the saddle. Those passed without further incident, and as they reached Pasaxtree, she grew excited at the prospect of finally meeting a Shaper who could mentor her.

She and Dhania had passed through the city, as it happened, on their way toward Selamus last winter. Nestled near the southern base of the Wyrmsmoke Mountains, Pasaxtree had nevertheless received a dusting of snow, normally reserved for the peaks. Its slanted rooftops had been capped in white, and when looking through its northern gates, Saffron had found the wooded land of Ifelian pure and full of possibility. They'd only spent a day there, replenishing supplies, but it had been her first striking realization of how different the world beyond the borders of Begnasharan could be.

This time, however, as she drew near the gap between the Wyrmsmoke and Wyvernwatch Mountains, Saffron could see the seasons had transformed the forests of Ifelian from a land of ice to one of fire. The foliage was brilliant in shades of gold, orange, and scarlet, and when gusts of wind rustled the limbs, the leaves rolled back and forth like crackling flames.

Saffron smiled and leaned forward to whisper to her horse. "I have a feeling this is where we are supposed to be." Sheen tossed her head, tickling Saffron's neck with her mane.

The sun had dipped below the mountains by the time the caravan reached the city, and once the merchants paid their entry tax, Saffron bid them a hasty farewell, hopeful she might find the Golden Crucible before it closed for the night. She remembered seeing the shop at the end of a snow-lined street during her last visit, though she had not gone inside. The gilded sign had caught her notice as it shimmered, even on a cloudy day, as though painted with liquid gold.

Pasaxtree presented differently now that the city wasn't covered in white, but she hoped her sense of direction would not betray her. The architecture was nothing like Selamus, where everything gave the impression of cohesive grandeur. Pasaxtree had no palace, for one thing, and no obvious focal point for the appraising eye.

Unlike the walled cities Saffron had seen in the Cradle, Pasaxtree was not designed with defense in mind. It was a way-station, a home to numerous powerful guilds and merchant houses who benefitted from its position near an important crossroad. They hired their own mercenary militias to keep the peace, though the groups continually vied for influence. Located at the southern end of the Ifelian Corridor, it served as the starting point and destination for travelers moving north and south between two mighty mountain ranges. Pasaxtree also lay approximately halfway between Talon Barge to the east and the borders of Begnasharan to the southwest.

As such, the city was shaped by various hands over time and reflected a variety of building styles within its numerous Wards. Rather than fostering confusion, Saffron found the incongruence quaint. She liked the idea of knowing where she was based on the look of structures around her.

She followed a vaguely familiar row of stout, wooden buildings with wide chimneys and porches. Their walls and roofs were a deep, chestnut brown, and their simplicity gave an air of comfort and welcome. Her memory rewarded her when, in the soft glow of a hanging lamp striving to fight off the oncoming dusk, she spotted the shining carapace of the Golden Crucible.

"See, Sheen, we didn't even have to stop and ask for directions," she said as she walked down the street, leading her horse by the reins. Plenty of other people were out on such a fine, brisk evening, but Saffron didn't want to draw extra attention before gaining a better lay of the land. Willem, the Shaper of Selamus, had imparted to her that Cauzel preferred keeping a low profile, and she wanted to respect his choice.

Despite her intentions, she garnered more than a few looks from passersby as she and Sheen approached their destination. She assumed it was because of her Begnari heritage, though she noted a mixture of pale and light brown faces, similar to her own bronze complexion, among the residents.

Once in front of the Golden Crucible, she looped Sheen's reins around a post supporting the overhanging porch, took a deep breath, and tested the door to see if the shop was still open for business. The portal was several inches thick, and heavy, but the wood swung in easily on its hinges. The interior of the building was even darker than outside, with only sporadically placed candles providing small halos of light.

"Can I help you?" The deep, scratchy voice reached Saffron before she noticed the movement of its owner. The man was clearly past his prime, yet appeared spry as he wound around stacks of full shelves toward her. Short silver hairs sprouted from his pale-skinned face, with more of the same atop his head.

"Salutations, sir. Are you the proprietor of this establishment?" Saffron blinked as she adjusted to the dimness.

"I am. Corwyn Fleabottom, and—whoa, my lady, you're going to want to cover up before you catch a sickness."

His comment caught Saffron by surprise and she quickly looked down at her outfit, worried that she'd somehow lost a garment or two without noticing. Her clothes were still there, however: a sky-blue wrap-around skirt covered her from the waist down, with a matching top that hugged the middle of her ribcage, leaving her shoulders and midriff exposed. She felt a sudden discomfort crawl across her skin at his assessment; the style was common enough in Begnasharan.

"I can recommend a tailor who should have something in your size, if you'd like. I surmise you're not from around here, but the autumn nights can chill the meat off your bones if you're not careful."

Saffron shook her head, shrugging off the subject of her wardrobe. "Master Fleabottom, my name is Saffron min Furasi, and I was told by an acquaintance that the owner of the Golden Crucible would be able to pass a message along to Cauzel Blackfeather on my behalf."

One of Corwyn's eyebrows arched, and he crossed his arms over his chest. "So you're trying to reach Cauzel, eh? Might I inquire as to why?"

Saffron flashed a smile, hoping to allay the shopkeeper's suspicions. "I was told he might be willing to take me on as an apprentice."

"Oh." Corwyn's arms unfolded loosely to his sides, and he shrugged before turning to straighten a few nearby jars filled with colorful powders. "Might be so, if you're not too late. He just recruited a new batch of apprentices within the last moon, or was it two? Either way, I'm not sure he has any room left in that tower of his. Still," he looked at her over his shoulder, "I can let him know of your interest."

"I would appreciate it." Saffron looked around the shop more closely, trying to assess exactly what kind of goods were for sale. The shelves were lined with bottles and jars, pouches and books. She reached out to touch one of the delicate-looking glass vials. "Are these magical ingredients?" she asked, her wonder evident.

Corwyn stepped behind her and carefully picked up the piece she was looking at. "They are implements of the arcane, yes," he stated softly. "You are welcome to come back tomorrow and spend more time perusing my wares, but for now, my lady, it's time to close up the shop." He replaced the vial on the shelf, its purple liquid casting a slight shimmer in the candlelight.

"Of course," she answered and shifted sideways, uneasy with his proximity. "Thank you for your assistance. I will return at midday." Without another word, she slipped out the door and closed it behind her. Almost immediately, she heard the locking bolt slip into place. Corwyn was right about her outfit, she decided, as a gust of chill wind gave her bare stomach gooseflesh. She would have to find something warmer to wear tomorrow, but for tonight, she just wanted to find a hot meal and comfortable place to rest her head.

Saffron unwound Sheen's reins and led her up the street the way they came. Before long, the alluring scent of roasting meat led her to a street vendor selling sliced rabbit on tiny spits. She bought some and took the vendor's advice on a nearby inn to spend the night.

She paid extra for a private room, where the soft bed disarmed her completely. The accumulated fatigue of weeks on the road claimed her shortly after snuggling beneath the blankets. She woke refreshed the following morning with plenty of time before her appointment at the Golden Crucible.

Most of her belongings were stowed with the caravan she'd protected, and her first order of business was having the trunk that held them delivered to her room. It contained the supple armor and shield she'd worn for most of the journey, a few changes of clothes, and hidden in a plain cloth pouch, her most precious possession: the pendant of Living Fire. Though guarded with a sturdy lock, she would have to find a new, safe place to store it now that the caravan was moving on. For the time being, she had some shopping to do.

Having no idea how long an apprenticeship might last if Cauzel decided to take her on, she wanted to make sure she shouldered the responsibility of her own upkeep. Sir Golddrake had given her a small purse for her service alongside the Order of the Rising Moon, but Saffron would have to start earning again before long. She still had the harp from Prince Falcionus; after she learned a little more about Pasaxtree, she was confident she could find opportunities to play for money.

First things first, however. After she paid a runner to retrieve her trunk, Saffron set off to buy warmer clothes. She noticed many of the fashions worn about town were dyed brown or green – colors of the nearby forest in spring. Autumn touched it now, though, and she had become increasingly partial to fiery colors of late.

Once she located a tailoring shop, Saffron solicited the advice of the finely groomed, dark-haired proprietor, who she was pleased to find was a woman. Together they picked out an amber-hued woolen doublet, which fit snugly over a pine-bark brown, long-sleeved cotton shirt. She eschewed her skirt for a pair of tawny leather trousers, capped by her sturdy riding boots. A pair of golden leather gloves completed her new ensemble. She decided to leave her long, dark hair down instead of weaving it into its usual braid.

After picking out her new outfit, Saffron moved on to acquiring a few other personal items. She indulged on a slim, handheld mirror, a small, partitioned box full of local seeds, and a pouch of sweet, dried apricots. She finished by purchasing a new travelling pack for future exploration of the forest, and a small set of lock picks from a tinker on a street corner. Rogan had begun showing her how to use his during their trip to Talon Barge, but she still had much practicing ahead to become competent.

With only a few coins remaining of her stipend, Saffron hiked back to the Golden Crucible to see if the owner had managed to contact Cauzel Blackfeather. When she entered the shop, she was greeted by the heavy scent of burning incense. Low voices murmured from deeper in the room, but her view was obstructed by the small maze of display shelves.

She closed the door silently and drew nearer to the voices before announcing her presence. "Hello? Master Fleabottom?"

A singular, sharp caw from near the ceiling startled her, and Saffron bumped into the nearest shelf, rattling its contents in a distinctly unsubtle demonstration. Looking up, she saw a large, black bird perched atop a bookshelf, regarding her intently.

"Noki, be good." A tall, slender man shifted into view from behind the furniture. His jet hair clung to his head in tight curls, and his long nose was hooked like a beak. His eyes struck her as kind, and while his face was not weathered, she had trouble determining his age. "You must be Saffron, yes?" He nodded assuringly, though kept his hands folded inside the sleeves of his loose, violet and black robe.

Saffron stood tall and cleared her throat. "I am."

His features relaxed, but fell short of a smile. "You can call me Cauzel. Corwyn and I were just having a nice chat. Please, join us."

"Pull the bolt on the door first, if you don't mind," Corwyn's voice called out. "We don't want our conversation interrupted."

Saffron did as asked, unsure from his tone whether the request was a jab at her own intrusion. Upon reaching the back portion of the room, she saw Cauzel and Corwyn already seated across from one another at a smoothly finished table. A cask of wine and three cups rested upon it, with a third chair vacant between the two men. Perhaps she wasn't interrupting after all. She took a seat and Cauzel filled her cup.

"Welcome, Saffron," Cauzel began, his voice even and unassuming. "Corwyn tells me you've sought me out to inquire about an apprenticeship."

She nodded. "I travelled all the way from Selamus, where Willem the Shaper recommended I visit you. He said you may be able to help me and gave me this letter to deliver to you." Saffron took the offered cup and ventured a tiny sip after handing over a small square of folded and sealed parchment.

The vintage was sweet, but spices she didn't recognize had been added to it, causing the flavor to change as she swallowed. She set the cup down.

"Help you learn magic?" Cauzel asked as he opened the letter.

"Help me learn more control, yes: to better manipulate my power, to change what it can do."

"So you have the gift?" Cauzel looked up briefly from his correspondence, obviously intrigued.

She nodded again, but he had already buried his long nose in the parchment. "Palomar taught me how to unleash my fire. How to let it burn through my song," she continued. Saffron couldn't help thinking back to the last time she saw the magnanimous Aasimar alive. She'd had no idea she should've said 'farewell.'

Wrinkles scrunched Cauzel's forehead as his eyebrows rose and he looked up, "Palomar?"

"Of course," Saffron closed her lids and shook her head, deciding where to start. "I am a performer," she started as she opened her eyes, "and Palomar was the Aasimar who showed me music could be a conduit for magic."

"Aasimar?" Corwyn finally contributed, shooting a glance at Cauzel.

"Fascinating," Master Blackfeather added, setting down the letter and leaning closer to Saffron. "Willem mentioned the Aasimar in the last letter he wrote. I would love to meet one in person. So, you use melody as your Shaping vehicle? It is not the usual way, but I am familiar with the Bardic tradition." Cauzel leaned back again and his thoughts seemed to turn inward. Silence lingered for a moment, then he sat up straight to ask, "I don't suppose you could provide a demonstration?"

Saffron glanced at all the shelves, lined with exotic wares. "I don't know. My magic is mostly related to fire, and I'd hate to damage the shop."

"Ah, I second that sentiment," Corwyn declared, peering at Cauzel to await agreement.

"You wouldn't have to cast an actual spell," Cauzel responded. "I have a good ear for this sort of thing. If you simply start singing as if you were going to manifest, you could stop before actually producing an effect. I would still be able to hear the magical potential in the notes. Come now, give it a try." He leaned over the small table, turning his ear toward Saffron.

Though she felt a little put on the spot, there didn't seem to be any harm if she just began a song. Saffron cleared her throat, resting a hand at the base of her neck. She remembered the time she used song to persuade the night-watch at the gates of Synirpa, and decided to try a few bars from that melody, figuring it safe enough.

With a low voice, slowly rising, she introduced the lament. Mid-way through the first stanza, though, Cauzel raised his hand to cut her off.

"That is enough. I feel the compulsion starting to take hold. You clearly have the gift," he said, nodding as he turned to face her once more.

She waited for him to continue, but he seemed to be carrying on an internal dialogue with himself.

"That was beautiful," Corwyn commented, tapping his fingers on the tabletop. "So, you know Willem, eh?" He drank deeply from his cup of wine. "I've heard stories of the war in the east. They say this King-priest of Chelpa was a Channeller … haven't seen that kind of magic in an Age. You fought in the campaign opposing him? It must have been terrifying, facing that kind of magic. I applaud your bravery, Lady Saffron."

"Magic is not the only reason Willem said I should seek you out." Perhaps bolstered by the compliment, Saffron decided to risk opening up further. She looked from Corwyn to Cauzel, whose bushy black eyebrows arched once again.

"When I left Begnasharan almost a year ago, I thought only of the dreams lying ahead of me. I had an invitation to play at the Court of Selamus, and was so excited about seeing more of the world that I convinced my parents to let my younger sister accompany me.

"Once our caravan crossed the River Chelhos, however, we were ambushed and my sister was taken as a slave. She was forced to do unspeakable things in the harem of the King-priest." Saffron kept her eyes on the table as she remembered the long months searching for her sister. Her mouth grew dry, and she paused to take another sip of wine.

"Even though we were eventually able to free her … twice," she managed a glance up at Cauzel to find him listening intently, "I realized there must be many others who don't have anyone so capable looking for them."

"I am deeply sorry for your sister's experience." Cauzel sighed and ran a hand through his hair. When he lifted his arm, Saffron saw fabric hanging off of the sleeve, cut into the likeness of feathers.

"Aye," Corwyn seconded before downing the rest of his cup.

"I can see where your story might be heading," Cauzel acknowledged. "I remember writing to Willem about the disappearances Corwyn first noticed along the Ifelian Corridor and how I suspect the travelers are being taken for nefarious purposes. Is that the other reason you sought me?"

Saffron nodded.

Cauzel bit his lower lip, then looked up at the bookshelf where Noki was nesting. "I think we may be able to help one another, Lady Saffron. Corwyn, why don't you tell her how it started?"

"Hmm, well, let's see." The older man clicked his tongue a few times, searching for the proper beginning. "Several months ago, a fellow merchant I'm on friendly terms with came to me with a story of misfortune, asking if I could lend him some money. A shipment of goods coming south from Korenland never arrived, and though documents assured it left, there was no further sign that the caravan ever existed. It was a total loss."

"I wasn't sure I bought his tale, but he was a friend and I decided to help him out. Not long after, more stories started circulating through the guilds of attacks along the Ifelian Corridor, targeting other trade shipments. Now, I know how rumors can gain a life of their own, so I wasn't paying too much attention, until my own delivery of exotic components failed to show up." Corwyn shook his head as he refilled his cup from the cask. "I took a big hit on that one – Ettercap silk glands are not easy to come by."

Cauzel cut in as Corwyn started paying more attention to his drink. "It was then Corwyn first asked for my help. He was getting nowhere with the guilds, as they all pointed fingers at one another. You see, traditionally, the Ifelian Corridor has been a very safe route through the forest. The nearby presence of the Eladrin discourages most brigands from raiding, though the road is far enough west that the Eladrin do not interfere with trade themselves."

"But then," Corwyn took over, "survivors started showing back up at Pasaxtree, reporting seeing lizardfolk during the attacks. Now, that doesn't smell like the work of the trade guilds to me." He reclined in his chair to take another sip, and a momentary silence fell over the table.

"So what does that mean?" Saffron finally asked, eager to reach the conclusion.

"I began my own investigation," said Cauzel. "I looked into whether specific types of goods were being targeted, or specific merchants or guilds. The attacks didn't present any obvious pattern to me, but I still hold there is some kind of purpose to them. Though it could certainly be an attempt at power consolidation from one of the guilds, none of the major ones were completely spared, and to some degree it hurts them all for merchants to lose so much business. I suspect, therefore, that the perpetrator is someone outside of Pasaxtree's society."

Saffron shrugged. "That makes sense, I suppose."

"However," Cauzel continued, "many are distrustful of those who openly practice the arcane arts, and I am known as such. So, not all of the guilds have been entirely cooperative in my investigation, which has hindered it significantly."

"And you think I may have more success with them, given my local anonymity?" Saffron spoke the thought for him.

Cauzel smiled. "I see I am not the only one adept at catching on."

"I could give you the names of guild contacts most likely to be useful," Corwyn offered.

"There is another possibility I have mentioned to Corwyn, but it should not leave this table. At least, not yet." Cauzel extended his arm and Noki flew down to perch on it. From a hidden pocket, Cauzel produced a few seeds and dropped them on the table. As quickly as they fell, Noki claimed them with his beak.

"Other research has brought to my attention the presence of an adolescent Nightwing, living deep within the swamps of Ergilad. They are known to be clever, and covetous, and sometimes exercise control over other reptilian creatures. I don't want to incite panic by spreading this, but it is possible she is beginning to exert dominance over her perceived territory. My theory would also explain the presence of lizardfolk at the ambushes."

"May the old gods save us if that's true," Corwyn declared.

"I've never seen a Nightwing," Saffron said, barely louder than a whisper.

"Few have and lived to tell about it, so don't go looking for it, if you want my advice." Corwyn smiled and clasped Saffron's shoulder. "I'm starting to warm up to you, which doesn't happen often, so I'd prefer if you weren't melted into a pile of acidic sludge."

Saffron finished her wine. "I appreciate the concern, Master Fleabottom, but I can look after myself. Give me a list of your contacts, and I will see what I can uncover from the guilds."

"That can wait another week, given the upcoming summit on Drachenmark, wouldn't you say, Corwyn?" Cauzel asked as he stood. "Given a little time with our new acquaintance, I may be able to aid in her espionage." Corwyn nodded his agreement.

Cauzel then directed toward Saffron, "I take it you haven't found a permanent place to stay yet?"

"I'm at an inn for now," she answered, standing as well.

"Good. How do you feel about a trip into the forest? I can make room for one more apprentice, I think. You're likely well beyond the others in practical experience, if not magical theory. You should meet them, though, as your training will require moving in to Blackfeather Perch. I want you to have a full understanding of what you're getting into before deciding for certain."

"I would very much like that," Saffron answered. "I bet there are trees and flowers here I've never encountered before."

"Flowers are for spring, my dear, but trees are something we have plenty of."

"Let me gather my gear and my horse, and I can meet you at the northern gates," she said.

Cauzel bowed his head. "The northern gates it is, Lady Saffron. Is an hour enough time?"

She nodded, the excitement of new opportunities flashing across her skin like a lightning storm.

Chapter 3

Blackfeather Perch

"You have a beautiful animal," Cauzel said from atop his own white mare.

"I hope you haven't been waiting long," Saffron replied as Sheen trotted up to the gate that marked the northern edge of Pasaxtree. Though the boundary consisted of handsome stonework and wrought iron, the gate was designed for aesthetics. The wall tapered to the ground several horse-lengths from where the gate was mounted. A wide road of flattened rocks extended as far as she could see to the north.

"It is no trouble, Lady Saffron. I rather enjoy the caress of the wind. I see you came prepared," he said, nodding at the spear and shield hanging at the ready on the left flank of her horse, "though I doubt you'll find need of them."

"Prudence demands it," she replied. "We are travelling the road where the disappearances have taken place, are we not?"

Cauzel nodded. "For a distance. We'll head further east before we reach the area where most of the ambushes have taken place. The journey should be safe enough."

"Well, then," Saffron smiled, "do lead the way." She'd used the last hour to not only gather and store her belongings, but write another letter to send back to Begnasharan with the caravan. The worry her parents must be feeling at the prolonged absence of their two daughters could only be imagined. What was expected to be only a few months had turned into almost a year. Saffron had half a mind to return with the merchants, but the world was a fascinating place worth exploring, and if she embraced the comfort of home so soon, she knew she might never leave again.

Sending them her love, she was sparse on providing details of their adventures, especially when it came to Dhania. She assured their parents they were both safe and planned to return, but she couldn't promise when. The news would bring heartache, but it was better than imagining their children were already dead. They had always supported her independence, after all.

Cauzel led the way north along the Ifelian Corridor, which Saffron noticed was both well maintained and heavily used. For the first hour they couldn't go far without passing a wagon or troop of riders heading home after a hunt. The weather was perfect for a stroll. Trees grew thick to either side of the road, their falling leaves dappling the sunlit path. It was as if the sky were raining gold, and each breath of the crisp air filled Saffron's lungs with new vigor.

"How long is the trip to your home?" she asked.

"Ah, Blackfeather Perch is my special sanctuary. We're not going to rush. Feel free to observe the land and ask any questions you might have along the way." She noticed Cauzel kept a tighter hold on the reins than necessary while he rode, and fought the cadence a bit as well, as if not fully comfortable riding a horse. "We'll take a day or so on the Corridor, and two more through the back-country," he finished.

Saffron looked at the foliage and the green grass peeking through where leaves had not completely smothered it. "That should be plenty of time. I've noticed how the land slopes upward to the west, but haven't had time to study any maps of the region. This is the beginning of one of the nearby mountain ranges, yes?"

"It is," Cauzel answered. "This is the southern end of the Wyrmsmoke Mountains. They curve north like the spine of the world, all the way to the Great Glacier. They're practically impassable, and form the western border of the Midlands. The Ifelian Corridor follows roughly parallel to the range, until the forest ends at the border of Korus."

"I see. We do not have woods like this in Begnasharan. The trees are beautiful. It must take an ocean of water to keep such large specimens thriving."

"We get a healthy amount of rain, but not overly much. I suppose the run-off of snow from the peaks feeds our numerous streams as well. I never really considered it, to be honest."

"Water is life, Cauzel."

After a moment of consideration, he looked at Saffron and nodded. They rode with comfortable silence between them for some time, though they gave polite greetings to travelers passing by. They made good time and stopped at a rustic inn Cauzel recommended, just as twilight painted the bright, autumnal colors with a touch of gray.

He paid for separate rooms, though Saffron offered to share. She had spent countless nights in shared quarters while travelling with the Order of the Rising Moon, and no longer thought much of it. Cauzel insisted, however, and she didn't push the issue.

In the morning, after a warm breakfast, they continued riding north. Ever fewer sojourners shared the road, and though Cauzel seemed just as light-hearted as the previous day, she found herself a little tighter in the saddle. She knew they had to be drawing close to where the attacks on caravans were reported.

Before they ran into any trouble, however, Cauzel declared it time to break east and leave the Ifelian Corridor behind. The ground on either side of the road had become damp, and the vegetation reflected a more water-saturated environment. Saffron made note of a distinctive willow with a huge knot flanking the road to the west where they left it.

Heading deeper into the forest, Saffron was struck by the impression that most of the trees must be very old. They had probably stood watch over their glades for centuries, and she wondered if they took kindly to intruders. After an hour of winding through the gaps between maples and poplars, oaks and sycamores, Cauzel reined his horse to a stop and dismounted.

"Is it time for lunch already?" Saffron asked. "I thought we might cover a little more ground before breaking—"

"We are not stopping to eat. There is something I must do."
Cauzel fetched an object out of his saddlebags. "Could you join
me down here, please?"

"What is it?" Saffron patted Sheen's neck and swung her leg
over the horse's hindquarters. "Is something wrong?" she
inquired, though Cauzel didn't seem alarmed.

"Have you ever seen an Eladrin, Saffron?" he asked in
response.

"Eladrin? You mean the wood-spirits?"

Cauzel chuckled, then reached two fingers into a leather
pouch to draw out a pinch of powder. "I suppose that means
'no.' The Eladrin are the Firstborn – they were here before even
the earliest members of humankind. They took shelter in the
primeval forests when humans began to systematically eradicate
them."

He stood directly in front of Saffron, and she noticed he was
only a shade taller. She had previously misjudged his height due
to his thin frame. "Please clear the hair from your forehead," he
said.

She gathered the loose sable strands off her face with one
hand.

Cauzel used the tip of his powdered index finger to draw on
her forehead. "Once the Eladrin established their ancient
sanctuaries, Trigilas, the Father of Spells, developed a powerful
magic ritual to protect them. Called the 'Veil of Trigilas,' the
ritual was a ward placed over the new forest realms of the
Eladrin. Any creature not inside the boundaries of the Veil at its
casting, or their subsequent birth, are overtaken by confusion
upon entering a protected domain."

"What do you mean by *confusion*?" Saffron asked.

"Intruders are unable to maintain a sense of direction or purpose. Essentially, they forget any reason they might have had to enter the territory, and are unable to effectively navigate within it. It is a powerful magic, and probably the only thing that allowed the Eladrin to survive in the wake of Arkmus's Revenge. Now, hold still." Cauzel placed his hand on top of Saffron's head, closed his eyes, and began mumbling in a tongue she didn't comprehend. When he was finished, he opened his eyes, removed his hand, and said, "There. I have bestowed my Shaper's Mark upon you, which will ward the confusion for one lunar cycle. I expect you not to betray this gift or despoil eladrin territory while under its protection."

"Of course not," she replied, raising her hand to her forehead. She could not feel any residue from the powder, nor any effect on her person. "What is *Arkmus's Revenge*?"

"You are not a student of history, then?" Cauzel observed. He moved to mount his horse as he spoke, so Saffron followed suit.

"It is often referred to as the 'Gift of Arkmus' in human lore." Cauzel paused, perhaps waiting for a spark of recognition, but Saffron hadn't heard that term either. "Eons ago, when the Avatars of the gods roamed Elisahd, Arkmus's fell in love with Eriane. She refused his advances, however, for her heart had already been captured by the Firstborn. Out of spite, or so the story goes, Arkmus incited a love of battle and the longing for strife in the bosom of humankind."

"Not a very nice thing to do," Saffron chimed in, mostly to show she was listening.

"Not very nice at all. Humanity turned its new lust for war against the Eladrin, who had only looked out for their younger brethren until then. They were caught unaware, and slaughtered by the thousands until they finally fled from all shared civilizations."

Saffron looked at the woods with a new sense of danger. It occurred to her that, if she was about to enter the realm of the Eladrin, they may not be pleased at her doing so. "That sounds awful. I had never heard this story before. I assumed the old gods were mythical, until I saw with my own eyes the power of Gholdur's War-priests. We do not tell such tales in Begnasharan."

"Willem mentioned news of the Chelpian leader threatening his homeland. You saw this King-priest yourself?" Cauzel asked.

Saffron shook her head. "We battled his forces in the provinces of Halidor and Rosegold. He was stopped, finally, at the Battle of Naresgreen, but I was not present."

Cauzel sighed, but she got the feeling it was a show of excitement and not deflation. "If the gods have renewed their interest in our world, the future will be shaped by it." He spoke aloud, but the words didn't seem directed at her.

Saffron kept her concerns private, but continued her watch on the woods, flinching every time the movement of a squirrel, gathering food for winter, jostled the dry leaves. She had no idea what the Eladrin looked like, but her imagination conjured creatures made from the wood of trees, watching from the hollows, threatening her with soulless eyes.

Several things Cauzel mentioned sat uneasily with her, but it took time to realize something he didn't mention perhaps bothered her most. "Cauzel" she said, finally figuring out what it was.

"Yes, Lady Saffron?"

"Are we in eladrin territory now?"

"We are. But you are safe with me," he answered.

"If you had to protect me from the magic of the Veil with your Shaper's Mark," she continued, "how is it you are unaffected? Who protected you? Are you not human as well?"

The silence in the wake of her question was deafening, and Saffron's muscles tensed as she waited for a lie to surface. She brought Sheen to a halt and reached for her spear, convinced she had been lured into some kind of trap. Was it a mistake to have brought her Living Fire pendant?

Cauzel's horse continued for another few steps until the Shaper realized Saffron was no longer following. He halted and turned his steed so they were looking face to face. His eyes assessed her, stopping on her left hand curled around the shaft of her weapon. His body slumped as he released the breath he had been holding. "I was born here," he finally said. "That's why I'm not affected."

"You were *born* here?" she repeated.

"Yes." He raised both his hands toward the sky. "I was born under the boughs of the Eladrin."

Saffron narrowed her eyes. Why was that something worth keeping secret? "I am too ignorant to know what that means." She kept the grip on her spear but didn't raise it.

Cauzel shook his head and shrugged. "It means I would be untrustworthy in the eyes of most humans, if they were to learn so. Perhaps it is the reason I was called to be a Shaper. Who knows?"

"I am a Shaper too, you realize. And a foreigner to this place. Why would I judge you for this?"

"I don't know," he replied. "I suppose I am just so used to dealing with suspicion."

Try as she might, Saffron had difficulty reading Cauzel's face. There didn't seem to be anything sinister behind his explanation, however, and she slid the end of her spear back into its support loop. "I'm sorry for that, but I am too used to men lying to me. How much farther do we have to go?"

"We still have another day of travel. Blackfeather Perch resides at the eastern edge of the forest, in the foothills of the Wyvernwatch Mountains."

"Shall we continue, then?" she said, squeezing her horse's flanks to get her moving. Saffron couldn't shake the feeling of being watched over the next few hours, but nothing came of it. With no inns this far into the wilderness, they slept under the trees. Slivers of moon and starlight pierced the canopy, reminders that the sky was still there.

Morning brought new energy with it, and Saffron's trepidation of the day before was replaced by curiosity and wonderment. Making it through the night without harassment allowed her to ease her worrying about an eladrin ambush and start paying attention to the variety of flora populating the woods of Ifelian.

They passed the hours in a friendly back-and-forth, Saffron spotting trees, bushes, and even wildlife she had never seen before, and Cauzel identifying them for her. He even allowed time for her to dismount on more than one occasion to collect and compare leaves, or feel the texture of strange bark that fascinated her.

Saffron enjoyed herself so much, she found it a shame her attention was about to be diverted by more social matters, significant though they were. She had already digested her midday meal when the land began to noticeably incline. The horses had to work harder for every step, and soon the trees began thinning as well.

Breaks in the leaves above allowed patches of a limitless blue sky to reveal themselves, and between a pair of boulders ahead, a well-worn trail began its winding ascent into the rapidly rising hills.

"Behold, the approach to Blackfeather Perch!"

Saffron heard the satisfaction in Cauzel's voice.

"Now, let's see what trouble my apprentices have gotten into while I was away." He winked and dismounted. From here on, they would have to lead their horses on foot.

After a pair of switchbacks in the path, they cleared the western side of a bulging hill, and Saffron spotted their destination for the first time. A slender tower of gray stone jutted upward from a looming cliff. It must have been a true labor to build in such a location, she thought. The tower rose at least five stories in height, and was capped by a balcony and turret with a conical roof. A white banner, bearing the likeness of a raven, flew in a stiff wind.

"I completely forgot about Noki," Saffron blurted. "Where has he been these last few days? Isn't he your pet?"

"My familiar," Cauzel corrected. "And I sent him ahead to bring word of our arrival. He should be here waiting, unless one of my apprentices used him to send another message."

Saffron shielded her eyes from the sun as she gazed to the top of Blackfeather Perch. "I think I see someone up there."

Cauzel glanced upward, then brought his concentration back to navigating the increasingly steep path. "That would be Iliana, one of my apprentices," he said. "The reason I brought up the Eladrin yesterday is because I wanted you to be prepared when you met your fellow initiates. They are not all human, you see. In fact, most of them aren't. Well, not fully."

"What do you mean by that?" Saffron looked up at the tower again, but whoever had been on the balcony was no longer there.

"Iliana and Thaelios are Eladrin, and their appearance can be … off-putting to humans, as ours is no doubt to them. You will get used to it, but I wanted to give prior notice. Aurus is a human lad from Pasaxtree, and Dyphina has fey heritage, by her account. We're still figuring her out – the approach to Shaping can be different from one culture to another."

"Fey? As in her father was a djinn or somesuch?" Saffron didn't know Cauzel well enough to gather whether he was just having a bit of fun with her.

"A wood nymph, actually. And it was her mother." She didn't detect a trace of humor in his tone.

Saffron decided to swallow any questions until meeting the other apprentices herself. She wanted a chance to make her own judgements as to their character, without undue influence from their master. These were to be her peers, after all.

The path wound like a snake around the hills, cresting several before ending in a tunnel of hedges, which lined a bridge over an expanse of open air to the edge of the tower. The thick greenery forming the channel blocked nearly all sunlight, and Sheen grew nervous halfway through. "Where are we stabling the horses?" she asked, unable to see anything beyond Cauzel except for a wide, wooden door.

In answer, he raised his right hand and placed it against the living wall of the tunnel. The hedge responded by peeling back to reveal a fresh passage. Cauzel turned and led his horse down the new corridor, and she followed. The tunnel soon opened into a spacious structure, smelling of pack animals and fresh hay. Sure enough, there were half a dozen stalls, some of which were already occupied by quarter horses.

"How is this possible?" Saffron asked, bewildered. "There was nothing outside of the hedge when we first entered!"

"Was there not?" Cauzel smiled as he walked his mare into one of the vacant stalls.

Saffron stood mute with a raised eyebrow as she tried to wrap her mind around the introduction of space from seemingly nowhere. When she realized no further explanation was coming from Cauzel, she followed his lead and found Sheen a place in the stable.

"One of the apprentices will be down to take care of the animals later. We should introduce you as quickly as possible, before Iliana creates an entire history for you." Cauzel read the question in Saffron's expression. "The one watching from the balcony – she has something to say about everything."

They returned the way they came on foot, finally reaching the door Saffron had noticed at the end of the original tunnel. Once again, all Cauzel did was place a hand on the surface of the portal. His palm radiated a strobe of white light, and the door opened of its own accord. "Welcome to Blackfeather Perch, Lady Saffron."

The inside of the tower reminded her of the Palace of Selamus – the walls of the first floor were smooth and white, the furniture ornate, polished wood. Plush cushions lined the dual lounges of the sitting room, and a set of stone steps climbed in a spiral around the inside of the outer wall.

"Please, make yourself comfortable." Cauzel opened a cabinet and selected a bottle of wine. He uncorked it and poured a glass, which he handed to Saffron. "If you wait here, I shall fetch my new apprentices. Keep in mind I am still getting to know them myself."

"Of course." She accepted the wine and took a drink to steady her nerves. "And thank you," she added, raising her glass.

Cauzel nodded, then took sweeping steps toward the stairs, ascending them two at a time. Once he was beyond view, Saffron exhaled and sat on one of the couches. She couldn't quite place why she felt so anxious. Meeting new people came naturally to her – as a musician, she was introduced to strangers after essentially every performance. Perhaps it was the fear of being judged by others she had no basis to judge in return. All she had learned of magic was from Palomar, who she now understood had a very different approach to Shaping than most. What if she couldn't learn what Cauzel had to teach?

Cauzel retruned while she was still in the throes of her rare bout of insecurity, leading a train of robed individuals down the stairwell. Saffron stood and smoothed the front of her doublet as the apprentices reached the floor and fanned out in anticipation of introductions. Cauzel stood behind them and cleared his throat.

"Everyone, it is my pleasure to present Lady Saffron, from Begnasharan. She is a veteran of the wars to the east, and is joining us to explore the talent manifested during that campaign. She has been referred by my honorable friend, Willem of Selamus."

"Arprah sith shael morethel?" a petite female declared in a fiery tone.

"Please speak in Illanese, Iliana," Cauzel requested.

The woman sighed before complying. "You heard me. Did she already take the trials?"

Cauzel shot her a disapproving look. "I am waiving the trials in her case. Saffron manifests in the Bardic tradition."

"That's not fair!" Iliana spouted. "Do you know how hard I had to study to beat out the other hopefuls?"

"Iliana, that's enough!" Cauzel took a moment to regain his composure while a wave of shame seemed to wash over his pupil's face. "As long as you are living at Blackfeather Perch, I am the arbiter of all things. What was your first lesson?"

Iliana pursed her lips, but relented under the invisible pressure of her mentor, rolling her eyes as she replied, "Respect our fellow Shapers."

"Correct. That applies to me, as well as to Saffron."

While Cauzel chastised his apprentice, Saffron took the opportunity to study the initiates' strikingly different appearances. Iliana, and the male next to her in the middle, were clearly the Eladrin. While some of their features were similar, their coloring was far from it. Though both short – a good head shorter than their human counterpart – Iliana was the more petite of the two. They all wore loose training robes, unflattering in her opinion, leaving only the skin of their necks and faces exposed.

Iliana's complexion was metallic bronze, with iridescent flecks sparkling when the light hit them, like she had been painted with tiny crystals. Her hair was long and black like Saffron's, except highlighted with streaks of violet. Her ears were almost twice as long as a typical human's, slanted, and tapered to a point. Yet her eyes captured the most attention. They were wider, more oval, and completely lacked distinguished pupils. Their entirety was a shade of purple mimicking the color in her hair. They rarely blinked, and Saffron found their scrutiny unnerving.

Like Iliana, the male Eladrin had metallic skin, but his was a reflective, pale silver. His hair was thick, shoulder-length, and just as silver as his skin, painted with streaks of ocean blue – the same color as his inquisitive eyes.

"Saffron," Cauzel moved on, "this talkative lass is Iliana Yurehileh, one of the sharpest students, and biggest pains, I have ever encountered. Beside her is Thaelios." He gestured to the male Eladrin. "They both came to me from Gilsage, the official capital of Ifelian. Of course, humans are not allowed there, so in my mind, this is a wonderful opportunity for you both."

Cauzel moved to stand behind the human. "This is Aurus Shadowguard, a natural talent, not unlike yourself." Aurus was newly into his adulthood, handsome, with a thin build and reddish-blonde locks that fell forward onto his face. He smiled widely at her, and Saffron could almost see the impure thoughts playing out behind his pale blue eyes.

She smiled back in spite of herself, then quickly shifted her attention to the final apprentice. Standing on the other end of Iliana was an undeniable beauty. It dawned on Saffron that Cauzel had not been teasing about her fey heritage. The woman had human features, but flawless, as if she were the gods' imagination made real. Despite the modesty of her robe, Saffron suspected her perfection did not end at its neckline.

"And lastly," Cauzel announced, "is Dyphina. She has travelled the farthest to be with us, and I hope to learn just as much from her as she does from me."

Dyphina blushed slightly at his words, her skin practically glowing with its own light. Her thick hair was a wash of green hues, like tree moss mixing with seafoam, and its natural waves were punctuated by several tight braids dangling from her temples, one of which gave her fidgeting hand something to do.

"It is a pleasure to meet you, Lady Saffron," Dyphina said while dipping into a polite curtsey.

"Yes, welcome to Ifelian," Thaelios added, his accent thick and lyrical.

Saffron nodded, and her eyes briefly shifted to Aurus's of their own accord. "I look forward to everything we can learn from one another."

"Well, now," Cauzel added. "I must check how they progressed on their assignments while I was away, but Saffron, perhaps you would like this opportunity to roam about the tower and get a feel for your prospective new home?"

"Certainly," she agreed.

"Excellent. I shall find you when we are done." Cauzel herded his apprentices back upstairs, leaving Saffron alone on the bottom level of Blackfeather Perch.

She sipped the remains of her wine, reflecting on how little she knew of the world, and basking in the excitement of this new place. She returned her empty glass to its tray and took a stroll around the open space of the tower's base.

As she browsed the first floor, it struck her that Blackfeather Perch could have been any affluent home – nothing obtrusive marked it as the abode of a renowned Shaper. A pair of ornate chandeliers hung from the ceiling, each holding dozens of small candles. There were tasteful murals on the wall, plenty of places to sit and study, expensive-looking décor, and the expected comforts of the wealthy. Noticeably absent were the mounted heads of fantastic creatures, bursts of colored light, and animated objects that she'd imagined.

Saffron decided to head upward and see what surprises might be in store on the higher levels. The stairway offered the Perch's first glimpse of the outside world, as an arched, paneless window, roughly large enough for a housecat to stand in, was hewed into the thick stone. The width of the tower this close to the base only allowed her to see a patch of blue sky, but she enjoyed the feel of the cool air circulating on her skin as she passed.

The second floor, less extravagant than the lower level, seemed more focused on practicality. A well-stocked kitchen, laundry, and storage pantries were sectioned off on either side of a central hallway. She hadn't seen any servants of yet, and wondered if Cauzel somehow managed to maintain the entire place himself.

A landing immediately off the stairs on the third floor ended in a stout, iron door. A raven was painted upon it, and she found it solidly locked, so she continued to the next level. The fourth floor had a welcoming feel. The interior walls were darkly-stained wood instead of stone, and sconces every few feet held tridents of candles. Thinking the proximity dangerous, she ran her fingers over one of the flames and noticed a complete lack of heat.

The soft glow of light off the wood lured her down a short hallway that ended in a rounded room. A large, circular table dominated its center, and upon it were personal items: a deck of cards, partially filled metal tankards, short stacks of books – some of which were open. A scarf and gloves were discarded on its surface, as well as what looked like a jewelry box, an ink quill, and parchment.

Curved benches, lined with cushions, surrounded the table, and four small hallways extended from the room like the spokes of a wheel. A cursory peek revealed wooden doors on either side of each hallway, all of which were closed. Saffron guessed these were the apprentices' quarters.

Not wanting to intrude upon their privacy, she ignored the hallways and slid past the table to the far wall, which was dominated by a large, rectangular window. This one was paned with glass, though latches suggested it could be opened to let in fresh air. The view it offered was impressive. Looking down, she saw the roof of the forest below: a sea of fiery colors extending in waves to the horizon.

She sat down on one of the benches and continued looking out over the woods, letting her gaze become unfocused until the colors bled together. Was she ready for this? The last year had taken her down a path she could have never predicted upon leaving Begnasharan, but wasn't that the point of leaving? She had already fought in a war, discovered an ability to conjure fire, met a slew of strange creatures, and fallen in love ...

She didn't want to think about Jaiden. Perhaps she was a fool for turning away Rogan, but he was good for Dhania, and she could only hope for their happiness. The time had come to turn a new page in her story, and she was determined to follow her heart – to pursue the things that gave her joy. For the time being, that meant learning more about herself. Becoming an apprentice to Cauzel Blackfeather and living with people she previously thought only resided in mythologies might be a fine start.

Saffron stood and made her way back to the stairwell, wondering where everyone else had gotten to. Her question was answered as she climbed further up the curving steps. Voices carried from the next floor and echoed against the stone of the outer wall. The fifth floor was the top, or at least as high as one could get from this set of stairs. They ended in a landing that bore a metal door similar to the one on the third floor. This one was cracked open, however, and painted with a single green leaf on its surface.

She pushed the door open further and saw all the apprentices at work behind broad tables, one for each of them, either writing on parchment with feathered quills or carefully measuring out liquids from one container to the next. Cauzel stood behind Dyphina, watching over her shoulder as she adjusted the strings of a lyre. Thaelios and Iliana were deep in an animated discussion while working separately, conversing in their foreign tongue.

Saffron had taken several steps into the room before Aurus looked up from his manuscript and smiled. "Welcome to the laboratory, Saffron."

Cauzel looked up after Aurus spoke and waved her over toward Dyphina's table. Saffron took in the rest of the room on the way, which seemed to be stocked similarly to the Golden Crucible. Nearly every inch of the curved walls were blanketed by bookshelves, and iron racks stood beside each table, covered with various implements used for experimentation. A ladder, leading up to a wooden trap door, hid in the narrow space between two of the heavy-looking shelves.

When Saffron drew closer, Cauzel lifted the lyre from the table and passed it across to her. "I thought you might check if the instrument is tuned correctly. Dyphina has attempted a simple enchantment upon it, but can't seem to get the pitch quite right."

Saffron nodded and accepted the lyre, not sure what they were expecting to happen. "I'll see what I can do. Anything in particular you want me to play?"

Dyphina shook her head, her flawless face tight with concern. "It doesn't matter. It just needs to be in tune."

Saffron used her thumb to strum midway across the strings, listening to the resonance of each note. She smiled reassuringly at Dyphina and made some adjustments before strumming a few more times. After another couple changes, Saffron settled her weight onto the tabletop and began plucking out a tune she learned early in her career, one she often used to warm up prior to performances.

To her surprise, once she started playing, the sound of her lyre was joined by a harmony of invisible instruments, giving the impression a full ensemble was playing. Saffron's fingers kept working from memory, though she looked down to see Dyphina beaming radiantly. Cauzel smiled as well from behind her, his hands delicately squeezing her shoulders.

"Wonderful," he announced, looking down at the top of Dyphina's head. "I knew you could do it."

Saffron caught movement out of the corner of her eye as the other apprentices ceased their previous activities and circled in closer to listen. She finished out one more stanza, then let the final note linger across the laboratory before handing the lyre back to an obviously pleased Dyphina.

"That was beautiful," Aurus said from behind her, and she turned to find him standing rather close.

"Thank you. It was nothing, really," she said, shifting to her feet and shrugging. "Magical instrument ..."

"Lady Saffron," Cauzel interceded. "Would you join me on the balcony, please?" He walked to the ladder against the wall and climbed, throwing open the trap door once he reached the ceiling. Saffron waited until he'd disappeared through the hole at the top to ascend herself.

She had thought the view from the window two floors down was incredible, but the vista from atop the tower took her breath away. A crenellated wall gave some protection from the wind, but she still had the impression she was a bird, hovering in flight. Open sky and clouds called from above, and she could see for miles in every direction. She circled around the circumference, drinking in the changing view from rocky peaks in the east to blazing forest in the west.

"What are your impressions so far?" Cauzel asked, ducking out of the wind. "I know you only had a brief introduction to your peers, but do you think you could work side-by-side without setting them aflame? Except for Iliana, of course," he smiled.

"They seem like a talented group," she replied. "I think I would be very lucky to have the opportunity to study magic under you. If you think I have potential, I would like to try." Saffron gazed over the mountains to watch a hawk catching a draft of rising air off the sun-warmed peaks. Like the hawk, she felt the lift of possibilities.

"Excellent," Cauzel answered. "I have yet to see what you can really do, of course, but I trust Willem's assessment implicitly. He is one of the wisest—"

Saffron saw what Cauzel had seen – Noki, approaching from the forest, ascending toward his master. His black form, agile and determined, climbed with every flap of his wings until he alighted on the Shaper's outstretched arm.

"There, there," Cauzel reassured his familiar, "what's got you returning in such a hurry?" He reached with his free hand to slide the curled message from Noki's leg carrier. The bird hopped along Cauzel's arm to take a steady place on his shoulder, allowing his master to unroll the parchment with both hands.

Saffron felt a bit slow. "I thought you'd already sent Noki ahead of us …"

"I did," he answered as he began reading, "but Iliana sent him back to the Golden Crucible immediately after with a request for scaveling tongues; patience is not her strength." After a brief pause, Cauzel sighed deeply and lowered the parchment.

"What is it?" Saffron asked, taking a step closer, fighting the urge to snatch the message and read it for herself.

"Corwyn's asked for my help," Cauzel explained. "Seems his nephew, Jorn, took a job escorting a merchant wagon. Master Fleabottom failed to talk him out of it, but gave him half a Yune Stone as a compromise."

"What's a Yune Stone?"

"Yune – Goddess of Destiny?" Cauzel asked, but Saffron hadn't heard of her and shook her head. "Doesn't matter. Corwyn's half of the stone turned red, which means Jorn will experience bloodshed by the next turning of the moon. He's afraid his nephew's likely to be ambushed and wants me to intercede."

"I'll go," Saffron offered without hesitation. "I'll find him and keep him safe."

Cauzel stared at her in silence, a gust of wind blowing Noki's feathers straight out, causing him to bury his beak in his master's bushy curls. "You know it might be dangerous …"

Saffron shrugged. She'd actually hoped for an opportunity to meet whatever they were up against firsthand, and maybe put her spear to use again. "Consider it my trials. I'll leave in the morning."

Chapter 4

The Winged Oracle

Be'naj folded her legs underneath her and sat on the patch of soft grass she'd cleared of fallen leaves. The Ifelian Corridor lay about a hundred strides to the west, and beyond it, the swamp of Ergilad. This was the spot that appeared in her trance-vision; all she had to do now was wait for the wagons to arrive. Everything was unfolding like before, except for this confounding pull. Some kind of energy – she didn't know what else to call it – was beckoning her to move further south.

Be'naj first felt the pull when her wings started coming in, but a few days ago it increased considerably and was strengthening by the moment. Not understanding the pull in the first place, for she had never succumbed to it, she had no idea what it meant. Yet the change was noticeable, and change scared her. Be'naj always looked a little different from the other Eladrin growing up around her: tall for her age, luminescent skin, and hair like polished brass.

When the other girls her age started bleeding for the first time, however, she began sprouting wings from her shoulder blades as well. She was called *freak, hunchback, bird-brain.* The teasing she could handle, but the worst part was realizing her mother had lied her entire life about the father Be'naj never knew.

The shame was too much for her mother to bear, and she left one morning, never to return. Once she was gone, the teasing devolved, for there was no one to stand up for or protect Be'naj. She abandoned her home in Gilsage, too, once the bullying became unbearable.

Years had passed, but she never dared go back, surviving on her own ever since. Her routine seemed to be working quite well, keeping to herself most of the time, but she'd started intervening on the behalf of travelers whenever her visions forewarned her of danger. The Eladrin codified distrust of humans, but those she'd saved so far seemed courteous and genuinely thankful for her assistance. They treated her better than her own people. Yet now, something beyond her control was about to cause a disruption, and Be'naj couldn't help worrying.

She tried to clear her mind of such concerns, however, and focus on accepting the will of Shecclad. Others may have found it odd, but embracing the religion she'd been exposed to during her childhood allowed some measure of peace and direction as an adult. Her devotion provided stability and motivation.

Among the pantheon of the Eladrin, Shecclad the Sky Lord was second only to Eriane in terms of reverence. Her choice only made more sense once her wings began to grow – though they never developed enough for her to fly. Be'naj attributed her occasional trance-visions to the grace of Shecclad and never got any indication she was mistaken.

The sound of hooves on the road and the groaning wheels of a loaded wagon reached her keen, elongated ears, alerting Be'naj to the approach of the merchant train well before it came within view. She stood and unsheathed the arming sword from its harness between her wings. With calm strides, she walked to the tree where she'd propped her shield and fastened it to her left arm. The gryphon emblazoned upon it eternally screeched a battle-cry, or so she liked to imagine.

If this vision's revelation was as true as the others, the northbound wagon would be set upon by lizardfolk any moment, and she would do her best to defend it. "Shecclad, give me mastery over my adversaries," she prayed, and then stalked from tree to tree, drawing nearer to the road.

The merchants were close enough for her to spy them beneath the lower-hanging limbs of her final hiding place – two covered wagons, no doubt laden with valuable goods, were flanked by four riders each. Surely some of them were brought along as guards, but there was no telling yet how many attackers lay in wait.

It didn't take long to find out. Not far from the road, on its western side, a bog spilled out into the lowlands beneath the slopes of the Wyrmsmoke Mountains. Its surface was punctured by reeds and other thick vegetation, which served as excellent camouflage for the semi-aquatic lizardfolk. A dozen of their muscular, scaled bodies broke from the swamp as if on signal, dripping brackish water as they frantically charged the lead wagon.

Be'naj glided from her hiding place as well, circling to catch the furthest of the lizardfolk from behind. She hoped the merchants were competent enough to hold off the creatures until she had time to thin their numbers. There were at least twice as many as last time.

Fortunately, the reptiles hadn't attached to the concept of armor, and judging from their crude weapons, metalwork of any kind seemed beyond their capabilities. That gave Be'naj an advantage, for the steel of her sword was sharp, and the interlaced chain links of her shirt and skirt could turn back swipes from the creature's long claws.

She waited just long enough for the lizardfolk to surround their prey – a tactic she anticipated based on previous encounters – before silently accelerating toward their unprotected rear. She held no desire to be cruel, and sought to kill with the fewest blows possible: one across the hind leg to disable, another to pierce the heart, and her first opponent fell.

The lizardfolk closest to Be'naj hissed when they noticed her presence, but she could already hear the protestations of the horses and shouts of the humans as they scrambled to defend themselves. Her best option was to focus on neutralizing those nearest her as swiftly as possible.

A pair attacked her in tandem. The force behind the stone-headed club as it *thunked* against her shield told her all she needed to know about the creature's ferocity. Her attacker was powerfully built, and its bulk considerably greater than hers. The second opponent tried to distract her, staying just beyond the reach of her weapon as it danced and clawed at the air. They weren't the only ones who could play the feinting game, however.

Be'naj rotated her body to face the unarmed reptile, showing her back to the clubber while watching from the corner of her eye. She waited until she'd lured it into raising both arms above its head, preparing to slam its weapon down for a killing blow. While its midsection was exposed, she spun back around, sword trailing her right shoulder and slashing across his chest. Tough as the beast's scales were, they were no match for the torque of her sharpened blade, and her adversary collapsed with a horrid death-wail.

With his partner bested, the unarmed lizardfolk had little chance. It leapt forward, counting on its aggression to catch her by surprise, but she merely used the momentum to impale it on the tip of her sword. Be'naj moved on to spar with yet another adversary wielding a crude spear, when the oddest sound reached her ears. There, in the middle of heated battle, she swore she heard *singing*.

A woman's melodic voice tickled the inside of her ear for a distinct moment before suddenly, out of the corner of her eye, she caught a bright flash of orange light. Be'naj raised her shield to provide an extra moment of defense, and dared to take a look back toward the wagon to spy how the fight was progressing elsewhere.

To her utter surprise, she saw a dark-haired woman in red leather armor, fighting fiercely with a round shield and short spear. The tip of the spear glowed red-hot and left a trail of flame as the warrior whisked it around with expert agility. The lizardfolk were clearly frightened by the threat of fire, and with two of their number dead at the woman's feet, the others were already taking long glances back toward the swamp.

Be'naj renewed her attack on the reptile in front of her, and after severing its crude spear with a hacking blow, she was able to quickly end its life with a well-placed thrust. No sooner had she squared her body to face another ambusher than the remaining lizardfolk hissed, one after the other in rapid succession. Cutting their losses, they all bolted toward the safety of the swamp, disappearing under the stagnant water before Be'naj could even consider what to do about it.

Satisfied the threat was over, she turned her attention to assessing any losses and getting a better look at the surprising, fire-wielding maiden. Be'naj found the woman staring right back at her, eyes wide and mouth agape. It was a reaction she had come to expect. A couple of the other humans were armed and had obviously been fighting as well, though they dropped their weapons and shouted as they ran to the side of a fallen comrade.

From first glance, Be'naj guessed he was dead, but she was still captivated by the woman in red taking tentative steps toward her. She knew it didn't make any sense, but it almost appeared as if the woman was happy to see her.

"Where did you come from?" the woman asked, speaking the same Illanese as the rest of the humans Be'naj had encountered, though with a different accent. Her features were also darker than the others. The tone of her question didn't seem suspicious, however, merely incredulous.

Be'naj responded in the broken dialect of a language she hadn't used since private tutoring sessions as a child. Illanese had been an impractical indulgence as a young Eladrin. "I saw attack from the forest. I help to fight." Now that the fighting was over, she also felt the pull calling to her strongly from where the group's horses were gathered.

"And you just happened to be walking by with a sharpened sword and shield at the ready? You're an Eladrin, aren't you?" The woman's spear was no longer burning, but Be'naj thought she could still feel heat coming off her. "But that's not all ..." she said, circling behind Be'naj, who rotated to continue facing her.

"Yes, me Eladrin. How you know?" Be'naj had never seen a human until a few weeks ago, and imagined it was just as strange for one of them to recognize a member of her people.

"I don't know how it is possible," the woman continued, excitement raising her voice, "but I cannot deny you appear to be part Aasimar as well!"

Chapter 5

Skywatch Haven

Saffron found it hard to believe, but while barely wider than her shoulders, the woman's wings were brilliant white, ending in bright, metallic feathers similar to Palomar's, only not quite so glossy. Their tips matched the hair on her head, which shone like liquid brass cascading down to frame her opal neck. "Is it true, then?"

"What is Aasimar?" the woman responded, her uniformly green eyes widening slightly.

Her speech was simplistic, but Saffron guessed that was only because she rarely had occasion to use Illanese. Her voice possessed the same lyrical lilt as Illiana's, but she was slightly taller than Saffron, who in turn dwarfed the thinly framed apprentice. Perhaps this woman knew that side of her heritage by another word; she was clearly not completely Eladrin.

While Saffron desired to delve into the mystery further, she also needed to address the matter of the ambush. The heavy-set, head merchant was already waddling over to join them.

"I have to look into the attack, but please stay," Saffron requested. "I would love to speak with you more. Do you have a name?" Saffron rolled her eyes at her inane question. Of course the woman had a name – she was a person, not an abandoned pet.

"I am Be'naj," she said, placing a hand on her chest.

"Be'naj," Saffron repeated. "That's a beautiful name. Mine is Saffron."

"Many thanks, both of you, for fighting off those horrible beasts!" The merchant didn't seem to care that he was interrupting. He rested a hand on his knee while leaning forward to catch his breath. "How did you know they were going to attack us?"

Given the language barrier, Saffron thought it easier for her to answer. "I didn't know for sure, of course, but there have been reports of ambushes along the Ifelian Corridor in recent weeks. As I said when I joined you, one of your guards has a concerned uncle, who asked me to keep an eye on him during this trip. Be'naj, here, deserves the greater share of thanks, I think." She looked toward the bodies of the four lizardfolk Be'naj had dispatched. "But you are most certainly welcome."

"That was quite a trick with the fire, and a clever disguise on your friend," the merchant added as he looked Be'naj up and down. "Are you travelling illusionists or something? If you're performing in Korenland anytime soon, I'd certainly pay to see your show."

Saffron looked from the merchant to Be'naj, unsure how much comprehension she had of the conversation. "I don't think we're headed that far north anytime in the near future." Probably easier to play along than try to explain things.

"A shame," he responded before clearing his throat. "Well, I really must be on my way. We've got a man to bury," he tilted his head back over his shoulder, "and I don't want to be here if those foul creatures return for their fallen. Let me give you a token of gratitude before we leave ..." He walked to the rear of his wagon and started sifting through a wooden crate.

Saffron used the opportunity to repeat the question he had originally asked, in a whisper. "How was it you knew there would be an ambush, Be'naj? I am not complaining, of course, but you appear to have been prepared for it." She tapped the blade of Be'naj's sword, stuck in the soft ground, with the tip of her spear. The woman didn't respond immediately, and Saffron wondered if she'd understood.

"I saw in a vision," she finally said.

Saffron hadn't expected that. "You saw the attack in a vision beforehand? Like a dream?"

"Yes, like dream, but Eladrin not sleep same as humans."

"Really? You dream, but you do not sleep?" Saffron asked, fascinated. She was about to follow with another question when the merchant interrupted again.

"A little something for your trouble." He smiled, though the sweat beading on his forehead indicated he might be going through more trouble than either of them. He handed a bundle to Saffron. She could clearly smell the calming scent of lavender when she unwrapped the white cloth, and inside was a wide candle with a long wick.

"Thank you, it's lovely." *And completely impractical for me to be carrying around at the moment.* It was heavy enough that she could probably use it to knock one of the lizardfolk unconscious if they returned.

"And for your friend …" The merchant held out an engraved, mahogany comb to Be'naj.

"Many thanks," she said, accepting the gift.

The merchant lingered as if expecting something further, but as the silence grew he took his leave. "Well, I must be heading on, as I said. Mayhap our paths will cross again!"

The other members of the merchant train had loaded the body of their fallen comrade onto the second wagon and mounted their horses by the time their leader assumed the reins once more. With a reluctant groan, the wheels began moving, and Saffron nodded at the guards as they passed.

"My thanks to you and my uncle," Jorn announced with a wave.

She'd only had an hour or so to get to know him, but he seemed like a good man, and she was glad he'd made it through the ordeal safely. Sheen followed for a dozen paces or so before realizing they were not continuing with the merchants.

Saffron met Be'naj's gaze and nodded toward the road, indicating she should keep her company as she walked. "So, you were telling me how your people don't sleep like humans …"

"Yes. Eladrin no sleep, we enter trance. Umm …" Be'naj seemed to be searching for a better word. "Meditation?"

Saffron smiled. "I think I understand."

She knelt over one of the lizardfolk Be'naj had slain and examined its body. It wore no clothing and its skin was cold. She sighed. They hadn't brought anything with them into the fray except a few, rudimentary weapons. Certainly nothing she could use to decipher their true motivation, or whether the attacks held a purpose beyond thievery.

Saffron looked up at Be'naj, who was watching her carefully. "Do you know what their diet consists of? What they normally eat?" She brought her hand to her mouth and chomped up and down to mimic feeding. "Would they want to take people for food?"

"I not know," Be'naj answered.

Saffron stood and made her way across the road, trying to follow the lizardfolks' path of retreat. She stopped when she sank to her ankles in the wet ground. Peering into the boggy waters, she could see no signs suggesting their attackers were submerged nearby. No bubbles of air rose to the surface, though the marsh was thick with vegetation.

"How were they planning on transporting the goods?" she wondered, this time mostly to herself. She thought she could make out where the pool ended, as the backdrop of the Wyrmsmokes rose, but no clear trails into the foothills presented themselves. Perhaps an underwater channel connected this bog to other lakes?

"Not much to go on," she whispered, taking a final survey of the environment west of the road. At least she'd confirmed lizardfolk were behind some of the attacks. From her understanding, the Ifelian Corridor had existed for quite some time, so it was unlikely that travelers were encroaching upon the creatures' territory, unless they belonged to a tribe that had recently relocated. All she could think to do was report what she had seen to Cauzel and Corwyn to see if they had any ideas. They knew the geography better than she.

Saffron's attention returned to the intriguing stranger. "You will have to pardon me, for I am new to the region. I would like to speak with you a little more – is there someplace safer we can go? Would that be all right?"

Be'naj stared at her, silently. It was almost impossible to read those pure green eyes. "Yes," she said, finally, but did not otherwise move.

Saffron waited for more, but when it wasn't forthcoming she contrived a gesture that was some combination of both nodding and shaking her head. "Good. We can ride my horse if you like. She can endure two riders as long as we aren't travelling far." Clicking her tongue brought Sheen ambling toward her.

While Saffron stowed her spear and shield, as well as the merchant's gift, Be'naj retrieved and sheathed her sword then strapped her own shield into place. Saffron mounted and urged her horse forward a few steps before extending a hand to help Be'naj climb on as well.

Instead of grasping her hand, however, Be'naj closed her eyes and began to tremble.

"Is something wrong?" Saffron asked.

Be'naj opened her eyes, though her lips still quivered. "I feel …" she put one, slender finger upon her bottom lip and exhaled, her body visibly calming as she did so. "I am meant to find you."

Saffron didn't understand, but it struck her as serendipitous to have such an encounter with a woman who seemed to bear some Aasimar traits. Not many others on this world, perhaps not even

Be'naj herself, would recognize such characteristics. Indeed, she was completely befuddled as to how such a blended person could exist. For, unless Saffron greatly misjudged her age, Be'naj was born before Palomar and his cursed brethren were banished from Mount Celestia.

"Well, then," she smiled, "let's go somewhere to get better acquainted, shall we?"

Be'naj grasped her extended wrist and vaulted into the saddle behind her. "I know a place," she said softly, then slid her slender hands along Saffron's hips for stability.

Saffron guided Sheen eastward into the woods, and Be'naj gave instructions along the way to lead them to her chosen spot. Much of the next hour was spent in comfortable silence, with Saffron very aware of the physical closeness between her and her passenger. She found it didn't bother her, like it might had Be'naj been a man. She considered the proximity of Be'naj pressing against her a search for security, rather than the sort of crude, sexual advance she was accustomed to.

"Just ahead." Be'naj pointed to a path worn through the cover of fallen leaves, and Saffron directed her horse to take it. They had to lower their heads to avoid a barrier of low-hanging branches, but once they broke past, the world opened up before them.

Saffron paused to admire the breathtaking beauty of the forest clearing. The scenery seemed more likely born from imagination than something created by the natural world. The most prominent feature was a hill, rising probably five times her own height, in the center of the clearing. From the top of the rise, a geyser spouted clear water. The spray dissipated over the side of the slope in a fine mist, creating a magnificent rainbow in the adjacent air. The surface of the hill itself was multi-hued: blues and reds and yellows swirled against brown, like the feathers of tropical birds she had seen in the markets of Begnasharan.

Pools of steaming water gathered at various heights along the decline of the hill, overflowing and feeding into lower pools all the way to its base. The top half of the mound was bare of vegetation, but the lower portion bore swaths of green grass, adding additional color and a hint of softness to the spectacular monument.

White, billowing clouds eased by overhead, with plenty of sunshine flooding the clearing. The blue sky lead to a meadow of purple and white wildflowers, still blooming, even this late in the season. Off to one side, Saffron spotted a raised plot of earth, sectioned off with lengths of wood to form what looked like a vegetable garden. A trellis supported a number of vines within the space. Huddled beneath the branches of an ancient elm on the far periphery of the glade, a simple shelter of logs, with a roof of layered pine needles, squatted in obscurity.

"This is where you live?" Saffron was both asking and guessing it to be the truth. "It's the most amazing thing I've ever seen."

Be'naj slid out of the saddle behind her and dismounted. From above, Saffron noted the chain shirt she wore had slits to let her wings through. She supposed all her clothes must have the same alteration. The overlapping links of the garment were of high quality, but the fit wasn't right. A bit tight around the shoulders, it also hung only just below her ribcage. While possibly her preferred style, Saffron suspected the armor was simply old and fit the woman before she hit a later growth spurt.

Likewise, the skirt was a little impractical, not quite reaching Be'naj's mid-thigh.

Saffron dismounted as well and looped Sheen's reins around a thick branch, picking one with ample foliage nearby to snack on. She watched as Be'naj unstrapped the shield from her arm and set it down in the grass. Next came the buckle of the strap around her torso, holding the scabbard in place between her wings. When her sword rested on the ground as well, Be'naj looked back at Saffron.

Holding her arms outstretched to either side, she declared in a musical tone, "Neldoren Erelonde." Seeing the lack of comprehension on Saffron's face, she amended, "Skywatch Haven."

"That's the name of this place?" Saffron realized she was going to have to work harder on her communication. She wondered how long it would take Cauzel to teach her the eladrin language if she asked. "Nel-dor-en Er-e-lond. It's truly wondrous."

Be'naj smiled and gestured to the patch of sun-bathed grass where she'd set her belongings. After she took a seat, Saffron followed suit.

"Do you live here alone?" She knew it wasn't the smoothest beginning, but Saffron couldn't help herself.

"Yes," Be'naj answered simply. She sat with her legs crossed beneath her, back straight.

"How long? I mean, do you have a lot of visitors?"

A look Saffron took for sadness washed over the half-eladrin's face, though the eyes still kept her guessing. Her chin tilted toward the ground. "No visitors. I am alone many seasons."

"But, you're amazing." The compliment slipped out as Saffron's empathy asseted itself. There must be some story about how such a unique creature came to live alone in a forest glade, but her instincts told Saffron it might not be a happy one. "Are there other Eladrin like you, Be'naj? With wings?" she clarified.

Be'naj's wings folded close in response to the question, along with a shake of her head.

"Do you know how you came to have them?" Saffron could see Be'naj was close to shutting down completely, but she felt an urge to learn the answer. She didn't know what it would mean if other Aasimar were roaming the world, but knew it had to be significant.

"I no have them when born," Be'naj explained, though she continued to look down as she spoke. "Mother tell me my father was eladrin soldier who died in the fighting, but I never know him.

"I was different – my skin," she touched her bare forearm, "my hair," she said, grabbing hold of one of her tight braids. Be'naj exhaled and looked up momentarily with an empty smile. "Too tall. I have no real friends, so I study books. I learn your language," she stifled a laugh, then shrugged. "Little."

She swallowed and the momentary joy completely left her voice. "When I come of age, my wings grow. I try to hide them, get them to stop, but they get bigger."

Saffron had always envied Palomar's wings. It hadn't occurred to her that under the wrong circumstances, such a blessing could be a burden. She reached over and placed her hand on top of Be'naj's.

Be'naj looked up at the sudden touch, but didn't pull her hand away. After a moment of uncertainty, she clasped her fingers around Saffron's and held them tightly. "I pray to Shecclad for what to do. He is Lord of Sky. The shrine's mystic was only Eladrin to accept me. My only friend. The other children call me names. I ask mother again to tell me who is my father, but she only cry and say he is gone." Be'naj shrugged. "One day, she is gone, too. I not know who my father is."

"It must have been a difficult way to grow up." Saffron squeezed her hand before releasing it. How could she tell Be'naj she thought she might know who her father was? Or at least, *what* he probably was.

"I was the one who left my parents," Saffron began. "I know they love me, and cared for me and my sister as best they could. We didn't live extravagantly, but I never lacked for anything, really. My mother is artistic, and fostered those attributes in her children. I started playing instruments when I was very young." Saffron's mind drifted back to the open rooms of her childhood home, practicing music while her mother sat nearby, keeping watch while arranging stones for the jewelry she crafted. The warm desert breeze that drifted through also carried her song throughout the villa. Practicing always seemed to sooth her as a child.

"My father adored me, indulging my curiosity by taking me to market. When I was a little older, he took my sister and me to a dancing demonstration. Some dances were meant for seduction, others were acrobatic, but one style fascinated me above all."

Saffron snuck a glance at Sheen, who seemed content dozing on her feet under the shade of a tree. Her weapons were still strapped to their harness, but Saffron imagined them in her hands, herself the balance between shield and spear. "There were warriors at the demonstration who danced with their weapons. It was unlike anything I had ever seen. They circled and leapt and jabbed at astonishing speeds. It was all choreographed, I know, but it struck me to see something meant for violence also appear so fluid, so graceful. The 'ghostdance,' it was called. I fell in love and wanted to learn, and my father couldn't deny me anything."

"I learn to fight as well," Be'naj responded, a touch of excitement lining her voice. She reached one hand over and placed it upon her scabbard. "The mystic teaches me. Shecclad demands mastery over enemies, so I learn."

"That's good," Saffron said, pleased to find something they had in common. "It's important to be able to defend oneself. Too many people try to take what they want, whether they have claim to it or not. It was probably my training in the ghostdance that swayed my father to finally let me go abroad. I left my homeland to play music, but also to see with my own eyes what lay beyond the desert of my youth." Saffron swallowed hard. "Perhaps I learned more than I bargained for."

She looked Be'naj directly in the eye. "I have also seen things I would not have dreamed possible had I merely heard of them from others or read about them in a book. When I rode with friends to the defense of a rebellious village in the Empire of Chelpa, I encountered a creature beyond my imagination. He was an Aasimar, and had feathered wings like yours, only much larger. They were mostly white, but ended in tips of gold."

Be'naj extended her wings again and looked at their ends, the feathers striated with bands of brass.

"He had skin bright as a pearl, and I noticed yours is more luminescent than the metallic shades of other Eladrin I have seen. Although, I have only seen two others," Saffron qualified.

"You think my father is Aasimar?"

"I don't know," Saffron shook her head. "Yes. It makes sense, although it doesn't. Palomar and the other Aasimar only recently regained their true forms, and they are not of this world. You are too old for one of them to have lain with your mother."

Be'naj opened her mouth as if to speak, then shut it. Her hands were trembling, but she reached behind her and gently stroked the tips of her wing. "I am drawn to you, Saffron. I feel pull before I ever see you. Perhaps …" Be'naj drew in air as if breathing was suddenly difficult. "Perhaps, because you know of my father?"

"I don't know what you're feeling," Saffron said, grasping Be'naj's hand once again, "but I will tell what I can about the Aasimar." She could see the emotion coursing through the woman's features and worried about overwhelming her. "Perhaps a break to eat first would help. I know I'm famished." Saffron didn't wait for an answer, but nodded encouragingly and stood. "I've got some rations in my saddlebags. Should we eat here, or would you like to show me more of Skywatch Haven?" She made her way to Sheen as she spoke, hoping Eladrin ate a similar diet.

She flipped back the cover of one of her bags and rummaged through her supply of food for options. "I have some dried figs, a few hard biscuits, some—"

"I have food." Be'naj was standing directly behind her. "Come. I make us supper."

"All right." Saffron closed her saddlebags and untethered her horse from the tree. Leading Sheen, she followed Be'naj across the clearing once she'd retrieved her sword and shield. The spray of the geyser created a backdrop of moving water as it fed the pools beneath, which Saffron found both soothing and hard to ignore.

As they walked across the meadow of untamed grass, nearer to the colored hill of many pools, Saffron noticed steam rising from the highest of them. "Is the water from the fountain hot?" she asked.

"Very hot," Be'naj answered. "I show you after eating."

Drawing nearer to the great elm, Saffron could see the shelter was actually a cluster of separate rooms, each with a purpose. A narrow hollow, with two walls and a roof stitched of branches and pine needles, served as resting quarters. A pile of worn blankets lined the hollow, and a moveable barrier of sharpened branches could be set in place to keep curious animals out.

Perpendicular to the hollow was what appeared to be a cooking area. Two stacks of rocks supported a thin sheet of iron, leaving a dug-out space beneath for fuel. No fire burned presently, but a nearby metallic basket contained a collection of rocks for heating. Saffron watched as Be'naj opened the third construct: a crudely made wooden chest, the size of a large coffin, which appeared to hold the entirety of the woman's belongings.

Be'naj deposited her shield and sword carefully into the dark box, as well as the comb she'd tucked into her belt, and withdrew a small stack of provisions. She set these on a flat slab of rock near the stove, then picked out a collection of dry kindling and grass stalks from a pile behind the shelter.

"Is there anything I can do to help?" Saffron asked.

Be'naj peered over her shoulder and smiled, but shook her head. Saffron took a seat atop the chest of her host's belongings, which looked sturdy enough to support her weight.

"Did you make all this yourself?" Saffron asked, both impressed and slightly saddened by the collection of primitive structures.

"Yes," Be'naj answered. She ignited the dried grass stalks on the heated rocks and set them beneath the kindling. In no time, a healthy flame burned under the sheet of iron, and she washed her hands in a water basin before assembling ingredients on her makeshift table.

Saffron knew she could have started a fire with a song, but there was something fascinating about watching this remarkable woman working efficiently in her familiar space. She looked around again at the entire setting, soaking in its serenity. Golden leaves and white bark framed a circle around the tranquil meadow of wildflowers, all paying homage to the hill of swirling color, capped by a natural fountain and overflowing pools of steaming water. This place held truer magic than whatever was inside her.

The remoteness of the location begged the question as to how Be'naj maintained her life. Was she really the only one who came here? "How do you get supplies?" Saffron asked. "Surely you must trade with someone – your weapons and armor, for instance."

"Kiruh, the mystic who teach me to fight. He give me armor when I leave home," Be'naj said as she transferred what looked like cornmeal wraps, filled with vegetables, onto the flatiron stove. "We meet in special place every spring and he brings gifts."

"So you only get fresh supplies once a year?" Saffron suddenly felt very spoiled. Before leaving her own home, she could have had new clothes, toys, or nearly anything else she desired simply by batting her dark lashes at her father. "Do you get any other visitors here? I mean, do you interact with anyone beyond the annual meetings with your mystic?"

With their food starting to sizzle, Be'naj stood and faced Saffron. "Not until my visions start. Sometimes, I see attacks before they happen. I find the place and help fight for humans on the road. Before you, I never see human use magic. Only Eladrin, as child."

"Oh, you saw the fire, then?" Saffron wasn't sure her display had been noticed during the fight, as Be'naj had seemed so intent on her own enemies. According to Cauzel, Eladrin were the first Shapers, so it might be possible Be'naj would know something helpful about the Living Fire. Saffron realized that bringing out her pendant might seem like flaunting wealth, but Be'naj appeared content without a need for material things. "I have something I'd like to show you," she finally said.

Saffron left her spot on the storage chest and made her way to Sheen, who was resting in the shade once again. From her saddle bags, she retrieved her water skin and a piece of folded, gray cloth. "What do you make of this?" Saffron handed the cloth to Be'naj, watching for her reaction as she unfolded the corners to reveal the pendant of the former King-priest.

Be'naj gasped. "This is where pull comes from." She looked from the bright crimson jewel, burning with its own inner light, up to Saffron and gasped again. "It is from the gods!"

"How do you know that?" Saffron asked.

Be'naj shook her head, perhaps struggling for an explanation herself. "I feel it, from inside." A popping sound from the stove prompted her to fold the cloth and quickly hand it back to Saffron. Once her hands were free, she carefully transferred their meal wraps from the iron to the flat stone.

"It's called Living Fire," Saffron explained. "Palomar, the Aasimar I spoke of earlier, told me it was formed when the Avatars still walked the surface of Elisahd, capturing some of their essence. He also said it was capable of enhancing the magic of its owner, but I have no idea what to do with it." She peeled back the cloth and ran her fingers over the ruby, its light dancing at her touch.

She laughed, feeling foolish as the memories of her travels to Pasaxtree swam into consciousness. "I tried singing to it. Over and over, actually, when I was bored and looking to pass the time. I don't know what I was expecting. Maybe Cauzel can teach me what to do," she mused.

"Why you not wear it?" Be'naj held one of the freshly cooked wraps out to her.

"Oh, thank you." Saffron set the pendant and her water down on top of the storage chest to accept the food. "It smells wonderful." The cornmeal was warm, but as she bit into the wrap, she realized its contents were much hotter. She pulled it from her mouth and blew into its center before tentatively trying again with just her teeth.

Looking over, she saw Be'naj watching her curiously, having little problem consuming her own portion. Ready for the heat the second time, Saffron managed to take a bite and chew. It tasted like beans, tomatoes, and some type of leafy greens, all seasoned with herbs she couldn't quite place. As she ate more of the wrap, she decided she quite liked it, and it tamed her hunger.

She was already half-way done before taking a drink of water and offering her bladder to Be'naj. They ate in silence, though Saffron's mind was a bundle of questions. Too many new experiences were making it difficult to sort through the past few days' events clearly. She was in a new country, meeting strange new people, trying to get to the bottom of who was behind a series of crimes she didn't fully understand, while embarking on her magical education.

"Thank you for supper," Saffron said upon finishing her meal. She peeked back toward the hill and noticed shadows from the trees had started to creep across it. "The hour is getting late, and I am weary from a full day. Is the water from the pools safe to drink? I need to care for my horse."

"There is stream of cool water, not far." Be'naj pointed further into the woods.

"Good. Is it all right if I share your clearing for the night? I don't wish to intrude, but we're some miles from the road."

Be'naj swallowed hard, like the words were stuck in her throat. "Yes, stay."

Saffron nodded and set to unburdening Sheen. She made a pile of her gear near the trunk of the elm: spear, shield, saddlebags, and saddle. She cupped a handful of oats and fed them to her horse before leading her under the dry boughs of the forest in search of the stream. It wasn't far at all, and while Sheen drank her fill, Saffron used the cool water to wash her face.

When she made her way back to the shelter, Be'naj pointed to her hollow of blankets. "You rest here."

"Oh, no, I couldn't. That's where you sleep. I'll make a bed of leaves."

"I insist, Saffron. I not sleep like you, remember? I trance."

"Well, that's very generous, Be'naj. It does look cozy." The truth was, Saffron felt weary, and if she could get even a partial night of good sleep, it would make all the difference. Tomorrow she would need to figure out her next step, something impossible to do with a fatigued mind. "Just wake me in a few hours and we can switch."

Be'naj nodded as Saffron crawled into the excavated space and pulled one of the blankets over her shoulder. "Sleep well."

Saffron wasn't sure if it was because they had already fought for the same purpose, or because Be'naj had shown such warmth and trust welcoming her to her home, but she felt comfortable enough letting her guard down to sleep as Be'naj watched over her. She began drifting off while Be'naj added more wood to the stove fire. The winged woman sat beside it, legs crossed and back straight, as Saffron's eyes closed to the crackle of the dancing flames.

They shot open as she was shaken awake. The full dark of night had fallen, though she could see the barest features of Be'naj's face in the red glow of the Living Fire around her neck.

"Come, you must see."

Saffron was still making the transition to wakefulness as she threw back her blanket and crawled out of the sleeping hollow. She forgot about the low roof and stood too soon, hitting her head. Be'naj's tone didn't suggest they were in danger, but Saffron had no idea why she was wearing the pendant. "Well, that's not where I left that," she mumbled, probably not loud enough for Be'naj to hear.

The flame under the stove was out, but a small glow exuded from newly heated rocks in the wire basket. She followed Be'naj as best she could, stepping carefully in the dark. Once they were out from under the trees, a magnificent mural of starlight painted the open sky. She stopped to stare at the spectacle, and saw streak after streak of white fire ignite and vanish against the black backdrop.

"This way." Be'naj grasped her hand and led her to the hill. They approached from the northern side, which seemed to be dryer, though she could hear the spray of the geyser from its top. As they climbed the slope, Saffron noticed from her companion's starlit silhouette that she had changed out of her armor into some sort of light, flowing gown. The feathers of her wings caressed Saffron's arm as they walked, hand-in-hand, to the crest of the hill.

Once they had nearly reached the top, Be'naj released her. "The stars are falling," she said, her voice full of wonder.

Saffron turned in a tight circle, her head tilted back to take in the panoramic view above. As the direction of the wind changed, the mist of the geyser blew across her, wetting her face with warm droplets. Although she wasn't sure it *meant* anything, she wanted to remember every detail of this moment for the rest of her life. She simultaneously felt insignificant, yet connected to something much greater than she could ever put into words.

While her reverie with the night sky absorbed her attention, she'd failed to notice Be'naj stepping around her until she heard a disturbance of the water. Leveling her eyes, she saw from the crimson glow around Be'naj's neck that she'd shed her gown and stepped into one of the pools.

The water only came above her knee, but steam rose from it, licking at the outline of her naked body. Be'naj turned to Saffron and held out a welcoming hand. "Come," she beckoned.

Saffron couldn't help but stare. She had seen other women in the nude before – she had bathed with her sister countless times – yet she had never seen the bare form of a half-Eladrin, half-Aasimar woman, lit by a night sky full of falling stars. Be'naj's skin was luminescent, stealing the glow of the heavens to shine from within, glittering even more brightly when she moved and reflected the light from above. Her frame was sleek with lean muscle, her breasts round and high with the Living Fire nestled between them, casting a scarlet glow across her chest. Her glossy hair fell over her shoulders to frame her face and white wings rose behind her, a reminder that she was not fully of this world.

Her right hand stretched out patiently in invitation; her left held the polished wood of the comb the merchant had gifted her that afternoon. "Is something wrong?" she asked, and Saffron realized she hadn't moved for several, long breaths.

"No," she said, her mouth suddenly parched. "I'll join you. A hot bath sounds wonderful." Saffron averted her eyes and started pulling off her boots. Be'naj lowered herself into the steaming pool while Saffron shed her armor and undergarments.

Once naked, she dipped a toe into the water and it nearly scalded her. "Ouch, that's hot." Deterring as the heat was, now that she was exposed, the night breeze gave her goosebumps. She summoned her bravery to give the pool another try. This time, she resisted the impulse to pull back and found that once she took a seat beside Be'naj and was waist-deep, the battling sensations of hot and cold were actually pleasant.

"It looks good on you," Saffron said once she'd settled in and relaxed, staring at the ruby pendant. "Come to think of it, Palomar was drawn to the Living Fire, too. He said its energy was what allowed him to remember the Song of Redemption and change from a Damper to his original self."

"What is *Damper*?" Be'naj asked.

Saffron sighed quietly. She wasn't sure she had the capacity to properly explain the history of the Aasimar. Still, even a little knowledge might aid Be'naj in her search for self-understanding, and Saffron couldn't deny her that.

"I'll tell you what I know, though it's not much, and I can't be sure of it myself. According to Palomar, the Aasimar live on another plane, called Mount Celestia. A group of them, Palomar included, were punished by their god and sent to our world. They look a little like you, only larger – especially their wings. They can soar into the air and sing songs of magic, which is how I learned what little I know.

"But they were cursed, as I said, and transformed into Dampers when they came here. The Dampers were stripped of their memory – lowly, weak, and eminently pitiable – the opposite of everything they used to be. But they were attracted to the Living Fire, and apparently, being around it returned their memory and songs to them. Eventually, it helped restore them back into Aasimar."

Saffron looked upward and caught another streak of shooting stars. She lifted her hips and leaned back until her lower body rose. She floated momentarily, the surface of the water just skirting her face. Exhaling slowly, she began to sink. Closing her eyes, she was enveloped completely by the warmth and wetness of the pool. It felt amazing. Her only regret was that she didn't have any wine with her.

When she resurfaced and brushed the wet hair and water from her face, she found Be'naj's eyes trained upon her. They looked soft and wet, as if she were about to cry or ask a question she was afraid to hear the answer to. It made Saffron uneasy, and she began talking again to provide a distraction.

"Your wings are beautiful. I was so envious of Palomar's. You said earlier you didn't always have them?"

"I hate them." Be'naj's lips trembled and her chin sank, not at all the reaction Saffron had hoped to induce.

"Why would you hate them, Be'naj?" Saffron waded forward, her desire to comfort almost overwhelming her. She gently lifted Be'naj's chin so she could look into her eyes from up close. "There is nothing wrong with you."

Once again, her words seemed to miscarry, as tears began spilling down the Eladrin's cheeks. Saffron moved even closer and embraced Be'naj tightly, wrapping one arm around her back beneath her wings while the other cradled her head against her shoulder. She felt the woman's heartbeat as she trembled and a pulsing heat from the Living Fire pendant resting between them. "It's going to be all right," she whispered over and over, willing the words to become truth.

She didn't know what had sparked this reaction, but Saffron couldn't help thinking of Dhania. If only her sister would have shown such vulnerability after her escape from the King-priest's harem, instead of responding with defiance.

Saffron eventually felt Be'naj's hands against her own bare back, returning her embrace, still holding the comb. That gave

Saffron an idea. When the crying calmed, she reached around to slip the comb from Be'naj's hand. "Here," she said, separating their bodies so she could slide behind Be'naj. "It always used to relax me when my mother combed my hair. Why don't we give it a try?"

She widened her legs and scooted forward, assuming the space between Be'naj's wings. Taking a handful of her shiny brass locks in one hand, she started gently working the wet comb through it. Saffron stretched Be'naj's hair repeatedly with long strokes of the comb, straightening the tangles. Eventually, her rhythm seemed to work, soothing Be'naj enough that she decided to speak.

"Before I leave home, everyone teases me for my wings. All the children hate me when they grow. In my thirteenth summer, a boy I like ask me to follow him to the kissing oak. I was so stupid," she bemoaned and sniffed, nearly beginning the cycle of tears again. "Three other boys wait for us there. I tell them I only like first boy, only kiss him, but they laugh and call me ugly. They hold me, down on the ground …"

Saffron stopped combing to listen as the crying won out, yet somehow, Be'naj continued through her tears.

"One, two, three, they count as they pull the feathers. I beg them to stop, tell them they hurt me, but they didn't until all gone. They leave me there in pile of feathers." Be'naj turned her head enough that Saffron could once again see the wet streaks on her cheeks. "I cannot fly, Saffron. My wings only make me ugly."

Saffron was crying, too. She had no more words. She reached both arms around Be'naj and held her tight, her cheek pressed against Be'naj's soft, wet hair. She felt wounded for her new friend, angry that others would be so wantonly cruel.

Bodies entangled, Saffron began noticing that the touch of her bare skin against Be'naj's was affecting her, quickening her heartbeat. She tried pushing such thoughts from her head as she was simply providing comfort, but the more she attempted to ignore it, the more she felt every point of contact – the curve of Be'naj's buttocks pressed against her inner thighs, her right hand laying across Be'naj's breast, her lips oh-so-close to the nape of Be'naj's neck.

Finally, she forced herself to let go and back away, feeling as though she'd crossed some invisible line she couldn't define. "I'm sorry that happened to you," she whispered, resting the palm of her hand on the space between Be'naj's wings. What sort of spell had come over her that separating from the touch of this woman's skin felt like a punishment? "We'll talk more in the morning," Saffron assured, eager to escape before her impulses got the better of her.

She stood and vacated the pool, the night air prickling her skin in the sudden absence of heat. Dripping wet, she folded her armor in her arms, not wanting to take the time to get dressed. Using the starlight, she made her way down the hill as best she could, stumbling a few times but keeping her feet.

Soon enough she was back in the hollow, shivering as she wrapped the blanket around her. She kept awake listening for a while, half of her hoping Be'naj would stay away until she was asleep, the other half hoping she would crawl into the hollow and help keep her warm. At last, sleep took over with no sign that Be'naj had ever left the pool.

When Saffron awoke, Be'naj was approaching the shelter with a basin full of water in her arms. She was wearing the same gown from the night before, though in the morning light, Saffron could see it was dyed the shade of an afternoon sky. She pushed down her blanket to rise, only then remembering her own nakedness.

Wrapping the blanket around her body, she crawled out of the shelter, responding to Be'naj's warm smile with a nervous one. Scuttling over to the elm trunk, she scoured through her saddlebags for a change of clothes.

"I should probably head back to Blackfeather Perch and give Cauzel my report of the ambush," she said as she pulled one of her waist-baring shirts over her head.

"You must leave?" The disappointment in Be'naj's voice was clear. She set down the basin and wiped the fallen strands of hair from her forehead.

Fully dressed, Saffron spun to face her host, who was still wearing the pendant of Living Fire. "I must." Why was she having trouble looking Be'naj in the eye? "But I will return to visit, soon."

"When?"

"Ummm …" Saffron's eyes rolled upward as she struggled over the calculation. "Well, it's probably two days cross-country to Cauzel's tower, then I really ought to return to Pasaxtree and interview Corwyn's contacts … maybe two weeks at the most?"

Be'naj's lids closed and she nodded her acceptance. "I see. Two weeks."

"But, you can keep the necklace while I'm gone, so you know I'll come back," Saffron offered. She stepped closer, but stopped short of reaching out to touch her. "I won't abandon you, Be'naj. You can trust me."

Be'naj stretched her wings to their full width, their brass tips vibrating slightly. "I do." She raised the ruby off her chest and looked down at it. "I sing to it while you gone." She broke into a wide smile, genuine happiness spreading across her face.

Saffron had witnessed so much emotion from her already, while knowing her for less than a day. She felt a sincere desire to bring more smiles to that lovely, alien face, though the sentiment seemed foolish after so brief a time.

"Two weeks, then." She saddled Sheen and loaded her gear, then decided to cut southeast across the forest before her resolve failed and she ended up staying in Skywatch Haven indefinitely.

Chapter 6

The Trials to Come

S affron's thoughts kept migrating back to Be'naj at Skywatch Haven, even after spending most of the day putting distance between them. The spot was, without a doubt, the most uniquely beautiful place she'd ever seen. What she found perplexing was that she could describe Be'naj in exactly the same way – uniquely beautiful.

Like her blood, Be'naj had a mixture of attributes Saffron wasn't used to seeing together. Vulnerable, yet strong. Independent, yet starved for attention. The way Saffron felt made her want to both run farther away and never leave Be'naj's side. But she'd left the Living Fire with the woman; she would have to return for the pendant. Was she foolish for trusting her so soon?

One thing was certain: Saffron would have to help improve her living conditions. While admirable that she managed to survive so far from another living soul, she appeared to be doing little more than surviving. With Saffron's help, there was no reason why Be'naj couldn't thrive for a change.

Saffron took notice as Sheen picked her way around a thicket of thorny vines. Ifelian was not short on trees. With the right tools, working together, she and Be'naj should be able to procure the lumber necessary to build a proper house. She could give music lessons in Pasaxtree to help earn money, and she still needed to look into possible patrons from the area who might be willing to pay for performances.

Perhaps, once she got a reputation established across Ifelian, she could add a school building to their yet-unbuilt cottage and teach students of her own at Skywatch Haven. She was musing over all sorts of possibilities when Sheen passed a copse of trees and came to an abrupt halt.

A shallow trench had been dug into the ground, only an arm's length or so wide, though with the earth built upward on the other side. Saffron was about to turn her horse to follow an easier path, but when she looked higher up the slope, she saw a thick rope tied tightly between two trees.

Suspended from the rope by a separate cord was a skull. Saffron heard movement on the fallen leaves to her right, but when she turned, nothing was there. "Probably just a squirrel," she said to herself as she dismounted, fearing it was actually an eladrin scout, or worse. She was unsure if she had crossed into their territory yet, but perhaps this trench and skull marked the boundary.

If the ancient story Cauzel told her was true, they were unlikely to look upon a trespassing human with much favor. She chided herself for leaving Be'naj with such haste that she failed to change into her armor. Keeping Sheen's body between her and the origin of the disturbance, Saffron loosened her shield and spear from their harness. Once she had them in hand, she decided to climb the slope to see if any clearer demarcations existed that she was crossing onto eladrin lands, or if this was something else entirely.

Saffron was able to leap across the ditch, and crawled on her forearms and knees up the embankment toward the rope. She kept on alert for further signs of movement, but all was still and quiet. When the ground leveled off enough to stand, she took another look at the skull. With relief, she saw that it wasn't human, but something smaller and animalistic. Perhaps a raccoon or large weasel?

From her higher vantage point, she saw that the pair of trees were joined by a third, forming a triangle, with other ropes connecting them. Furthermore, the trench she had crossed was part of a moat that encircled the triad. After ducking under the rope and into the heart of the triangle, she noticed the bark had been stripped from the inward face of one of the trunks. Carved into the smoother layer beneath was the symbol she recognized from the black banner she saw during her ride to Pasaxtree – a clawed hand with strange runes on either side.

The fallen leaves had been swept from the raised clearing, and near its middle were the remains of an unrecognizable creature, torn to pieces and sacrificed. Saffron's gut said this was no eladrin ritual, but what did it mean that the symbol carved into this tree was the same one etched on the door of the farmhouse where her sister had been taken? That was way on the other side of the Wyvernwatch Mountains. Was it possible the same demon who bewitched the leader of the Black Hill orcs was operating his cult in the heart of Ifelian?

Whatever the truth, this week was turning into one of the strangest she could remember. She decided to leave things as they were and pry what information she could from Cauzel when she reached his tower. After taking one more look around to determine if she was being watched, she skidded back down the slope the way she came. Saffron climbed onto her horse but kept her shield and spear in hand, just in case.

Pulling Sheen's reins to the left, she guided her around the circumference of the trench, continuing east. Although it might mean a little longer on horseback, heading for the base of the mountains seemed safer. Skirting the edge of the heavier forest might make her less of a target for territorial Eladrin.

She lit a fire when night came, but was so on edge she slept very little. The only disturbance, though, turned out to be an annoyingly active owl who hooted every time Saffron was finally about to doze. The next day, she scoured the ridgeline as she rode, and in only a few hours was able to make out the shape of Blackfeather Perch, jutting from the rocky cliffs. She knew Cauzel wouldn't be expecting her back so soon, as she had planned to return to Pasaxtree when she left, and hoped her early arrival wouldn't be an inconvenience.

By the time she'd gotten closer and wound her way around the boulders marking the base of the ascending trail, Noki was there to greet her. He cawed twice, making sure he had her attention, then flew up toward the balcony of the tower.

Saffron had only been there once, but following the path into the hills seemed oddly like coming home. She felt like there was so much to tell Cauzel, and so much to ask as well, though part of her wanted to take a long nap to gather her strength first.

When she reached the tunnel of hedges, she entered as before and found the side-passage to the stables already open. She led Sheen to an empty stall and took the time to unburden and care for her, then carried her armor and another change of clothes with her into the tower.

Cauzel was waiting on one of the couches in the front room when she entered. He stood and approached with a glass of wine to greet her. "The timing of your arrival is unexpected, though I'm happy you're safe. I hope your swift return isn't because you ran into trouble on the way back to Pasaxtree."

Saffron accepted the wine and drank deeply. "In my experience, finding trouble is sometimes the most direct route to a solution."

Cauzel's bushy eyebrows arched. "And what did you find, I wonder – Corwyn's nephew still alive, I hope?" Cauzel's hand absently stroked his beardless chin in anticipation.

"He's alive. And I found more than I bargained for, in some respects." Saffron's mind couldn't help conjuring an image of Be'naj's shimmering body, outlined in starlight. She closed her eyes and shook off the thought before opening them. "We were ambushed by lizardfolk – nearly a dozen of them. They were lurking beneath the surface of a pond by the road until we drew close."

"You were able to fight off that many and remain unharmed?" Cauzel's tone suggested he was impressed.

Saffron wasn't sure she was ready to discuss Be'naj's circumstances yet. "We received unexpected succor from another traveler. The lizardfolk fled once we'd halved their numbers. I doubt they were expecting strong resistance. Although, with the attacks continuing, more merchants may end up hiring additional protection."

Cauzel hummed contemplatively and returned to his seat on the couch. "So it was lizardfolk, after all?"

"Without a doubt," Saffron answered.

"And their intent seemed to be thievery, rather than simply violence?"

Saffron thought on it. "Well, they retreated once it was clear they were outmatched and lacked the ferocity I'd associate with killers. Their tactics were more consistent with subdual. One of them had a net, for instance, and I don't recall seeing any blades."

Cauzel shook his head. "What I know of lizardfolk culture simply isn't consistent with these attacks. They prefer to be left alone and would normally become aggressive only to prevent encroachment on their territory. They wouldn't bother those simply seeking to pass by. Furthermore, they don't value property the same as human cultures. Lizardfolk have little interest in material objects beyond those which aid their survival, so some of the goods reported missing after these raids makes little sense.

"The most logical explanation seems to be the one I fear the greatest – some other force is driving the lizardfolk to carry out these attacks on its behalf."

"You think it's the Nightwing?" Saffron completed his thought, remembering their conversation in the Golden Crucible.

Cauzel sighed. "It seems plausible, though I don't know if a little banditry is worth provoking a dragon. On top of these concerns, I received a missive yesterday from the Keeper of Gilsage. It appears he, and possibly other important figures in the region, were sent declarations of the so-called *Lord of Drachenmark's* intentions to begin levying taxes on all who use the Ifelian Corridor, starting in the new year."

"Excuse my ignorance, but who is the Lord of Drachenmark?" Saffron asked.

"There is no such place, as far as I'm aware," Cauzel replied. "Some fellow named Thuvian Skullreaver signed the document. It sounds preposterous to me, but I've been summoned to Gilsage to weigh in on the matter and provide assessment of possible threats as a Shaper.

"As such, I shall be leaving again in two days, possibly for a week or more, and am arranging tasks for my apprentices to complete by my return. I was wondering if you might stay and assist. It would expose you to some of the methods used in the employment and research of the arcane arts, and I admit I'd feel more at ease with you keeping an eye on them."

Saffron finished off her wine, buying a moment to consider the offer. "You mean you don't want me to continue looking into the ambushes along the Corridor?"

"Not for now," Cauzel said. "I should probably discuss my Nightwing theory with the Keeper before proceeding, and this meeting will give me a chance to do so."

"Then I would like to stay," Saffron admitted. "At least for a week or so."

"Excellent. I think it will be a worthwhile endeavor on your part – a chance to begin working with and getting to know your fellow apprentices."

Saffron nodded her agreement. "The Keeper of Gilsage, that's an eladrin position, is it not?" She hoped to steer the conversation in such a way that she might gain more insight about Be'naj. "You seem to be fairly well-connected in the eladrin community for an outsider. Didn't you say they were distrustful of humans?"

"Well, yes, that's true for the most part." Cauzel picked at the couch's upholstery. "I have acquired a level of standing with the Eladrin of Ifelian because of my Shaping abilities. It is a strong tradition with their people, and respect is given to any who prove themselves worthy within the discipline."

"Can I ask you, then – have you ever heard of a union between an Eladrin and a member of another race yielding offspring? I've seen such a thing possible between orcs and humans while in the Northern Provinces." Saffron sat on the couch opposite Cauzel and kept her eyes trained on him, defying him to change the direction of the conversation. For some reason, talking about the Eladrin seemed to fluster him.

"I, uh, well …" Cauzel brushed the fingers of one hand absently along his opposite, bony elbow. "I suppose humans and Eladrin could breed, if you ever found a pair willing to do so. There are mentions in the histories of such a sub-race, before the Revenge of Arkmus, called the Ellafous."

Saffron cocked her head to one side and spoke as if merely musing at possibilities. "What about races not of this plane? Could an immortal race, such as the Aasimar, have children with the Eladrin, or even humans for that matter?"

"Well, Dyphina is an example of such a union, if you remember. My studies have uncovered numerous examples among humankind, where one parent has bred successfully with a member of another race. I doubt I have ever seen an exhaustive list on the matter, but I wouldn't be surprised if such heterogeneity extended to anthropomorphic members of the outer cosmos. It is an interesting subject to say the least. I would encourage further research if you hold a passion for it."

Cauzel's response seemed sincere, and she leaned forward to communicate her own interest. "Do you have any books among your collection I might read for more insight?"

"Hmm ..." He considered her request. "I'm afraid the only tomes in my library concerning such things are written in Eladrin. Perhaps one of our first endeavors upon my return should be instruction in the mother language of magic."

He stood abruptly and made his way toward the stairs. "For now, though, I must begin making arrangements for my departure. I would like to perform an official assessment of your knowledge tomorrow, and I still have work to do setting up the apprentice challenges for while I'm away. As a consequence," he said while beginning to climb, "I have given them the rest of the afternoon off, if you'd like a chance to socialize before the rigor of their assignments spoils their mood."

"There was one more incident I think worth mentioning," Saffron recalled before losing his audience. Cauzel halted, waiting silently for the rest of her tale. "On the way back to Blackfeather Perch, I came across what appeared to be a site of ritualistic sacrifice. I was worried at first it might be the Eladrin communicating their distaste of my presence, but then I spied a symbol carved into a tree – one I had seen before.

"The same mark was on the door of a farmhouse where some sort of demonic cult gathering was taking place. I saw the emblem again on a banner just south of Pasaxtree. I thought it odd the same symbol should appear across such distances."

Cauzel nodded gravely. "I will give this news proper attention. Would you draw the symbol for me later?" Saffron nodded and he said no more, no doubt saving his wind for the numerous winding stairs leading up to his quarters.

Saffron had been alone with her thoughts for the better part of two days and decided a distraction might be welcome. Unsure of the apprentices' whereabouts, she figured she could get some exercise climbing the stairs herself, given her recent time in the saddle.

When she reached the second floor landing, she spotted Dyphina in the kitchen. Aware of her own hunger, Saffron sauntered in to see what the stunning apprentice was up to.

"Getting something to eat?" she asked, drawing closer.

Dyphina glanced over and smiled while putting the finishing touches on her plate. "Just stocking up on a little study food," she said, which appeared to be a collection of melons, grapes, and cheese. "Would you like some?"

"Fresh fruit this late in the year? How does Cauzel get it? And yes, I would, if it's not too much trouble." Saffron gathered her hair and swept it to hang over one shoulder.

"No trouble at all," Dyphina responded, doubling the portions on her plate and packing the remainder back into the larder. "Cauzel Blackfeather is a resourceful individual. His renown as a Shaper has earned him a lot of friends, as well as enemies. He does favors for all sorts of aristocrats and powerful merchants, who in return make sure his material needs are met.

"Please, help yourself." Dyphina nodded toward the stacked plate while she finished putting away the food. "I don't mind sharing," she smiled.

"Thank you," Saffron said, plucking a green grape and popping it into her mouth. Her thoughts swept to Be'naj, who had been so kind with her own food stores, and how hard growing up without knowing one side of her mixed heritage must have been. "I apologize if this is too personal, but do you know both of your parents, Dyphina?"

"Sort of a strange question," she answered after squinting. "But, yes," she nodded. "I grew up mostly with my father, but he takes me to visit my mother fairly often. They both agreed this was a wonderful opportunity to study under Cauzel. What about your parents? Did one of them teach you to play the lyre like that?"

"What? Oh, no." Saffron was not expecting the conversation to shift toward her. "My parents are wonderful, but my father paid for lessons when I was young. Once I grasped the basics, I pretty much taught myself to play."

"Well, I hope to become half as good someday." Dyphina selected a slice of cheese and draped it across her tongue. She even made eating seem sensual.

"I'm sure you will," Saffron imparted, choosing a large cluster of grapes from the plate.

"Got what you want?" Dyphina said, flipping her thick, green hair over her shoulder before lifting the platter from the counter. "I'm heading back up to the laboratory to study. The others are relaxing in the fourth floor commons, I think. You should stop by and say hello. I know Aurus, for one, would enjoy that." She giggled. "He has hardly stopped talking about you since you left." Dyphina winked and breezed past Saffron toward the stairwell, hips swaying as she walked.

Saffron had a feeling she could learn a thing or two about seduction from the young Shaper, though she still didn't know much about the half-fey. She plucked another grape from its stem and looked around the empty kitchen, then trailed Dyphina back to the stairs.

"Oh, you really got her with that one, Thaelios!" Aurus's voice carried into the stairwell as he got up from the common room table and headed toward his sleeping chamber. He turned and spotted Saffron approaching the commons just before disappearing from view, then quickly popped his head back around the corner to consider her more thoroughly.

He turned completely and skirted through the commons, down the candlelit hall to meet her before she entered the circular space. "Saffron, where have you been? You left the other day without saying goodbye."

"She said goodbye, Aurus, just not to you personally." Iliana spoke without raising her head or diverting attention from a selection of cards spread across the central table. Thaelios sat across from her, equally focused on the cards.

"What are you two doing in there?" Saffron casually slipped by Aurus, who didn't make a move to get out of the way, causing their bodies to rub together as she passed.

"It's a game called 'Memory Whip,'" Aurus provided, speaking from directly behind her. "And these two *hate* to lose. Especially to each other."

"How is it played?" she whispered over her shoulder, not wanting to disturb the Eladrins' concentration.

"Each of the cards has either a spell or arcane component displayed on the down-facing side." Aurus leaned in and whispered in Saffron's ear, tickling it with his breath. "Some of the spells only have one related component, but some have two. The players take turns flipping over three cards, and if they match the correct spell to its ingredients, they remove the set from play – most sets wins. The complication is that your opponent gets to swap the position of two cards after every turn, so you really have to work to keep track of things."

"Sounds like you would have to know your arcane formulas pretty well, also."

"Indeed," Aurus confirmed. "But that's not really a problem for these two. It's really not fair," he said, tilting back from her ear to speak loudly enough for Thaelios and Iliana to hear. "These two don't need to sleep like normal people, so they get to spend all those extra hours scouring over their spellbooks, memorizing incantations."

"Don't blame me for not being as lazy as you, Aurus," Iliana contributed, still not looking up from the table. "I've known cats that sleep less."

"The only reason you question my work ethic, Iliana, is because you're intimidated by my talent," Aurus jabbed.

"Talent?" Iliana finally looked up after flipping over her third card. "Is that what you call that smoldering log of smoke you mustered yesterday?"

"Bah," Aurus dismissed with a swat of the air. "Come on, Saffron, let's go somewhere we're not likely to die of boredom."

"Oh, well, I suppose—" before she could finish her thought, Aurus grasped her wrist and tugged her toward the stairwell. "Where are we going?" she protested, yanking her arm free.

He quickly recovered with a disarming smile. "I just thought we might be able to talk a little more intimately away from the twins," he said, pointing back toward the commons, then leading the way up the stairs. "How about the laboratory?"

"Are those two related?" Saffron asked, still undecided on whether to forgive Aurus for grabbing her.

"Not literally, but they are alike in many ways." He waited until she followed up the steps. "They both take the studious aspects of the process more seriously than they should. Magic is more than knowing what to do and when to do it. You feel it; you Shape the energy into what you want. You understand that, right?"

"I think I know what you're talking about. The one who taught me always started our lessons by having me visualize what I wanted to do. I would then compose a song that reflected my vision." When they reached the laboratory, Saffron was glad to find Dyphina reading a book at her worktable. A dozen or so lit candles gave the large space an intimate glow.

"Oh, I didn't think you'd be up here, Dyphina. You know Cauzel gave us the evening off, right?" Aurus walked over to her table and whispered something as he leaned toward her.

Dyphina giggled at what was said, then responded in a voice loud enough for Saffron to hear. "I don't think that would be a good idea. I just want to be as ready as I can for our next trials. Cauzel told me whoever did the best would get a chance to accompany him the next time he visited Gilsage."

"Did he tell you anything about what the trials would entail?" Saffron wasn't sure she'd have a chance to win the reward, given her informal role in the process, but since encountering

Be'naj, she was very interested in taking a trip to the capital of Ifelian to learn more about the Eladrin.

Aurus spoke up first. "I heard they were going to be similar for each of us, but entail three specific tasks, which we would be performing in an alternate order."

"Oh you *heard* this?" Dyphina laid a string down to mark her page, then closed her book. "And who exactly did you hear it from? I'm sure Cauzel is the only one who knows what's going to happen, and I doubt he'd tell you and not the rest of us." Her green eyes narrowed and her nose scrunched. "Or have you been meddling with that clairaudience incantation?"

"Maybe you should be the one to tell us about secret information, Dyphina? It's not like *I'm* trying to sleep with our master ..." Aurus's eyebrows shot up and his lips pouted into a perfect 'o.'

Dyphina's jaw dropped and she reached across the table to slap Aurus's gut. "Why don't you just leave me alone? I'm sure Cauzel will tell us everything we need to know soon enough."

"I've had quite a long few days myself," Saffron said. "I really want to get to know each of you better, but it sounds like we'll have an opportunity starting with these trials. I think I'm going to retire to bed early."

"We could always do both," Aurus said with an innocent tone.

"Both?" Saffron repeated, confused.

"We could retire to bed early *and* get to know each other better ..."

Saffron fought back a smile of her own. Normally such brazenness would annoy her, but she couldn't help thinking of

Jaiden's similar ineptitude at wooing her. "Thanks, but I'm okay."

Saffron dreamt that a ghostly presence chased her through a dark wood. The trees themselves were evil and grabbed at her as she ran, looking for Be'naj. She eventually tripped over something, but instead of a protruding root, it was Palomar's dead body, lying on the ground. The trees snatched her as she'd stopped moving, and she could feel the cold of the chasing specter drawing near. When she looked up into the night sky, screaming to be set free, the stars started blinking out, one by one.

She sat up in bed when she woke, not remembering where she was. Her forehead was beaded with sweat, but she felt a draft chilling her body. Saffron forced herself to steady her breath, and as her heart slowed, it came back to her that she was in Blackfeather Perch. She felt an urge to see the stars.

Not wanting to wake anyone, for it was black as death in the tower, she eschewed singing and lit the candle the merchant had given her with flint and steel. Grabbing the blanket from her bed and wrapping it around her shoulders, she picked up the candle and peered into the hall outside her already cracked door. Everyone else seemed to be sleeping.

On the pads of her feet, Saffron walked to the cold stone stairs, then up to the laboratory. The halo of her candle made strange shadows dance across the room as the flame sputtered on the wick, and unsettling details of her nightmare returned. She needed to know the stars were still there.

Unsure she could balance the thick candle while climbing the ladder, she set it on one of the worktables and ascended the rungs with haste. Swinging the trap door open, she exhaled a frosty breath of relief at the sight of the fiery multitudes still lighting the sky.

The vivid constellations served to remind her of Be'naj, and her mind swept back to the two of them bathing in the hot springs together. She knew she'd felt uncomfortable, but maybe that was because of what else she was feeling – a connection unlike anything she'd experienced before. Why did she have to run away from the moment? If she had only stayed, perhaps she would be closer to learning what she'd truly left home to find in the first place.

Saffron stared at those stars until assurance of their permanence sank in again. She decided that, if Be'naj gave her the chance, she wouldn't run again.

Eventually, the late autumn wind made staying outside too averse, and she crept back down the ladder. Her eyes having better adjusted to the dark, Saffron blew out the candle and skirted quickly across the floor to the stairs, where she found just enough moonlight creeping in from the window below to navigate the steps back to the apprentice quarters.

In the morning, Saffron awoke in her tiny room still feeling tired, but too preoccupied for further sleep. She knew Cauzel was a busy man, so she hurried to wash and get dressed. After grabbing a meager breakfast from the larder, she padded up the stone steps to the laboratory. Master Blackfeather sat at one of the long study tables, pouring over a book. All the other apprentices were still sleeping or at breakfast.

"Ah, Saffron. Wonderful." Cauzel stood and waved her over. He read a few more lines in his book before marking his place with a thin cord and shutting it. "I was just reading this chapter on transmography – a favorite subject of mine. I was thinking more on the connection between Nightwings and lizardfolk, and remembered a reference in this book of shape-shifting magic. Did you know dragons are sexually mutable?"

Saffron had almost reached the table when he plied his question, and wasn't sure if her testing had already begun. "I don't even know what that means," she admitted.

"Apparently, they can sire or gestate offspring with nearly any other animal species, including humans," he carried on as if the subject was innately fascinating. "Of course, the act of copulating may be challenging, but that's where magic comes in. A few, powerful specimens have learned alteration magic that allows them to take other forms temporarily, though most dragons purportedly look down their snouts at other species, so the practice is rare."

Unsure what reaction was appropriate, Saffron raised her lower lip and nodded as she placed her forearms on the tabletop.

"But enough of that." Cauzel clasped his hands together. "Thank you for meeting with me this morning. I wanted a chance to see where you stood in your knowledge of arcane concepts before leaving, so I could begin designing a worthwhile curriculum of study during my trip." He inhaled deeply, drawing Saffron's attention to his oversized nose. It really did remind her of a beak. "Why don't we start with you telling me what you've been taught already? Your previous mentor was an Aasimar, you say?"

Saffron cleared her throat, trying to decide where to begin. "Certainly. Yes, everything I already know was taught to me by Palomar, though I've built upon the concepts he delivered on my own."

"Fascinating." Cauzel had conjured up a blank scroll and quill without her seeing and began to scribble notes. "Go on."

"Well," she began, momentarily extending her neck to try and see what Cauzel was writing. It was no use, as the script was foreign to her, so she relented. "Palomar told me that my songs could produce either effects tied to one of the elements, or ones that influence the mind. I was most strongly bound to fire, so that is the focus of most of my songs."

"Interesting," Cauzel nodded. "And how many magical songs do you know?"

Saffron swallowed hard and started to relax as she thought back on her lessons with the Aasimar. "Palomar said there were seven instigating notes that a talent could bind their magic to, but I have not yet developed melodies for each. So far I know *Set the Spark*, *Fire Blossom*, *Burning Weapon*, *Fire Nova*, and *Enrapture*."

Cauzel looked up momentarily. "You named these songs yourself?"

Saffron nodded. "I did. Palomar told me it was important to visualize what effect I wanted to create, and apply my will to each composition."

"Yes, yes, of course," he agreed while continuing to write. "And how similar are your results from one casting to another," he asked, once concluding his note-taking.

Saffron shrugged. "Fairly similar, or at least I haven't noticed otherwise."

"Hmm. Would you be willing to try something for me?" Cauzel asked.

"Certainly."

Cauzel looked around the table until his eyes fell on the very candle Saffron had been given for helping drive off the lizardfolk, and had left behind the previous night. Staring at it once again returned her thoughts to Be'naj.

"I want you to light this candle with a song," he stated as he slid the thick column of wax to the middle of the table. "Can you do that?"

"Of course," Saffron responded, swiveling in her chair to face the candle dead-on. She concentrated on the idea of producing flame, and began singing the tune she'd dubbed, *Set the Spark*. She felt a brief rise of heat within, and as it coursed outward, the wick lit by magic.

"Outstanding!" Cauzel remarked, the hint of a smile flashing across his thin lips. He reached his hand below the surface of the table, seeming to search for something. When his fingers reappeared they were holding a coin. "This is platinum," he said, grabbing a set of metal tongs from further along the table.

He clasped the coin between their ends and held it over the tip of the candle flame, which broke into tongues to lick across the flat surface. "The melting point of platinum is beyond the normal heat exuded by a candle. I want you to raise the intensity until we see the metal start to bend."

"What?" Saffron asked, looking at Cauzel as if he'd just asked her to milk a fish. She shook her head. "I don't know how."

"I understand, but consider this your first lesson." Cauzel stood and edged around to the same side of the table as Saffron, still holding his coin over the candle. "Amplifying magical effects is a technique few succeed in mastering, though it is not so difficult. It does, however, require both patience and more of your own energy.

"Now, I want you to stare at the flame: really study it. Note the precise regions where the color changes. The shape. The heat." Cauzel was directly beside Saffron as he spoke, his voice turned soft and calming.

Saffron did as instructed, gazing at the teardrop of fire surrounding the blackened wick. It danced ever so slightly, with occasional minute flickers in color along the corona.

"Remember the note you used to trigger the spell?"

Saffron nodded, keeping her eyes on the flame.

"I want you to concentrate on the aspect of heat. Imagine it intensifying. Then, begin humming that first note." Cauzel waited until she'd begun. "Good. I know you feel something inside – a warmth, perhaps?"

Saffron nodded again, still humming.

"Use that. Lock onto that feeling, and now give that note your full voice." Cauzel took a step to the side, further from Saffron, so he could switch the tongs from one hand to the other.

Saffron opened her mouth, transitioning from a vibration of her lips to release of the note directly from her throat. In response, the thin blue of the fire's outer edge thickened.

"Perfect!" Cauzel exclaimed, delight clear in his voice. "You can take a breath when you need to, just don't let your concentration slip and pick back up again as soon as you can." He waited for her to do so, then continued his guidance. "Really put that inner warmth into it, and then, staying with the same note, raise it an octave."

Saffron glanced ever so briefly at her mentor, then back at the flame. She could feel what he was talking about and wondered if their experiences were similar, or if he just understood the nature of magic so completely. Again, she did as instructed and changed pitch, releasing further energy into the spell.

The flame's color deepened to purple and the coin's surface began to hiss. A bubble or two appeared as Saffron continued, and a new rush of accomplishment surged through her as the pressure of the tongs Cauzel was holding started to push into and bend the platinum.

"Excellent," he commented as a smile widened his face. When it was undeniable she had succeeded, he pulled the coin back from the candle and straightened his posture.

Saffron took that as a sign of completion and let go of her note. Her face felt flushed, and she noticed for the first time the increased heat of the flame had sent rivulets of wax cascading down the outside of the candle, where they were hardening into beautiful streaks of vibrant color.

"Well, how do you feel after your first lesson?" Cauzel asked.

She exhaled. "I wasn't expecting that."

Cauzel's chin rose in concert with his bushy eyebrows. "I mostly wanted to see how you took instruction, but you also proved to me that you have significant natural talent." He shook his head. "To think you might never have discovered it." He set the metal tongs back on the table and picked up the book she'd interrupted him reading.

"I have more preparations to make for my journey, but I look forward to teaching you, Saffron," he said as he made for the laboratory's exit. "I'd let it cool first, but you're welcome to the coin as a keepsake, if you'd like."

Saffron watched him leave, still processing what she'd just achieved, inwardly giddy at the promise of more lessons to come. Was he just complimenting her, or did Cauzel truly think she had what it took to become an adept sorceress? She held onto the possibilities as she blew out the candle, pocketed the coin, and climbed the ladder to the tower balcony, suddenly thirsty for a cool autumn breeze.

Chapter 7

Gaining Leverage

The image of the face appearing on the smooth surface of Annoxoria's scrying pool was distorted, smeared like the blood its owner'd spread across his Speaking Stone to facilitate their conversation. She didn't know who had bled for the privilege, but she preferred it that way. Magic always came with a cost – that was one of the first lessons she learned as a young sorceress.

"Master Blackfeather is leaving his tower for a week, but something is afoot. He's recently taken on a new apprentice, and has her looking into activity along the Corridor. Now is the time to act if you want to gain leverage on the Shaper. His apprentices will be taking turns performing exercises outside the tower."

"Lord Skullreaver and I will decide whether or not to act," she intoned. Members of this cult shared the annoying trait of believing themselves equals – perhaps because they referred to one another as family. She would discuss the matter with the Lord of Nightwing Castle, of course, but had no doubt he would see things her way. They had known since the inception of their plan that Cauzel Blackfeather was a possible adversary. Steps needed to be taken to ensure he could be controlled when necessary.

"Where, precisely, will the apprentices be three days from now?" she asked the blond Shaper who, from his distorted projection, looked barely into his manhood. He thought they were part of the same team, no doubt, as her pact with the corrupted Izefet indicated. She would play the ally to get what she wanted, but would never be one of them. She would never bow to anyone but her Thuvian.

"We've been assigned partners for a test that requires open space," the young man explained. "There is an archery range in the woods southwest of the tower. Two of us should be there in the afternoon that day – I'll make certain I'm not."

"Yes, that would be wise," Annoxoria needled. "Very well, *brother*, continue your observations." She touched the water's surface with a finger and the smeared face vanished with the ripples.

She would have to go herself. There may only be a pair of apprentices to deal with, but even a novice Shaper with any talent could prove difficult to control. She couldn't trust such a task to underlings. Before making any preparations, though, she would have to inform her lover.

Annoxoria considered her image in the reflective surface of the now-still pool. She smoothed out the shading under her eyes and took stock of the sparkle of her ruby earrings. She wanted to look perfect before visiting Thuvian – he deserved no less from his mistress. Satisfied in her appearance, she left the room and locked the door to her personal quarters behind her.

Thuvian had spent the morning hunting and would likely still be out on the southern lawn. It would be wise to catch him before the regular tour of the mines began. Poor progress put him in a sour mood, and little had been made lately. He would also be on edge until hearing back from the dignitaries he'd sent word of his intentions to. Their reactions would shape the progression of Thuvian's plan.

Annoxoria strode through the castle's long stone halls until she reached the entry for the high terrace. The heels of her boots made their signature click against the polished marble as she headed for the stairs. Her view of the inner courtyard revealed that Thuvian had indeed returned from his hunt. The proud, downward curve of his horns stood out as he bent over an elk's carcass, gutting and stripping its body. At least his trip was successful. They usually were, for Thuvian was strong, determined, and clever.

He relied upon those same traits to carve out a country of his own. He was crafting a nation from the backbone of the Wyrmsmoke Mountains, territory no one else claimed because other nations didn't consider the land habitable. The forging of Nightwing Castle proved them wrong, and its foundation was bought by the gems they harvested from the mountains' roots.

"My Love," Annoxoria called from the steps when she was half-way down.

Thuvian turned his head at her greeting, simultaneously reaching his hand into a slit in the elk's belly and yanking out its intestines. He stood straight and dropped the body parts into a pile, then handed his knife to an attendant to finish the job. The half-Nightwing rinsed the blood from his hands in a basin while Annoxoria descended the remaining stairs, then walked over to greet her as she reached the grass-covered portion of the courtyard.

"It is a fine kill, My Lord. We shall eat well tonight."

He immediately took her in an embrace. He was rough, forceful in his desire as he kissed her, and she wouldn't have it any other way. One strong hand slid down her back and cupped the curve of her buttock, pressing her against his hardness – a clear indication of how badly he wanted her. She would let him take her right there in the courtyard, if that was what his passion dictated, but he pulled back from their kiss after another moment. Her hands slid against the textured black scales of his back as they separated, reveling in the wondrous complexity of their surface, missing the press of his body already.

"The hunt always helps clear my head," he said in his deep, haunting voice. It was almost as if he spoke with two of them: one civilized tone overlain with a feral counterpart, a clear reminder that, no matter what he said, he was always dangerous. "It is nearly time to check on production. Have you come to join me?"

"I will join you, my Lord, but I bring another bit of news first." Annoxoria was already nervous about his possible reaction, for he was beyond her ability to predict – a fact that excited her immensely.

"Good news or bad?" he asked, clasping one of her relatively tiny hands in his as they walked to an arched entryway on the ground floor of the castle.

She wasn't sure how to answer his question, so just dove into the narrative. "I have been keeping eyes on Cauzel Blackfeather as we discussed, and it appears he cannot keep that bony nose of his out of our affairs. He is investigating the ambushes along the Corridor, something the merchant lords of Pasaxtree have been unwilling to do thus far."

"Or perhaps he acts on their behalf?" Thuvian pointed out.

"That is a possibility," she admitted, "but regardless of his motivation, he will probably discover the involvement of the lizardfolk before long. And that might lead him to our doorstep."

"Or Sepathia's, like we intended. If the blame were to go to my sister, we might find Cauzel and his allies aligned with our cause."

"True. We knew this day would come, but we cannot further control which direction he looks. I have a proposition to mitigate future interference from Cauzel, should his investigation not go in our favor. But, it must be acted upon quickly." Annoxoria started to feel more relaxed. So far, Thuvian was remaining completely calm, with no outward signs of his draconic aggression kicking in.

"Hmmm," his throat rumbled. "And what sort of devious scheme has my Lady planned for our unsuspecting neighbor?"

"The Shaper of Ifelian is taking a trip away from his tower, leaving his apprentices to perform tasks while he is away. Some of these tasks will leave them vulnerable, beyond the protections of Cauzel's magical wards." Annoxoria glanced at Thuvian to gauge his reaction, knowing he could see where she was headed before saying the actual words. His face remained its normal, scowling mask of slightly protruding fangs and deep-set, amber eyes. Unreadable.

"It presents a perfect opportunity for us to take possession of something we know is dear to him," she continued. "He has invested a lot of energy into teaching his pupils, no doubt, and they would make valuable hostages to prevent his meddling in the future."

"Or, such an act could provoke him to action," Thuvian countered, though it seemed more like a consideration than direct challenge to her proposal.

Annoxoria stopped walking and turned until she was face-to-face with her lover. "I am completely devoted to you, my Lord, as you know."

He stared at her, face unflinching, the lighter gray scales of his chest rippling slowly with each controlled breath. "I do, Nox."

She fell to her knees before him, still clasping his hand tightly. "I think acting now is the wisest strategy. Besides your sister, a Shaper of Cauzel's ability is the biggest threat to the rise of Drachenmark. I would like to lead the expedition personally to make sure there are no mistakes, but I subject myself to your will, as always."

Her submissive position brought her face in line with Thuvian's waist. She couldn't help lowering her eyes slightly while waiting for his response, fixating on the bulge beneath the chainmail sheet that hung from his belt. She thought she saw it twitch, and again, part of her hoped he would force her to service him right there in the hallway, taking what he wanted. Instead, he moved his hands gently into her tight curls until he caressed the sides of her head.

"You have my leave to go, then. It is never wrong to act from a position of strength. Let those who surround us fear us first – then we shall have their respect." He drew her up from her knees and bent to kiss her mouth. "Come, let us get the production check out of the way. I have unspent energy, and you are too tempting to resist."

She smiled at his words and practically floated the rest of the way to the mines, looking forward to the pleasure she would give her lover, her Lord.

Like Thuvian, Annoxoria much preferred the dark of night when stalking her prey. However, the apprentices were only likely to be out during the day, so she had to make do. She didn't want to involve Izefet, or even suggest she might need his help on a mission for the benefit of Drachenmark. She was going to handle this the same way she had everything else before ever hearing of the 'Name of the Beast.'

Although her power alone was formidable, adding an element of brute strength gave adversaries more to contend with, and she didn't want to underestimate Cauzel's students. Grellock, her ogre captain, could certainly handle any physical threats they might pose. Since the intent was to capture their opponents, she decided it couldn't hurt to bring along a handful of lizardfolk as well. They were indebted to Thuvian for his protection from Sepathia, and loyal beyond whichever slaves might have been suited to the task.

It was fortunate they understood Draconic, because they didn't have brains large enough to learn a second language. Grellock wasn't much smarter, of course, but simple phrases in Illanese had always been enough to ensure his compliance. She knew he enjoyed hurting others, so she'd have to remain vigilant to keep the apprentices alive should they resist too strongly.

The weeklong journey east had proven a nightmare so far. Having been born within it, she failed to account for the Veil of Trigilas, which she only now realized had been more than just a folktale. Her charges kept wandering off once they crossed the border of eladrin territory. She was forced to tie a rope around each of their waists and lead the awkward procession through the woods.

When Grellock stopped intermittently, however, or started to pull in another direction, there was no moving him. She had to wait until he became aimless again to correct their course. She worried about how her charges would react once the ambush began and started working on a contingency plan. Regardless, they would head north once the prisoners were in hand, as that was the shortest distance to the eladrin boundary.

Finally, as she approached a line of trees, she heard the sound of a female voice, singing. She told Grellock to wait and untied the rope from her waist, creeping forward. Careful not to make any noise, she slithered around branches until she reached the trunks of the trees that were set along the top of a cliff. A landslide of some sort had ripped the earth away beneath them, though the ground sloped downward in both directions around the drop. It eventually leveled off into a sizeable field from which most of the trees had been cleared.

In the field were two human women and an eladrin male. Bales of hay with targets upon them had been set up on the northern side of the field, and midway between them and the southern end, a woman sang while anchoring one end of a magical rainbow. At the opposite end of the archery range, the Eladrin held the other end of the prismatic bridge and was chanting words of sorcery while manipulating the air.

Between them, the second woman, dark of hair and wearing a red leather outfit bearing numerous slits, offered encouragement. "That's it, Dyphina, now raise your voice to the next octave."

As the woman did so, a new band of yellow color sprung from her hands and arced across the field toward the Eladrin.

Excellent, Annoxoria thought. For the moment, at least, the apprentices were in the middle of casting and completely preoccupied. There would likely be no better chance to take them. With the cliff acting as a natural barrier, her forces could approach from both sides to hem them in.

Annoxoria returned to her cohorts and untied the rope connecting them while explaining to Grellock what to do. When she finished giving the ogre his simple instructions, she spoke to the lizardfolk in Draconic. Adept at fishing, she'd armed them with familiar nets. They were to fan out and approach slowly, blocking any escape in the direction of Cauzel's tower. She hoped to capture her prey before Grellock got too zealous in his pursuit.

Not wanting to chance a bout of directional confusion, she herded the half-dozen lizardfolk with her around the north end of the cliff, using the autumn trees to mask their movement. Once everyone had gotten into place, she waited for her captain to make his move.

Peeking around the trunk she was using for cover, she noticed that a pair of bows were stored within close reach of the male. Eladrin archers were known for their accuracy – Annoxoria hoped this one focused enough on his magic to eschew that aspect of his cultural heritage. The thought just passed when she heard the gurgling roar of Grellock spread across the field. Time for action.

Annoxoria slipped out from behind her tree to see Grellock's fearsome figure waving an iron-headed cudgel above his head, raising a commotion. The young Shapers' concentration was shattered and their cooperative spell vanished with it. The woman in red was the first to react.

Instead of running in fear, however, she drew a dagger from the back of her belt and shouted to her companions. "Thaelios, behind me!" She stood perhaps a dozen strides from Grellock but wasn't taking cover. She began singing in some strange language, facing down her opponent.

Annoxoria was surprised, but at least the ogre had captured their attention. *"Ellenof shegree contemnus,"* she chanted, pointing toward the green-haired woman after pulling a tuft of bat fur and a tiny lump of coal from a pouch fastened at her belt. Just before she finished her spell, Annoxoria caught a glimpse of a small bloom of fire launching from the dark-haired woman toward her ogre. Incendiary magic could be a problem.

An instant later, however, Annoxoria's swirling sphere of clinging shadows cut off her view of the apprentices. Centered on the one closest to her, she knew it engulfed the Eladrin as well, though probably didn't extend far enough to reach the fire-summoner. Annoxoria yelled in Draconic for the lizardfolk to close in and take their prey while she approached the edge of the darkness herself.

The shadow hissed as it churned around and around, diminishing both the sight and hearing of those within. The lizardfolk's keen sense of smell would give them the advantage, but they took longer than she hoped to respond and not all of them came at once. "It's that damned Veil," she muttered, trying to decide if she needed to compensate.

"*Ishniel vorkalu!*" She ordered the lizardfolk into the Sphere of Shadow to cast their nets, but as they entered, a small deer sprung out of the dark mass, bounding east toward Blackfeather Perch.

Annoxoria narrowed her eyes at the fawn. "Very clever, apprentice." A slight shimmering of the image gave it away as an illusion to her trained eye, though she couldn't be sure whether its caster was still in the shadow or had disguised herself and fled. There was an easy way to find out. "You brought this on yourself, dear."

She reached into another pouch and withdrew a rhubarb leaf and the dried stomach of an adder. "*Nattara hufstrem.*" A bolt of green shot from her open palm like an arrow, striking the fleeing fawn with a splattering sound.

The illusion vanished, revealing the green-haired woman lying on the ground, wincing. She reached toward a hole in her brown dress over her thigh, but dared not touch it. A compound like acidic spittle bubbled from the skin under the hole, and she clearly didn't want to risk spreading.

Annoxoria noticed one of the late-arriving lizardfolk approaching from the cover of the eastern trees. "*Vorkalu,*" she said, and it tossed its net over the woman sprawled on the grass.

With that one immobilized, Annoxoria circled to the other side of the shadow spiral to see how Grellock had fared.

His cudgel lay on the ground, and part of his leather breastplate and right bicep were blackened, but he held the woman in red between his gigantic hands. Her arms were pinned to her body and Annoxoria could see he was squeezing tightly, trying to make her pop.

She was about to shout an order for him to stop when she heard the whistle of an arrow as it flew through the cartilage of the ogre's oversized, left ear. Grellock instinctively dropped the woman and she fell to the ground, unmoving.

Retracing the flight of the arrow, Annoxoria saw the silver-haired Eladrin fitting another onto his bowstring. She had underestimated the courage of Cauzel's apprentices, as well as their concern for one another. This one must have run back toward the ogre to retrieve a bow once she cast her spell.

While Grellock had his attention, however, she needed to decide how to best incapacitate him. The Eladrin would be of no use if he was squashed into jelly, and her ogre would be of no use with a few more strategically placed holes. As she reached into her pouch for inspiration, however, another solution presented itself.

A well-aimed bola from one of the lizardfolk just emerging from the hissing shadow struck the Eladrin mid-calf, entangling and toppling him over. The arrow fell loose from its string, and before Annoxoria even had time to begin chanting, a net was cast over the prone apprentice.

Annoxoria surveyed the field to make sure the commotion hadn't attracted any further adversaries. Satisfied they were alone, she commanded the lizardfolk to not only bind the hands and feet of their prisoners, but gag them as well. She dismissed her Sphere of Shadow with a wave of her hand, then ordered her subordinates to once again rope themselves to one another for the journey home.

Grellock groaned his complaint as she examined his ear, but as it had pierced clean through, she simply snapped the arrow in two and threw the pieces to the ground. "You were lucky," she said, and left it at that. She checked to make sure the woman in red was still breathing, and upon confirmation, directed her ogre captain to carry her over his shoulder, once tied.

"Hurry, now," she said, tying the free end of the rope around her waist as her lizardfolk lifted the other prisoners. "I want to be out from under this accursed Eladrin spell as soon as possible."

The heat in the mines wouldn't have been so unbearable if the air hadn't also been so stagnant. Fresh air barely reached this deep, even with the ventilation shafts, and the sweat of the toiling workers left a persistent stench that took getting used to. Annoxoria's strategy for dealing with it was to wear as little as possible during the daily performance inspections. She wouldn't dare be seen without her black, over-the-knee leather boots, but today her thin, sleeveless dress held tight to her body and only reached mid-thigh. Rust colored and riveted with tiny scales, she didn't bother wearing anything underneath. Every now and then she got a little thrill from reminding the slaves what joys remained beyond their reach.

She was joining Thuvian for the inspections momentarily, but Annoxoria wanted to pay a visit to her newest prisoners first. She opened the door to find five pitiable souls, including her recent captures, chained together in the bleak, putrid-smelling quarters. It was difficult to differentiate between them in the dimness; the only light to reach the room was the soft, red glow of the smelting fires from deeper in the mines, playing off the rough, stone walls.

"I know you think you're special," she began, standing in the doorway with a wide stance to give the full effect of her backlit outline, "but I am here to remind you you're not. You may know a little magic, imagine you have powerful friends – but down here you're as ordinary as the other laborers unfortunate enough to be chained to you. I'm sure they can tell you what happens to workers who don't do their jobs. I am Lady Annoxoria Nefzen, and I have sole control over your lives."

She could feel their eyes on her, soaking in what they were told, and it made her warmer still. "You are here for the digging. You will be shown a routine. Follow that routine, and you will be fed. Find enough rubies, and you will earn other small comforts. Find one of the rubies that shines from within, and you shall have a place in this kingdom beyond our mines. Disobey those with authority over you, and you will be punished … creatively."

Annoxoria took a step toward reuniting with her Lord, then thought of one last piece of advice. "Forget your magic. Mine is stronger, and using it will only bring you ruin." With that, she gave the newly captured slaves no further thought and left the sleeping quarters to rendezvous with Thuvian for the beginning of their tour.

She loved being half of the most intimidating couple in the Midlands. These daily walk-throughs of the mines were not only an opportunity to stay abreast of which areas were producing at a faster rate, but to remind those who labored why they were toiling under the earth and not wandering free above it.

Just as Annoxoria cultivated a look designed to inspire lust, her partner's presence delivered a powerful dosage of fear. Though Thuvian Skullreaver was naturally protected by hardened scales and bony plates, he often wore steel shoulder guards and a chainmail loincloth to emphasize his armored physique. His front was cast in muddy gray scales, straining to contain his lean musculature. His arms and back were rougher, sharper, and colored the coal black of his Nightwing heritage.

He was fond of wearing a blood-red cape in the presence of others – he'd declared it made him appear more regal. Thuvian claimed his father was an Eladrin, but the only trait suggesting it was the eyes. They were oversized, solid amber, and set in the front of his face, though he did possess the narrowly slit pupils of his mother's side. His mouth was narrow, but deep, with sharp teeth more suited for tearing meat than gnashing. His tongue was wonderfully long and skilled; she shivered just thinking about it.

He stood waiting for her with the ogre overseer, though if his patience was tested by her late arrival, she knew she was forgiven as soon as he saw her hips swaying in her tight dress. Thuvian was propped up by Viper's Kiss, the weapon she'd spent a fortnight enchanting as an engagement present.

A staff of ironwood, it was capped on either side by foot-long, double-edged, serrated blades. When commanded, their glowing heads hissed and turned green, secreting an acid corrosive enough to eat through steel. She wondered if he was aware of it melting through the stone floor as he leaned upon it now.

"Sorry to keep you waiting, my Lord. I wanted to see how our little birds were adjusting to their new nest." She braced her hands on his strong chest and stood on her toes to kiss his bony cheek.

"I would wait a thousand sunsets for your beauty, my Lady," he responded. "But now that you are here, shall we proceed?"

She knew it wasn't really a question, but nodded regardless. Thuvian gestured for the overseer to lead the way.

The mines were too expansive to cover their entirety every day, so a few tunnels were selected each morning as part of a rotation that comprised the bulk of the operation. While Thuvian inspected the contents of the baskets and carts filled by the workers, for both quantity of gems and the size of individual deposits, Annoxoria kept her eyes mostly on the laborers themselves.

Her interest was rooting out laziness, deceptive practices, or those who might be plotting to either escape or do their masters harm. No such behaviors could be tolerated, and she would rather err by punishing an innocent than reap the consequences of inaction.

"Has the presence of that Aasimar yielded results yet?" Thuvian asked, drawing her attention away from a pair of slaves she thought might be whispering to one another.

"He has been directing some of the new tunneling efforts, supposedly guiding them toward where he feels the strongest pull, but we have yet to claim a single Seed of the Avatars." She still hadn't told her lover the true reason the strange, winged creature was helping them. It was the only secret she kept from him.

"Take me to where they are working," Thuvian commanded the ogre.

The overseer grunted and nodded in response, then turned down a side tunnel to his right. They had not yet cleared the tighter passage when the sounds of excited shouting greeted them from ahead.

"I found one! I found one!"

The ogre picked up his pace to reach the source of the commotion, but Thuvian continued with his normal gait. Annoxoria fought the urge to rush past him, envious of the firm control he seemed to have over his emotions. Or perhaps, his heart was simply not beating as quickly as hers.

When she finally reached the end of the tunnel, emerging into a workable section of the mine with more open space, she saw the Aasimar standing on a ledge of rock beyond the height of Thuvian's reach. He had a look of awe on his face as he stared into a bright red stone, balanced between two of his fingers.

Annoxoria knew what it was, even from a distance, for it shone with a swirling light of its own making. They had uncovered their first piece of the Living Fire!

Chapter 8

The Mines of Living Fire

L ying in chains gave Saffron a greater appreciation for what her sister had been through at the hands of the Black Hills orcs. She sat on an uneven stone floor, the air around her hot and dark, matching her mood. Only the dimmest red glow of firelight from beyond filtered into their room through the barred, square cut-out of their door. Thaelios and Dyphina were settled in lumps to either side, resting, signs of their presence reduced to ragged breathing and the occasional tug of chains against her leg.

They'd been joined with another pair of hostages upon arrival, though their peers smelled to have a few weeks of experience already behind them. At least she was now confident about where the travelers abducted along the Ifelian Corridor ended up. Annoxoria had been boastful during their journey, and once Saffron saw the size of the mining operation, everything made sense.

"I need to get out of here," Saffron stated aloud, though not to anyone in particular.

The voice that answered was gruff and scratchy. "You and every other poor bastard stuck under Nightwing Castle. But," he paused to stretch his limbs into a new position, rattling the chains lightly, "it's unlikely to happen, unless you count the crematorium a viable escape route."

"I *would* rather die than remain as a slave, toiling without hope or the freedom to determine my own fate." Saffron couldn't allow even the hint of resignation to find root in her mind.

"A woman after my own heart," the second prisoner chimed in. His voice was more even and full of bass. "I am Phaerim, by the by, and that optimistic sack of potatoes is Faulk. Are you three merchants, or just cursed to be in the wrong place at the wrong time?"

Saffron ran her tongue along her lips, trying to wet them, but her mouth felt hopelessly dry. "I'm a musician," she replied, content to leave it at that. "How long have you been kept down here?"

"My train was ambushed a tenday ago," Phaerim answered. "I was a guard, but we were about four guards short of what we needed. Faulk's been here longer – he's a tough old codger."

"Not that old," Faulk countered, "but I do what I have to."

"And what about your friends," Phaerim continued, "are they musicians as well?"

"What do our professions matter now? We're all miners from this point on." Saffron didn't want to be off-putting, but she wasn't eager to trust two strangers with too much information. She certainly didn't want to speak for the other apprentices.

"It may matter if we're going to actually trust one another and try to break out of here. We will have to work together, obviously, and planning would be easier if we knew what skills we were each contributing."

"I think they're sleeping," was all Saffron added.

"Well, you might as well wake them," Faulk said. "They're going to round us up for our shift shortly, and the ogres aren't a patient lot."

The memory of the hulking creature nearly crushing her to death reminded Saffron of the pain in her ribs. She wasn't sure she could survive whatever punishment their brutish sensibilities dictated they dole out, day after day. Though only their first morning waking underneath the castle, she was especially worried about Thaelios and Dyphina. Neither seemed particularly built for hard labor, but after seeing how her sister coped with imprisonment, she knew better than to make assumptions about what others could endure.

She leaned over in the dark and felt the soft curve of Dyphina's back. She was folded up with her legs tucked into her chest. Saffron nudged her gently, and Dyphina woke with start.

"I was dreaming," she said, leaving Saffron surprised how quickly she acclimated to being awake.

"How is your leg, Dyphina?"

Saffron could hear her tentatively moving a hand to check the injury she'd incurred on the practice range. Saffron saw the damage when the wound was still fresh – it was sticky with a mixture of fluids – but the journey to the castle had taken nearly a week, and she'd had a sack over her head with only a narrow slit to see through for most of it.

"It's not too bad. A scab has formed, so as long as I can avoid infection it should mend."

"Aye, this is not the place for open wounds," Faulk stated. "If there's corruption, it will more than likely get you before all's said and done. You sound like a nice lass, so I hope you heal properly."

Dyphina didn't have an opportunity to respond before the door to their chamber swung open. "On your feet!" The command seemed ornery enough on its own, but was accompanied by the motivating whip-crack of the ogre's lash.

The rattling of chains filled the room as the slaves hurried to comply, and when Saffron reached over to wake Thaelios, she found he had silently stood. She still wasn't used to the fact that Eladrin didn't really sleep.

Faulk was at one end of the line and took the lead in filing out of their chamber. Once into the main corridor, the light of widely spaced torches provided more to see by. Saffron got a better look at the two additions to their team, if only from behind. Phaerim's shape was sleek, yet leanly muscular. His shirt was torn from obvious confrontations with the whip. Dark hair shielded the back of his head in thick, loose curls.

Ahead of him, Faulk was short and stocky, though obviously possessing great physical strength. His forearms were wide, his ragged sleeves pushed above them, and his thinning blonde hair pulled back in a ponytail.

The ogre lingered until all his charges were clear of the room. Saffron was alert, attempting to absorb every detail of her new surroundings. The floor and walls had been hewn from the stone of the mountain, though not with great care. The passages were serviceable but uneven, leaving her thankful for the thick soles of her boots. A long, lonely passage with no offshoots, only occasional doors to other cells, led them away from their block of slave quarters. With no route to escape, no guards were wasted along the route until they reached a larger hub of tunnels.

Her leather armor was stifling hot, but after seeing the tears in Phaerim's shirt, she couldn't be too sorry for the protection it afforded her. She was thankful once again for Natrone the armorsmith's skill and the suppleness of kank hide, for her suit was able to pass as heavy clothing and had not been confiscated.

She paid attention as Faulk shuffled them past several forks – left, then right, then right again – until they reached a more open chamber with stores of empty baskets and tools. Faulk grabbed a pick and Phaerim a hammer, but the latter grasped Dyphina's wrist when she reached for an implement as well.

"Just take a basket," Phaerim said. "We'll gather the rocks, and you can sift through them. Keep anything that sparkles and we can sort the lot at the end of our shift."

Dyphina nodded silently, picking up an empty basket and placing it against her hip. Overhearing Phaerim's explanation, Saffron handed a basket to Thaelios as well, though she took a hammer for herself. She wanted to get a sense of its weight in her hand should she need to use it as a weapon, and figured she could use a little exercise since she'd been unable to train in days.

The day turned into a grueling set of repetitious tasks. Faulk, Phaerim, and Saffron hammered and chiseled the walls of the mine, while Dyphina and Thaelios collected the fragments and sifted through them in their baskets. Without speaking, they quickly fell into a rhythm of teamwork.

Faulk had an uncanny knack for picking out prime spaces with enough room for all of them to operate smoothly, then scouting out a new one to move to once the prospects went down. Phaerim worked efficiently and told them to pace themselves, for the day was long. Though they would be evaluated on production, he advised against dwelling too much on it. Keeping a steady pace would be enough to get them by, and in the draining heat, overexertion could be a silent killer.

They all did enough work to keep from being whipped, yet Saffron wondered what the threshold for such treatment was, as she heard more than one snap of the lash, answered by moaning, from other areas of the mine. She devised ways to look busy, even if she needed to relax and rub out her muscles before continuing.

Her forearms throbbed by the time they earned their first break, which seemed to fall innumerable hours after beginning. Other slaves came through the passages, handing out biscuits for what felt like a midday meal, though Saffron could only guess at the actual time. For all she knew, it could have been their dinner the following day, and she suddenly had to fight off an acute desire to sleep.

Despite Thaelios and Dyphina performing lighter work, Saffron was impressed that they kept at it and didn't complain.

At the very least, she felt responsible for the other apprentices and couldn't let them waste their potential in this mine.

Cauzel would realize soon enough that they were missing and surely wouldn't stand for such an affront. Would he be able to discover what became of them? Saffron could scarcely even consider what her failure to show up would do to Be'naj. Would she ever trust another person again? Saffron didn't know if she could live with such guilt. She decided she wouldn't, because she would either break free or die trying. She made a decision right there to trust their new chain-partners and begin the work of planning an escape.

Not much had changed by the end of their work shift. Saffron was exhausted, and the muscles in her arms and back cried for relief. With no transition from sun to stars, the passage of time was measured in hammer strokes and streams of sweat.

Bowls of cold porridge waited for them when they shuffled back to their personal quarters, but they were forced to eat in the near dark. Her eyes made adjustments to the dimness over their shift, however, and even the timid glow of the torches nearest their room now allowed her to distinguish the shapes of her companions.

She slumped to the ground, giving her weary legs a rest, and cradled her bowl of mostly tasteless sustenance while she thought. "From what I could tell, there seem to be about five groups of chained prisoners for every ogre. And what are those others creatures – the hairy ones?"

"Rauglor," Faulk answered. "Mean-spirited bastards. Almost makes them worse than the ogres. They're larger cousins of the Rauggin, and used to living underground. They harbor a collective hatred of anyone who doesn't spend their miserable lives beneath the mountains."

"Well, they'll be a problem, too." Saffron had seen more than one act aggressively toward their charges. "I figure one for every group of prisoners is about right."

"And they see hells-better in the dark than we do ..." Phaerim paused. "Those of us who are human, anyway."

It occurred to Saffron that her new companions had likely never seen an Eladrin before. She was finally growing accustomed to the strangeness of their striking features. To their credit, neither Faulk nor Phaerim had made a disparaging remark or treated Thaelios with disdain.

"I see better in the starlight," Thaelios spoke what might have been his first words of the day. "Not so, underground."

"Are you ... one of the firstborn?" Phaerim prodded further.

"I am Thaelios Dunwarden of Gilsage, and yes, I am a son of the Eladrin."

"How did one of your heritage come to be stuck here with the likes of us?" Faulk asked.

Saffron tensed while awaiting Thaelios's response. Again, she worried their interest was perhaps more than natural curiosity. What if they were spies of whoever captured them, planted to extract vital information? Her earlier decision to trust now seemed hasty.

"I am unsure as to the *why* of it," Thaelios answered in an even, measured tone. "Perhaps learning more about our captor would provide a glimpse at the reason. As for the *how*, we were ambushed in the woods. I doubt our story differs greatly from the majority of this mine's inhabitants."

"Sooner or later these villains have to draw the wrong kind of attention," Phaerim said between mouthfuls of porridge. "You know, if one of the trade guilds loses enough money or the nephew of some influential lord goes missing, someone would have to come put a stop to it, wouldn't they? Maybe the right move is just keeping our heads down and waiting this out."

Saffron sighed. "I doubt time is on our side, Phaerim. How long before one of those Rauglor decides to take its aggression out on one of us? Or we slip and fall in the dark, or are too exhausted to continue filling our quota?"

She didn't mention her fear that she might be responsible for Cauzel's apprentices being targeted. She knew the previous attacks had all been perpetrated along the Ifelian Corridor, and the obvious answer staring down her conscience was that she was somehow watched after her battle alongside Be'naj. Why else would their captors suddenly deviate and take a group so far from the thoroughfare? They could not have been mistaken for merchants, after all. It made her worry about the danger Be'naj was in, as well. If Saffron didn't find a way to warn her, she might be chained to their legs one of these mornings, or worse.

"You're right," Phaerim conceded. "This is no way to live, worrying each day if it might be your last."

"We're not the only ones to contemplate escape," Faulk scoffed. "I assure you that. And yet, I'm comfortable in my certainty that no one has achieved the feat. Why would we be any different? And don't tell me it's because we're special. There are men with spikes running through them who probably felt so."

Saffron wasn't sure how to respond without revealing who they were. Phaerim beat her to it. "But they *are* special, Faulk, don't you see? The queen came to visit them here, not address them in the throne room – have you ever heard of that happening? And she said something about not bothering to use magic … shadows of the deep!"

Saffron could see his outline turn to face Dyphina, who was next closest to him.

"You're all Shapers, aren't you?" Excitement, and perhaps a little hope, flavored the question.

"We are learning to be, yes." Dyphina's voice was timid, but Saffron couldn't blame her for revealing the truth. Besides, their captor already knew of their magical affiliation.

"What does that mean, exactly?" Phaerim continued. "What can you do?"

"I …" Dyphina trailed off, unable to provide an answer anyone wanted to hear. "Without my spellbook, not much."

"Well, where is your spellbook?" Faulk asked, as if she might have hidden it somewhere in their holding quarters.

"Perhaps I can explain a little about arcane theory to the uninitiated," Thaelios offered, coming to Dyphina's aid.

"By all means." Phaerim put his bowl down and settled his back against the rock wall.

Saffron did the same and was pleased to find its surface slightly cooler than the surrounding air.

"The world, you see," Thaelios began in his soothing, melodic voice, "has always provided the potential for magic. There is an energy created by the heart of the world that is released at places of natural wonder – a tumbling waterfall, a giant chasm in the earth, the most ancient mountains and trees. You see it unleashed during thunderstorms, or the raging of a volcano, or the crashing of waves upon the beach, and think little of it.

"When the Avatars visited Elisahd a dozen centuries ago, their divine presence only added to this magical energy. It seethed from them and built up in the atmosphere, waiting to be tapped. Trigilas, the Father of Spells, was the first mortal to learn to manipulate this energy to achieve fantastic effects. He taught the other Eladrin, and the gods became worried they would no longer be needed."

"Sounds like stories to me," Faulk interrupted momentarily, but Phaerim shushed him.

Thaelios continued, undaunted. "Trigilas's manipulation was called 'Shaping,' and it involves using a combination of the right words, movements, and aligned materials to achieve certain outcomes. In the generations following his first discoveries, various other methods of manipulating magical energy have been developed.

"Lady Saffron, for instance, follows the bardic tradition, using musical frequencies, combined with intention, to unleash the energy's potential."

"Who is Lady Saffron?" Phaerim asked.

Saffron lifted her hand in the near dark, though it was unlikely anyone noticed. "That would be me," she said with a resigned tone. There was little point in holding back such information now.

"What this means for us here, under our current conditions, is that we are limited," Thaelios soldiered on. "New spells must be researched and studied, and the specifics can be complex, which is why we scribe the methods into our spellbooks. Without these formulae, never mind the confiscation of our ingredient pouches, we are reduced to those few incantations already fully committed to memory that require no material components. Unless, one of you happens to have hidden a cache of fox fur and almond shells?"

Was that a stab at humor, Saffron wondered? Thaelios gave more of an explanation than she had gotten from Cauzel, though the master of Blackfeather Perch clearly had other concerns on his mind. Dyphina had some background in the bardic tradition as well as employing traditional methods. Palomar had simply referred to his casting method as *Harmonious Release*, which suited her for an explanation.

"To form a plan of escape," Saffron said, steering the conversation toward fruitful action, "we need to gather information. We need to know, as best we can, how many of the enemy will be guarding us, and their movements, if possible. Is there a time or location better suited for us to act? We also need to know where most of these tunnels lead, if we're going to use them to escape – not to mention what lies beyond. From your experience, are there any opportunities to wander, or do the ogres always dictate where we go?"

Faulk coughed to clear his throat. "They lead us to a starting point, but we have some freedom to migrate when areas are fully harvested."

"Good," Saffron responded. "We'll use that to start a systematic exploration of the mines. Any plan we make will be useless if we can't find a clear route out of this hellscape."

"We'll also need a way out of these chains. It will be too difficult to fight or run if we're tethered together," Phaerim added.

"And we'll need to arm ourselves," Faulk contributed. "No sense in getting caught too early, but once we decide on the timing, we should smuggle some of the mining tools to use as weapons. Still, I don't know. Have you ever seen one of those ogres angry?"

"I was nearly crushed to death by the one who attacked us," Saffron offered, remembering the enormous strength of its embrace. She was completely helpless once in its grip.

"My point, exactly." Faulk let out another fit of coughing. "We're going to need something more than a pickaxe to take one of them out."

"Maybe we can create an opportunity when none of the ogres are around?" Thaelios mentioned.

"We'll work on that part of the plan," Saffron said, shaking her head. She knew they needed to take on one problem at a time, or the combined obstacles would seem insurmountable. "I think our first step needs to be familiarizing ourselves with the tunnels. We'll worry about other problems later. Perhaps I can practice a few songs in the meantime."

With no argument, they tabled the discussion to get some rest before their next, grueling shift. As much as she craved sleep, Saffron had trouble putting her active mind to rest. She alternated between thoughts of what tomorrow held, solving the problems that blocked their escape, and her desire to alert Cauzel to what became of his pupils. Mostly, though, she imagined Be'naj's face, illuminated by starlight, waiting to see her again.

It seemed she had just closed her eyes when the bellowing of their ogre overseer roused Saffron from sleep. Her muscles ached even worse than before she rested, and it was a struggle to stand during the disorienting first moments of wakefulness. She gathered her faculties and tried to begin memorizing the various twists along their path, noting particularly where corridors split or ladders indicated another level.

The mining was difficult, but the idea of progressing toward freedom made it more bearable. If she had cared about such things, she might have taken pride in the amount of rubies they were uncovering during their shift.

She remembered descending when they were led from the castle to the mines, and supposed they were somewhere below the fortified structure. Heading higher would no doubt bring them closer to the entrance, but it also likely meant more security and eventually, Annoxoria herself.

Faulk seemed to have the same notion and kept them exploring systematically deeper into the mountain. He pressed further laterally as well, whenever they weren't under close scrutiny, searching for some kind of back door or ventilation tunnel that might lead to the surface.

Shifts passed, one always leading to another. Some expired without ever having the freedom to progress in their search. Sometimes the ogre lashers and Rauglor lording over them asserted their authority, telling them precisely where to dig for the day. During a run of bad luck, one of the Rauglor got particularly rough with Thaelios, whom they seemed particularly keen to torment.

"Uhr mannor!" the creature yelled at the Eladrin, shoving him in the shoulder and jarring loose the basket he carried. It fell to the ground and toppled sideways, spilling its contents across the rough floor of the mine.

None of them had any idea what it had said in its foul language, but Thaelios made the mistake of casting a disapproving look over his shoulder before dropping to one knee to gather his losses. The Rauglor reacted swiftly, thrusting the butt of his spear against the back of Thaelios's head, the *crack* of the impact knocking him out cold.

"No!" Dyphina screamed, dropping her own basket and huddling over her fallen neighbor to protect him from further abuse.

Saffron's grip tightened on her rock hammer, her frustration nearly boiling over. The Rauglor seemed to sense her hatred and turned to face her, eliciting a menacing gurgle that sounded even parts taunt and laugh. He was a head taller, probably twice her weight, and no doubt lacked the imagination to consider her any sort of threat.

She wanted nothing more than to teach this miscreant a lesson, but she caught sight of Phaerim discreetly shaking his head before tilting it to the left. Shifting her eyes to follow, she spotted a second Rauglor pushing another group of chained miners into their vicinity from an adjacent tunnel. Phaerim was right – as much as she burned to act, now was not the time.

Saffron lowered her eyes, signaling to the Rauglor that he'd won, and thankfully he moved on. Faulk and Phaerim started scooping mineral clusters back into Thaelios's basket while Dyphina cradled his head and lightly tapped his cheeks to bring him around. The incident slowed them for the rest of their shift as they all attempted to keep one eye on their overseer to ensure they weren't blindsided again. Saffron still felt flushed when the time came for their dinner. Instead of impotent retaliation, she tried to channel her emotion into ideas for a new song.

Back in their group chamber she practiced singing, and taught Dyphina some of what she'd learned as well. They focused on *Enrapture*, with Phaerim their willing subject. He seemed to enjoy the soothing Begnari refrain, and everyone else remained silent while the performance was in progress. As an escape from their typical drudgery, it was difficult to tell if the resulting passivity was due to magic or simply willful indulgence in escapism.

When not teaching Dyphina, Saffron crafted a new melody, applying the little that Cauzel had shown her. She had to be careful during its practice, for this music possessed a soul eager to burn. She used her desire for freedom and the longing to spare Be'naj from future pain to fuel it. She used the knowledge of what had been done to her sister, Dhania, over and over in the harem of Hope's End, to shape it. Her practice was promising, but she would wait until necessary to fully unleash it.

Fortunately, Thaelios's rivalry with Iliana led to him committing much of his spellbook to memory. By his own admission, there were only a few spells he knew that didn't require material ingredients, but he demonstrated one that was eminently useful.

"*Otreritus penicul,*" he pronounced, while concentrating on the manacle around his ankle. Saffron's eyes were starting to see much better in the dim light as the days passed. It was not an adjustment she wanted to become permanent. In the pregnant silence that followed Thaelios's spell, she heard two faint, metallic clicks.

"And there you have it," he declared, reaching down and removing the now opened lock from its iron ring. He spread the hinges and slipped his leg free of the bond.

Saffron excitedly grasped her own and did the same. She stood and walked to the other side of the room, free for the first time to wander more than an arm's length from her companions. "Do you know what this means?" she asked, genuine joy flowing through her voice. "Everyone doesn't have to shuffle with me to the other side of the room when I have to shit!"

Faulk laughed, followed by the desperate rattling of chains. "Hey, why is mine still locked?" The levity had run from his voice. "Let me out of these!"

"The magic only works within a small range," Thaelios explained. "To get them all at once, we will need to circle close."

"Come now," Phaerim aligned with Faulk's sentiment, though his voice retained a small measure of patience, "you have to try again and set us all free."

Thaelios sighed. "One moment." He walked over to the three people still in chains and repeated his spell. "*Otreritus penicul.*" A short breath later they had all discarded their chains.

"Why haven't you shown us this trick before?" Phaerim asked with obvious incredulity.

The eladrin Shaper shrugged. "There is nowhere to go, unless *you* want to wrestle an ogre. You're aware this is only temporary, right? We will have to put them back on before we sleep so they don't suspect anything."

"We know, Thaelios," Phaerim said, shaking his head. "But let us enjoy the feeling a while."

Another dozen shifts passed and their optimism waned. They had all been whipped over the last several days, usually due to their output suffering while trying to unobtrusively position themselves to better scout new corridors. Saffron feared for Dyphina and Thaelios's health. None of them received adequate nourishment, but the toll of their injuries weighed heavier on the slighter apprentices. Saffron's armor helped blunt the bite of the lash, but it still stung when her blood mixed with fresh sweat after a strike.

And then, one day, she saw it. Before they were corralled back toward an open shaft by a growling Rauglor, she spied a straight, smoothly carved tunnel ending in an iron door. None of the other tunnels had doors, and this one had an armored Rauglor posted in front of it.

She whispered the news to Thaelios first, and then Dyphina, who passed it down to Phaerim beside her. They had been waiting so long for this moment, no one seemed sure what to do next. Phaerim and Faulk had pickaxes already, and Saffron was armed with a small-headed rock hammer. Only one ogre was within sight, and he stood down an incline, harassing another crew of laborers. He would have to cross the chamber and then climb up to their level, which would buy them time.

Saffron could only see two Rauglor nearby, plus the one posted outside the door. It was probably the fewest lashers they had seen on a shift all week. Her hands shook with nervous energy. Everything seemed to suggest an opportunity. She didn't know for sure where that door led, but if they could get past it, they might be able to barricade it from the other side.

Saffron made eye contact with each of her fellow prisoners and read the same thought in all their faces. They might be scared of what was to follow shedding their bonds, but were resigned to finding out. She saw Phaerim nudge Faulk, and the two shared a look at the Rauglor, silently agreeing to their task.

Saffron rested a hand on Dyphina's shoulder, hoping to both steady her and ascertain if she was ready. Without speaking, Dyphina licked her lips and nodded.

Finally, Saffron turned to Thaelios and nodded as well. Perhaps it was the trick of his solid, indigo eyes, but he alone seemed as calm as if he were about to pour a cup of tea. He shifted toward Faulk, closing in the circle so they were all close. As previously discussed, they each extended their right feet into the circle, making sure their locks were proximate.

"*Otreritus penicul.*" No sooner had the words been spoken than the crack of a whip against Thaelios's shoulder blade caused him to grunt. A light spray of blood carried over and splattered across Saffron's cheek.

"Back to work!" the Rauglor insisted in his savage dialect of Illanese.

Saffron dipped down and pulled the opened locks from their manacles in rapid sequence. As soon as she was done, Faulk howled and charged the offending Rauglor, with Phaerim just behind.

"Dyphina, the ogre!" Saffron urged as she caught sight of the huge lasher bounding toward them.

Dyphina turned to face the growling monster and clenched a fist upon her chest as her voice sprang to life. Saffron spared a look up at the half-fey from her crouch, struck again by her commanding presence, despite skin caked with dirt and hair frayed from constant heat.

The ogre slowed to a lumbering halt, then stood, slack-jawed, staring at Dyphina. Two other groups of slaves in the area stopped working, all watching the apparent revolt with vacant eyes.

To Saffron's left, Phaerim and Faulk had engaged the Rauglor, who was surprised at the sudden uprising. He drew back his whip to strike them, but they closed too quickly. Faulk smashed the shaft of his pick down against the creature's forearm, raised in defense. A crack of bone betrayed the extent of the damage, and Phaerim followed by driving his implement into the Rauglor's ribs with a two-handed swing.

The second Rauglor joined the fray just as his partner fell, this one armed with a spear. He thrust it aggressively at Phaerim's chest, who would have been impaled had he not dropped to the ground like a fallen stone.

After quickly checking to make sure Thaelios wasn't in need of immediate assistance, Saffron rushed over to help against the Rauglor.

Faulk kicked over the body of the lasher who had fallen to his knees, causing the spear-wielder to jump back in avoidance. That bought Phaerim time to push to his feet and fall back, just as Saffron slipped in front of him. She powered straight for the Rauglor, swinging her hammer and not giving him time to mount an attack of his own. Preoccupied with parrying her rapid blows, he had no answer when Faulk dove forward, driving his shoulder into the Rauglor's midsection and tackling him.

Weeks' worth of mistreatment boiled to the surface, and Saffron pounced astride the Rauglor's body, overtaken with wrath. With a blood-curdling yell, she swung the rock hammer down upon the skull of her grappled enemy, driving straight through its eye-socket. The creature stopped moving and Faulk looked up at her in amazement.

Her chest was rising with deep breaths, a couple of which passed before she'd recovered from her rage. "Get to the door!"

She left the hammer impaled in the Rauglor's face and picked up his spear, its shaft comforting her grip like the hand of an old friend, while Faulk scrambled to his feet. She still heard singing, and saw that the ogre remained motionless a couple strides from Dyphina and Thaelios.

Saffron knew they were raising a huge commotion, and it would only be a matter of moments before reinforcements arrived to check on the disturbance. "Dyphina, follow me. The magic will linger as long as we don't aggravate the ogre." She hustled back along the ridge of the tunnel until reaching the spot where she had spied the door.

With the rest of her companions close behind, she dipped the head of her spear and proceeded into the smoothly-hewn corridor. The final Rauglor stood between her and the door to freedom, she told herself. She would do whatever it took to reach it.

The corridor was narrow, leaving only a little room to maneuver on either side. Upon noticing her, the Rauglor snarled and smacked the flat of his scimitar's blade against the steel of his breastplate. He took a defensive stance, daring her to engage.

Saffron wanted to end this quickly. She shifted to an overhand grip on her spear and broke into a full run, which seemed to surprise the Rauglor. He responded by slightly raising his weapon, preparing to bring it down in a slicing arc.

She read every shift perfectly. One-two-three-four-five strides covered the distance between them, where she planted her right foot and lunged to her left. Her left foot pushed against the wall, sending her back to the right just as the Rauglor's weapon started downward toward the newly vacant spot. The Rauglor's head and eyes turned faster to follow Saffron, however, and she caught their disbelief as she also sprang off the other wall with her right foot, centering over his body.

Downward momentum added power to her strike as she drove her spear into the vulnerable space just above the guard's collarbone. It penetrated with satisfying friction as her knees collided with the Rauglor's lower body, pushing it into the door with a thud. Once she landed and the guard slumped lifelessly onto the floor, she checked the handle. Locked.

Aware of the need to hurry, she called to Thaelios as she rummaged around the corpse for keys. "Can you unlock it?"

She heard footsteps behind her. Thaelios chanted his incantation as her search came up fruitless. A sharp click signaled the lock was no longer a problem, and Saffron slid her arms under those of the dead Rauglor to drag him from impeding their escape. The others squeezed past as she removed the body.

"Remind me to never block your way to a door," Phaerim said as he took position behind the bulkier Faulk, who grasped the handle with one hand, holding his pickaxe in the other.

"Ready?" he asked. Once Phaerim nodded, he puffed out a held breath and yanked the door open.

Through the backs of her companions, Saffron couldn't see much of what lay beyond the door, but she saw the brown hide of an ogre. She immediately dropped her load and pulled the spear from its neck.

"Close the door!" Phaerim yelled in a panic. Faulk did just that, yet no sooner had he lain his shoulder against its iron surface than a pounding thud dented the door and pushed him back the length of a hand. Phaerim drove his weight against the portal as well, shutting it once more.

Dyphina turned to Thaelios. "Can you lock it?"

He shrugged. "I have not memorized such a spell," he stated, still seemingly calm. "Can you *Enrapture* the ogre?"

"That only works when they're not aggressive!" she retorted.

"Well, we have to do something!" Phaerim gritted his teeth as another blow from the ogre struck the door, jolting them back. The door's upper hinge also bent inward at an unhealthy angle, jarring debris from the stone supporting it.

"I know a song," Saffron said clearly, yet unsure whether her new composition was ready. "Keep the door shut as long as you can. When I lift my spear, back away."

She envisioned the ogre behind the door as the recipient of her hateful gift and began a turbulent melody, invoking a litany of injustices perpetrated by the wicked. As always, she sang in her native tongue, its words seeming more suited to the fire she already felt coursing through her. It warmed her veins more than blood, and though it wasn't yet actual, it carried the unborn soul of the flame she would soon release.

Saffron was so inwardly focused, she couldn't tell how long she'd been singing when the door finally burst off its hinges. Phaerim and Faulk flew backward onto the ground, while Dyphina and Thaelios hugged the walls to give Saffron as clear a path as possible through the tunnel.

The heat had been building inside her, and when she finally saw the arm of the ogre reaching through the vacant doorway, she knew it was time to unleash it. A rush of cool air surrounded her as if she had just stepped free of a furnace, and then an explosion engulfed the ogre.

Pum-pum-pum-pum, the inferno climbed in a series of graduated pops, narrowing from bottom to top, but all encasing the ogre in a wreath of red-orange flame. He stumbled back into the room behind him, dropping his maul and flailing his arms in a desperate attempt to put out the fire. Saffron watched, her arm outstretched, while the creature howled and his skin blistered and peeled under the intense heat.

It didn't take long for the howling to stop. The ogre fell to his knees and then face-first onto the floor, though the flames persisted around his body. An odd silence fell about the corridor as no one moved or spoke a word in response to what had just occurred. Only the crackle of the slowly receding fire indicated her ears still worked.

And then, she heard singing from behind. Saffron first glanced at Dyphina, who also turned toward her, but the woman's lips were not moving. Already fatigued from her effort, she felt the music sapping her strength further. It took all of her resolve to merely shuffle her feet so she could find the origin of the song.

Right before collapsing in exhaustion, she spotted the movement of large, feathery wings through her closing lids. She knew it didn't make sense, but could have sworn the person singing was an Aasimar.

A deluge of putrid water, dumped over her head, brought Saffron back. Manacles were once more chained around her ankle, but they were joined by a second pair around her wrists. A cloth gag, tied behind her head, made it difficult to cough up the liquid that trickled into her open mouth.

Her friends were all in a row beside her, and they were sitting on the floor of what appeared to be the throne room of

Nightwing Castle. Annoxoria, the sorceress who orchestrated their capture in the woods of Ifelian, looked down upon them.

"You have certainly been a disappointment," she derided from the safety of her throne. She sat with her long, booted legs crossed, her skin a shade darker than Saffron's. She was not Begnari, though, nor even Chelpian. Her shadowy make-up and the small horns protruding from her hair certainly appeared sinister.

"I was hoping you might prove yourselves useful to have around. I cannot, however," Annoxoria said as she uncrossed her legs and leaned forward, "tolerate you poking your noses where they don't belong and immolating my ogres."

Another figure, wrapped in a black, hooded robe with gold trim, shifted a few steps toward the prisoners. A malodorous, sickly green fog hovered about him, originating from under his hood and sinking to the floor, dissipating a few feet beyond. "I will take them," he said, his voice like a hissing echo.

"What would a ghast possibly want with my trouble-making prisoners?" Annoxoria asked. "You don't intend to devour their souls, do you? I have heard tales about how your master fuels his magic."

Saffron detected true distaste in the sorceress's voice. Whoever this mysterious, fetid stranger was, their captor didn't enjoy his presence either.

"Nothing of the sort, I assure you," he responded. "If these prisoners are capable enough to escape your mines—"

"They did not escape, Gullagion," Annoxoria corrected. "As you can see, they are still in chains."

Gullagion turned his shrouded head toward the sorceress, then back to the prisoners. "Nevertheless, the Wolfspider has use for such capable slaves, and I can deliver them to him. Fear not, you shall be compensated for their flesh." He reached an emaciated hand into the sleeve of his robe and then cast a handful of gold ingots onto the floor.

Annoxoria stared at her guest, and Saffron could see the anger burning in her eyes. "I didn't say you or the Wolfspider, whoever that is, could have them. They are my slaves, and are mine to deal with."

"Many pardons, Lady Annoxoria, but didn't you already say they were intolerable?"

"I have my own uses for them," she argued. "Their safety can be leveraged if their master becomes too much of a nuisance."

"Isn't keeping them more likely to make him one? I will take them far beyond his reach, and he need never know of your involvement. Once you find more of the Living Fire, Hadrian No More's gift will assure no mere mortal will ever be a threat to you again."

A silence filled the room while Annoxoria weighed the black-robed figure's words. Saffron was unsure of what she wanted the Lady to say. On the one hand, she might finally be free of these accursed mines, which is what she'd been so desperately trying to achieve. However, being sold off to this inhuman specter of decay was not appealing in the least. She found herself holding her breath until Annoxoria finally spoke.

"The Shaper of Blackfeather Perch will no doubt be weakened merely by the loss of his pupils," she said at last. "If he is able to magically divine their location, taking them farther away may prove just the lengthy distraction we need. Very well, Gullagion, have it your way. Take them with you when you leave."

Chapter 9

Visiting the Perch

Every few days, Be'naj traveled west to watch over the
Ifelian Corridor, but at night, under the stars, her
thoughts found their way back to Saffron. How could a
fortnight take so long to pass?

She filled many of her idle hours sprucing Skywatch Haven
for her guest's imminent return: cutting and stacking more
firewood, harvesting vegetables from her garden, scrubbing her
flatware in the stream. Whenever she left her familiar clearing
for the road, she took the time to set some snares for checking
on the way back. It would be nice to serve meat the next time
she and Saffron shared a meal.

A few days before Saffron's promised return, Be'naj received a vision during her restorative trance. Though normally silent, this vision was accompanied by a voice. She'd always held the visions to be gifts from her revered Shecclad, god of the Sky and Mastery, and so assumed the voice to be his.

It spoke in a powerful, rhythmic cadence as a scattering of images transitioned through her mind's eye: a sandstorm blowing across a vast desert, a large sphere of polished black marble resting on a pedestal, a doorway of stone leading to a torch-lit tunnel, and finally, a horned beast with sharp teeth and a long tongue.

"The Eladrin have been marked for death,
Their Keeper to fall by winter's last breath,
'Less you follow the dance of Living Fire
'Cross distant realms to a ruined spire,
Wherein lies the truth of Broken Names,
A secret trove, and devilish games.
Go to Ancient Tarmuth, beneath the sands,
Through portals three, and strange, new lands.
Yet beware the cursèd Name of the Beast,
Spreading like a plague from greatest to least,
Out from the depths and across the far hills,
To envelope Elisahd, by the half-breed's will."

The completion of the verse ripped her from her trance. The words stuck clearly in her mind, so she felt in no danger of forgetting, but they were unsettling and left her unsure of what action to take. With her other visions, she simply went to the place she saw in her mind. They were always within the confines of Ifelian, somewhere within the woods of her homeland. She felt a certainty upon reaching the spots, as she could match what she saw with her waking eyes to the recollection of her trance-vision.

She had never seen a land with so much sand, however, and didn't have any clue how to get there. She remembered Saffron talking about how she had travelled widely to play her music, and decided to consult her friend about the vision.

The night before Saffron was supposed to return, it rained. Be'naj, already wet, decided she would be happier warm than cold and took a soak in one of the thermal pools on the colorful hillside. As she bathed, Be'naj thought about the time spent in those same waters with Saffron – how patient and tender she had been and how comfortable her presence. Be'naj couldn't remember feeling so close to another person since her mother left half a dozen years before. She wanted that feeling to continue.

The following day was born to pass slowly. The rain had pushed through but left a chill in the air behind it. She lay in her hollow, wrapped in blankets, waiting for the sun to rise enough to start casting shadows. Half of the leaves had fallen from the deciduous trees, and the previous night's moisture clung to them, making the ground cover slick to walk on.

She put on a pair of brown leather pants and a hunter green halter top with bark-colored, oak-leaf designs sewn in. Charcoal-grey cloth sleeves rolled up from her wrists to biceps, keeping her arms warm. Be'naj tied up her brass hair with green ribbons, exposing her slender neck and the rise of her wings.

Dressed and ready to greet Saffron, all she had left to do was wait. And, she waited. Her stomach began to growl sometime after noon, but she didn't want to eat, lest Saffron arrive hungry. She walked the perimeter of the clearing twice, not wanting to stray further in case she missed Saffron. The third time, she measured heel to toe with each step, counting how many lengths of her feet comprised the circumference of Skywatch Haven.

She sat amongst the wilting wildflowers, listening to the geyser atop the hill until the sun passed all the way over to the eastern rim of the trees. Finally, she made herself a small portion of dried rabbit and green beans, though she ate with her ears primed to catch any approach through the woods.

The sun set, and still no Saffron. The next day was the same, except Be'naj started worrying about all the possible tragedies that might have befallen her only friend out in the wide world. Perhaps more lizardfolk had tracked her down and overwhelmed her. Maybe she tripped on a root and struck her head against a tree trunk and was lying unconscious in a ditch somewhere. It was possible she had been mistaken for a criminal by the authorities of Pasaxtree and was rotting away in their dungeons, awaiting justice.

The day after, her thoughts shifted to what she might have done to scare Saffron from returning. Saffron was such a worldly woman, obviously, and Be'naj lived in squalor compared to what she was likely accustomed to. She didn't fully understand what it was like for a human to sleep, but she was fairly sure they didn't normally do it in dug-out trenches of dirt.

Why hadn't she built a sturdier shelter by now? Her childhood home in Gilsage was modest by eladrin standards, but it at least kept out the wind and cold. Be'naj tried not to dwell on the comforts she'd left behind, but maybe she'd grown too comfortable being destitute. She thought the food tasted all right, but maybe Saffron didn't like her vegetables, or thought her cornmeal too bland. Or maybe, just like the Eladrin she'd grown up with, Saffron didn't want to spend any more time around a freak with wings who couldn't even fly and didn't know who her real father was.

Be'naj curled up in her hollow, crying, desperately trying to smell a trace of Saffron's hair on her blanket. At last, another thought occurred to her, one that stemmed her weeping and returned some sense of control to the emotional spiral she was caught up in – Saffron had willingly left her pendant. She wouldn't have let Be'naj, a virtual stranger, hold onto something as valuable as the Living Fire obviously was, if she didn't intend to return for it.

Something had to be preventing Saffron from fulfilling her promise. Be'naj stood and wiped the tears from her cheeks. If that were the case, it was her duty to take action and help the friend who had shown her such kindness. If it wasn't, and Saffron showed up while Be'naj was gone, then she would have to understand why her friend left in search of her.

She changed into her mail shirt and skirt, ignoring how the cold penetrated her suddenly bare legs, fastened her sword across her back, and strapped her shield to her left arm. The day was late for a start, but she didn't care if she walked through the night and then some. She filled a small satchel with food from her stores and slung her drinking bladder across her shoulder to balance it out. The first place Saffron said she was going was Blackfeather Perch, two days away. Be'naj remembered the direction she'd headed, and figured a tower should be easy enough to spot once she got close.

She walked until the sun went down and came up again, her acute eyes able to draw enough starlight to see by. It occurred to her then that Saffron's two days of expected travel were on horseback, though she couldn't imagine the steed moved much swifter through the thicker parts of the forest than she. After a few hours to trance and rest her legs, she started again.

Sometime in the early afternoon, she heard the telltale bird calls – she had crossed into the ancestral lands of the Eladrin and they were notifying one another of her presence. Of course, she was Eladrin too, and though she had chosen a life of exile from her people, she didn't suppose she was in any danger for intruding. She was still far from any settlements she knew of, though perhaps a border outpost existed nearby.

She determined to pay it no mind and ignore the Eladrin, so long as they kept hidden. Her business was with Saffron, and if she was not present when Be'naj arrived, then with the master of the tower, Cauzel Blackfeather.

Be'naj continued walking into the night once again. The heavens were almost completely obscured by clouds, and the terrain was proving difficult to navigate in the dark, so she decided to stop and put a little food in her belly. She was just about to transition into a meditative trance when the sounds of a branch snapping caught her attention.

Her hand immediately went to the hilt of her sword as she looked for the source of the disturbance. It could have just been some small, nocturnal animal on its nightly search for food, but a feeling came over her of being watched by something with keener night-vision than herself. She held still as a stone and listened, waiting for the stealth of whatever was out there to fail again.

The next sound she heard was the whoosh of an arrow through the night air, moving too quickly for her to react. A horrid gargling signified she was not its target, however. She spun to see that a darkly colored, diminutive creature with wide, yellow eyes had broken cover and bounded toward her. The profile of an arrow protruded from its back. It cursed her, showing off a row of sharp teeth. Be'naj readied her sword, though even upright, the creature was perhaps only breast high.

Another arrow ended its charge, piercing its heart from behind. The mongrel fell face first onto the leaf-covered ground, several paces short of Be'naj. She'd never seen anything like it. She scanned the forest, searching for signs of other attackers as well as the archer who'd defended her. Only the normal chorus of indistinguishable nocturnal sounds paraded her ears. She didn't catch any movement, either.

"Pen'ell," Be'naj said as loudly as she dared, offering thanks to whom she assumed was an eladrin longbowman. She knew how steadfastly her people protected their lands from intruders. Unnerved by the attack, Be'naj decided to continue on for another hour or so before stopping to rest. She kept her sword unsheathed while she walked. When she could barely keep her eyes focused in the dim light, she found an undisturbed spot and put her back against a thick trunk before entering her trance.

The night passed without further incident, and when morning came, the woods appeared far less treacherous. The terrain began to slowly rise and fall as she entered the foothills, and she kept a lookout for signs of habitation. She had to be drawing close to where the tower was located, though she'd received no vision, and had only Saffron's vague description to guide her.

Every deer path she encountered, every worn swath of dried leaves, seemed a possibility, and Be'naj wasted time investigating them all. At last, her determination produced results. An east-west trail, worn into a slight ridge of raised earth, passed by a large boulder and ascended into the hills. Following it around a curve, she came clear of the tree cover and spotted a stone tower rising from the first mountain cliffs of the Wyvernwatch.

A banner flew from the pinnacle – a raven upon a white field – and her heart increased its pace. "Blackfeather Perch," she affirmed. This is where Saffron had gone. Her stomach churned at the thought of having to talk to the type of important people who must live in such a place.

Though a steady climb awaited, Be'naj barely felt her feet touch the ground as she drew nearer her destination. The trail wound around and was not overly wide, making it a difficult place to reach with more than a couple people side-by-side. Not easy to assail by force, she noted. The final approach was marked by a tall, green hedge, shaped to form a tunnel, and she looked around the hills one last time to see if she was being watched.

With no sign of anyone at all, Be'naj walked with as much confidence as she could through the verdant passage, which led to a wide, painted door. A heavy knocker of wrought iron hung from the middle of the portal, with a square cut out above it. Tiny, vertical bars of iron blocked the hole, which was backed by a sliding panel. Be'naj lifted a quivering hand and struck the knocker twice against the door.

She brushed herself off while she waited in case she had somehow collected leaves or any other unsightly debris during her journey through the woods of Ifelian. Several long moments passed, and she was about to strike the door again when the rectangular panel suddenly slid aside and she found violet eyes assessing her from behind it.

"Who are you?" the female voice asked in a decidedly unwelcoming tone. She spoke Illanese, but Be'naj recognized eladrin eyes when she saw them.

"I am Be'naj of Silthoron," she responded in Eladrin, using her mother's town of origin instead of her own, but thankful to be able to converse in her native tongue. Her tutoring in Illanese had been stunted when she fled home. "I am seeking a human woman named Saffron."

The woman on the other side of the door took a moment to answer. "You're Eladrin," she said in their native tongue, "but not entirely." It seemed more an observation than a question, so Be'naj remained silent. "What is your connection to Saffron, and why do you seek her here?"

"We fought together to save a merchant from lizardfolk along the Ifelian Corridor. She mentioned her teacher was the Shaper, Cauzel Blackfeather, the master of this tower."

"Hmmm." The purple eyes blinked and the woman tilted her head slightly askance. "I overheard Saffron talking about you, but I didn't hear her mention what you were. You are still a stranger to me, and I'm not sure I should grant you entry, given the circumstances."

"What circumstances?" Be'naj retorted, trying to suppress her indignation.

"The master of the tower is late returning, while Saffron and the others have disappeared. Everything has gone wrong since she first showed up, and now it is my duty to watch over this place until Cauzel returns. I don't think letting in someone with a sword and … whatever your blood taint is, would be a wise decision. Especially if you're friends with Saffron," she added.

Be'naj's jaw dropped at the woman's audacity. She burned to let all manner of insults fly, but didn't want to get stuck on the wrong side of the door. "Don't you think you might need help finding your friends if they've all gone missing? There is probably a reason they've done so, and simply waiting for them to show up when they're past due doesn't sound very wise." Her argument didn't seem to sway the woman, and the last thing Be'naj wanted was to spend time alone in a tower with another judgmental Eladrin, but she knew she probably needed this person's cooperation to find Saffron as quickly as possible. It sounded like she might be in danger.

She remembered the pendant of Living Fire and withdrew it from her satchel. Lifting it to the door-hole, she tried to keep her voice calm and pleasant. "I think this may have something to do with the disappearance of your peers. Please, will you let me in so I can help you find them? I swear to Shecclad the Sky Lord I will not do you harm."

"What is that?" the woman's eyes narrowed.

"It is Saffron's magic necklace. It possesses a power that called to me, and she let me hold it for safe-keeping while she was gone." Be'naj wasn't sure the two were connected, but she had to say something that would get her inside. "Perhaps someone else knew she had it and came looking for her? Please, I need your help to find her."

Be'naj could see that the brilliance of the pendant's jewel intrigued her interrogator. Finally, she relented. "If you don't keep your word, I will call down a curse so bad you'll wish you never set eyes on this tower."

The panel slid closed, and after a series of locks shifted and clicked, the door swung inward. "I am Iliana of Gilsage. Be'naj, was it?"

"That is correct." Be'naj stepped inside the tower and looked around its spacious interior. She knew this Cauzel fellow was famous, but he appeared wealthy as well. Face-to-face with Iliana, Be'naj was reminded how much slighter of build full-blooded Eladrin were. She was so much bigger now – it was difficult to imagine how she had ever let them pick on her.

"You can leave your arms by the door," Iliana instructed. She waited until Be'naj had removed her sword and shield before stepping back and allowing further access to the room.

"Thank you for admitting me, Iliana of Gilsage. Do you mind if I eat? In my eagerness to arrive, I did not indulge in much nourishment during my journey." Be'naj opened her satchel to replace the pendant and find something light to consume.

"Of course not. But please …" Iliana made an awkward gesture toward the stairway that wound around the rim of the tower. "You are a guest under this roof now, and you should refresh yourself with something from our stores."

Such was the rule of eladrin hospitality. Be'naj nodded her appreciation and followed Iliana to the second floor. There, a large kitchen and packed larder offered all sorts of simple delicacies.

"I was just carving a boar shank when you knocked, if you would like some." Iliana barely waited for a nod before returning to the carving platter and skillfully cutting thin slices of roasted meat. She added a few green stalks of sweet reed to each of the plates and handed one to Be'naj, followed by a cup of cool water she poured from a jug.

"When did you last see Saffron?" Be'naj asked, after they'd both had a chance to swallow a few bites of their meal.

Iliana looked her over again, apparently trying to come to a conclusion about her wings. "Question for question?" she asked.

Be'naj sighed. She didn't want this to become about her, but realized she couldn't expect to receive without giving back. "All right."

"A tenday ago, give-or-take, Thaelios and Dyphina were beyond the tower walls performing a trial left by Master Blackfeather. Saffron was supposed to be helping them. It was my and Aurus's turn the following day, only they never came back." Iliana took a deep drink of her water.

"All three of them vanished?"

"They did," Iliana confirmed. "The only trace I found was Saffron's dagger on the ground. I know it was hers because it was curved in the Begnari fashion. Now you. Where did Saffron say she got that necklace you showed me?"

"She did not say," Be'naj replied, somewhat surprised by the question. "I suppose that means you've never seen it before?" She felt a twinge of satisfaction that Saffron had shared such an important relic with her and not her peers at the tower.

"It is obviously magical." Iliana seemed eager to put her deductive powers on display. "If she acquired it by legitimate means, it stands to reason she would have shown it to her arcane mentor. I never heard Cauzel give mention of it, either. She probably stole it, and its rightful owner came to claim it. Now, Thaelios and Dyphina have paid for her thievery as well."

Be'naj grew hot once more. "Saffron would not have done such a thing. If she stole it, why would she leave it with me? And how does that explain your master not returning? There has to be something else we don't know." She tried to think back to everything Saffron had said about why she was guarding the merchant in the first place.

"Saffron said she needed to tell Cauzel about the lizardfolk attacking travelers along the Corridor, like it was a clue to who was behind them. Maybe she figured it out and they got too close and ended up in trouble?"

"Cauzel Blackfeather is the greatest Shaper in Ifelian. Everyone knows that," Iliana objected. "He doesn't just 'get into trouble.' It's more likely Saffron was an agent of whoever these people are, and she's the one who took Thaelios and Dyphina. Then Cauzel found out, and he's gone after her to bring them back."

"What do you have against Saffron?" Be'naj blurted out. "She is a kind woman. And wait, you said you were alone in the tower – what about the one you were partnered with? Has he gone missing, too?"

"Aurus? He's human, and he went to Pasaxtree a few days after the others went missing to see if he could gather any information from his contacts there. It's the logical place for them to surface if someone took them as hostages." Iliana's eyes narrowed as she stared straight at Be'naj. "And everyone just *loves* Saffron. She shows up without ever having proven herself and takes a spot as one of Cauzel's apprentices. You tell me that isn't suspicious." Iliana's tone rose to a whine, "And she plays the lyre, and has those pouty lips and warrior's physique the men seem to be crazy about, and I bet it all came completely natural to her. She doesn't have to study magic, but that's perfectly fine because she can just sing and everyone falls in love with her."

Be'naj recognized that tone, and suddenly, it all made sense to her. It was the same way girls in her village would talk about her when she was younger, growing up taller and faster and stronger than them. Instead of making her more furious, understanding melted her frustration and she found a place of calmness from which to respond.

"I don't think Saffron has ever done anything to try and hurt you. Maybe if you remember that, you can spend your energy trying to ensure your friends return safely and not waste it finding ways to blame her for whatever problems you think you have. I had hoped we might have answers to help one another. Either way, I thank you for your hospitality. If you'll allow me a few hours of respite to trance, I will gladly continue my search for Saffron elsewhere."

Iliana stared at her, mouth slightly open, as if Be'naj was the first person to ever dare confront her. Instead of responding verbally, however, she groaned in mock disbelief and stalked out of the kitchen.

Be'naj did not know how to take the response, so she assumed it was general agreement. She finished her food and decided she would leave with the first light of morning. Maybe Aurus would discover something in Pasaxtree, but Be'naj knew she couldn't show up in the largest human city in the realm and expect a warm welcome. Her best choice, though she knew it would be dangerous, was to try and find one of the lizardfolk settlements in the swamp. It could be that's where the prisoners were being kept, though she worried they would only last as long as the creatures' bellies remained full.

Not wanting to intrude further upon her host's begrudgingly-given hospitality, she wandered back downstairs and picked what she thought was an out-of-the-way corner to enter into her trance.

"And, what do we have here?"

Be'naj shifted her vision from mind to sight, exiting her trance to find a lanky, dark-haired man with sharp features regarding her curiously. Before she could respond, Iliana came tearing down the stairs, followed by a cawing raven.

"Master Blackfeather, you've returned!" she called, just as she passed the second floor landing.

"I have," the man responded. "And who is this lovely creature meditating at the edge of my sitting room?"

Be'naj stood, then bent in a shallow bow. "I—"

"This is Be'naj," Iliana cut her off. "She came looking for Saffron. Oh, Master Blackfeather, I have so much to tell you. What took you so long to return?" She had reached the bottom of the stairs by the time she asked her question, and the bird landed on the edge of the railing, quiet and content to watch.

"Looking for Saffron?" Cauzel posited, shifting his attention to his apprentice. "But not finding her?" His eyes darted back to Be'naj, who shook her head before Iliana answered.

"Master, she was with Thaelios and Dyphina, performing the trials you left for us. None of the three returned. We were expecting you back over a week ago."

Cauzel's brow furrowed, though he appeared outwardly calm. He walked over to the wine cabinet and selected a bottle. "Shall I pour you some, Be'naj?"

She shook her head again. "No, thank you."

Iliana, on the other hand, seemed thoroughly flustered. "Cauzel!" Her voice was insistent, dropping all sense of formality. "Your apprentices have gone missing. Don't you think we should do something besides standing around sipping wine?"

Cauzel seemed not to take notice of Iliana's outburst and removed the cork from a bottle. "What about Aurus?" he finally said as he poured himself a drink. "Is he too, gone? Was he with the others when they disappeared?"

"What?" Iliana closed her eyes and breathed loudly through her nose several times. "No, Aurus and I were partnered for that task. He's in Pasaxtree, trying to find if they were taken there."

"I'm almost certain they weren't," Cauzel offered.

Be'naj finally gained the courage to ask, "You speak Eladrin?" The mystic in Shecclad's shrine told her their language was a mystery to humankind, but here was one conversing in it fluently.

"I do," Cauzel answered. "I speak a number of tongues, as it happens." He held his glass up to his nose and inhaled deeply. "And now I see why Saffron was interested in finding that book." He gave Be'naj a comforting smile before taking a sip of his vintage. "Tell me – you are obviously half-Eladrin – do you know anything about the rest of your heritage, Be'naj?"

She looked down at her feet and her cheeks flushed with warmth – a familiar feeling when asked such questions. "I never met my father," she admitted.

"Well," Cauzel responded, keeping his voice cheery, "I think it's safe to say he must have had wings."

"Saffron said she thought I was part Aasimar – that she had met some in her travels."

"Indeed, I don't doubt the truth of it," Cauzel remarked, "though I couldn't say for sure, not having seen one myself."

Iliana stamped her shoe against the stone floor, drawing their attention. "Why are we discussing Be'naj's possible ancestry when Thaelios and Dyphina are missing and probably in danger?"

"Saffron, too," Be'naj felt compelled to add.

"Iliana, what is the first thing one does when encountering a new problem?" Cauzel asked the question as if it was a lesson already dispensed.

Iliana shifted her weight and rolled her eyes. "Gather as much information as possible."

Cauzel bowed his head and brought his free hand upward in a gesture suggesting this was all obvious. "I'm gathering information. Be'naj and Saffron clearly have some connection, and she may know something that will help us figure out where my apprentices are. If they are all alive, and I have no reason to think otherwise thus far, then most likely they are together.

"Iliana, have you determined where your fellow apprentices were, when taken?"

She nodded. "I found Saffron's dagger on the grass of the archery range. One of the bows was out of place, and there was some blood nearby as well."

Cauzel inhaled deeply, this time without a glass of wine under his arched nose. "All right, then. That is where we shall start."

Be'naj reached for the ruby pendant then drew her hand back. These were strangers, but Saffron must have placed faith in her mentor, and since Be'naj needed help finding her, she decided to commit. "Master Blackfeather? I have something to show you."

Given the teachings of her youth, she found it ironic that she more easily trusted humans than her own kind these days. Be'naj brought out the Living Fire pendant and extended it. "Saffron had this in her possession until recently, and I wonder if it might be what whoever did this was after. She said it was magical." Be'naj couldn't help smiling, thinking about Saffron first showing it to her. "She said she sang to it."

Cauzel set down his wine and carefully accepted the jewel as if it was delicate as a newborn. "And what have we here?"

"Saffron called it—"

"The Living Fire," Cauzel answered his own question. "Where did she get such a treasure?"

Be'naj stayed silent, for it seemed Cauzel may have been asking himself again.

"She probably stole it." Iliana's contribution drew a stern look from Be'naj.

Cauzel ignored the comment. His eyes were lit with wonder, like he was holding a piece of history in his hands. "They say the Living Fire trapped the magical essence of the gods' Avatars, back when they roamed Elisahd. In the hands of a potent Shaper, such a gem could amplify spells significantly. Obtaining one would certainly be a motive for anyone with magical prowess."

"Only, I've had it," Be'naj corrected. "At least for the past fortnight."

"If Saffron did *sing* to it, as you say, it may retain her arcane signature as the last person to activate it. I think I can use it to locate her. May I be allowed to try?" he asked.

Be'naj was surprised by the request for permission. The pendant wasn't hers, after all. "Certainly. Anything to help find her."

"Good," he said. "That will take some time to accomplish, but I promise to take care with it. First, to the archery range."

The raven on the bannister squawked and took off higher into the tower, while Cauzel locked the ruby pendant in a nearby cabinet. Be'naj followed Cauzel and Iliana, looking back at the cabinet then grabbing her sword by the door on the way out, just in case.

They followed the path she arrived from, back through the hillsides, to the edge of the forest. From there, it only took about a quarter of an hour to reach the large clearing. A side trail she wouldn't have noticed on her own broke away from the main path, leading to the field.

"This is where I found the dagger," Iliana offered, leaping forward a few steps to an area of flattened grass.

An elongated, dark stain lay within the region of matted blades, and Be'naj knelt down to examine it. The blood had dried, but it was almost black and distributed from what looked like powerful spurts. "This isn't human or eladrin blood," she said with some relief.

Cauzel nodded, apparently taking her word for it. He walked to a pair of wooden stands with pegs for holding quivers of arrows and slots for longbows. One of the bows was strung, lying on the ground, as if carelessly tossed aside. A quiver was also out of place, its former contents scattered around it.

"One of them used the bow to defend themselves, probably wounding whatever left that blood behind. My guess is Thaelios, given his proficiency and the position of Saffron's dagger." Cauzel picked up one of the wayward arrows and ran his fingers over the fletching. "Whoever did this had to know who they were targeting and where to find them. If they did hope to get that pendant, they also had to be patient and determined enough to risk eladrin intervention, waiting for Saffron to leave the tower."

"That does seem bold, given the Veil of Trigilas," Iliana speculated. "We know the Eladrin wouldn't attack those under your protection, Master, but who else besides an Eladrin would be able to navigate the Veil?"

Be'naj had to agree. "And how long could they expect to stay safe? There must be an eladrin outpost not too far from here, for I was being watched the moment I crossed into their territory."

Cauzel nodded, looking around and still toying with the feathers of the arrow. "Part of my arrangement with the Keeper of Gilsage when Blackfeather Perch was built was that I take responsibility for protection of the lands adjacent to my own tower. This includes narrow bands of approach in each of the cardinal directions. It seems like there are two possibilities: either whoever did this knew exactly what paths to take to avoid the Eladrin, and there aren't many who do, or powerful magic was utilized to evade detection. Unfortunately, I can only think of one likely answer as to who is behind this, and it's not one that pleases me at all."

"Who?" Be'naj asked.

Instead of answering, Cauzel pointed toward a holly bush. "Look!" They followed the direction of his finger until certain of what they were seeing.

Be'naj lifted a scrap of torn netting, just like the kind she saw the lizardfolk use during her skirmishes along the Ifelian Corridor.

"It's like I told the Keeper of Gilsage during our council," Cauzel sighed. "I think we're dealing with the Nightwing dragon, Sepathia."

Chapter 10

From Wyrmsmoke to Wyvernwatch

Saffron and Dyphina, their ankles and wrists still bound, were led by a female servant to a room on the base level of the castle. An armed Rauglor trailed them, but once they reached the room, he freed their hands from the chains. The woman, looking completely disinterested in their plight, handed them each a small scrap of cloth and a sliver of soap.

"Wash yourselves," she said, nodding at a large bucket in the middle of the room. "You'll be taken to the courtyard in a quarter hour, so do not tarry."

The Rauglor crossed his arms but remained at the doorway as the prisoners shuffled in. The woman continued deeper into the castle, leaving them in the washroom by themselves.

Saffron considered singing for a moment, but it was too risky. She could not protect Dyphina, and there were likely more guards within shouting distance. Instead, she stripped off her boots and armor, eager to remove weeks' worth of dried sweat and grime from her body. Dyphina shed what was left of her dress as well, though it had already been torn in several places.

"I wish I had worn more practical attire for our trials," she said, noticing the poor state of her filthy dress as she removed it. Even though she was covered with soot and dirt, the half-fey woman retained a glow to her skin. She was still undeniably beautiful.

"How is your leg?" Saffron noticed the scab from Dyphina's acid wound had peeled, leaving a long, narrow scar on her thigh.

Dyphina took a step into the large, curved basin and dipped a bronze pitcher into the oversized bucket of water. "It doesn't hurt anymore," she said, twisting her torso so Saffron could see the still-red welts across her back. "These, however, sting quite a bit."

Naked, Saffron stepped into the basin as well. "Here, let me clean them," she said as Dyphina dumped the pitcher of water over her own head, gasping at the sudden cold. "The last thing we want is for your wounds to become infected."

Saffron bent at the waist and dipped her cloth into the bucket, then rubbed her sliver of soap against it until suds bubbled up. Dyphina swept her hair over one shoulder, and Saffron delicately dabbed at the lash stings with her cloth. Dyphina winced a few times, but on the whole remained stalwart.

"There," Saffron said as she finished cleansing the length of Dyphina's wounds. She wrung the blood from her cloth before her friend could see, then filled the pitcher again to rinse the soap and blood away.

Dyphina turned and locked eyes with Saffron. "Thank you. For everything. I know I wouldn't have survived this long without you here."

"No need for thanks." Saffron didn't think it would be helpful to add that she was fairly sure Dyphina wouldn't even be here if not for her. "We'd better hurry, I'm sure we don't have much longer."

Dyphina nodded and they both set to scrubbing themselves as thoroughly as possible before the servant returned. When she did, they were relieved to see she brought fresh clothes for each of them. The pale gray tunics and brown breeches weren't particularly flattering, but it was nice to have clean fabric after their bath. Saffron folded her armor and clutched it to her chest as the chains were put back on their wrists, but Dyphina made no effort to salvage her own dress.

They were led through a series of corridors to a thick, arched door, already open to let in the cool, autumnal air. A wide courtyard lay beyond, and as she was led out, Saffron saw that Thaelios, Phaerim, and Faulk were already present, dressed similarly to her and Dyphina.

Upon reaching the foot of the steps leading down from the door, a Rauglor shoved a pack into each of their arms. Opening it quickly, Saffron found a full water bladder and a sack of rations – at least enough for a fortnight. She stuffed her folded leather armor into the pack as well, its supple bulk filling out the rest of the space.

"Are you two all right?" Phaerim asked, though she barely recognized him.

She nodded. "You clean up well." He had taken the opportunity to shave his face, and now that it was clean, she could see a scar along his jawline. Faulk, on the other hand, kept his blonde beard intact, which was growing longer by the day. For the first time it struck her that Thaelios had never grown facial hair during their imprisonment, and she wondered if that was a trait common to Eladrin.

Saffron turned as Phaerim stiffened. Entering the courtyard on a phantasmal horse seemingly composed of black smoke, was Gullagion. The strange green fog still hung about him, and he pulled his hood back so they could see his face. Mottled flesh was drawn tightly over partially exposed bone. His eyes burned red as hot coals. As he opened his mouth to speak, she could see his teeth were sharp, like those of a predator.

"You are henceforth the property of the Wolfspider. If you play your role well, you will find this a significant improvement to dwelling in the mines here." He nodded to a Rauglor who trailed his horse, and the creature stepped forward, its arms burdened with wide, metal rings.

"I have heard of your escape attempt and realize the chains around you now may not be sufficient. Worry not, for I come with a solution."

Starting with Thaelios, the Rauglor placed a ring around each of their necks. They closed with a snap as one end fit into the other, leaving no external lock to pick. Saffron found the metal cold, but not too heavy.

"I am Gullagion, Lieutenant of the Dread Lich, Hadrian No More. He created these collars, and they are warded against magic. They have an explosive spell placed upon them. Should you crack or find a way to open them, the spell shall be released. If I, or any of Hadrian No More's lieutenants speak but a few words, the spell shall be released. If you run, rebel, or simply cause me too many problems, the spell shall be released. If the spell is released, you will not survive. Understand?"

Gullagion paused. Saffron considered asking who Hadrian No More was but didn't think it wise, given the newly introduced threat. Perhaps death would prove preferable to this new slavery, but she could always decide later.

"Human property is not allowed in the adjacent lands, I am told," Gullagion said, audibly disappointed. "Therefore, you will not interact with anyone we encounter along the road. You are not to speak to travelers unless I instruct you." He replaced the hood of his black cloak over his head and tilted the reins of his horse to the left. "Now, we march."

A Rauglor shoved Saffron's shoulder and she fell into place behind Gullagion's steed, making sure to leave a fair distance between them. The awful stench of rotting death lingered around Hadrian No More's lieutenant. Linked by the chains around their ankles, Dyphina followed on Saffron's heels, and the men, similarly bound, took up positions beside them.

Phaerim looked at Saffron, smirked, and gave a shrug. "The collars aren't entirely unfashionable." He inhaled deeply and let the breath out through his mouth. "I'll take the fresh air and walking over that stuffy, cramped mine any day."

Saffron nodded. "We'll see if that attitude changes once we're trying to sleep on the freezing ground tonight. We have no bedding and no warmer clothes."

Phaerim shrugged again. "Maybe. But at least we won't be sleeping in the same room where we piss and shit."

Saffron couldn't argue that point. This transfer to the ownership of the Wolfspider, whoever that was, seemed to be an improvement in their fortunes.

Nightwing Castle rested in a concealed valley of the Wyrmsmoke Mountains, and the path back to the Ifelian Corridor was not an easy one. Though the sun fell fully upon them, their altitude cooled the air. It wasn't an unpleasant environment for walking. The exertion of climbing, especially without full use of her hands, broke a sweat across Saffron's brow and neck, but the cool mountain breeze quickly licked it off.

The nightmarish steed of smoke, with red pinpoint eyes to match its rider, didn't seem bothered by the terrain. In fact, Saffron wasn't sure what passed for its feet ever completely touched the ground. As a result, the pace set by Gullagion proved difficult to maintain. She sued for occasional breaks, which he begrudgingly granted.

Hours passed before any of her fellow prisoners spoke another word. Whether that was out of fear or just a conservation of breath, she wasn't sure. For her part, Saffron was filled with questions threatening to overflow. During one of their breaks, she sought out Thaelios, who seemed the most likely repository of such knowledge.

"Did you see this creature's face when he pulled back his hood? Do you have any idea what Gullagion is? And who is this *Hadrian No More* we're all supposed to be frightened of?"

Thaelios gestured for her to lower her voice, even though she felt she was whispering. "Hadrian No More is known as the

Dread Lich," he said, barely loud enough for her to hear. "He is one of the most powerful and dangerous individuals on Elisahd. He was once a Shaper who performed a forbidden ritual to grant himself immortal un-life, though stories of his rise suggest the process drove him mad. Gullagion must be one of his undead thralls."

Saffron sank back. That didn't seem like good news at all. She shifted her attention to Dyphina, who she could tell was having an especially rough time keeping pace. "Don't worry, we'll be out of the mountains early tomorrow at the latest. Is your leg giving you problems?"

Dyphina massaged the outside of her left thigh. "I'll fight through, thanks."

Saffron hadn't heard a word from Faulk since they left the courtyard, though she could see a storm brewing in his eyes. "Everything decent with you?" she asked, stretching as far toward him as she could without dragging Dyphina along.

Faulk moved his eyes toward her, but kept the rest of his body motionless. "It will be decent once I'm out of these chains and free."

She decided not to agitate, nor was there time for it, as Gullagion urged his steed forward again, ending their break. The prisoners rose to their feet and continued the arduous trek through the mountains.

Sunset came early this time of year, and though Saffron doubted their undead guide had any problem navigating in the dark, he seemed to appreciate the mortals' need to bed down for the night. There wasn't much level ground within sight of the path, but at least Gullagion didn't object to them building a fire when she asked.

The men gathered fallen branches and kindling from the meager, woeful trees, while Saffron and Dyphina arranged loose rocks in a circle to contain the blaze. The work was slow with only a hand's span of slack between their wrists. When Saffron had organized the fuel in a neat pile within the stones, Faulk, looking on, remarked sarcastically, "A very pretty thing. Now, how are we going to light it?"

Phaerim knelt near the pile. "We might be able to strike our manacles together to get a spark."

"I don't believe we have to worry about it," Thaelios observed dryly, just as Saffron began humming a somber tune.

As the humming grew to a full vocalization, an ember began to glow within the heart of the kindling. Soon, its heat ignited the dry wood around it. Once a true flame sprung up, she ceased singing. Gullagion stood beside his horse, perhaps ten paces away, running a decayed hand over the flap of a leather saddlebag, which was draped over the steed's ethereal flank. Though he didn't say a word, Saffron had a feeling he was watching them from under his hood.

The dry rations in their packs wouldn't benefit from cooking, but the heat of the fire felt nice as the temperature dropped rapidly with the sun's departure. Saffron had scouted a patch of high grass before choosing where to build the fire, and once they were done eating, she rested a hand on Dyphina's hip and guided her to the spot. Protected from the wind on one side by the sloping rocks, it was near enough to the fire for them to soak up its warmth while it lasted.

"Here," Saffron said, lying in the grass on her side and directing Dyphina in front of her. "We should sleep now. We'll need all the rest we can get – and all the heat."

Dyphina tore some long stalks of nearby grass and matted them to serve as a pillow, then snuggled back into Saffron as they settled into as comfortable a position as they could find.

Saffron saw Phaerim staring at them from the other side of the fire and wondered if she would find the three men similarly bundled by the time she woke in the morning. She smiled at the image, but doubted its likelihood.

Of course, she found Thaelios already risen when she awoke, scanning an unrolled parchment scroll. Just sitting up robbed her of the warmth of Dyphina's body, but she felt an urgent need to empty her bladder.

She gently shook her sleeping partner awake so they could find an out-of-the-way spot to relieve themselves. "What's that?" she asked casually, still not cognizant enough to worry about the unnerving presence of their black-clad escort.

"It was in my pack, along with a few arcane ingredients." Thaelios spoke calmly, but his face betrayed unusual tension. "I noticed it yesterday the first time we stopped for water, but I wanted to wait until everyone was asleep to investigate further. Gullagion confirmed earlier this morning that it contains an illusion spell." Thaelios swallowed with some effort. "He wants me to cast it upon our group, to disguise us."

"He what?" Phaerim asked, sitting up and pressing his palms against his eyelids.

"Obviously, if we're going to be travelling along the Ifelian Corridor, it wouldn't do for five people in chains to be seen walking behind the undead, riding on a conjured horse of smoke. Suspicions would rightly be raised."

"Of course they would," Faulk grumbled, not bothering to sit up. "That's why you can't do it. Someone noticing us and alerting the authorities in Pasaxtree is probably our best chance to be rescued."

"While that may be true, Faulk, you cannot expect Thaelios to outright refuse our captor," Saffron argued. "Not with these blasted collars around our necks." She wasn't prepared to act rashly so early into their journey. The longer they survived, she reasoned, the greater the chance an opportunity for escape would come, especially now that they were travelling in the open.

She looked at Thaelios's alien eyes, wishing he was easier to read. "But why rely on one of us to cast the spell? Did Gullagion not conjure that beast he's riding? It most certainly isn't natural."

"You speak the truth – the steed is no doubt magical, but it could have been bestowed by Hadrian No More, whose Shaping is unrivaled."

"Pardon the break, but the privy beckons." Saffron was already crossing her legs and could delay no longer. She and Dyphina wandered behind the curve of the hill to squat. The relief of pressure in her bladder stimulated the clarity of her thinking.

Being new to the region, Saffron knew little about the forces working against her. Many of the players seemed beyond reach, and it appeared even Thaelios was relying mostly on lore. The Dread Lich was purportedly a master of dark magic, but there was always the chance Gullagion was only using his reputation to beguile them. She had no evidence the collars they wore were enchanted at all. Defying the undead creature seemed a heavy risk at this juncture, but was there a way she could safely test him?

"Dyphina," Saffron asked as they headed back to the center of camp, "do you know anything about undermining the undead?"

She shook her head. "I grew up in the woods, isolated but for my family. My mother had a talent for nature-magic, common to Fey, and passed it along to me, but I had little formal training before coming to Blackfeather Perch."

Gullagion approached the blackened ring of their extinguished campfire, preventing their conversation from continuing. "Time to march," he said in his raspy voice, the green mist seeping from him bringing tears to her eyes as it cascaded downhill.

The slaves gathered their packs without another word, pausing long enough to allow Gullagion to mount his horse and gain ample separation before following on foot. Saffron's assumptions of the terrain proved correct, and after an hour, they crested their final rise before the trail sloped downward. Her knees stiffened with the added strain, but shortly after noon the trees thickened and the ground leveled off. An hour later they emerged from the curtain of autumn foliage to find themselves along the Ifelian Corridor.

Gullagion circled back toward them, and the walkers took the opportunity to retrieve their water bladders for a drink. "It is time, Eladrin," the ghost ordered in his rattling voice.

Thaelios extracted the scroll from his pack and studied the words one last time.

"Don't do it," mumbled Faulk, staring hard at Thaelios.

Thaelios looked at him briefly, but quickly shifted his gaze to Saffron. She noticed Phaerim watching her as well and had the acute realization that they must see her as some sort of leader. Pursing her lips, she nodded to Thaelios.

He placed what looked like glass beads onto the earthen road at his feet and began reciting the incantation. *"Elinos columin sharak."* He repeated the phrase once for every member of the party, then crushed the glass under his boot.

The ink vanished from the parchment as he finished reading the words, and a spark of multi-colored light shot from Thaelios's chest to Phaerim, who was standing closest. Surprise had just registered across his features when the spark jumped to Faulk. It followed by coursing to Dyphina, then Saffron, and finally Gullagion.

Saffron tracked from face to face as the light struck each person, looking for some effect beyond their reaction of surprise. She barely registered that the spark striking her failed to correspond with any sensation. She noticed no difference in anyone's appearance.

"Ha, it didn't do anything," Faulk noted triumphantly.

Gullagion didn't respond except by turning his smoky-black steed southward to continue along the Corridor. Phaerim shrugged and fell in line, causing Thaelios to abandon his look of disappointed confusion.

They continued at a healthy pace, the ease of the road a welcome respite from the morning's shifting elevation. After only half an hour, Saffron spotted the first travelers heading their way, north along the road. The prisoners shared glances with one another, then at the back of Gullagion, who seemed unconcerned. For all their hope, they dared not speak. As the couple on horseback neared, Saffron found she had been holding her breath.

The riders gave no indication of fearing the black-cloaked Gullagion on his devil-steed, and soon drew near enough to spot the slave chains – Saffron lifted her wrists to make sure they couldn't miss them. She implored them with her eyes to lend them aid. Surely, they would question such an unwholesome scene and intervene.

Yet the man and woman smiled right at them. "Lovely day for a ride, no?"

"Safe journey to you," Gullagion responded, looking back at his chattel, daring them to speak.

Saffron could not have found the words even if she wanted to. Her disbelief transitioned to disappointment as the riders faded across the northern horizon. Had the spell worked after all? What had the man and woman passing them seen?

She caught Dyphina's eye and saw the crushed hope all over her countenance. They travelled in silence for another hour, and Saffron's thoughts drifted past the autumn trees to Be'naj. What she wouldn't give to be back at Skywatch Haven now, luxuriating in the hot springs and laughing with her graceful, winged friend. She couldn't help hoping that Be'naj missed her, too.

It was the same each time they passed new faces on the road. The disappointment dulled alarmingly fast, and as the filtered beams of sunlight withdrew and shadows grew long under the trees, Gullagion ordered them off the road. They cut east around the trunks of majestic oaks, and Saffron suspected they were somewhere between the tower of Blackfeather Perch and the city of Pasaxtree.

"Are we going to set up camp soon?" Phaerim asked once the road was no longer within view.

Saffron's feet ached and she was eager to get off them. How many days were they going to keep up their march? She had no idea where this *Wolfspider* that Gullagion referred to even lived.

"Soon," was the ghast's only reply.

Soon turned out to be another hour, and Saffron had already stumbled several times over exposed roots in the falling darkness. At last, Gullagion stopped within a circle of trees and told them they could rest.

Saffron edged toward Thaelios while they were setting up their meager camp. "Are you able to tell whether we're in eladrin territory? Wouldn't they likely intervene if we were?"

"They would," he nodded hopefully, "though the Veil of Trigilas might fail to confuse Gullagion, given his nature. How do you feel? Is your sense of direction failing you?"

"No," Saffron admitted, "but wouldn't Cauzel's mark still protect me?"

"It might have worn off by now," Thaelios conceded, "though Phaerim and Faulk are unprotected." They both looked at the wiry Phaerim, standing only a few paces away, acting oblivious to their conversation. "We must be south of Gilsage, though maybe my brethren will visit us under the stars tonight."

The night was clear and chilly, though not so cold as the previous one in the highlands. Saffron curled up with Dyphina again to conserve body heat, but she found it difficult to fall asleep. Her hearing, especially, was on alert, anticipating the arrival of eladrin bowmen with every snapping branch or falling acorn.

Gullagion maintained his distance during the night, evidently aware of the effect his presence had on the living. With no need for rest, however, he stayed on his steed, watching them, turning over whatever thoughts went through the heads of the damned. He betrayed no hint of concern about their location, leaving Saffron wishing for better mastery of the local geography.

The sun rose without anyone coming to their aid and with Saffron still weary after only a peppering of sleep. By noon, they veered south again and clouds rolled in. The forest, beautiful as it was, seemed to deaden around them as they walked, no doubt silenced by the unnatural presence of their guide.

The Eladrin seemed to be giving them a berth as well, though Thaelios was at a loss to explain it. "My people would not tolerate such an intrusion – there must be other magic at work." Saffron subtly asked both Phaerim and Faulk which way they had come from Nightwing Castle, and the two men could not find agreement. It certainly seemed they were passing through lands under the protection of the Eladrin, without reprisal.

That prompted another question to surface in Saffron's mind. "Why didn't your folk intervene when Annoxoria attacked us outside Blackfeather Perch?" she asked after making her way back to Thaelios.

He shrugged. "Part of the agreement allowing Master Blackfeather to maintain a tower within the Ifelian Forest came with a responsibility for him to protect the surrounding territory. There is a narrow stretch of wood leading to the Ifelian Corridor that is left unguarded by the Eladrin for his use. Very few know of it beyond his own apprentices, but perhaps she found it using sorcery? How else would she have known when we would be outside the protection of the tower as well, or that Cauzel would be away?"

Saffron couldn't help feeling like she'd been caught up in schemes far greater in scope than any of them yet realized. She thought of the animal sacrifice she'd come across during her return from Skywatch Haven. Could the cult be performing rituals that somehow affected the perception or disposition of the Eladrin?

After the second day of keeping their southern course, Saffron surmised they must be travelling parallel to the Ifelian Corridor. Keeping to the forest slowed them down, but Gullagion must have had a reason not to pass too close to Pasaxtree.

If she hadn't been scanning the forest regularly for Eladrin coming to their rescue, she might not have noticed the eyes. Bright with a yellowish tint, they stared at her from the shadow of an elm trunk – or at least she thought they did. She blinked and peered harder to make sure, but they were gone.

"Did you see that?" she whispered to Dyphina. "I think we're being watched."

Dyphina swiveled her head. "What am I looking for?"

Saffron stared hard back at the tree, willing the eyes to reveal themselves, but saw only vacant shade. "Just be ready," she cautioned.

Less than an hour later her suspicions were strengthened when Thaelios sidled up to her and confided, "We're being stalked. I've heard disturbances among the trees flanking us for some time, but I don't think they're Eladrin. My folk would more likely select a spot ahead to engage. Whoever follows us now is biding time. We must be nearing the southern border of the Ifelian forest as well, for I fear this means we have left the territory of Gilsage behind."

Saffron's heart sank with his assessment, though she'd ceased expecting a rescue from outside forces. Her gut told her that if they were going to regain their freedom, they would have to win it for themselves.

As the day wore on, the terrain grew rougher. A floor of stone started poking through the softer layer of leaves and forest decay, and hillocks cropped up from the formerly level ground. And again, Saffron spotted the eyes. Once, watching from the low boughs of a sycamore, and then from beside a boulder shaped like the hardened face of a giant. Unsure of whether to feel fear or relief, she looked to Gullagion each time she saw the orbs in the shadows, but he showed no signs of noticing.

Eventually, the difficulty of the terrain required all of Saffron's attention. Constrained by their chains, Saffron had to remain within a few paces of Dyphina or risk losing her footing, and the same was true for the men. They occasionally had to use their hands to gain leverage through gaps of rock, and their progress slowed significantly.

In one such spot, while their groups were separated by the necessities of climbing, their stalkers finally showed themselves. Twilight had fallen and shadows loomed long. Gullagion sat atop his phantasmal horse some body lengths ahead, waiting for Faulk and Phaerim to assist Thaelios up a steep rise, when Saffron spotted a creature dashing from the darkness toward their stationary captor.

It had the shape of a man, though sleek and colored as if formed of the very shadow it stole from. Saffron held her breath, fighting her instinct to call out a warning, but the creature didn't seem intent on harming Gullagion. Instead, it snatched something from the saddlebag resting behind the ghast's sickly leg and bolted back into the brush, heading down the hillside.

Before Gullagion could do more than stare in the creature's direction, two more emerged, peeling from the shadows of freestanding objects. They ran toward Phaerim and Faulk, who had their backs to the on-comers as they hoisted Thaelios up. When they drew closer, Saffron could see that their skin appeared covered in tight scales like fish, and she was about to call out a warning when Dyphina screamed next to her.

"Watch out!"

Saffron turned just in time to catch one of the strange creatures behind her, lifting a rock in both hands to smash her skull. Without thinking, she stepped left to avoid the blow, but her sudden movement jerked Dyphina off balance. She slipped and the chain linking their ankles snapped taut, sweeping the feet of the creature out from under him. He dropped the rock and fell to his knees with a painful-sounding crunch.

The trail erupted into a chaos of cries as each group of travelers struggled against their shadowy assailants. Saffron didn't have time to worry about anyone beside herself and her partner, though, as her fallen attacker grabbed her calves and pulled her to the ground as well. Her head smacked against the hard ground, and in the following moment of disorientation, he scrambled on top of her and pinned her arms.

She stared into a face mostly human, yet undeniably feral. Aside from the dark, scaly skin, his eyes were yellowed with slit pupils and his bared teeth filed down to points. If this was a person, what sort of transformation had he undergone?

His eyes moved down Saffron's face to her throat, and she got the impression he was deciding whether to bite her. His hesitation proved his undoing. Suddenly, Dyphina's arms looped around his head and she pulled back, catching his throat on the chain connecting her manacles. He expelled a shrieking croak as his body yanked backward, though it did not save his windpipe.

Saffron scrambled to her feet, surprised to find that the irons around her wrists and ankles had become unclasped. Dyphina struggled underneath their flailing attacker, her desperate pull having drawn him on top of her.

Saffron acted quickly, seizing the loose chain that had connected her to Dyphina and looping it several times around the creature's ankles. She stood and used the chain to drag him off. One of his hands clenched his crushed throat while the other grasped madly for purchase.

"Dyphina, the rock!" Saffron nodded toward the small boulder the creature had dropped. While she used the chains to leverage his legs and keep him on his back, Dyphina seized the stone, lifting it to her chest with some effort. She looked at Saffron with an expression of doubt, as if knowing what was expected but hoping she was wrong.

Saffron met her eyes and nodded. "Do it!" she urged, unsure how long she could keep her stronger opponent subdued. Dyphina flinched but returned the nod, stepped forward, and pushed the rock toward the creature's head.

He snarled and wailed at the blow, as Dyphina had shut her eyes just before releasing the stone and failed to hit him squarely. Its weight and rough edges had still succeeded in scraping off the side of his face.

Saffron released the chain, dropping his legs to the ground. She pounced on top of the pitiful creature, straddling his waist, and picked up the rock. She was sure he could no longer see through all the blood, and he beat ineffectually against her body with one hand. Saffron exhaled, clenched her jaw, and brought the rock down forcefully, cracking through the creature's skull. His arms and legs ceased flailing and fell limply to the ground.

Looking up, Saffron saw the body of another creature strewn across the boulder the men had been using for leverage, though Faulk's face was covered with bleeding scratches. Gullagion appeared behind them, on foot. As the green fog that poured from him cascaded over Phaerim, the human seized and emptied the contents of his stomach onto the rocks.

Gullagion, about to speak, noticed and took a step back before addressing them. "Two more escaped, and they have stolen the property of Hadrian No More."

Faulk scrunched his scratched face as if insulted that he should give a damn. "And we just had to fight for our lives!"

Gullagion turned to him. "I have opened your bonds, temporarily, so that you might pursue and recover my satchel. Tracking humans is not my strength, but that satchel is more precious to me than all your lives, so you will recover it or die trying."

Phaerim, who had taken a few steps further from Gullagion, spit the remaining vomit from his mouth. "I understand such nuances may be beyond someone in your … state, but I don't think those things were human."

"They are Thralls of the Nightwing," Thaelios announced, "or I miss my guess."

"Thralls of the what?" Phaerim asked.

"The Nightwing," Thaelios repeated. He turned to Saffron. "I read about the practice in *Lore of the Dragon*, at the library in Gilsage. They are fanatic devotees of Nightwings, who they deify as living embodiments of the nether realm." He rubbed his wrists where the manacles had bound them. "If they are unlucky enough to find a Nightwing who accepts them, they drink her poison, diluted with other ingredients, and over time their bodies transform. In return for her gift, they serve their matron like zealots."

"Lovely," added Faulk.

"You are wasting time!" Gullagion interrupted. "Return the satchel, unopened, by nightfall, or you will all pay with your lives."

"He's quite the motivator," Phaerim quipped. "Anyone know where we should start? I think they headed west, but beyond that I have no clue."

"I have some experience tracking," offered Faulk, "but we'll need to move quickly." He shot a glance at Dyphina. "Not sure we all need to go if there are only two of them. Might slow us down."

Saffron thought of Dyphina's hesitation with the rock. Sparing her a chase that might end in more violence was probably wise. "Dyphina, do you mind staying behind?"

"I'll stay with her," Phaerim put in, a little too eagerly. "In case more show up."

Dyphina smiled and looked down.

"All right. Faulk, lead the way. Thaelios, we may need your knowledge of the creatures and territory. Are you fit to run?" Saffron was curious to have a peek into that satchel and see what was so valuable.

Thaelios nodded and, with a grunt, Faulk headed west down the rise. Saffron and Thaelios followed without a word, leaving Phaerim and Dyphina with Gullagion. Faulk wasn't concerned with explaining himself, but Saffron noticed every now and then he would point to a scuff in the moss or consider some broken, leafy stems in the brush and mutter under his breath.

They moved quickly with no complaints, but Saffron had no idea if they were gaining ground or not. Were the Thralls heading back to a camp where she would have to reckon with a hundred more, or would they stop and consider themselves in the clear after a mile or two? Whatever the case, up to this point, their apparent carelessness suggested they were hurrying.

After what seemed at least an hour, if she could trust her pounding heart, Saffron was about to beg for a moment's rest when Faulk suddenly pulled up and raised a finger to his lips. Saffron ceased running and tried to quiet her gasping breath. She crept forward to join Faulk behind a thick trunk as stealthily as her throbbing legs could manage, and Thaelios was behind her a short moment later.

They had been following a game trail for the last mile or so, and ahead, stooped over in admiration of something between their faces, were the Thralls of the Nightwing. Saffron spotted Gullagion's leather satchel on the ground, forgotten in the awe of whatever it was they held.

This was clearly the best opportunity they would have to surprise their prey, but they had no weapons. Saffron considered singing to bring her fire magic to bear, but that would alert the Thralls to their presence. The look on his face suggested Faulk was considering the same problem about what to do next.

Thaelios removed the dilemma. *"Eonos jubilex throst."*

Saffron snapped around to warn the Eladrin to be quiet, but turned back when she heard a pair of thuds from the direction of the Thralls. They had both collapsed on the trail, apparently unconscious.

Faulk looked at Thaelios with an open mouth, then nodded his respect. "It must be handy to be a wizard. Why haven't you used that trick on our pal, Gullagion?" he asked, stepping closer to their quarry.

"The sleep spell has no effect on his kind, nor mine for that matter, but it's quite useful on humans." Thaelios wore a rare grin, obviously pleased with himself.

"I'll have to remember that," Saffron said, duly impressed.

"It will only last a few moments, though," Thaelios cautioned. "We still need to find a way to incapacitate them further.

"That shouldn't be too much of a problem," Faulk said, searching the side of the trail. "Saffron showed a pretty useful trick of her own back at the ambush." He picked up and cast aside several stones after hefting them, unsatisfied with their weight. "There we go," he said at last, prying a broad, moss-covered specimen free from its muddy bed.

Saffron's mind raced to find another solution, uneasy with murdering a pair of sleeping victims who had not even harmed them. She looked along the trunks of nearby trees, speculating whether there were enough vines to possibly bind the Thralls. But, as Thaelios said, they only had a few minutes, and Faulk's solution seemed the safest. He knelt beside one the sleeping creatures – no, men – and raised the stone above his head.

"Wait!" Saffron extended an arm toward Faulk.

"What? Do you want the honor?"

Saffron looked at Thaelios for an alternative idea, but he had already turned his back on the scene. She lowered her arm and spoke softly, "Just get it over with." Turning her back as well, she flinched after each disturbing *crunch* that followed.

"Well, look what we have here?" Faulk said a moment later, stepping between Saffron and Thaelios with his own hand extended. "So this is what that abomination wants so badly. Not surprising, given where we're coming from."

In his palm was a nearly fist-sized, uncut, red crystal. Even with minimal facets, it shone brightly, but its light came from within. Saffron immediately recognized it as a piece of the Living Fire.

"Reckon that's worth a small fortune," Faulk said with a covetous gleam in his eye.

"We have to give it back, though," Thaelios insisted. "We're all at risk if we don't return it."

"We could just say we found them and it wasn't here. Or that we didn't find them at all. Hells, we don't even have to say anything." Faulk closed his fist around the gem and tucked it into the satchel now resting across his shoulder. "Just consider it back-pay and keep heading west to Pasaxtree. It should still go pretty far three ways."

"You're not only forgetting our friends," Saffron interjected, "you're forgetting these." She gently tapped a finger against her throat, wary of putting too much pressure on the metal collar around it. "If we don't go back and hand over the ruby, Gullagion won't hesitate to incinerate us. Not sure about you, but I'm fairly fond of *my* head."

Thaelios nodded and stared at Faulk as if nothing else needed to be said.

Faulk smiled, a grim expression considering the red tracks across his face. "I was only teasing," he said, pulling the strap of the satchel over his head and handing it to Saffron.

She took it uneasily, wondering if it wasn't part of some further trick to undermine them. "Good," she finally said as she donned the leather pouch. "Now, we should head back. Sunset comes early, and we don't want to risk Gullagion getting antsy and exploding us anyway."

Saffron and Thaelios turned up the trail but had only taken a few steps before Faulk called out, "I'm still not going back."

"What?" Saffron wasn't sure if she'd misheard him. "Don't be foolish. If you don't come back, you'll die."

"Perhaps, perhaps not," he shrugged. "We don't know that we can trust this Gullagion to make good on his threat. The whole collar story could be a tactic to keep us in line. Maybe there's no spell at all. He had to have Thaelios here cast that illusion, didn't he?"

Saffron followed his eyes to Thaelios, who gave an apologetic nod and shrug. "While it is certainly likely Hadrian No More has the kind of power to craft such cursed objects, we have yet to receive proof the Dread Lich is actually behind Gullagion," he admitted.

Saffron could scarcely believe what she was hearing. "I thought of that, too, but he's a blasted talking corpse riding a horse of smoke! You don't think there's dark magic involved? You want to risk your life on that hunch?"

"Either way," Faulk said calmly, smiling at her reaction, "I'm not sure having my head explode is going to be any worse than whatever they have planned for us."

Saffron couldn't argue that. She wanted to, but she couldn't. The idea of being a slave sat very poorly with her as well, but she didn't have it in her to just give up. Not yet. What if her sister had when she was taken by the King-priest of Chelpa? Saffron never would have forgiven herself.

"Just tell them I was killed by the Thralls," Faulk added. "With any luck," he swallowed hard, perhaps having second thoughts about his decision, "as long as Gullagion gets the ruby back, that will be enough for him. Get going, now. As you said, Saffron, sunset comes early."

She stood still for another moment, taking in Faulk's expression, wondering if it was worth trying to change his mind. "Are you sure?" she said, finally.

He nodded. "I'm sure. Now get going, both of you. I'll try to put some more distance between us in case there's a maximum range to this thing," he said, pointing to the collar.

"Farewell," Thaelios offered, sounding far from hopeful.

Faulk nodded and headed west, downhill, putting more of the Ifelian woods between him and their captor. Saffron watched him for a hundred paces or so before turning resolutely. "Come, Thaelios, we need to make good time." They started at a brisk jog back up the path they had come, no longer needing to slow for Faulk to decipher signs of passage.

Regardless of her efforts to concentrate on the trail, Saffron's mind couldn't break free of Faulk and his decision. She hadn't known him that long, after all, but they'd shared struggles, and when at last she and Thaelios emerged back onto the southern trail, she found she was weeping.

"Where's Faulk?" Phaerim asked as he and Dyphina took turns embracing the returning pair. Saffron noticed Gullagion was creeping closer as well, though he kept enough distance not to induce purging. The red pinpoints of light floating in his eye sockets seemed fixed on the satchel slung across her torso.

She removed and tossed it to the ghast. "He fell to the Thralls," she lied, nearly choking on her words.

"Such a shame," Gullagion responded, his attention attached to the leather pouch as he peeked inside.

Phaerim momentarily stared down the ghast, then slowly shook his head. "What a piece of work," he said under his breath. "Did he go easy, and are you two all right?"

Saffron forced a smile. "We're fine, and Faulk's in a better place now." She couldn't keep her eyes from flitting to Gullagion, waiting to see how he would react. He replaced the satchel in his saddlebags and hoisted onto his mount.

"We are almost to the edge of the forest. I shall allow camp once we are clear of it. Now," he said, looking back at them, "put your irons on."

"What?" Dyphina looked as if he'd just told her she was an ox.

Saffron took up her complaint. "We just hunted down your precious satchel and returned it to you ... and you still don't trust us?"

Gullagion seemed to be seething, though it was difficult to tell. When he spoke, his voice held an edge it had previously lacked. "I expect you to obey my commands. I can make this journey *much* harder on you if you wish. Do you desire to test me?"

Saffron folded her tongue to prevent speaking. She *desired* to say a lot more, but knew it could only hurt them. After staring down Gullagion to make clear her disapproval, she returned to where their chains had been discarded and set to replacing the manacles. As before, the others followed her lead.

When everything was in place, Gullagion pointed in their direction and spoke a single word she couldn't catch. She heard the locks click back into position. Before they started off again, Gullagion lifted that same hand into a fist in front of his face. "*Etmos mortis*," she barely made out. "I hope you said farewell to your friend."

Chapter 11

Return to Gilsage

Be'naj sank to a knee at the news, her body mimicking the reeling of her heart. Was Saffron now in the clutches of a dragon? Cauzel's deduction resonated with her own instincts; dragons were known for their love of precious things, and if Sepathia thought Saffron possessed a jewel such as the Living Fire, she would be a target. Nightwings were also rumored to be especially cruel and cunning, and the idea that one had conspired against Saffron left Be'naj in the throes of despair.

"And what evidence, Iliana, led me to such a conclusion?" Cauzel remained calm, determined to turn even this devastating realization into a teachable moment.

Iliana faltered, clearing her throat and looking at the torn net before offering her observation. "The blood came from something neither human nor Eladrin, and lizardfolk favor the use of nets such as this for catching both fish and sentient prey."

"Good. And …" Cauzel encouraged.

"And lizardfolk naturally inhabit swamps and jungles, which are also the preferred territory of Nightwing dragons." Iliana lifted her head, a smile of satisfaction lighting her violet eyes.

Cauzel built upon his pupil's explanation. "Nightwings are known to bully lower species into performing tasks they find beneath them, and lizardfolk are some of the most commonly terrorized in that regard."

The Shaper's deductive exercise allowed Be'naj time to reclaim her spirit and set her resolve. She stood and placed a hand on the pommel of her sheathed sword. "Then you will have to teach me how to pursue and slay this Nightwing. We have no time to dally."

Cauzel tapped a finger against his lips and tilted his head. "We may have more time than you think. If, indeed, Sepathia is responsible for the disappearance of my apprentices – and I'm only holding her as the probable perpetrator at this juncture – she will have, by now, determined that Lady Saffron was not in possession of the pendant she covets.

"That being the case, she will likely have either already disposed of her prisoners, I'm afraid by violent means, or will attempt to use them as leverage in order to acquire the piece. If that is the case, I'd reason Saffron, Thaelios, and Dyphina are not in immediate threat of harm."

Be'naj wasn't interested in arguing, she simply demanded an outlet to pursue her purpose. "What do you propose, then? We cannot simply wait to be contacted by a ruthless dragon in order to hear her demands ..."

Cauzel opened his mouth to speak, then shut it without doing so, seeming to reconsider his position. "You are correct that this is no time to be idle. There are a number of fruitful endeavors we might undertake." Iliana turned to listen to her master as he folded his hands behind him and began pacing.

"First," he said, "I must locate Aurus to ensure he is not also in danger. A powerful Nightwing's reach might even extend to Pasaxtree. If someone else is behind the attack, he could be in other sorts of trouble. Iliana, you can assist with the homing spell, if you like."

"Of course," Iliana replied.

"Something that will take a fair turn longer, though, is trying to use the Living Fire to do the same for Saffron. I have a focus for each of my other apprentices – it was one of the first tasks performed upon acceptance – but neglected to do the same for Saffron." Cauzel shook his head. "Regrettable, especially under the circumstances."

"I am hopeful it can be achieved, but it may take some days to succeed. While that percolates, you and I, Be'naj, can study strategies for how to best outmatch Sepathia. It was a course I intended on pursuing very soon, anyway. Is that satisfactory?"

Be'naj would have preferred a proposal sounding more like action than contemplation, but held enough wisdom to know taking on a Nightwing wasn't something to do ill-prepared. "All right. As long as we begin immediately."

"I wouldn't have it any other way!" Cauzel exclaimed, and the small contingent returned to Blackfeather Perch.

Be'naj left the Shapers to their magic, trusting they would be able to find Saffron faster than she could on her own. The bulk of her day was spent practicing swordplay while visualizing the defeat of her imagined opponent.

When she was nearly exhausted, she ascended the high balcony of the Perch and stared across the vast wilderness. The view made her wish even more that her wings were strong enough to carry her aloft on the winds. She would soar over the sprawling forests of Ifelian, letting her heart guide her to where Saffron was assuredly waiting.

Her eyes inevitably turned south, toward Gilsage, the eladrin capital where she'd spent her youth. The vision of prophecy she'd received a few days back weighed on her mind, though she felt it beyond her capacity to interpret. An uncomfortable churning in the pit of her stomach coincided with the thought of returning to Gilsage to share the message.

The Mystic of Shecclad who trained her had always been gentle, but that could not be said for the majority of Eladrin she grew up with. Memories of the distrustful looks, teasing, and often unrestrained cruelty affected her still. She had hoped to never go back.

Perhaps she didn't have to. Cauzel, though human, seemed to know a great many things, and perhaps his knowledge extended to the interpretation of portents. Be'naj decided to first tell her Shaper host of the words bestowed on her and listen to his advice. It would be foolish, after all, to take an unnecessary journey to Gilsage when the quest to save Saffron might pull her in another direction.

She resolved to seek out Cauzel after her next trance so as not to interrupt his efforts to locate his absent apprentices. In fact, she waited for an hour after sunrise to seek him out, knowing that humans tended to rest most heavily during the dead of night. On her way upstairs to his private quarters, however, Be'naj came across Cauzel and Iliana in the kitchen.

"Good morning, Be'naj," he said. "I trust you tranced comfortably?"

"Thank you, I did." She was going to ask how he slept, but the answer appeared to be "not well." Cauzel's black hair was disheveled and there were dark circles under his eyes. He cradled a mug of steaming liquid, breathing in its aroma as if it were the only thing keeping him upright.

"Would you like some tea?" Iliana offered. She seemed much perkier than her mentor.

"My thanks," Be'naj nodded, and Iliana set about finding an empty mug to fill with hot water. "Was it an especially long night?" Be'naj asked, unsure of what that might actually feel like for a human. She had heard the phrase uttered by harried caravan riders she'd escorted along the Ifelian Corridor.

"A difficult one, to be sure," Cauzel responded.

"Were you able to hone in on your apprentice's location? Is he not safe?"

"He won't be when I see him again," Iliana muttered as she dipped a collection of herbs into Be'naj's mug.

"What does that mean?" Be'naj asked before accepting the hot drink. "Thank you," she added.

"You are welcome," Iliana replied, grabbing a pair of buttered rolls from a pan and handing one to Be'naj.

"It means Aurus was not exactly where he said he would be." Cauzel took a delicate sip from his mug and swished the liquid around his teeth.

"He was not in Pasaxtree, you mean?"

Iliana failed to stifle a sarcastic laugh. "It's not that he wasn't in Pasaxtree that is the problem. The traitor was at the Court of Skullreaver."

"We don't know that," Cauzel corrected. He looked directly at Be'naj. "I traced him to a valley of the Wyrmsmoke Mountains, which happens to be the site of a foreign castle that's recently been brought to our attention."

"And nothing else!" Iliana exclaimed. "There is no good reason for him to be in those mountains."

Cauzel bowed his head and sighed. Be'naj got the impression they had already hashed out this discussion prior to her arrival. "What are you going to do?"

"He was on the move in our direction, so I have every confidence he intends to return to Blackfeather Perch. Assuming he does so, I must have a very serious conversation with him." He looked over his shoulder at his apprentice, "Which Iliana will not be present for, nor shall she make any effort to speak to Aurus first."

The Eladrin repeated her sarcastic laugh, but continued devouring her breakfast.

Be'naj angled her body so only Cauzel could see her face, and spoke timidly, "There is another matter I wished to speak with you about, Master."

"Of course." He straightened and stretched his eyes open, raising his bushy eyebrows almost to his scalp. "We can speak in my laboratory." Cauzel gestured toward the stairs and followed Be'naj as she ascended. He looked back before they had climbed more than a couple steps and called, "Arcane

Defenses, Iliana. I expect you to be well-versed by the time Aurus returns."

When they reached the third floor, a short entryway led to a shimmering, metallic door. It was not constructed of iron, having more in common with the crystal-flecked skin of the Eladrin. Be'naj allowed Cauzel to move ahead of her, and when he grasped the handle, a sigil in the top-center of the frame shone the color of pale green moonlight. The door unlocked with a *click*.

Cauzel held it open for her, and Be'naj walked into a short passage that split into two large rooms, one on either side. "To the right," Cauzel instructed, and she followed his directions. The room she entered was well-lit by sunlight from a panel of windows in the curved wall. She was surprised to find that art, predominately with a raven motif, covered most of the other available surfaces.

There was a large desk, plenty of bookshelves, and rolls of curled parchment distributed across a plain-looking table. Everything seemed to have an order to it, though, unlike his apprentices' collective workspace on the top floor.

"So, Be'naj, what was it you did not want the ears of Iliana to be privy to?" Cauzel asked as he sat on the corner of his mahogany desk.

She crossed her arms over her chest, suddenly feeling as if she were back at lessons and not wanting to reveal too much ignorance. "When I lived in Gilsage as a child—"

"Did you?" Cauzel intruded, surprise tinting his voice.

"Um, yes. When I lived there, I showed certain … tendencies, and my mother had me train under the mystic in the Shrine of Shecclad. Unlike humans, we Eladrin have no need for true sleep, but enter a restorative trance to center our thoughts and revitalize our bodies."

A playful smile passed like a wave across Cauzel's lips. "So I've heard."

Be'naj paused her narrative, wary of his amusement.

"Please, continue. I shall cease my interruptions." Cauzel set his mouth in a firm line.

"Many times, my trance held prescient visions of the near future." Be'naj unfurled her wings, then folded them back. "A gift from the Sky Lord, the mystic told me. I had such a vision several days ago: one I found disturbing, especially since it was accompanied by a voice, declaring what sounded to me like prophecy."

"I see," Cauzel eventually responded when she failed to continue. "Have your trance-visions prompted you to action in the past?"

"Usually they simply prepare me to do so, for I have no direct knowledge of when the occurrences will come to pass. I might recognize some scenery that alerts me to what is about to happen, but beyond that, they mostly prime me to accept the future."

"But this time is different, you feel?"

Be'naj grew more comfortable discussing the topic, as Master Blackfeather gave no indication he wasn't taking her seriously. "I think so, yes. The vision was on a much grander scope, and I've never heard words accompany one. I have to wonder – if my visions are a gift from Shecclad, was it perhaps His voice I heard?"

Cauzel stood and paced, walking to the windows and back. "A fascinating prospect, to say the least. My dear, I must admit the divine is not my province, though if you are willing to tell, I would be interested in the details of your vision. Who knows, perhaps I could shed light on one aspect or another?"

"I would like that," Be'naj admitted. "The words are etched in my memory," she said as she walked closer to the windows, staring out over the sea of trees as she recalled the voice once more:

> *"The Eladrin have been marked for death,*
> *Their Keeper to fall by winter's last breath,*
> *'Less you follow the dance of Living Fire*
> *'Cross distant realms to a ruined spire,*
> *Wherein lies the truth of Broken Names,*
> *A secret trove, and devilish games.*
> *Go to Ancient Tarmuth, beneath the sands,*
> *Through portals three, and strange, new lands.*
> *Yet beware the cursèd Name of the Beast,*
> *Spreading like a plague from greatest to least,*
> *Out from the depths and across the far hills,*
> *To envelope Elisahd, by the half-breed's will.*

"Several images accompanied the lines as well: a sandstorm, blowing through a desert, a sphere of black stone, and a horned creature, among them." Be'naj turned back to find Cauzel furiously scribbling onto a piece of parchment.

"Fascinating," he said. "Ancient Tarmuth … it sounds like old Eladrin to me. A starting point, at least. The Keeper's library in Gilsage would be a cogent place to begin research." Finally, finishing his transcription, Cauzel set down his quill and regarded Be'naj. He sighed.

"I know there are other pressing matters at hand: finding my charges and securing their safety is of utmost importance, I assure you. But I do love a puzzle, I admit, and this sounds like a challenging one. As far as interpretation goes, I would defer to the mystic. Yet the Keeper and the Eladrin in general were mentioned, and I have sworn allegiance to them, so I can justify giving it my attention as well.

"Here is what I propose: while I must wait here for Aurus's return, you need not. In a few more days, I should not only have his explanation, but the outcome of whether Saffron's pendant will suffice as a means of tracking her location. In the meantime, perhaps you should consult your mystic, and I can meet you in Gilsage to follow-up on research in the Keeper's library."

Be'naj followed his plan until the point he suggested she travel to Gilsage. She had already considered it, of course, but the idea still terrified her. If anyone but the mystic confronted her, she had no idea how she would respond. "Can't I just wait and travel with you?"

"You could," Cauzel admitted, "but that would not be very efficient. I could use your help in the library, so it would be preferable if your other business was concluded by my arrival. I have means of travelling much faster on my own, so it would further slow us down for you not to have an ample head start."

Be'naj swallowed past the lump in her throat. "I see."

Cauzel seemed perplexed by the source of her hesitance. "Saffron's steed is still stabled here – I am certain your friend would not begrudge you borrowing her horse in order to save her."

He was right – how could she refuse. The fate of her people might rest on unravelling the meaning of her vision. Perhaps going home was a trial Shecclad had set before her. He did reward mastery, after all. "Yes, a horse would be welcome," Be'naj said, finally. "I will leave soon."

Sheen seemed to remember Be'naj and didn't object to her riding. "I know you must miss Saffron," Be'naj whispered as they took the trail leading away from Blackfeather Perch. "I do, too." She patted the horse's neck and Sheen whinnied her agreement.

Not long after the tower was obscured by the fiery autumn canopy, Be'naj felt eyes upon her again. She was quite comfortable knowing the Eladrin were watching as long as they did it from afar, though she wondered what the scouts hiding behind the foliage made of her. Did they see themselves in her eyes, or merely an oddly familiar outsider?

The day passed uneventfully, with Be'naj mostly buried in thoughts of rescuing Saffron. She imagined entering glorious battle with Sepathia and somehow arising victorious, even against long odds. She halted Sheen as the sky grew dark, not wanting to tire the horse or have her injure a leg. They started again at first light, however, and covered respectable ground, though she was by no means rushing to her destination.

It took some time to gather her bearings, not having been this close to her childhood home for ages, but eventually, recognition bloomed and she counted down the miles to the Shrine of Shecclad. She tried recalling her days in the sanctuary, for they were some of the fondest memories she had.

As Sheen picked a path over the roots of oaks and elms, bringing them ever closer, Be'naj worried about what she might do should others react poorly to her return. At last, she saw it:

the white and blue of the painted shrine stood out starkly against the backdrop of orange and brown leaves, its ivory spires reaching toward the realm of the Sky Lord. She knew it only consisted of a modest chapel and a few simple rooms, but somehow it looked smaller than before she'd left.

Though it rested on what could be considered the outskirts of Gilsage, she expected other Eladrin to be present, or at least visible, walking along the path to the more heavily settled areas of the capital. Yet, the hum of nature hung undisturbed; the wind playing in the branches and the songs of birds mingled peacefully.

Be'naj brought Sheen to a halt within sight of the stained windows, which filtered the sun into bright colors for those basking inside. A rustle in the trees drew her attention, but it was only a squirrel leaping from branch to branch.

When she looked back toward the shrine, however, a man stood in the middle of the entry path. His copper hair was trimmed uncommonly short for an Eladrin, and he leaned upon a tall, wooden staff with both hands, staring up at his visitor.

"Mystic Kiruh!" Be'naj called, a note of fondness mixing with her surprise at his sudden appearance.

"I had a vision of your arrival, child, though I scarcely believed it." He let one hand fall from his staff and ambled closer, his blue-trimmed, white robes concealing what Be'naj knew to be a thin frame.

She dismounted and walked Sheen forward, meeting the mystic at the border of the path. "Where is everyone? Has service to Shecclad waned so in the last few years?"

"I dismissed them once I was certain you were coming today. Seemed like it would make for an easier visit, no?"

Be'naj couldn't help herself and embraced Kiruh.

"Oh my," he said, seeming surprised, though he placed his empty hand gently on the top of her head. "Have you been receiving the supplies I've cached for you?"

"I have, thank you."

"Please, my dear," he said, pulling back from her embrace to look at her face, "don't cry. Save those tears for a sad occasion. Tie up your horse and come inside, won't you? There are still prying eyes all around."

Be'naj nodded, wiping the tears that had come unbidden, and did as the mystic asked. Once they were under the painted roof of the Sky Lord, they each took a seat on one of the meditation cushions. It felt as if no time at all had passed since she last sat there.

Mystic Kiruh clasped both her hands in his. "So, what is urgent enough to bring Be'naj all the way back to the scene of her childhood? It wasn't a very merry one, if I recall."

"It was not, Mystic." Be'naj's wings fell open slightly as she relaxed, their brass tips glinting in the afternoon sunlight that bathed the shrine. "I have continued receiving visions since I left, though recently one bestowed such a troubling impression, I felt compelled to seek your guidance."

"Indeed, you always had the attention of the Sky Lord," the mystic smiled. "It does not surprise me in the slightest he would choose you to deliver news of import. What was the nature of your vision?"

Be'naj recounted the words and scenery delivered during her trance, and Kiruh listened closely to everything she had to say. When she was done she waited, hoping her mentor's wisdom would be able to provide insight.

"It sounds," he began after clearing his throat, "like you have a journey ahead of you, child. It is no coincidence Shecclad has spoken to *you*, Be'naj. You are special, you are capable, and you are not tied to this realm in the same way most Eladrin are. Aside from our Keeper, who I shall warn personally, I don't know what the things or places mentioned in the prophecy are. And I have no doubt this is prophecy, my dear. You must follow the clues the Sky Lord has given you, or I fear we all may regret it."

Be'naj extracted her hands and bowed her head. "But there is someone else who needs me, Mystic. Someone who has shown me kindness, when so few have. I cannot go on this journey and abandon her."

Mystic Kiruh sighed. "Be'naj, sometimes we face difficult choices in life, where we have to decide between what makes us feel better in the moment and what will allow us to respect ourselves later on. Other times, the choice is made for us, and that can be difficult to live with as well. Shecclad has given you this task, Be'naj, and you cannot turn from it, even if you wish to. That which makes you who you are will not allow you to leave your family to calamity, even if you do not feel fondly toward them."

Be'naj was about to protest, to challenge the idea of what true family was, but the doors to the shrine suddenly swung open with a bang. Through them walked a flustered Cauzel, huffing for breath.

"My apologies for interrupting, Your Divine Holiness, but I needed to tell Be'naj that we were wrong. Saffron and my apprentices are not prisoners of Sepathia!"

Chapter 12

Property of the Wolfspider

S affron had no way of knowing what became of Faulk, but she and Thaelios decided before they returned not to tell the others of his choice. She didn't like keeping such a secret from Phaerim, and especially Dyphina, but worried no good could come of it.

Travelling was easier once they were clear of the forest and left Ifelian behind. Thaelios was sure the illusion spell he cast over them had expired by now, but it no longer seemed to matter to Gullagion. They had entered unclaimed territory, where no law prevailed.

Gullagion only hinted at their destination, but Saffron had travelled this road after leaving Rogan and Dhania in Chelpa and knew it well. The irony of her situation didn't escape her. She had headed west along this same path to bring an end to the slavery she was now subjected to, heading east to Talon Barge.

Everyone along the salt road gave them a wide berth due to the obvious devilry surrounding Gullagion. With no sovereign in charge, no one had motivation to contest the presence of the undead, unless it was to steal his charges. Since he only held four slaves, and none of them looked particularly robust, Saffron knew there was little chance that equation came out in their favor.

So, they walked for five days along the road with little deviation from their routine. Mounted caravans passed them, and though they received blatant stares, no one drew close enough to even exchange words. At last, they arrived in the town of Lirole Run, resting on the western bank of the River Chelhos. They caught a ferry across the river to Talon Barge, where they booked passage on a larger ship heading downstream. Where the ship was heading wasn't clear. If they were taking it all the way to the sea, they might end up anywhere. Whatever slight hope Saffron had held onto that Cauzel might appear and rescue them was left on shore as she stepped aboard their floating prison.

Once below deck, their chains were mercifully removed, though the collars remained. They stayed down with the cargo, though they weren't the only souls to do so. Another dozen or so men shared the candlelit space with them, and Saffron got little sleep. She recognized the hungry looks she and Dyphina received from their neighbors, which had little to do with the meager rations they all received.

They were outnumbered, and Phaerim didn't seem to scare any of them, though he tried his best to appear menacing. If anything, Saffron found the general suspicion toward Thaelios – with his large, solid-blue eyes and silver skin – did more to steer would-be molesters elsewhere. Despite constant vigilance to stave off the aggressions of the below-deck undesirables, Saffron considered it a blessing that they saw nothing of Gullagion.

Days passed, their minutes delineated by the regular rocking of the ship's hull against the waves, and if it weren't for the reminder of their collars, Saffron had no proof the lieutenant of Hadrian No More even existed. It became clear at some point they had made the transition from river to open ocean, but with no time topside, she had difficulty discerning their location.

Thaelios wasn't taking the movement of the ship as well as the others. A constant green tinge tainted his metallic countenance, and he sat for long periods with his head tucked between his knees. Phaerim eventually started interacting with a couple of the other passengers in a non-aggressive manner, and returned to the group one day with the news they were headed for the port of Zeblon.

"Zeblon?" Saffron responded, sitting up on the moth-eaten blanket that constituted her bed. "I wonder where that is. Certainly not on any map I've studied."

Thaelios shrugged when she looked at him. "It's nowhere I've come across in my readings."

"Well, according to my new friends over there," Phaerim tilted his head toward the other side of the deck, "they certainly have no problem with people owning people. Even make some of their slaves fight."

"Fight?" Dyphina asked, straightening her posture. "What for?"

"For sport," Phaerim added nonchalantly. "Seems they have an arena and quite the pervasive gladiator culture to go along with it."

Dyphina bit her lip, a look of concern washing over her face. "You don't suppose that's where we'll end up, do you?"

Phaerim shrugged. "Very little would surprise me at this juncture. I mean, how did we come to be on this accursed boat in the first place? Fate is a fickle mistress, as my father used to say."

Saffron didn't add anything to the conversation but started piecing threads together in her mind. Given their violent disobedience in the mines of Drachenmark, she could imagine Annoxoria's perverse sense of justice seeking to parlay their crimes into participation in a foreign blood-sport. The thought didn't frighten her personally, so much as raise worry for her companions' well-being. The other apprentices were not trained for such endeavors. Horrible as killing for entertainment would be, she also remembered the harem at Hope's End. At least for Dyphina and herself, options less palatable than fighting loomed as possibilities.

Over the next few hours, Saffron's mind wandered between conjurations of the myriad troubles awaiting her and sweeter memories of her recent past. Strange though they were, she was starting to find a home amongst her fellow Shapers at Blackfeather Perch. She knew she had been on the path to discovering great things, learning to harness the fire of song that burned within.

And then, of course, there were the tender moments of her blossoming friendship with Be'naj. Was it friendship that connected them? Be'naj was selfless and strong, yet so vulnerable. She was strange, awkward, yet undeniably beautiful, and Saffron ached at the thought of her accepting she'd been abandoned again. Drowning in all these thoughts was going to make Saffron crazy. She needed to escape her own head.

Craving a change in routine, and unsure how much longer they were going to be stuck underneath the wooden roof of the main deck, Saffron took the initiative to make sure the four of them at least maintained some fitness. She started leading them in calisthenics daily, or at least what she guessed was a day, given their lack of access to the passage of the sun. The other prisoners eyed them suspiciously as they exercised, some watching intently, wetting their lips as they stared her down.

Saffron did her best to put it out of her mind and not acknowledge the behavior. Phaerim's tenuous new friendships seemed to be forestalling any direct confrontations, as he confided that he'd misrepresented his relationships to both women in order to prevent their neighbors from becoming too demonstrative. Though not graphic in his retelling, Saffron understood that it may only be a matter of time before she and Dyphina were forced to physically defend their virtue.

Blessedly, before that time came, after what she guessed was a fortnight on the water, the ship finally dropped anchor. The hatch leading up to the top deck was unlocked and opened. A square of bright sunlight shone above, and after ample time for the prisoners to look to one another in confusion, the heavy boots of a man tapped down the stairs to their level.

"Form a line, organized by your owners!" he shouted. He was broad-shouldered, with skin dark as coal and teeth that flashed bright white. "You will give your name to be checked against the manifest, and my second mate will direct you to the correct representative. Don't give any trouble, and you won't get any trouble."

Eager to access the fresh air as soon as possible, Saffron hurried to form the front of the line as soon as he stopped talking. Thaelios and Dyphina followed, with Phaerim acting as a buffer at the rear.

Saffron was happy to find that more chains were not yet awaiting them, and Gullagion was nowhere to be seen as she emerged into the sunlight. She flattened her palm to screen her eyes from the intense glare and breathed deeply. The air was salty from the sea and gulls weaved over the masts, filling her ears with their calls.

The second mate directed her and her companions to a man dressed in immaculately pressed robes of fine cloth, waiting beside the boarding plank. Saffron was surprised to see that he looked Begnari. She led the others with tentative steps and offered a greeting in her native tongue when she reached him.

"*Hazan. Migberiigdin, Saffron min-Furasi.*"

"And I am Harzhim," he responded, also in Begnari. "Consul of the Wolfspider's gladiatorial pens. Follow me." He turned without looking back at them, apparently secure that they would, indeed, follow. Once they reached the boardwalk, Saffron could see why. Half a dozen guards in light mail, wearing dark capes and black-plumed helms, filed into place on either side of them.

They held their spears rigidly vertical and displayed obvious discipline in their formation.

Their ship had docked in a busy harbor, packed with bright-sailed galleons and fishing boats alike. A crescent-shaped boardwalk ran along the coastline, and long piers jutted out over the water. Obviously Zeblon supported a significant amount of sea trade. Toward either end of the crescent, Saffron could see rows of large warehouses, and between them, a bustling marketplace. Beyond the wooden planks of the boardwalk, avenues of baked sand separated sections of the city.

Harzhim led them along a path that skirted the edge of the market toward a huge structure, unlike any Saffron had seen before. Not a castle or palace or tower, it possessed curvature that suggested a nearly circular outer wall. The walkway led around one side of it, where manicured lawns and a broad, tree-lined street were flanked by some of the most impressive mansions she had ever seen.

Their path linked up to this street, which took them to the entrance of the circular monolith. Harzhim stopped and faced them once he reached the huge, swinging doors. "This is the Arena of Zeblon, your new home. For some, it will deliver great glory – for others, it will be your grave."

Phaerim tapped Saffron on the shoulder. "What's he saying?"

She quickly translated as two of their guards stepped forward to open the doors.

"Oh, wonderful," Phaerim responded, turning his worrying look to Dyphina. "At least we got that question answered straight away."

They followed Harzhim into a broad tunnel. On the other side of it, Saffron could see bright sunlight reflecting off a floor of white sand. They turned to continue along the ring-shaped perimeter and came shortly to an iron cage protecting a staircase, heading below the floor. Two more guards stood alert on either side of it.

Harzhim produced a key from a chain tucked under his shirt and unlocked the cage, then gestured for them to go first. Down the stairs, a series of stone hallways lined with lit torches, crisscrossed before them. More cages, some quite large, perforated the hallways. Harzhim took the lead again and navigated one of the halls before unlocking a cage door.

"This is where you will live," he stated plainly. "You are now Gladiators of the House of the Wolfspider. Your fellow gladiators can tell you anything else you need to know. Meals are served twice a day, but the next will not be for several hours." He gestured for them to enter the cage.

Saffron hesitated, trying to get a clearer bearing of her surroundings. From her current vantage, she could see no other exit from the tunnels besides the way they came.

"I am a busy man – do not make me wait ..." Harzhim dropped the previously casual tone and nodded slightly toward the cage.

"I suppose this is where we stay for now," Saffron relayed to her companions in Illanese before forcing a smile at the Consul. She led them into the pen, which was irregularly shaped to create the effect of several adjoining rooms, though no other doors separated the spaces. Benches lined a few edges of the enclosure, and straw mattresses lay in small rows throughout the pen.

A handful of other gladiators populated the cage, though they remained at the far end until the door was shut and locked. Once

Harzhim and the guards vacated, a massive, shirtless Illanese man, muscular and bald-headed, strode over, trailed by a second, less impressive Begnari.

The hulking man's sun-darkened chest bore a large, brown, scorpion tattoo, and smaller symbols decorated the skin behind his temples. Starting with Saffron, he looked each of them over in turn, not bothering to explain himself. When his calm eyes finished their assessment of Thaelios, he finally spoke. "What an odd fellow you are."

The statement didn't sound derisive – merely curious. Saffron noted the man chose to speak Illanese, even though he was in mixed company. Perhaps the people here were mostly bilingual? She could only guess that, being a port of some size, Zeblon attracted visitors from a variety of cultures.

Thaelios didn't seem to quite know how to respond, his face remaining blank even as he took a half-step back from their new neighbor, who looked especially giant compared to the thin-framed Eladrin.

"Are you the one who's supposed to tell us what in the Nine Hells is going on?" interjected Phaerim, who stepped forward and boldly struck eye contact.

The man laughed – an unexpected, jovial expulsion that shook his entire upper body. "Of course, where are my manners? I should have expected Harzhim not to give you a proper orientation." He flattened one broad hand against his bare chest and introduced himself. "I am Zygrim the Bull, the most accomplished fighter in the Pens of the Wolfspider, which simply means I've managed to survive the longest. Behind me is my sometimes fighting partner, Charilo." He gestured to the wiry Begnari man who remained in his wake. Charilo's thin, dark facial hair quivered as he broke into a half-smile and gave a courteous nod. "Charilo's primary claim to gladiatorial fame is that he's managed to allow me to save his neck at least a handful of times." Zygrim indulged his full laugh once more. "Welcome to your new House."

"Pleased to meet you, Zygrim. My name is Phaerim, and these are my capable companions: Saffron, Dyphina, and the mysterious Thaelios."

Saffron looked sideways at Phaerim, wondering if he hadn't really been a merchant in his previous life. "We have so many questions, as you can imagine, and would be grateful for any answers, Zygrim. Shall we sit and get more comfortable?"

"Why not? Idle time is something we have in plenty, here." Remaining polite, Zygrim indicated a collection of benches along one of the walls and waited for them to be seated before adding, "I can see that, like me, you have no doubt been brought here from some distance. I am sorry for your change in fortunes."

Saffron noticed, as they rearranged on the benches, that Zygrim and Charilo bore collars similar to hers. Looking deeper into the cage, she noted the same of the other prisoners. "And where are you from, exactly?" she asked, hoping to mirror Zygrim's courtesy.

"I hail from the fertile land of Lystia, but on my way to the jungles of Xyanarind, some months ago, my ship was smashed to pieces on the rocks littering the cape. Would that I had a better navigator ..." Zygrim's head tilted upward as if he was reliving a memory.

"I was lucky enough to swim to shore," he continued, "but my lungs were so full of water I nearly drowned, even so. I passed out from exhaustion and awoke a prisoner of the Wolfspider."

Dyphina looked incredulous. "They can do that here? Just, take a person they find on the beach as a slave?"

Zygrim shrugged. "They saw I was a foreigner and shipwrecked. I guess they figured no one was going to stop them." He flashed a sudden smile her way. "I certainly didn't make it easy on them, I can assure you."

Phaerim sniggered, sizing up their host. "I believe you on that."

Saffron was still trying to piece together exactly where they were. She had never heard of Lystia, either, so that was no help. They must have headed east, though, because she'd seen maps of the lands between Begnasharan on the western coast and the Cradle of the World, where she'd spent the last year fighting against the King-priest of Chelpa, and none were populated by her people, save her home nation.

"Have you seen this *Wolfspider*?" she asked. "I presume he's actually a man."

"Oh yes, he's a man," Zygrim confirmed. "The most ruthless and influential Guild-Lord in the region. Rumors have him backed by none other than the Dread Lich, Hadrian No More."

Had everyone else on Elisahd heard of this creature but her? Saffron didn't understand the connection to their predicament. "Why would a guilder keep a stable of gladiators? Does he not have legitimate businesses?"

"Oh, make no mistake," Zygrim answered. "The Arena fights *are* a legitimate business in Zeblon. Or at least what passes for one, here. It's a fundamental pillar of their society, in fact. We fight not only for the pleasure of the crowds, but for the interests of our House. The Wolfspider runs but one of the four major competitors of the Arena. Our victories are an integral part of the shifting power between these Houses. It is the reason that, for the most part, we are treated well – much better than the common slaves of the city."

"So slavery is a part of Zeblon's way of life?" Saffron felt her skin flush with surfacing anger.

"Very much so," Zygrim confirmed. "All the major households are slaveholders. Enormous amounts of money change hands based on the outcomes of our fights. The more successful gladiators attract sponsors, who use that connection as influence in other aspects of their lives. That should be your goal – attracting a wealthy sponsor. You will increase not only your quality of life here in the pens, but your likelihood of holding onto it."

Zygrim leaned closer, as if what he was about to say was not to be discussed openly. "Don't think for a moment that the fights are fair. The odds are swayed in many ways, and you don't want to be the one caught on the sour end of a rigged contest."

"So, let me see if I understand correctly," Phaerim announced. He stood and paced in a short line. "We are supposed to fight against people like you, who are obviously built for it," he extended an upturned palm at Zygrim, "on top of which, the odds may have been further stacked against us?"

Zygrim nodded.

"Well, where is the suspense in that?"

Saffron shook her head, wanting to learn more about sponsorship. "So who, exactly, are these sponsors? Fickle nobility? Wealthy merchants? Bored sycophants trying to attain glory by living vicariously through the deeds of gladiators?"

"All of those and others," Zygrim confirmed.

Saffron was about to follow-up, but was unnerved by Charilo's unwavering stare. She finally met his eyes. "Is there something you'd like to say?" she asked in Begnari.

He shook his head as if emerging from a stupor and offered a weak smile. "My apologies, Lady Saffron" he answered in their native tongue, "but you are obviously educated and highborn. I was just wondering how a noble daughter of Zeblon came to find herself in such company. It is surprising to encounter even a single woman in our ... profession. To have two of such beauty," he said, glancing at Dyphina, "introduced at once is especially rare."

Saffron switched to Illanese, assuming Charilo could understand. "I am not a 'daughter of Zeblon,' as you put it. My family has longstanding roots in the Sultanate of Begnasharan, and my friends were taken against their will in Ifelian. None of us, beautiful or not, educated or not, deserve to be here, fighting at the whim of the mongrels of Zeblon."

She hadn't intended to let all that out, but couldn't deny it felt good to give it voice. Charilo looked frightened that he had offended her, and Zygrim's eyebrows had risen halfway up his bald head.

"Well-said," the Bull replied. "Just a word of advice, though," he said, leaning toward her and using his conspiratorial tone. "You will want to be careful of who overhears such thoughts. Even some of your fellow gladiators would use any advantage to curry favor with the right people." He stood upright again when he'd finished.

"So, who runs the other Houses we're competing against?" Saffron asked. She had a good mind for politics and was eager to find some angle she could use to their advantage.

Zygrim's face screwed up a bit as he recalled the list and counted out on his thick fingers. "The Wolfspider, the competing Temples of Hellig-nok and Pnemonesis, and the Caliph of Zeblon all maintain their own stables. Each House possesses particular strengths and ways of handling things."

Thaelios spoke for the first time since they entered the cages, catching Saffron off-guard. "So, do you fight against gladiators from the other Houses?"

Zygrim tilted his head and smiled, as if Thaelios's melodic voice was a special sort of music, just for him. "Often, that is the way of it," he finally said. "Sometimes we fight alone, other times in groups. Occasionally, I've even fought against wild beasts and unnatural creatures."

Full realization seemed to be seeping in for Dyphina. "Are you jesting? Do you mean to say that I could be put out there, on my own, and forced to stand off against a panther or wolf? With a crowd of screaming lunatics watching me being eaten alive!" Her mouth remained open and she looked at Phaerim, who wrapped his arm around her shoulder but offered no words of comfort.

"How often do you fight?" Saffron asked soberly.

Zygrim bit his lip, perhaps grasping that the level of fear among the newcomers was greater than his own by at least an order of magnitude. "There are battles once a week, but not everyone fights each time. We are told our schedule a few days in advance."

Saffron nodded. "And how many days until the next fights?"

"Five," he answered. "You'll likely find out the day after tomorrow if you're going to be involved. Either way," he added, in an apparent attempt to find a silver lining, "you'll have at least a couple of days to train beforehand."

"I don't imagine a month of training would make much difference." Despite his words, Thaelios didn't sound dejected. He was merely presenting an honest assessment.

"No doubt your first match will be tough, my exotic friend." Zygrim, this giant of a man, managed to express a tone of pure compassion. "In addition to your opponent, your first time is as much about mastering your fear and not becoming overwhelmed by your surroundings: the roar of the crowd, the sun reflecting off the sand into your eyes. In truth, there is very little we can do to prepare you for that."

Saffron thought it best not to dwell on such things for the moment. The days ahead would hold plenty of time for worry. She stood and walked a few paces to get a better look around their new home. The other handful of slaves showed no interest in introducing themselves. She saw one reclining on a mattress, another lifting and lowering his body from the bars overhead, and a third appearing to be engrossed in silent meditation. "So, how do you pass the time when you're not fighting or indoctrinating new prisoners?"

Zygrim straightened his posture and flexed his impressive arms to either side, stretching his chest. "I exercise and use my allotted training time to my best advantage. I am lucky enough to have a sponsor who visits me occasionally … and then there's always the Den of Sin."

"Den of Sin?" Saffron's interest was piqued.

"Yeah, it's an illicit playground of sorts, for all manner of questionable pastimes. There's gambling, drinking, whoring, that sort of thing. Lots of unsavory types, of course, but we can't afford to be too picky, can we?

"You can get contraband there if you talk to the right person, and it's a good way to release some of the pressure of regularly fighting to the death. The Wolfspider operates it, so there's direct access from the tunnels down here. You can earn passes by being victorious in the Arena, or sometimes sponsors will purchase you one as a favor."

"Isn't the Wolfspider afraid some of his property will use the outing to escape?" Phaerim asked.

"Not really," Charilo chimed in. "There are guards, and his gladiators are well known. Then, of course, there are these." He tapped a fingernail against his metal collar. "It would be foolish to run. At least in the Arena, everyone has a chance."

"Just get through your first fight," Zygrim said as he shrugged. "If you can do that, we can teach you how to navigate the world down here. We all have a better chance at succeeding, the better our House is positioned. Sometimes, sponsors with enough clout can even get you time on the outside – though it usually comes with a price …"

It sounded to Saffron like he was speaking from personal experience.

"I know it's a lot to consider. Come, Charilo. Let's give them some time to themselves." After one last, lingering look at Thaelios, Zygrim ambled back toward the far side of their spacious new cage, and his partner followed.

Saffron considered the rest of her companions. It was going to take some serious work to get them ready for armed combat.

She only hoped that, when the fighting assignments for the week came out, they would somehow be spared.

Chapter 13

A Thrall in Nightwing Court

"**I** don't like to be kept waiting," Annoxoria declared as her chamberlain led Izefet once again into the throne room of Nightwing Castle.

"*Who does?*" the half-demon projected. "*But I have many obligations, and all of them take time. Yet, I am here now, My Lady.*" He looked around the throne room, which was practically deserted. "*And your Lord is still absent?*"

Annoxoria's face flushed with warmth. While she hated keeping secrets from Thuvian, she was not ready to divulge what she privately hoped to gain from this unpalatable partnership. Izefet didn't need to know that, however. "Lord Skullreaver is attending business elsewhere. He, too, has many obligations."

"*Of course,*" Izefet responded, the hint of a smile coming across even in his voiceless projection. "*Then we may speak plainly, no?*" He walked closer to the throne and looked over his shoulder at the chamberlain, who Annoxoria dismissed with a wave.

Only a pair of guards remained at the room's secondary entrance, and those she had picked personally for their loyalty. "We may. You know, I presume, that we have already provided the Dread Lich's lieutenant with a shipment of Seeds of the Avatars. Are you ready to uphold your part of the bargain? Have you come to facilitate my transformation?"

Annoxoria brushed her hands against the top of her leather boots, which rose to the middle of her thigh. She had no idea what form such magic would take – ritual, potion, or something more … unpleasant. She had researched extensively and seen examples of dubious procedures bordering on torture.

"*I have come to address it, My Lady, but you must remain patient. The Living Fire you provided is only the first step in the process.*"

Annoxoria frowned and slouched back against Thuvian's throne, which extended well above her head. "I should have known. Do not try to extort me for more concessions, Unholy One. I will not abide two-tongued negotiations, nor be manipulated by the likes of such an abomination. We made a deal, and I expect you to keep the terms."

Izefet stood rooted in place, though he folded his arms, tucking his clawed hands into the sleeves of his black robe before responding. *"Tsk, tsk, tsk. Such a sharp tongue you have. And here I thought we were friends."*

Annoxoria narrowed her eyes and folded her arms as well, waiting for something with more substance to emerge.

"As I was saying," Izefet finally continued, *"The Living Fire you delivered is only the first step. Hadrian No More requires additional gems in order to craft the talisman necessary to act as a conduit for his ancient power. In addition, there is something else you will need to provide for the spell to work as you hope."*

Her tongue shot to the roof of her mouth, ready to let loose another tirade, but Annoxoria held back momentarily, waiting to see what ridiculous caveat the half-demon was trying to create.

"You will need a token of the creature you wish to become in order to complete the transformation. In this case, a single scale from the body of a living Nightwing."

"Are you jesting?!" Annoxoria's scornful epithets were forgotten as her mind wrestled with the news. "Why not try something less dangerous, like hurtling myself from the top of the castle? How am I supposed to get that?" Even as she complained, she realized the requirement made sense.

Possessing a piece of what she intended to become should have occurred to her before Izefet even mentioned it, but that didn't make her disappointment any easier to swallow. If only a scale from her lover would suffice, there would be no problem. Alas, she possessed the soul of a true dragon, and not something in-between. As much as she loved Thuvian, being *half* of anything would not make her whole.

"Of course it sounds like an impossible task, but if there's one thing I've learned in my time on this world, it's that there is

always a solution to get what you want, if you're creative enough." Izefet's crimson eyes offered no comfort, however.

"Bah, enough of your platitudes. Do you have anything else useful to tell me?"

"*I trust the presence of the Aasimar is making your search for the Living Fire more efficient?*"

Annoxoria sighed and relaxed her shoulders. "It is. They are sure we've located more, we're just having an issue retrieving it. Slaves aren't always the most creative in *their* solutions."

"*Well, I trust that's a problem you will also solve. Unless there is more you need of me, I will take my leave, Lady Nefzen, and return in a fortnight. As I said, I have many obligations. I will send an agent to await delivery of the Living Fire when you've extracted it.*" Izefet gave a courteous nod and made for the exit, not waiting on Annoxoria to actually demand more of him.

She was glad to be rid of his presence, though. His telepathy was unnerving, and although he usually remained polite, she could feel the vibration of his underlying malice. He was certainly not to be overly trusted. Still, if he could deliver what she wanted, there was nary a price she would be unwilling to pay.

Annoxoria stood and descended the steps from her Lord's throne. She had plenty of work to do: not only to figure out how to rob a living Nightwing of one of its scales, but to learn more about the half-demon who made, then changed, the conditions of a potent promise. What were his true motivations, and what could he actually deliver? These were worthy questions.

Her first stop was the holding cells. One reason she was annoyed by Izefet's tardiness was that her audience with him interrupted the interrogation of a recent capture. Some creature, more or less human, had infiltrated their vale and was found lurking around the grounds not far from Nightwing Castle. Whether an enemy agent intent on reconnaissance, or simply a wayward mutant of some sort, she didn't yet know. The creature's appearance, however, gave her a quiet rush.

Its skin was a slate grey, wrapped in a pattern resembling small scales. Instead of round, its pupils were vertically slit like a snake's … or a dragon's. The idea had hardly escaped her and returned stronger after the disappointing news Izefet delivered. Perhaps this creature held the key to another way of getting what she wanted – one not requiring a death wish, or even dealing with such an untrustworthy aberration as the half-breed.

Annoxoria practically bolted down to the dungeons where Thuvian's spymaster, the extremely competent Pereen Guillory, had been left to extract as much information as he could from their newest guest. As she approached the doorway to the block of cells where the interrogation was taking place, she could hear an animalistic snarl, followed by the smack of metal on metal.

The jailor unlocked the gate upon seeing her, bowing as Annoxoria passed. Pereen, a middle-aged man with a solid but thin frame, held a pair of iron tongs in his hands, and was just releasing something from them onto a small table at the edge of the room when she entered. Scanning the area, she found the prisoner had been moved and now lay horizontally spread upon a pair of crossed, oaken beams, his ankles and wrists bound in irons.

"Ah, Lady Nefzen," Pereen greeted her, his tone casual even though he employed her title. He was one of the few she respected enough for this not to bother her. "You just missed the most interesting conversation."

The prisoner spat a reptilian hiss at the spymaster's remark.

She leaned over as Pereen set down the tongs, to find that the object he'd dropped was one of the creature's teeth. He picked up a small glass vial and extended it toward her.

"He was carrying this, hidden on his person. It was his only possession outside of the dagger taken from him during capture."

Annoxoria lifted the vial in front of her face to inspect it. A putrid-green liquid filled half of its scant capacity. "Do you know what it is?" Her first guess was poison. Perhaps he'd meant to imbibe it when caught and never got the chance. Perhaps he'd intended to commit murder.

"Nightwing venom, apparently, though he wouldn't divulge its purpose." Pereen gestured toward the bound prisoner. "This is one of Sepathia's Thralls, though, so we can hazard a guess."

Annoxoria looked at the creature's face more closely. Blood trickled from its mouth and nose. "So, Thuvian's sister hasn't given up." She'd attempted to eradicate her half-brother before.

"It would seem not," the spymaster answered.

She tucked the vial into her cleavage. "We need to know if she's planning a move against our Lord. Find out what you can from this vermin, and make sure no more of his kind are skulking around the castle."

Pereen nodded, stroking his pointed goatee.

"Once you finish that, I have another task for you," Annoxoria continued. "I need to know more about a group that's been operating in the Corridor recently: 'The Name of the Beast,' they're called. I want to know what they've been up to, how strong their influence is, and anything specific you can find out about an agent of theirs named 'Izefet.' He's some sort of half-fiend."

The spymaster couldn't keep a smile from creeping across his scarred face before once again giving his casual bow. "It is my pleasure to be in your service, My Lady."

Annoxoria kept her face an emotionless mask. "I'm sure it is." She turned on her heel and left the dungeons, heading for her personal study. She recalled seeing some mention of Thralls of the Nightwing in her research on transformation and wanted to revisit the topic after meeting one in the flesh. Determining truth from mere legend, or the embellished whimsy of folktales within her lore books, was a skill she was yet mastering.

As her boots echoed along the stone hallways toward her destination, she took a moment to consider all she and Thuvian had built. His force of will drew many to follow him – others, he compelled through fear. She respected both aspects of his personality. He knew what his gifts were and used them. This castle was a testament to his leadership and dominion.

But she took pride in her contributions as well. Her support legitimized him in the eyes of many. She was shrewd and cunning, knowing how to entice some subjects into loving her while taking pleasure in making the recalcitrant suffer.

Her attention to detail was expressed in the transformation of their home from a functional structure of stone into a monument to her Lord's heritage: the iron braziers decorated with wings, the ceiling reinforcements shaped like exposed bones, the curved spaces and black, hanging cloth to deaden sound, the scaled walls and strategic gold filigree all spoke of her dedication to their desired place in the world. Together, she and Thuvian were a force careening toward a reckoning.

When Annoxoria reached her study, she closed and locked the door behind her, then selected the volume entitled *Draconis Arcana* from the bulging shelves. She was fairly sure it was where she had read the story. Setting the text on her desk, she opened its ancient, leather binding, thumbing through pages until she came to a section with the heading: *Servants of the Serpents.*

A number of entries and diagrams populated the parchment, all of which she'd considered at some point in her research, but none of them went far enough to satisfy her. She could feel her draconic heritage coursing through her veins; her blood boiled with magic, after all. For now, though, Annoxoria scanned through the text until she found what she was looking for: Thralls of the Nightwing.

As magically adept creatures, dragons had a long history as centers of ritual and ceremony among lesser beings. They were sometimes seen as instruments of the gods, or demons come to haunt and destroy, or even deities in their own right. Nightwings, especially, were surrounded by some of the darkest traditions.

Thralls of the Nightwing, her book maintained, were the result of demon-infatuation, nurtured by the indulgence of the object of worship. When groups of fanatic humans willingly subjugated themselves into the service of a Nightwing, she occasionally rewarded them with a painful alteration. Poison, extracted from the dragon's tail stinger, was diluted with other elements and made into a potion, which the Thralls imbibed during a special ceremony.

Some died during the process, but over time, the result for those surviving was a drastic change. The Thralls' skin became dark, hardened, and scaled like their matron. Their eyes became reptilian and sensitive to the light, but their senses of smell and hearing were enhanced, not to mention the ability to feel the vibrations of other creatures. The Thralls always, according to the *Draconis Arcana*, served the interests of their Nightwing matron.

Annoxoria leaned back against her tall chair, considering what she'd just read. She had seen firsthand proof that Thralls of the Nightwing were real. She retrieved the vial of confiscated poison from her cleavage and inspected it again. Did it hold the secrets of transformation? Perhaps she could figure out the other ingredients or even make slight variations to get better results. The question certainly demanded further inquiry.

For now, she needed to make her rounds in the mines and make sure the budding animosity between the Aasimar and her ogres wasn't causing another cave-in.

Annoxoria's anxiety made her feel as if every hair on her body was standing on end. It pained her to leave Thuvian's arms, considering how often he had to be away these days, but she needed to know what the spymaster had found after his weeks-long investigation. Her regular ingestions of the concoction she'd distilled using the Nightwing venom were not having a visible effect, other than making her muscles spasm uncomfortably every few days. It looked more and more like she might have to trust Izefet, and she wanted to know exactly what his "Name of the Beast" was up to.

Hurried as she was, she still took the necessary time to go through her dressing routine before leaving Thuvian's bedchamber. Her scaled, leather boots and corset were polished until they reflected the torchlight. Her nails were immaculately manicured to suggest talons, and her dark makeup suggested sunken eyes that mirrored her partner.

The walk down to the dungeons seemed longer than ever, and she was ready to claw out the jailor's eyes when he fumbled his keys trying to let her in. She hissed at his apology and stormed deeper into the dungeon, where she was told Pereen was conducting more interrogations.

"Well?" she said as soon as she saw the back of the spymaster's cloak. "What were you able to find out about Izefet and his machinations?"

Pereen Guillory turned to face her, and as she drew closer, she could hear sniveling coming from the open cell he was standing in. He was holding those familiar metal tongs, only now they clenched what looked to be a bloody tongue.

Pereen followed Annoxoria's eyes down to what he was holding and tried to conceal it behind his back. "Apologies, My Lady. I would have come to meet you had I known you desired an audience so soon."

"I heard you retuned over an hour ago." She looked back to Pereen's face, ignoring the distraction of the whining prisoner.

"Indeed." Pereen stole a glance at the former owner of the tongue he held. "I had a few loose ends that needed tying." He gestured toward the hallway behind them, so they might leave the presence of the captive. When they were out of casual earshot, the spymaster broke into his revelations.

"Lady Nefzen, the Name of the Beast is apparently some sort of dark cult, though whether this *Izefet* is the object of their adoration or merely a practitioner, is uncertain. Regardless, it has spread in popularity and has a sizable chapter in Pasaxtree, though it apparently originated in the east." He shifted his weight, bringing the tongs back into view, and Annoxoria found her eyes drawn to the dangling tongue while Pereen spoke.

"What the cult wants, exactly, is not clear. They seem to be decidedly anti-Eladrin, and there is some talk of invading the refuge of Gilsage. But they don't seem to like those with authority anywhere, from what I'm told. This is something worth monitoring as our Lord starts exercising his power more outwardly."

"I knew it! That accursèd trickster." Annoxoria felt vindicated by her instinct to distrust the half-fiend. "He's trying to stage an uprising that would destabilize the region, just as Thuvian enters the political arena." Her mind churned, turning over dozens of possibilities in rapid succession. "Perhaps that can be used to our advantage, though."

"There's more, My Lady." The spymaster's warped smile tickled the corners of his mouth.

"Speak your mind, Master Guillory."

"Izefet, in particular, has been trying to locate the ruins of Rinn-Rhulian, beneath our very noses."

Annoxoria snapped her head around suddenly, making sure no one else was listening. "Do you know why?" she asked in a harsh whisper.

"The obvious reasons, I'd suspect. But he clearly doesn't want you to know of his intentions to do so, or he would have simply asked, don't you think?" Pereen's eyebrows arched as if he were a very clever man, indeed.

"No one but us and Thuvian knows how to get in, spymaster, so I don't want to hear about Izefet finding out. Understood?"

Pereen looked severely wounded by the insinuation. "Of course, My Lady. I would never betray the Lord and Lady of Nightwing Castle."

"Very good." Annoxoria believed him, but it couldn't hurt to be clear. "If that is all, then, I will leave you to your work." She glanced down at the bloody tongue once more and turned to leave as the spymaster bowed.

Chapter 14

Enter the Arena

L uck didn't appear to be on their side. When the fighting assignments for the week were handed out, Saffron learned that she, Phaerim, Thaelios, and Dyphina would be battling against another group of novices from the Caliph's stables – a little bit of gamesmanship between the two rivals.

Harzhim delivered the news, then led them to a sparring area where they could train with wooden weapons. "Three hours today and three tomorrow," he said. Saffron translated for the others after he'd gone and tried to decide how best to spend their training allotment. She looked over the available armaments, having no idea if their implements for the actual fight might vary.

Spears and shields were included upon the rack, so Saffron decided to start with them. "Assuming we are being pitted against other slaves and not hardened warriors, I should at least have an advantage over our first opponents. We'll make this as simple as possible. Your job, until we make noticeable progress, is not to get killed."

"Aww, where's the fun in that?" Phaerim teased. "I don't know about these Shapers, but I have every intention of using this opportunity to release some aggression."

"As you like it," Saffron responded, selecting a shield and wood-tipped spear. "But we should still learn as much as we can about our allies' fighting styles, so we can react quicker to threats and fight cooperatively."

"What about magic?" Dyphina asked. "I know we don't have our spellbooks to study from, but I've memorized a few tricks, and I'm sure Thaelios has as well."

"I'd only use it as a last resort," Saffron suggested. "We don't know yet how these fights are arranged. I am afraid that if we show too much promise too soon, we'll find ourselves pitted against more experienced foes."

Dyphina didn't argue, but her face showed lines of concern. "I'm just not certain I can get the hang of using these," she said, gesturing to the weapon racks.

"Well, let's give it a try first, shall we?" Saffron forced a smile and waited while her fellow apprentices grudgingly selected their spears and strapped shields to their arms. Phaerim seemed more interested as he hefted his shield, getting a sense of its weight. Dyphina looked uncomfortable, and Thaelios appeared to struggle under the burden.

"The first thing we want to work on is adopting the correct defensive posture …" Saffron spent the rest of their practice time showing the others how to stand steady, move their shields to best protect them, and make simple thrusts with their spears. Concentrating on the bare essentials, she didn't waste effort on counterattacks, offensive use of their shield, or other, more advanced techniques.

They all generated a healthy sweat, and Saffron could see from their flushed faces, heavy breathing, and drooping limbs that Dyphina and Thaelios were exhausted by the time they finished. Phaerim fared a little better, but Saffron knew they would all be sore later. To their credit, none of them complained of their fatigue, perhaps because they realized it was their own lives at stake and whining would be counterproductive.

"I think that went well," Saffron commented as they were escorted back to the main pen, trying to be positive. In truth, she worried whether Cauzel's apprentices would have the stamina to hold out in a protracted engagement. The pressure would be on her to dispatch their opponents as quickly as possible.

Phaerim pulled her aside once the others were resting on the benches, massaging their weary arms. "That was interesting, to say the least. I've never trained with a shield before. Seems like it could be useful, once you get the hang of it." He tilted his head toward the apprentices, then brought his voice down to a whisper, "How do you feel about their chances?"

She looked into his eyes, wondering if he was testing her resolve. "I like all our chances, Phaerim. Of course, there's no accounting for the quality of our opponents at this stage."

"How was your first day of training?"

Saffron and Phaerim both turned as Zygrim's voice boomed across the cage. He had stopped next to Thaelios, resting a broad hand on the Eladrin's narrow shoulder.

"Ah, muscles a little weary, no doubt?" Zygrim said, not waiting for a response. He straddled the bench Thaelios was seated on, sliding close and moving both hands to the top of his shoulders. "Here, let me see what I can do about that."

Thaelios's eyes opened wide, but he remained speechless as Zygrim the Bull vigorously massaged his shoulders and back.

Dyphina regarded them longingly. "Oh, can I be next?" she asked, rotating her shoulders to indicate their stiffness.

"Sure," Zygrim capitulated, his eyes bright as they moved down to focus on his task. "I saw that you four will be fighting as a group. Sorry it came so soon, but that probably means you will be fighting other novices, like yourself. Just watch over one another and you should have an honest chance. Too many gladiators end up fending for themselves in group matches, not realizing how their chances suffer once an ally falls."

"Thank you for the advice, Zygrim," said Dyphina, blinking a few times in close succession.

"I noticed your name was not put in peril this week," Saffron added from across the room. "I was wondering if gladiators not involved in combat still have the opportunity to watch the fights. I would be interested in hearing your assessment."

"Harzhim allows it, though many of us prefer not to. We get enough exposure to bloodshed as it is."

"Oh, I see. I hadn't thought of that," Saffron admitted.

Zygrim smiled. "I don't mind, however. I'd be happy to give you any suggestions I can."

"My thanks. I must say, Zygrim," Saffron crossed the space between them as she spoke, "I wasn't really expecting anyone here to be so helpful."

"Well," Zygrim drew his hands from Thaelios to regard her more directly, "I remember how lonely it was when I first arrived. Most relationships here don't last long, as you can imagine. I'd like to help if I can."

Dyphina took the opportunity to scoot the thoroughly befuddled-looking Thaelios out of the way and take his place on the bench in front of Zygrim. "My turn!" she said. "I think I can feel some real knots in there."

Saffron rolled her eyes and headed toward her mattress, choosing to stay clear of whatever scheme Dyphina was perpetrating. She wanted to spend some time visualizing their coming battle, anyway, seeing herself pivot and jab in her mind's eye, fighting her way to victory.

The group's second session of training went more poorly than the first, as Thaelios's and Dyphina's less-seasoned muscles prevented them from pushing as hard. When Phaerim questioned their effort, Dyphina snapped back before throwing down her shield and stalking off.

"Alright, let's change things up a bit," Saffron butted in before Phaerim could find a clever retort. "It's been a long day and we don't want to ruin our strength completely before battle. Let's put our weapons aside and work on cooperative formations. We don't want to trip one another, but staying close will keep any one of us from being surrounded." Over the rest of practice, she showed them the proper footwork and operating distance to allow for maneuvering without opening the circle to unnecessary attacks.

Finally, the day of the games arrived. Saffron's group was bound by manacles and led out of their pen. Harzhim took them down a series of torch-lit corridors to the arming room, where they received final instructions.

"Today is a great day," he began. Saffron could hear the rumble of the crowd, somewhere above and beyond the doors on the far wall, stomping their feet and demanding entertainment. "Either you will win glory from your victory in the Arena, or you will die upon the sand, feeding the ground with your blood – a truly great death."

"Is it?" Phaerim whispered to Saffron from the side of his mouth as she translated. "I was always partial to old age."

"You will have a few moments to arm yourselves as you wish while the crowd continues to build. As novices, yours is the first fight of the day. You will whet their appetite!" Harzhim spread his arms to the ceiling. "Not much is expected from you, in truth, though a wise man might see that as an invitation to surpass expectations, no?" He unlocked the manacles from their wrists, one by one. "Good luck, and fight proudly for the House of the Wolfspider until all your foes are slain!" With that, he exited the doors they'd entered through, which swung shut and were barred from the other side.

"Find what you need, quickly," Saffron urged after sharing her own, brief version of the Consul's speech. "We don't know when those doors will open." They had not been given any clothes to change into, and Saffron was thankful again for her supple, kank-hide armor. She'd changed into it before they gathered that morning, but the rest of them had only their travelling clothes, which offered little protection from weapons.

She selected a bronze-tipped spear, shaking the shaft to test its flexibility. Satisfied, she moved on to pick a round shield with as few notches in it as possible. She had tied her hair back in a braid that morning after doing the same for Dyphina, and tested it one last time by shaking her head from side-to-side. Her growing nervousness threatened the steadiness of her hands, so she turned her attention to assuring the others were ready.

She noticed Dyphina had picked weaponry similar to hers, which was essentially what they had practiced with. When she looked to Phaerim, however, she saw he was holding a pair of long daggers, trying one out with each hand.

"What are you doing?" she asked. "That's not what we've been working on."

"I know," Phaerim said, unrepentantly, "but we didn't have these available in the training room, and they're going to keep us alive." He grasped the hilts of the daggers tightly and made a deft, outward-slicing motion to demonstrate.

"They have a bow! I'm much better with that, Saffron," Thaelios cooed in his lyrical lilt.

Heat radiated off Saffron's face as she felt her carefully envisioned plan crumbling around her. "How is a bow going to keep you safe, Thaelios? You can't aim one and use a shield at the same time!" But the Eladrin was already plucking the string, and they had run out of time.

The heavy, swinging doors that lead to the floor of the Arena swung open, bathing the southern end of the chamber in sunlight. Two guards, dressed in polished, ceremonial armor and scarlet cloaks, thrust their helmed heads into the doorway, yelling "Come Out!" in Begnari.

Saffron was suddenly met by three other pairs of eyes, and she nodded to her companions, trying to maintain an air of confidence. With slow, deliberate steps, she walked toward the near-blinding light, as if this were not the single strangest moment of her life. She lifted her shield to block out the sun, giving her eyes time to adjust to the contrast. The crowd surged around her, rising up as she entered their view.

The sand beneath her feet wasn't too deep, though she recognized it might slow her down at a full run. An oval wall, shaped of thick bricks, encircled the Arena floor, separating gladiators from spectators. Seats rose for several stories behind that wall, packed with more people than Saffron had ever seen in one place.

Thousands of voices chanted and screamed in Begnari, eager to see the blood of strangers spilt for their amusement. Saffron quickly looked behind her to make sure the others had followed, just in time to see the swinging doors close, with the guards disappearing behind them. Only the combatants remained on the sand.

Across from them, perhaps a hundred paces away, was another quartet of hapless prisoners, bearing weapons and looking up at the crowd in awe. Saffron felt a twinge of guilt, knowing their foes were likely just as innocent, but fought to squelch it. "It's them or us," she told herself. Neither side seemed eager to engage.

And yet, a scant breath later an arrow struck the sand a mere body's length in front of her. Saffron raised her shield – one of their opponents had chosen a bow as well.

She looked back, confirming that Thaelios had enough wits to grab a quiver of arrows before leaving the arming room.

"You've got it, you might as well use it!" He quickly drew an arrow. "The rest of you, follow me, but don't let them past you. Phaerim, if one of them makes a break for Thaelios, it's on you to protect him."

Phaerim nodded, crouching as he followed her like a shadow, no doubt wishing he'd chosen a shield after all. Another arrow sailed over Saffron's head as she worked her way forward, Dyphina at her left flank. So far, their opponents seemed content to remain stationary while letting their archer take unmolested shots, but he didn't appear especially proficient.

Saffron assessed the men with her eyes, now adjusted to the mid-morning sun, while her ears filled with echoing calls from the excited masses. One of their competitors crouched in front of their archer, his shield protecting the lower half of the man behind him, while a spear jutted out to discourage a charge. The remaining two gladiators stood on either side of the bowman, brandishing shields and short swords. None of them looked comfortable.

An arrow struck the shield of one of the standing men, causing him to flinch. Thaelios was clearly a more reliable shot. A rivulet of sweat ran down Saffron's temple, and she registered for the first time that the climate was noticeably warmer than in Ifelian. She had been too preoccupied when disembarking to notice.

She'd cut the distance between them to thirty paces. A second arrow from Thaelios struck the shoulder of their archer, just before he released another shot. In conjunction with their increased proximity, this spurred their opponents into a new strategy. The three with shields charged, abandoning their archer, who'd become essentially useless.

Considering the man with the spear the biggest threat, given his advantage in reach, Saffron singled him out. She raised her shield to deflect his high thrust and countered with a jab to his thigh. She scored only a glancing blow, but the bloodletting turned him more cautious.

The two with swords spread wide as they closed, seeking to flank them. Saffron spared a glance at Dyphina, who was clenching her spear tightly as she hid behind her shield. Saffron returned her attention to her opponent, who'd taken a more defensive tack, but heard the strike of steel against Dyphina's shield.

"Use your spear to keep him at a distance!" Saffron yelled in Illanese, hoping their enemies didn't understand. She struck out again, but her opponent blocked her blow. Their archer snapped the arrow embedded in his shoulder and circled the periphery of the melee, trying to keep his allies between him and Saffron's team.

The vibrating thud unique to an arrow striking wood pierced the din of the crowd. Another stolen glance confirmed that Thaelios was covering Dyphina with his bow. Turning back to her personal engagement, Saffron decided it was time to get creative. She doubted this man had ever encountered the *ghostwind.*

Twisting her feet and launching into the air, Saffron spun completely around while airborne, extending her spear and using its momentum to whip her unsuspecting opponent's weapon from his hand. While he was still mesmerized by her movement, Saffron landed and immediately lunged toward him with her shield, smashing it against his own and knocking him off his feet.

She was about to finish him off when Dyphina screamed for her. "Saffron!"

She turned to see the man who had been attacking Dyphina sprinting toward the unprotected Thaelios.

"Phaerim!" Saffron yelled in response, as he'd agreed to guard the Eladrin. Looking in his direction, she saw he was entangled with his enemy, grasping the wrist of his sword-arm in one hand while his other attempted to pry the man's shield away from his body. There was no way he would be able to disengage and make it to Thaelios in time, and every step mattered.

With no time to consider, Saffron took off toward Thaelios, granting a reprieve to her nearly beaten opponent on the ground. The Eladrin saw the approaching danger and was lining up one last shot with his bow. He let it fly, but his foe intercepted the missile with his shield. Saffron knew he would not have time to draw again.

The gladiator raised his sword as he bore down on Thaelios, screaming a battle-cry. Instead of lifting his bow to protect himself, the apprentice raised a hand in front of his face, his first two fingers extended. Saffron saw his lips moving and hoped he knew what he was doing.

Just before the man could slice into Thaelios's undefended torso, additional versions of the Shaper expanded to either side, making it appear as if there were five of him, rather than one. The crowd collectively gasped as the faltering attack of the gladiator cut through the thin-air of an illusion instead of the real thing. The image disappeared as it was pierced, leaving only four versions of Thaelios, but the trick had done its job.

Saffron caught up as the man seemed to be choosing where to strike next. He thrust his sword into the chest of another illusion, causing it to vanish, then turned as Saffron's shadow descended upon him. The movement opened him up to her strike, and she didn't hesitate. The crowd erupted into gleeful chaos as the bronze tip of her spear buried into the man's sternum. He looked up at Saffron and coughed, spitting blood onto his chin before collapsing backward onto the warm sand.

"Are you all right?" she huffed at the collection of spinning, mirrored images, unable to tell which was the true Thaelios. They nodded in unison, prompting her to spin and reassess the opposite side of their artificial battlefield.

Phaerim straddled the still form of his opponent, who lay on the ground with his arms spread above his head. Phaerim's hands were tight around the hilt of one of his daggers, which he removed from the dead gladiator's throat. The injured archer had backed against the far wall of the Arena, his left hand clutching the wound on his sagging right shoulder. He didn't appear to want any part of the battle and was not a threat.

Dyphina, on the other hand, had plenty of trouble. The man Saffron had earlier knocked to the ground had recovered his spear and managed to disarm the apprentice. She clutched her shield with both hands, one holding the handle and the other grasping the arm strap, desperately blocking exploratory jabs from her attacker.

Each new thrust elicited a shriek from Dyphina, which seemed to be a source of perverse pleasure to the man with the spear. With a wide grin plastered across his face, he backed her ever closer to the wall. Soon, she would have no more room to give. Saffron sprinted toward them.

Then, a curious thing happened. Dyphina and the man locked eyes, and she lowered her shield. Instead of pressing his advantage, however, the gladiator lowered his arms as well, continuing to stare straight at Dyphina's face. Saffron was almost there.

She skidded to a halt, however, as she drew near. Dyphina's countenance, beautiful on its own, was glowing with a fey aura that further enhanced her allure. This was certainly new.

Suddenly, the man cried out, "Ahhh!" He dropped his spear to cover his eyes. Saffron noticed the crowd had gone quiet. They were all leaning forward, trying to get a clearer glimpse of what had caused this strange turn of events.

"What did you do?" asked Phaerim, who had retrieved both his daggers and joined them.

When the man moved his hand away from his eyes, they were covered with a white film.

"I can't see!" he said, reaching out as if to make sure something of the world remained.

Dyphina's mouth dropped open and she blinked rapidly, clearing her own vision. Her skin no longer emitted the same radiance from a moment before. "I don't know," she finally answered. "I was frightened and he was looking right at me, and I … I don't know," she repeated.

"Well, what do we do now?" Phaerim asked, directing his query at Saffron.

"How should I know? It's not like I'm an expert at blood-sport etiquette." The crowd was growing restless at the lack of violence, and she could hear many of them calling for the Wolfspider's team to finish it. She held out the tip of her spear and tapped the shield of the blind man to get his attention. "You there," she spoke in Begnari, "do you surrender?"

"Yes, I surrender," he said, dropping his shield. "Please, give me back my sight!"

"Sorry, but I don't know how," she said. Saffron turned in a circle, shouting at the crowd, "They surrender! They surrender!" She was answered by a chorus of boos. At last, as Thaelios joined the group, both sets of gates from which the gladiators had entered opened again, and four guards jogged forth from each to surround them. They were escorted back to the Wolfspider's pens, where they returned their weapons before a healer inspected their wounds.

"You've got blood on your chin," Saffron said to Phaerim, brushing her own to indicate where the stray liquid had landed. Trivial matters were all she could manage, still wrapping her mind around what she'd just been through. Killing another slave, bearing witness to the birth of new power in Dyphina, and calculating the possible outcomes of Thaelios's magical display kept her thoughts turning as the Begnari nurse looked her over.

None of them suffered more than a few bruises, though the continued vibration of the ceiling as the next fight began served as evidence that what they had just experienced was real. After receiving passing marks from the healer, they were shuffled back to their main cage, where Zygrim's smiling face greeted them.

"You won!" he said, much too loudly for Saffron's liking, and Charilo delivered a congratulatory nod as they entered. "Not only that, you all lived!" He clasped Saffron's wrist in greeting, as she was the first to enter, then gave a smothering embrace to Thaelios as he stepped into the pen. "And you!" Zygrim pulled back and gripped Thaelios firmly by the shoulders, searching his enormous blue eyes for a reaction, "You are going to be the talk of the city. Not only a chance for them to see a true-to-life Eladrin, but that trick you pulled! It was wonderful. I have no doubts you'll soon have a line of noblemen waiting to sponsor you."

Saffron took a seat on one of the benches, watching and listening with curiosity. She had forgotten about that aspect of this grotesque theater. Her focus for their first fight was getting everyone out alive, but it seemed like the eventual solution to their captivity may stem from outside political connections. "Zygrim, can you tell me more about how that works?"

"Sure," the hulking Zygrim replied, taking up a spot in the center of the chamber. "As winning gladiators, tradition dictates you will receive one of these passes." He produced a palm-sized, clay disk from the pocket of his significantly shredded breeches. It had the initials "DoS" inscribed over the image of a spider's face. "Harzhim will likely bring yours later, after the day's fights have concluded. These get you into one of the most popular haunts of the city, the Wolfspider's own 'Den of Sin.' It will be especially crowded tonight."

"How did you get yours, if you didn't fight today?" Saffron asked.

Zygrim smiled. "I had my sponsor deliver one as a favor. I didn't want to miss the chance to celebrate with my new Housemates." He shot a look in Thaelios's direction. "Many of the best connected citizens will also be there, looking for the chance to rub elbows with victorious gladiators. It's the perfect opportunity to strike up a relationship with someone on the outside. It's mostly about status for them. They gain prestige among their peers for establishing formal connections with successful fighters – but they can do *you* favors."

Phaerim perked up, moving closer to Zygrim after leaning lazily on the wall of the cage for most of the conversation. "What sort of favors?"

Zygrim shrugged. "New clothes, better food, specialized weapons for the Arena. Contraband, under some circumstances. Medicine, if you're sick or wounded. Possibly even monitored trips outside the confines of these pens. All sorts of amenities, really. It's part of the culture."

Though Saffron shared a language and ethnicity with many in Zeblon, the culture seemed a drastic departure from her home in Begnasharan. What she wanted was someone who could buy their freedom or at least get them out of their collars. There didn't seem to be a better route toward escape for the immediate future, so she resolved to keep an eye out for the best possible connection. Maintaining patience, however, would be hard.

A weary-looking Harzhim visited them a few hours later and fulfilled expectations by presenting the victors with passes to the Den of Sin for the evening. "You will be taken to the baths to prepare. Women first." He unlocked the cage and motioned for Saffron and Dyphina to step through the gate.

Saffron explained to her friend where they were going, an overdue pleasant surprise. Travelling down several corridors of the labyrinthine bowels of the Arena eventually led them to a spacious, square room.

Tiled from floor to ceiling, the room's perimeter was lined with polished, wooden benches. A large, square, copper basin, wide enough to swim across, occupied its center. A trough underneath the basin showed the glimmer of hot coals. Glorious steam rose from the surface of the water, filling the air with a rare humidity.

"I'll give you one half-hour, then bring the men," Harzhim said, handing them linens and a small, bronze container.

"We'll take it," Saffron responded, eager to scrub the accumulated filth of their journey and training from her body. As soon as he left, Saffron draped her towel over the edge of the tub. Dyphina was already stripping off her sweat-crusted clothes.

"I don't suppose we'll get a chance to wash these any time soon ..." she said disappointedly.

Saffron sighed and started peeling off her armor, which took considerably more time. She could hear Dyphina moaning in contentment as she stepped into the heated basin, and worked a little faster to remove her leather shell. Once naked, she waded into the warm water also, slowly descending as her skin got used to the temperature. She couldn't help but think back to her time at Skywatch Haven, sharing the natural hot springs with Be'naj.

The water was deep enough that if she sat in the center, her head would be completely submerged. Saffron held her breath and plunged under the surface, imagining she was entering an entirely different world where all the hardships of her recent past couldn't touch her. When she arose, the air touching her wet shoulders seemed much colder than before.

"Here," Dyphina said, handing her a small, coarse-haired brush she'd selected from a rack on one side of the tub. "Take turns scrubbing backs?"

"Sure," Saffron responded. She sat behind Dyphina, close to the sloped edge of the tub, and pulled her closer. Working in tight circles across Dyphina's back, she saw her friend's shoulders relax as she coaxed out another moan.

"That feels so nice," Dyphina exclaimed. "I'm still so tense from our battle earlier. Thank you for getting us through that," she said, glancing behind her. "I kept seeing the face of that Thrall I smashed with the rock and could barely hold my spear straight. I think I'm getting too used to you saving my life." She released her green hair from its pony tail and pulled it in front of her shoulder.

Saffron understood how the scars of trauma could linger. "I am only doing my rightful part," she replied after swallowing the lump in her throat. "You have such unusually colored hair," Saffron pivoted, choosing not to dwell on thoughts of strife. "Do you get it from your mother?"

"I suppose so," Dyphina answered, leaning forward to grab some oil from the lip of the basin. "Her hair changes color with the seasons. Dad's hair is mostly brown, with a little bit of copper and a strand or two of grey, though he wouldn't admit it," she giggled as she began washing her own. She had never brought up the subject of her parentage on her own.

Saffron paused her scrubbing. "So, your mother's not human after all?" she asked, more bluntly than she'd intended.

Dyphina shook her head slightly, and her voice grew subdued. "She's fey. I suppose that's the most likely explanation for what happened out there today – though it's never happened before, I swear."

"Oh, I didn't mean anything by it!" Saffron inwardly cursed herself and began brushing again. "I just … met someone else recently who has mixed parentage, and our current situation reminded me of her." That seemed awkward – now had she said too much?

"It's alright," Dyphina reassured. "Here, would you like to switch?" She turned and took the brush from Saffron, then stood up so they could trade places.

Saffron couldn't help looking over her friend's physique as they shifted positions. She swallowed hard, then muttered, "I envy your beauty. You must have a thousand suitors back home."

"Ugh," Dyphina voiced her frustration as she settled in behind Saffron. "And yet how long has it been since anyone's touched me? I've really missed physical intimacy since arriving at Blackfeather Perch. How about you? Have you had any ... suitors recently?"

"Ha," Saffron laughed nervously and shook her head, surprised by the question. "No. Not since ..." her mind wandered back to the regretfully drunken night with Rogan at the palace in Selamus, "... a while."

Dyphina gave a commiserating sigh as she went to work scrubbing Saffron's back and shoulders. "You're very beautiful too, you know." She left a pregnant pause hanging for a moment. "Have you ever considered, well, being with a woman?"

Saffron's chest spasmed. "What? No. Well, what do you mean?" Why were her mind and mouth suddenly having trouble working together? She had only been with men, and only a couple times at that, but didn't think of women in that way. Though, she certainly felt *something* with Be'naj ... "Have you?" She looked over her shoulder and spied a betraying smile as Dyphina lowered her face.

"Once or twice, just for fun," Dyphina admitted. "The touch of a woman is often gentler than a man's and can feel nicer, in my experience. Would you like me to show you?"

Saffron was frozen by the question. It didn't seem like something she should indulge in – Begnari culture strictly forbade men and women lying with their own ilk. And yet, she had never heard a satisfactory explanation as to why it was wrong and couldn't personally think of one. She had not been touched in so long, either, and it was only the two of them in the bath. No one else would have to know as long as they didn't take too long, and Dyphina was the one offering ... Saffron finally nodded, almost imperceptibly, her face still not fully turned toward Dyphina.

"Here, why don't I bathe you and you can tell me if you like it?" Dyphina suggested, trading in the coarse brush for a hard soap of olive oil and flower petals. She didn't require a response, immediately drawing the wet soap down the curve of Saffron's neck to her shoulder, circling forward across the collarbone, working toward a bubbling lather.

Saffron closed her eyes and exhaled through her nose, trying to relax and focus on Dyphina's soothing touch as the soap cascaded around her chest. The bar slid between her breasts, then underneath them, Dyphina's empty hand joining in to spread the lather. Her fingers titillated as they roamed Saffron's belly, sides, then up and underneath her arms. Saffron melted beneath the sensations, and images of Be'naj's naked body under her own hands started flashing across her consciousness.

She suffered an overwhelming urge to feel soft lips upon hers, and turned so that her torso was facing Dyphina, though her eyes remained closed. She puckered her lips slightly in invitation, though was unsure Dyphina would read it as such. Saffron didn't have to wait long before finding out. Dyphina's arms hooked underneath her own and curled around her back, drawing her closer until Saffron felt the soft crush of the half-fey's breasts against hers, and slick, plump lips covering her mouth in a kiss.

The kiss felt gentler than a man's, as Dyphina had hinted, and Saffron's lips parted just enough to let her tongue barely sneak past them to find Dyphina's doing the same. Whether it was the steam or her passion boiling up, Saffron became light-headed and opened her lips wider to grant full exploration of her mouth to Dyphina's tongue. She couldn't deny the woman knew how to kiss.

"Ahem!" A harsh, fabricated cough drew Saffron's attention from Dyphina's mouth, causing her to turn and separate. The slick soap fell from Dyphina's grasp as they looked across the room to find Harzhim standing at the entrance with clothes draped over his arm. "It's time to dry off, ladies. The men will be arriving soon. I brought clean outfits for you to wear tonight since you will be representing the House of the Wolfspider. We must have you looking sharp, no? Please, try to hurry."

He set the new clothes on the bench near their old ones and turned to leave the bath. Saffron and Dyphina shared a look and immediately began laughing.

Chapter 15

The Den of Sin

The outfits Harzhim brought for them were essentially long, black tunics that reached the middle of their thighs. Trimmed in gold, the cloth draped to a low neckline and golden cords cinched them at the waist. They were also provided with dark sandals that tied up to the middle of their calves, and Saffron was grateful not to have to change back into dirty clothes after their hot bath.

The men turned out to be much quicker at bathing, for she and Dyphina were still combing the tangles out of their damp hair when they heard Zygrim's and Phaerim's boisterous conversation carrying down the corridor. As they turned the corner, Saffron saw they were dressed in new outfits of black and gold as well, though their tunics reached a little further, to the top of their knees.

"Hello!" Phaerim said when he saw them, and Saffron noted how much more exuberant everyone seemed to be. A planned night of carousing was almost enough to remove the awareness that they were still expected to fight for their lives on a weekly basis. Everyone seemed keen to forget that several gladiators from their opposing House would never have the same opportunity.

Zygrim embraced Saffron and Dyphina simultaneously with his wide arms. Beside Thaelios, who singularly appeared to be his normal, subdued self, Saffron noticed a pair of men she had not yet met.

Phaerim read her look and promptly delivered introductions. "Wemic and Nueril, these are my other partners from this morning, Ladies Saffron and Dyphina. They only speak a little Illanese," he added as an aside in Saffron's direction.

"Well, the night is off to an even better start," Wemic said in Begnari, flashing a smile as he reached forward to kiss each woman's hand. "And you're both gladiators?" he posed.

He was handsome, Saffron decided – tall and leanly muscular. A dusting of black facial hair followed the line of Wemic's jaw, and his skin was just a shade darker than hers. Those flashing eyes, however, were what really stood out. "We're a little more than that," she said, leaving him to interpret what she might mean, "but yes, we fought today."

"Wemic fought in his first solo challenge today and also won," offered Zygrim. "It's an important step toward really getting noticed. He should be proud."

Once again Harzhim interrupted, something he seemed adept at. "Excuse me, is everyone gathered? Do you have your passes? It is time for you to make an appearance. Follow me to the Den of Sin."

They all filed out after the Consul, and Saffron paid attention to their route. They eventually wound along a curving hallway, lined with torches on one side, that abruptly stopped at an unmarked door. Harzhim unlocked it with one of the keys around his neck, then pushed it open and grabbed the last lit torch from its sconce.

Beyond the door waited darkness – pitch black, except for Harzhim's flame. They passed a short landing, then descended a series of wide steps and down another long corridor before coming to a thick, wooden door framed in bronze. The Consul waited beside it until all seven of his charges caught up and gathered close.

"For those who have never been, the Den of Sin lies beyond. Once we enter, newcomers can follow me to the accounting table. While you are encouraged to enjoy yourselves, there are certain expectations of you as well.

"First, do not incite or react with violence. While you may not notice them, there is plenty of security, and they will respond harshly to unacceptable behavior. There will be ramifications within the House as well, and of course, there are always your collars as a last resort. Second, everything you see within the confines of the Den of Sin is to be kept in strict confidence. This establishment does not believe in the limits of typical morality, and members expect for their particular proclivities to remain private.

"Beyond that," Harzhim gave a leering smile at Saffron, "you can do almost anything you like. Gather on the other side of this door in four hours, and you will be escorted back to your pens."

Saffron faced her companions. "You three are going to seriously have to consider learning Begnari." She quickly explained the rules, and when she finished, Harzhim opened the door.

The noise and commotion hit her all at once: a dominating combination of laughter, music, a hundred conversations, and movement. The space itself was cavernous, dimly lit by chandeliers hanging high overhead, and the smells of perfumes, spirits, and perspiration mixed into an exotic blend of hope and desperation.

As she followed Harzhim, she stole glances around the room to get a sense of the different diversions available. A large bar took up almost one entire wall of the hexagonal establishment. Bottles, barrels, and casks were stacked in organized sections, with racks of tankards, mugs, goblets, and cups available within arms' reach of the bartenders.

The opposite wall recessed to allow for a large stage that jutted out slightly over the main floor. Currently, a trio of belly dancers gyrated across it as a small band of musicians played behind them. Several intoxicated members of the crowd leaned over the edge of the stage, waving their arms in vain attempts to grasp the dancers, though Saffron spied a guard in the ceremonial armor of the Arena keeping a close eye on them, within striking distance.

After taking them down several levels of steps, Harzhim spoke to a man behind an enclosed counter, whose workspace opened up further behind the abutting wall. He returned with a handful of small, clay disks, which he portioned out to Saffron, Phaerim, Dyphina, and Thaelios. They were marked with a '5' on either side, and he gave them five disks each.

"Compliments of the Wolfspider," Harzhim said, though only Saffron could understand. "Don't lose it all at once!" After dispensing that final advice, he left with obvious intent toward the bar, weaving through the crowd and leaving the Wolfspider's new gladiators to fend for themselves.

"Any idea how far each of these tokens will go?" Phaerim asked, lifting one near his face and closing one eye to inspect it.

Zygrim squeezed his way to the counter and asked the teller in Begnari to retrieve his deposit. While the man was in the back, checking the vaults, Zygrim proposed a plan of action. "There is a lot of ground to cover here, especially on your first night. Given the language barrier, why don't we split up? I'll take the men and translate for them until they get their feet wet. Saffron can speak for the ladies, and we'll all meet up again in a couple of hours. How does that sound?"

Saffron shrugged. "It works for me," she said, hoping Dyphina would agree. She wanted to talk more intimately about what had happened in the bath and what it meant between them, and having to constantly speak for three other people in a crowd like this was going to get old quickly. Over Phaerim's shoulder, she saw the backs of Wemic and Nueril as they wandered off toward the gaming tables.

"Sure," Dyphina nodded. Phaerim looked pleadingly at her as if he wanted to be invited along, but eventually raised his hands.

"Why not? Let's go have some fun," he said, slapping a palm each onto Zygrim's and Thaelios's shoulders.

Left to themselves, Saffron and Dyphina scooted off, arm-in-arm, heading in Harzhim's wake toward the bar. "I wonder if these chips are enough to buy us a drink," Saffron mentioned. "I could really use a goblet of wine after today."

Dyphina laughed, shaking her head before nodding. "I concur."

Making their way to the ordering line, they generated stares from men and women alike. Saffron wondered whether that was simply because they were female gladiators wearing the garb of the Wolfspider, a rare-enough sight she was sure, or because Dyphina's green hair and exotic beauty drew their curiosity.

Whatever the cause, they seemed to have attained a measure of notoriety. The men waiting ahead of them in line parted and allowed them to order first. After Saffron called for two goblets, she fumbled with her tokens, inquiring how much the drinks would cost them. The server shook his head and told them a gentleman further down the bar had already taken care of the charges.

Saffron and Dyphina shared a look, silently agreeing not to question this unexpected generosity, then raised their cups in the direction of the slender man who was raising his at them. "Oooh, that's so good," Saffron purred after taking her first sip, even though the vintage was quite ordinary by her normal standards. "Day-old bread and water for every meal really makes you appreciate variety, no?"

Dyphina was still taking a long swig, but nodded over the top of her goblet. "Shall we try to grab an empty table?" she asked once she'd swallowed. Saffron agreed, and they put some distance between them and the dense swath still in pursuit of alcohol. Saffron claimed a small, round table with two chairs just as another couple departed, and it felt great to rest her weary legs.

"So," she began, unsure how to broach the subject currently occupying her mind. "Thank you for that demonstration in the tub earlier ..."

Dyphina licked her lips and set down her goblet. "You're welcome, of course. How did it feel?"

Dyphina was sitting tall, chest slightly out, her wide, doe eyes roaming freely over Saffron's face and body. She seemed different, full of the confidence Saffron usually possessed during most interactions. "It felt nice. I just wanted to make sure you knew that, given how abruptly things ended." Saffron mumbled the last part, lowering her eyes and taking a deliberate sip of her wine.

"It felt nice to me, too." Dyphina smiled and reached across the table, placing her hand over Saffron's. "It's okay, we can talk about it – it doesn't have to be strange. Are you trying to say you'd like to explore further?"

Saffron looked at Dyphina's hand on hers and felt it squeeze. She raised her gaze to meet her companion's, then lifted one eyebrow and squinted with the opposite eye. "I don't know. Maybe? I don't want to rule it out, but it feels like a lot right now with everything else going on. It seems like it might complicate things while I'm trying to concentrate on a strategy to get us out of this mess." She hoped that didn't sound like a rejection.

Dyphina released her hand, though. "Sure, I understand that. We've got more important things to worry about. Although ..." she drifted off, her eyes elevating to a spot behind and above Saffron's head, "... it doesn't look as if Nueril does."

Saffron turned in her chair to see what Dyphina was talking about. The wall behind her, still a fair distance off, was pocked by a dozen doors, rising over several levels. A zig-zagging, wooden scaffold provided access to the portals, each marked by a number on their frames. A woman in a cropped, white top and airy, silk pants led Nueril by the hand along the landing to a door on the second level, then took him inside.

"Is he ...?" Saffron's mouth fell agape. She quickly recovered and shrugged as Dyphina giggled. "I hope she's at least being compensated well."

"How much do you think they charge for it?" Dyphina asked.

"Hopefully more than what Harzhim gave us," Saffron replied. Her eyes already trailed over the crowd at the base of the scaffolding, though, seeing if anyone else she recognized was in the midst of bargaining for some time alone. She didn't see Zygrim or the others, but her eyes were inexorably drawn toward a man in a strikingly bright set of robes.

His hair was greying but he owned a thick, brown mustache, which joined with other facial hair leading up to his sideburns, though his chin was left bare. He spoke animatedly with another patron, his waving arms creating a hypnotic pattern of color as his robes shook. They were a garish blend of yellow, orange, green and purple, but the cloth did not seem delineated according to any sensible structure.

Saffron stood to get a better vantage, curious as to what would lead this man to dress in such a gaudy way. Her movement prompted a pair of swarthy men to spring forth and offer their introductions to her and Dyphina.

"Good evening, ladies," one of them said. "Are the two of you searching for *companionship*?"

The way he emphasized the last word rushed Saffron to the conclusion that the answer was "no." She tried not to frown and responded, "I'm sorry, but my friend does not understand Begnari, and we're already spoken for."

The second man smiled and shrugged. "That is not a problem. I actually wasn't looking for a whole lot of conversation." His eyebrows moved up and down quickly to accentuate, in case she had not understood.

"If you are already spoken for," the first man added, "is there some sort of list we should be on to have our turn?"

Saffron's hands clenched into fists and she blew hard out of tightened lips to release some of the pressure rising to her face. Dyphina was looking at her with wide eyes, no doubt awaiting a translation that would never come.

"The only list you are going to find yourself on is the one I intend to start keeping so I can later apologize to the parents of those I have eviscerated," Saffron hissed, staring a challenge directly into the man's eyes.

Though his friend's face fell as he backed away from Dyphina's chair, the man she'd spoken to searched Saffron's eyes, looking for weakness, perhaps. "You know, I don't like it to be too easy," he said calmly, just loud enough so she could hear him.

"You might not like it at all, my friend," came Wemic's voice as he walked up beside Saffron. "You know we're gladiators, right?"

She turned to find him looking relaxed, a toothpick dangling from between his lips, though his gaze stayed fixed on her conversational partner.

"House of the Wolfspider," Wemic added when the man had nothing to say.

He looked back at Saffron as if to show he wasn't intimidated, when he clearly was. "You know, you're not even that attractive," he said, before stepping backward and gathering his friend to slink off into the crowd.

"Well, sorry if I interrupted your fun," Wemic stated once the men were gone.

"It's fine – my threshold for challenges is substantially higher these days," Saffron replied, then shifted to Illanese to speak to Dyphina. "I could use some more wine, what do you say?"

"Sounds good to me," Dyphina answered, getting up from her chair.

"How about you?" Saffron switched back to Begnari to ask Wemic. "Would you care to join us for a drink?"

"I'd be honored," Wemic replied, placing a hand on his chest and flashing a playful smile.

After refreshing their drinks at the bar, the three of them wandered the Den of Sin for a while, talking and taking in the sights. Saffron found that Wemic possessed a wonderful sense of humor, and he did a fair job spreading his attention between her and Dyphina, though much of his interaction with the half-fey involved teaching her short phrases in Begnari.

After watching a dance performance and listening to some music, they headed toward the gaming section, where Saffron once again spotted the man in colorful robes, whispering in a corner to a man shrouded by a black cloak.

"Wemic, do you know who that is?" she asked, nodding in the direction of the rainbow-clad stranger.

He stopped walking and peered toward the indicated corner. He lowered his voice to a conspiratorial tone, "That would be Ayez, the Many Colored – he's one of the Twelve."

"And who, exactly, are the Twelve?"

Dyphina leaned in and whispered, "What are you two talking about?"

"The Circle of Twelve? You've never heard of them?" Wemic seemed incredulous, but Saffron reminded him she hadn't been in the country that long.

"They are a Cabal of Shapers, Mystics, and devotees of the Temple of Pnemonesis," he explained. "They own estates atop the highest plateau of Zeblon, overlooking the sea, and are the subject of many rumors. Some think they are trying to wrest control of the region from the Caliph; others say their primary rival is the Wolfspider, himself."

Saffron was intrigued. "Do they get involved with the Arena very much?"

Wemic looked back at Ayez, then around the room, before responding. "You can be certain ours are not the only eyes on Ayez this evening. Members of the Twelve are usually a reclusive bunch, and hardly ever show themselves without a purpose. They don't have a fighting stake in any of the Arena Houses," he continued, "but Ayez attends the fights regularly, and I've seen him here before, though I have no idea why he comes."

"Sounds like just the sort of sponsor we need," Saffron said, more to herself than her companions.

Apparently tired of her exclusion from the conversation, Dyphina grabbed hold of Saffron's hand and started pulling her toward the gaming tables. "Come on," she said, "I see Phaerim and Thaelios."

Thaelios was seated at a card table with a large stack of tokens in front of him, wagering on a game involving cards and dice. Phaerim cheered from behind, yelling and shaking Thaelios's shoulders as he won another hand.

"Have you been playing cards this entire time?" Dyphina asked Phaerim as they reached him.

He turned and kissed Dyphina on the cheek in his excitement. "Not the whole time," he yelled above the boisterous onlookers, "but Thaelios is on quite a run. He's got a much better sense of this game, so I gave him the rest of my tokens to wager with. We've won a small fortune already!"

"What do you need all that money for?" Saffron asked. "It's not like there are a variety of options to spend it on. Unless," she reconsidered, "you're intending to purchase some … intimate companionship."

"What?" Phaerim squinted. "No!" He put an arm around Saffron and drew her close so he could whisper without being overheard. "I met this man who deals in less than savory materials. I'm going to buy some red centipede poison from him – you know, for the Arena. It's potent stuff, from what I'm told, but it's not cheap."

Phaerim released her, turning his attention back to the game, which had moved on to the next hand. Thaelios considered his cards and made his wager. Saffron saw four players currently involved, but had no idea how the game was played. She watched until the end of the hand, won by a squat man in a broad hat, then told Phaerim she would see him later, back in their pen.

Everyone else seemed keen to stay a little longer, but Saffron was weary from the long day and wanted somewhere quiet to think. She left the rest of her tokens with Dyphina, then found a guard near the door who agreed to escort her back. The tunnels seemed extra silent on the return trip, after the cacophony of the Den of Sin, but that was fine by her.

The guard informed her she could not wear the excursion outfit she was leant for the evening back into the cage, and it would have to be left with him. When she explained she had no other clothes to change into, he took pity and rummaged through the wardrobe room, emerging with a simple but clean wool tunic for her to wear. The cage was dark when they reached it, and those left behind were already sleeping. Saffron lay down on her mattress in the warm blackness, and before she managed to focus, her mind flooded with unbidden thoughts.

First came Be'naj's face, streaked with tears at her latest abandonment, for which Saffron was responsible. Next came her spear, stabbing through the man's heart in the Arena earlier that day. She saw him choking on his own blood, over and over, before collapsing to the ground. She tried to banish the images, but the only thing that would do it was the thought of Dyphina touching her in the bath, kissing her as she became more aroused.

Saffron let out a grunt and sat up on her mattress, though she was still in the dark. "The future, Saffron," she said to herself. "Think of the future." Her mind shifted to Ayez, the Many Colored and the so-called Circle of Twelve. If there were Shapers among them, possibly one held the knowledge or power to counter the magic on her collar, or at the very least, identify whether they were truly enchanted in the first place.

She had to devise a way to convince one of the Twelve to sponsor her … a plan started forming, and she was finally able to fall asleep while turning it over again in her mind. Her slumber was deep, for she didn't even stir when the rest of the gladiators returned. She awoke with the call for their morning meal and found Dyphina and Phaerim asleep on their mattresses, flanking hers. Thaelios was already up and about, of course, and Saffron broke bread with him while the others slept off their late night.

"I was thinking about sponsorship," Saffron mentioned as they unenthusiastically dabbed at their porridge.

"Aye, I would like someone who could bring me something to read," Thaelios offered. "And after last night, especially, I would appreciate immensely if you could find the time to instruct me in the Begnari language."

Saffron nodded. "Of course. How did the gambling go?"

"I was able to bank a sizeable amount, even after lending Phaerim a fair sum for a transaction he was keen on. Now, what I'm going to do with it, I haven't a notion at the moment. It seemed prudent, though, to acquire currency, especially when the other participants seemed so eager to throw it in my direction. That was only my first night playing Knots & Locks, but you'd think the locals would be better at it."

Cradling a bowl of his breakfast in one huge paw and wearing nothing more than a glorified loincloth, Zygrim approached while Thaelios expounded on his grip of gaming strategy. He nodded to Saffron and asked, "May I join you?" before sitting on the bench beside her, across from Thaelios.

"Certainly," she replied, scooting over to make more room. "That's quite the statement you're making there," she said with a hint of laughter in her voice, bobbing her head toward his barely covered groin.

He looked down and shrugged. "Laundry day," he blurted before shoveling a large scoop of porridge into his mouth. "My sponsor made me choose between a pass to the Den of Sin last night or a new tunic, and I felt like celebrating with you." Zygrim looked across at Thaelios and smiled. "It was a fun night, no?"

"Wait a moment," Saffron interjected after swallowing a mouthful of her own breakfast. "We have a laundry day?"

Zygrim laughed. "Yes. You can leave whatever you want cleaned in a pile near the meal gate, and they will return it in the evening."

"That's good to know." Thaelios sniffed at his own shirt and breeches. "It's been so long that I don't really notice anymore, but I'm sure these things are filthy."

"What do you know about the Circle of Twelve, Zygrim?" Saffron thought Thaelios might be interested to hear about them as well, and assumed Zygrim could pass along more information than the little she'd heard.

Zygrim moved his tongue around the inside of his mouth for a moment, gathering stray bits of food before swallowing. "The Circle is a dozen of the most influential people in Zeblon, outside of the Patriarchs of the four Houses, of course."

"Did you see Ayez, the Many-Colored, in the Den of Sin last night? Wemic said he's seen him there before, and he comes to all the fights."

"I did. I've never talked to him in person, but he's supposed to be quite eccentric." Zygrim tilted his head to either side, stretching his neck. "His tastes tend to run toward the …

unusual. You left early last night, were you not enjoying yourself?"

"I had my fun," Saffron answered. She shifted her eyes sideward to see how Thaelios was reacting. "How about you two?"

"Oh, I had a great time," Zygrim answered first.

Thaelios nodded and shrugged at the same time. "It was interesting. I felt like half the room was always staring at me."

"I know what that's like," Saffron commiserated. "These two ogres tried to convince Dyphina and me to get private rooms with them. They did a poor job of it," she continued before either of the men could inquire about the outcome. She decided to steer the conversation back toward her intended subject. "So, does anyone know the Circle of Twelve's agenda? Do they ever sponsor gladiators, Zygrim?"

He lowered his bowl and studied Saffron, weighing his words. "I don't think anybody knows exactly what they're up to, and they haven't sponsored anyone since I've been here, but they could just be waiting for the right fighter. Hard to say. Are you searching for something specific?"

Saffron sighed and considered the sleeping Dyphina. "I'm looking for a way out, honestly. Don't you think a collection of powerful Shapers would have a better chance at getting these damned collars off safely than some wealthy merchant? I just want to know if they can be trusted."

"Well, when you put it like that, I suppose it makes sense," Zygrim admitted. "Not sure any mortal Shaper can match Hadrian No More, though. Still, there are stories of exceedingly popular gladiators with the right connections having the opportunity to buy freedom. I'd like to see that day as well, but for now, I'm just focusing on what I can control – staying alive in the Arena and making my life here more comfortable for as long as I can keep it."

"You are clearly gifted, my friend: strong, fierce, and nimble," Thaelios contributed. "The urgency I think Lady Saffron feels, but is too polite to mention, is because she, and I with her, don't know how likely it is for us to continue surviving the Arena. We were not all born to fight with our bodies." The Eladrin finished his statement with a sad half-smile, as if accepting the likelihood of his approaching end.

"Come now," Zygrim said dismissively. "I saw you out there." He reached across and tapped Thaelios's arm. "You were wonderful, and full of surprises. Don't count yourself out."

Saffron shook her head slightly. "Thaelios is right. We cannot afford to wait. Do you think they would let me volunteer ahead of time to fight this week?"

Zygrim's mouth fell open. "I suppose so," he said, after a pause. "Are you sure you want to do that?"

"I've got to make an impression on the Twelve, quickly. And maybe, if I offer myself up, it might buy the others a week off?" As she spoke, Saffron made up her mind to do it.

Upon waking, Dyphina asked Saffron where she got her new tunic, and Saffron agreed to lend Dyphina her travelling clothes when they came back from being washed. She kept an eye out for Harzhim all day, and though he didn't show, she let the men who brought their evening meals know that she wanted to speak with him.

When he stopped by their pen the following day, Saffron volunteered to fight the coming week, and went further by asking for something more challenging. Harzhim regarded her as if she'd lost her mind and argued that he didn't want to lose a promising fighter so early on, but eventually capitulated. He even agreed to temporarily spare her friends.

That week, on her training days, she not only practiced with spear and shield, but hummed and sang soft tunes when she had privacy, working on building a slow fire within, harnessing the heat of her arcane flame. She wanted to be ready to put on a show that no one in the audience would be able to forget.

At last, fighting day arrived. Saffron changed into her armor, and everyone in her pen wished her luck as she made the lonesome trip to the arming room. Once more, the rumble of the crowd overhead got her blood pumping quickly. Her hair was tied tight in its signature, single braid, and she took a moment to reflect on her goals: finding freedom, re-uniting with Be'naj, and bringing a just end to the slavery under Nightwing Castle. As the large doors leading into the Arena swung open and the sunshine poured through, she realized she may have to add the liberation of Zeblon's gladiators to her list.

She'd asked for a challenge, and Harzhim assured her she'd get one. During her first fight, she'd been so focused on her opponents and defending her friends that she hadn't taken much time to observe her surroundings. Stepping into the late morning sunlight, she breathed in the fresh air and looked up to notice how blue the sky was. White, feathery clouds were sparsely painted across the southern sky, moving calmly on high, unfelt winds.

The cheering multitudes were another matter. She turned in place, looking out over the thousands of indistinguishable faces, not a one of which seemed silent or still. They didn't know her, yet were already yelling for her to succeed or fail with a fervor she could scarcely believe. Saffron couldn't imagine what their daily lives must be like to allow such a frenzy to build by the end of their week.

She wanted to play to the crowd, however, and lifted her spear and shield in a gesture she hoped projected confidence. Perhaps some of the Twelve were in attendance. She mentally measured the height of the surrounding walls to determine whether her plan would pose any danger to the crowd. She figured they would be safe as long as she remained near the center.

Once the opposing gate started swinging open, she readied herself. Saffron lowered her shield into a defensive posture and sang, fairly certain the cheers of the mob would drown out her growing melody. She kept her eyes on the gate, singing and watching as her foes stumbled into the bright light.

There were six of them, and while the number surprised her, she was more shocked by the fact her opponents weren't human. Only a touch over waist-high, but thickly muscled, the creatures had mottled, brown skin and large eyes, which they shaded with both hands. They took in their surroundings with obvious confusion, but scuttled forward when the guards began prodding them with spears.

Saffron's only thought was that they must be rauggin, creatures she'd only heard about in tales. They were unarmed, but she had no illusions about their lack of compunction toward using their nails and teeth to savage her. She kept singing, feeling the heat rising through her entire body, until it became uncomfortable to hold it in.

The crowd quieted somewhat as the rauggin approached, perplexed by her apparent lack of aggression, for Saffron merely walked calmly to the Arena's center. As she hoped, the creatures decided to use their numbers to their advantage and quickly encircled her.

At last, the viewers fell almost completely silent, the mood changing from vicarious participation in violence to one of true concern. Saffron's voice lifted above them at last, no doubt drawing further confusion about how a woman could be singing at such a time, facing her oncoming demise.

As if sharing a collective, hunting mind, the rauggin charged at once, snarling and squinting in the bright sunlight, extending their hands to tear into her. Their action sparked Saffron's own, however. She hit and held a high note, coinciding with a quick rise and fall of the butt of her spear against the sand.

With its strike, a red-orange wave of flame erupted, exploding outward in a ring around her, knocking the rauggin off their feet and immolating them in a nova of arcane fire. Two more ripples followed, extending the distance of ten paces before dissipating into the heated air in rings of smoke.

Saffron stood silently, as did the crowd. The unprotected flesh of the rauggin was blackened, and they showed no signs of life. Saffron lowered her shield and cast her eyes in an arc around the populace, watching for any reaction at all. Slowly, pockets of unsure applause started echoing throughout the Arena, growing until vocal cheers caught on as well.

She raised her spear once more in victory as the gate to her entrance opened and the customary guards emerged to escort her back to the arming room. The cheers swelled even louder as she exited. Zygrim wasn't waiting to greet her this time when she returned to the pen, for he had a fight of his own and was already in preparation. The others met her with excitement, however, and asked how the fight had gone.

"We shall see," she replied. "I used some unmistakable Shaping. Perhaps I'll find out tonight if it was enough to whet the appetite of the Twelve."

Thaelios nodded while Phaerim folded his arms in a mock pout. "Too bad we won't get to go to the Den of Sin with you tonight."

An hour passed, and Saffron sat on a mattress with Phaerim and Dyphina as Thaelios explained the rules and strategy behind Knots & Locks, the combination card and dice game he'd played last week, when she heard Charilo's voice from the other side of the cage.

"Zygrim, is that your blood?!"

Saffron was the only one to understand, but she quickly announced that Zygrim was hurt, and they all rushed to the far gate to investigate.

"Ahhh, you should see the other guy," Zygrim winced as the guards let him through. He wore a large bandage wrapped over his torso and his left shoulder, but there were smears of drying blood across the expanse of his chest and arms. "It looks worse than it feels, I promise."

"I should hope so," Saffron quipped, "because it looks terrible. Are you going to be alright?"

Charilo walked ahead of Zygrim and cleared a space for him to sit on a nearby bench, previously littered with playing cards. "You're going to be fine, my friend," he said in Begnari, so rapidly Saffron could barely make it out.

Zygrim still winced as he sat, however. "Tried to block his blade with my spear and it cut right damn through."

"So I guess you won't be joining me in the Den of Sin tonight?" Saffron was disappointed, but happy Zygrim managed to survive.

"Are you jesting?" he forced out a toothy grin. "I wouldn't miss it for the world."

Sure enough, dressed once more in the black and gold of the Wolfspider's House, Saffron saw Zygrim walking gingerly down the hall on her way back from the baths. As the only other victorious fighter from their faction that day, Saffron was glad to have a familiar face accompanying her.

Clean and covered in his fine tunic, it was impossible to tell Zygrim was injured – except by the careful way he moved and the fact he avoided extending his left arm. He had a modest amount of tokens stashed in his vault and offered to buy Saffron her first drink, stating the acquisition of alcohol was his absolute priority to start the evening.

"I feel the same way, and thanks," she added. With a goblet of wine in her hand, and something stronger called a 'Sandstorm' in Zygrim's, they casually walked the perimeter of the establishment, sipping their drinks.

"Are you looking for something in particular?" he asked.

Saffron had been craning her neck at various intervals, marking the comings and goings of patrons. She frowned and shook her head, though only because she had yet to see who she was looking for: Ayez, the Many-Colored. He would be easy enough to pick out of a crowd if wearing the same robes as last week, and he was the only member of the Circle of Twelve she knew to look for. "Let's go see what's happening on the stage."

Zygrim nodded and followed as Saffron cut a path through the crowd. Upon reaching the adjacent seating area, she saw an illusionist in a shimmering blue cape on stage, performing tricks for the onlookers. A harp played a haunting melody in the background, adding an element of intrigue to the performance. She tried to follow along as the man made a large diamond disappear and reappear, accompanied by puffs of grey smoke. People clapped as the performance came to an end, the gem ending up inside a previously empty and locked, painted box.

"Ah, if it isn't the Crimson Scorpion herself!"

Saffron heard a raspy voice from behind and turned to find Ayez regarding her with interest. He was about her height, a middle-aged Begnari man with lightly salted facial hair and pronounced crow's feet around his eyes.

"I saw you perform a neater trick than that this morning," Ayez mentioned casually as he joined in applauding the illusionist.

"What was that you called me? The 'Crimson Scorpion'?" Saffron asked, disappointed she'd allowed him to sneak up on her.

Ayez presented his palms in a gesture of innocence. "That is what the crowd dubbed you, madam. I apologize if it offends. Please allow me to introduce myself: I have a nickname too, you see. I am known as Ayez, the Many-Colored." He bowed shallowly.

"My name is Saffron min Furasi, and this is Zygrim the Bull."

Zygrim took a step closer, doing his best not to appear too intimidating.

"Yes, of course, two of my favorites. You are looking in much better health than when I saw you last," Ayez announced to Zygrim. He looked uncomfortably at the crowd around them. "My dear, I would sincerely like to share a word with you, but I do not relish being overheard, and I assure you there are many watching and listening. Would you consent to entering a private room with me?"

Saffron looked at Ayez sideways. Surely he didn't think she was that gullible. "You're not the first person to try that, though I will give you credit for being more clever than most."

Ayez's lips vibrated in amusement. "While I would be a lucky man indeed to receive your favors, I give you my word the only thing on my mind is a conversation." He looked up toward the scaffolding servicing the privacy chambers. "It is the only way we can escape eavesdroppers for certain."

Saffron considered the man for a moment longer, then nodded. "I give you my consent, but Zygrim will be watching the door."

"Yes, I will," he confirmed.

"Excellent! Shall we procure a key?" Ayez extended his arm, allowing Saffron to lead the way. Once he paid for the room, the two of them climbed the wooden stairs and walked along the squeaking planks of the switchbacks to their door on the third level. Saffron felt like the entire establishment was watching her shameful parade toward ill-repute, though she dared not spare a glance back over the crowd.

Inside, Ayez closed and locked the door behind them as Saffron took a seat on the bed. No other options were afforded in the cramped space, which reeked from a musk of sex and sweat.

"What did you wish to speak with me about?" Saffron asked, feigning ignorance. She had no intention of letting on so early that she had been hoping for this precise scenario.

"I know you are new to Zeblon," he began, taking a seat beside her on the worn blanket, "so first allow me to tell you something of the city's history. Our current Caliph is still young, but his father was a greedy man and cared more for building his own fortune than for his people.

"When the temples came into popularity a decade ago, they started extracting tithes from followers who flocked to their services, drawn by the allure of apparent miracles. At the same time, the Caliph opened up the port and provided concessions to the trade guilds in order to increase his revenue from newly imposed taxes.

"Wealth was pouring in from foreign lands with each new ship, and combined with the allowances regarding slavery of debtors and the condemned, the city flourished – at least for those who had their hands in the coffers. Impressive mansions and shrines were erected, the Arena was built ... though as I'm sure you can guess, there was a cost."

Saffron nodded, aware that great achievements were almost always born on the backs of the downtrodden.

"As the trade guilds brought in money for the former Caliph, he didn't want to pass laws or intervene in any way that would cost them business. Trade wars began, and violence spread as the stakes grew higher and tactics more brutal. The Wolfspider emerged as the most adept in this new environment, in large part because he draws support from Hadrian No More.

"My cabal, the Circle of Twelve, have reason to believe the Wolfspider pays for this support by providing the Dread Lich with innocent lives to sacrifice. We oppose Hadrian No More's influence in our realm, the Wolfspider and his brutal business tactics, and to an extent, the Caliph for his lack of motivation to intervene on behalf of his own people."

"I see," replied Saffron, still working through the various relationships in her head. "And what is your interest in me?"

Ayez hesitated, taking measure of Saffron after sharing his position. "Shapers are rare, and there are some in my cabal who think it is no coincidence one has been delivered to our doorstep in the bonds of slavery. Our position as powerful men and women exempt us from sharing the circumstances of those we seek to help. You, however, could act on our behalf as an insider."

Saffron leaned back, feeling a shift in power now that Ayez was the first to ask for something. "What would acting on your behalf entail, and what do I get out of the bargain?"

"You want to be free, don't you?" Ayez leaned forward, taking up the space she had forfeited, his hypnotic robe seeming to shift colors as he moved. His tone acquired a note of urgency it had previously lacked. "Acting on our behalf would be working toward that end by disrupting the Wolfspider's influence, in one way or another. We may not be able to defeat the Dread Lich directly, but if we can oust the Wolfspider, then Hadrian No More's conduit to Zeblon would be severed as well."

"So, you're saying the Circle of Twelve would like to sponsor me?" Saffron did want to help, but she wanted to arrive at specific terms before agreeing to do so.

It was Ayez's turn to sit back. "You mean as a gladiator?"

"That's what I am at the moment, whether or not I'm also a Shaper." Saffron found the admission of her servitude distasteful, regardless of its truth. "You said you're trying to make a difference with the poor, and it seems that supporting me would be a good place to start."

Ayez folded his arms across his chest, as if they could somehow protect him from being swindled. "What is it you had in mind?"

"Well, I'm not alone down in those pens, and the conditions could be better. I don't want to become a target, but a few amenities for me and my friends would go a long way. I also don't want to necessarily wait until the Wolfspider is toppled, whatever that means to you, to regain my freedom. I was not born a slave, and this is not my natural state, whether or not you think it serves your needs." Saffron meant to hold back, but found her resolve waning.

"As you may be aware, the Wolfspider's gladiators are all fitted with these collars – supposedly gifts from Hadrian No More. We were told there is an enchantment upon them that would mean the wearer's death with only a word from our masters. I need to know if this is true, and if so, whether your cabal possesses the means to neutralize them."

"Fascinating!" Ayez moved closer on the bed to get a better look at her collar. "I always assumed they were merely adornments, symbolic of ownership."

"I assure you, having one strapped around your neck is the opposite of fascinating," Saffron said. "So, do you think you can counter the magic? Are we able to find terms?"

Ayez stood. "My Lady, I certainly hope we can. I will relay our discussion to my peers so that we might reach an agreement.

More research will have to be done regarding your collar, and we may need an opportunity to take a closer look. I will send word as quickly as I can with the Circle's decision."

Saffron took his cue and stood as well. They clasped wrists and Ayez moved to the door, unlocking it with his heavy key. She had reason to be hopeful, but now that she'd met Ayez, Saffron knew that waiting to hear back from the Twelve was going to be its own kind of torture.

Chapter 16

The Keeper's Library

"How did you catch up to me so quickly?" Be'naj had numerous questions for Cauzel, but she was so surprised to see him that this was the first to escape her mouth.

Cauzel shrugged, "I flew. I wanted to make sure I found you before you tried to enter the capital." He looked around to make sure no one was listening, but Mystic Kiruh was the only other person present. "There may be agents of the cult looking to do us harm."

"You flew?" Be'naj asked. She fluttered her wings, wondering if Cauzel might care to elaborate.

Kiruh took a step closer to Be'naj. "Is there anything I can do to assist? You're welcome to take sanctuary here."

"A gracious gesture, Mystic," Cauzel responded, though he'd started pacing and wringing his hands, "but the lady and I have important research to do. We must make our way to the Keeper's Library in the capital – the sooner the better."

"Did you discover what you needed to about your prophecy?" Cauzel asked Be'naj.

Be'naj was still distracted by his revelation of flight and took a moment to shift orientation. "I think Mystic Kiruh is right: I need to trust in Shecclad to reveal what is necessary, and pursue that as best I am able."

Cauzel nodded his acceptance. "You are ready to travel, then?"

"I am." Be'naj embraced her mentor. "Farewell for now, Mystic Kiruh. My thanks for the help you've given over the years."

"We are both servants of the Sky Lord, my child," he said as they broke. "Keep faith, and I have no doubt you shall find yourself giving much more than you take."

Almost as soon as Be'naj and Cauzel were outside the shrine, the Shaper resumed talking. Not being much used to conversation, Be'naj got the impression he could speak enough for the two of them.

"Do you mind if we share the horse?" Cauzel asked. "It would be easier if we stayed together on our way into Gilsage. My presence might make the journey go smoother, in any case. Well, dissuade strangers from asking too many questions, that is."

"I know what I look like," Be'naj retorted, not bothering to face him. "And yes, we can both ride Sheen ... unless you would teach me to fly as well?"

Cauzel paused to give a nervous laugh, "Eh, I don't suppose it's that easy, is it?"

Be'naj smiled to herself. She liked that she could make this sorcerer think twice about his choice of words. Time would tell if it rubbed off. She led the way to Sheen and mounted first, then offered Cauzel a hand to help him into the saddle. He hesitated before taking it, but doing so gave Be'naj the strange sensation of seeing something larger than what her body felt – as if the touch of Cauzel's hand didn't match her expectation of it. She didn't have long to consider the oddity because the man was already talking again.

"Sorry to interrupt your time with your friend, but I really do feel we should accomplish our goal as quickly as possible. This whole 'Name of the Beast' group I've heard mentioned is adding up to more than a nuisance. There have been rumblings in Pasaxtree for a while now, and after my interview with Aurus – that's my other apprentice – I worry their spreading influence is something we must be vigilant for."

The paths toward the center of Gilsage were well marked and familiar enough to Be'naj, even after all her years away. She tried listening closely to Cauzel's voice instead of dwelling on the negative memories this place had given her.

"I decided to let Aurus come to me on his own terms, in order not to give away any of the suspicions Iliana's been spouting this last week," Master Blackfeather continued. "He spun a fascinating tale, though I suspect it was rehearsed. I was able to find more than one hole in the narration. He's definitely hiding something ..."

"What did he say? Were you able to locate Saffron?" Be'naj couldn't believe it was taking the man so long to get to the important parts.

"My apologies," Cauzel responded, reaching around her to grab the reins and urge Sheen to halt. The autumn woods surrounding them had mostly transitioned from brilliant fire to bare branches, exposing eladrin structures that peeked out between them. Plenty of evergreens flourished this close to the foothills of the Wyvernwatch, meaning the settlement was never fully revealed. "This way," Cauzel nudged them left down a stone path partially concealed by moss, which brought them nearer to rows of log and masonry houses. Sheen ambled leisurely while investigating the unfamiliar trail.

"Aurus told me he'd gone to Pasaxtree to stir up information about what might have happened to his fellows, and in doing so, apparently drew notice from the Name of the Beast. He claimed abduction by a group of cultists, who took him into the wilderness to question him further. He was able to goad them into bragging about taking my other apprentices as well, including Lady Saffron."

"But you don't believe him?" Be'naj asked, looking over her shoulder to catch Cauzel's expression, though he sat too close.

"Oh, I believe parts of his story, especially after managing to attune Saffron's pendant for my location spell. It appears she, Dyphina, and Thaelios are all still alive and together, though on the move. We can assume it is not a direction of their choosing, since that would bring them back to Blackfeather Perch."

"How did he escape the cultists?" Be'naj asked out of politeness, only mildly interested in the answer. They'd progressed far enough that the buildings were growing more regular and Eladrin were stopping to stare as they passed. She wanted to keep Cauzel talking as a distraction. Be'naj's palms were sweating against the leather of the reins, and she felt a heat rising in her cheeks.

"That is part of the tale that doesn't sit particularly well with me." Cauzel seemed oblivious to her state of distress. "I've been fairly vigilant in overseeing the magical instruction of my pupils, and for Aurus to have used the spells he named during his escape stretches credibility. I will ask for a demonstration when there is sufficient time."

"Mmhmm," Be'naj answered, though she was barely listening. Her eyes were locked on the face of an eladrin man at the market, staring her down, a basket of vegetables in his arms and an uncomfortable expression on his face. Surely cucumbers didn't inspire such malice?

"Ah, just up the hill!" Cauzel declared with an air of satisfaction before nudging his heels to Sheen's flank. "We're almost to the Keeper's estate."

He held tighter to Be'naj's waist as they climbed a rise of green earth, up a path flanked by the trunks of thick trees. When it leveled off, starlight globe lamps marked the way down several branches off a central, stone-lined road. Each of the smaller paths led to buildings with ample grounds between them. The main path led to the largest timber home Be'naj had ever laid eyes on. The Keeper of Gilsage's estate, and even the surrounding quarter of the city, had been off-limits during her childhood.

Cauzel selected one of the lesser paths, however, and within moments they dismounted before a sturdy, stone chapel at least as large as the shrine to Shecclad. A pair of soldiers in light, silvery mail flanked the doorway. Unmoving, but presumably watching them, their eladrin eyes made it difficult to discern intention.

"I don't think they're going to let us in," Be'naj whispered to Cauzel. "In fact, I'm surprised you haven't been arrested yet. Unless things have changed, humans aren't allowed in Gilsage."

"Oh, not to worry, they know me here." Cauzel reached into the neckline of his black robe to retrieve something. "I have the Keeper's Seal," he said, flashing a bronze medallion at the soldiers as he approached the door. They nodded almost imperceptibly and didn't move to bar him as he grasped the silver-plated handle. Cauzel held the door open and gestured for Be'naj to enter ahead of him.

Her feet didn't move. "What about the horse?" she asked after a moment of getting over her surprise.

"Quite right." Cauzel blinked deliberately as if chiding himself for missing something so obvious. "Forgive me, I don't usually travel to Gilsage on horseback." He turned to address one of the guards. "You lads will make sure our horse reaches the stable, won't you?"

One of the men nodded, then rigidly stepped forward to take hold of Sheen's bridle.

"There, it's taken care of," Cauzel declared, still holding the door open.

Be'naj finally obliged and passed through. "The Keeper's Seal?" she asked once they were inside and the heavy door shut. The sound of its closing echoed around a spacious room, punctuated by rows of tall, book-lined shelves. "However did you manage that?" Be'naj's question trailed off, however, as she took in the library.

Beams of afternoon sunlight filtered in through a row of high windows, set between angled layers of the timber roof. The walls were mostly grey stone, but supports of dark wood added a welcoming feel. The shelves and furniture were constructed of the same two materials, so that the entire building seemed born of one design.

Several long, wooden tables, their upward faces polished smooth, populated the space before the shelves. These were lined with comfortable chairs she could imagine spending hours in without complaint. So many bound books filled the room, she found it hard to believe *that* much had ever been written, let alone collected into one place.

Cauzel had remained silent while she looked around and waited for her to absorb the weight of gathered knowledge before answering. "I have known the Keeper for some time, and proved long ago that I have the best interests of his people in mind."

Be'naj wasn't sure what that meant, but didn't press it. She felt momentarily stung by the thought that her people's leader could accept an outsider into his home while her own neighbors never accepted her differences. It passed when she remembered her decision to no longer care what the Eladrin thought of her.

Cauzel advanced down the few steps into the central part of the library, making his way over to the first set of shelves. Be'naj followed, overwhelmed at the prospect of searching through all these volumes.

"What is it we're looking for, exactly?" she asked in a low voice, holding the same reverence for the Keeper's Library as she did Shecclad's Sanctum.

"There are several topics to be investigated, as I see it," Cauzel explained, trailing his fingers over the tops of book spines, narrowing down to his first selection. "You," he said, plucking a tome from the shelf with a sigh of satisfaction, "should learn all you can about Nightwing Dragons in the event Sepathia is somehow masterminding this whole operation." He handed her a book, entitled *Flying Shadows*.

"As I was getting to earlier, my apprentices are still alive and together, though heading east past the mountains, away from prime Nightwing territory. Other nefarious elements dwell in that direction, but it's too soon to jump to conclusions. If it is the cult who has them, as the now unreliable Aurus contends, we need to find out what they're hoping to accomplish by travelling along such a difficult path." Cauzel nodded.

Assuming it was a gesture to assess her agreement so far, Be'naj mirrored him, prompting Cauzel to head around the corner toward a new set of shelves. "We should have the library mostly to ourselves today, so feel free to talk openly." When she caught up with Cauzel at his next stop, he was unrolling a piece of parchment, which she recognized as the notes he took when she recited her prophecy.

"Hmm, we are forewarned of the 'Name of the Beast' by your vision. They seem like a new group to me, but I will endeavor to find any records of past activity, which might indicate a motive. Still, my main interest is in 'Ancient Tarmuth beneath the sands.' It seems odd that any location bearing an eladrin name should lie in the desert, as your people typically took refuge among the deep forests during the Revenge of Arkmus ..." Cauzel scanned the shelves once more, and Be'naj decided she would leave him to it.

One assignment was enough for her, for it had been years since she'd handled a book, and she wasn't sure how easily the practice of study would return. She wandered back near the front of the building and selected a comfortable chair near where a square of sunlight painted the surface of a table.

She began reading. She enjoyed her book, for it was not at all the dry exposition she expected, but rather started as a story. Ekleon the Explorer was an intrepid, if perhaps foolhardy, eladrin scholar who chased legends of dragons from site to site. He cataloged some of the Nightwings' more terrifying features: horned faces with sunken eye sockets reminiscent of bare skulls, acidic spittle that could burn straight through the hide (or even armor) of their foes, and of course, venomous tail stingers that paralyzed their victims, who were often eaten alive.

As the story unfolded, it became clear that Nightwings were also shrouded in superstition. Because of their ability to fly silently and blend in with the night sky, they gained a reputation as spies and shapeshifters who could adapt to any environment. Ekleon doubted this to be true, though tales persisted of Nightwings encountered in human form, who turned back into dragons when an advantage presented itself.

The book's Explorer protagonist relayed a frightening episode of witnessing a conclave of Nightwing-worshipping fanatics. They whipped themselves into a frenzy while dancing around a huge bonfire, and ended up tearing the flesh from one of their own as a sacrifice, using only their sharpened fingernails.

She finally got to a chapter on defeating the beasts, which she read slowly and carefully. An eladrin soldier, weary of his community living under the shadow of fear cast by one of the beasts terrorizing the region, infiltrated her lair by posing as one of her fanatic servants. With his true identity secret, he tainted her offering with an elixir concocted by his herbalist wife.

An hour after consuming her meal, the Nightwing went temporarily blind, and in her confusion and rage, he was able to slay her. As a cautionary ending, however, Ekleon noted that the dragon's sense of smell was still acute enough to locate her attacker. Before she succumbed to her wounds, she delivered an impaling strike with her tail, killing the hero.

"Fascinating!"

Cauzel's exclamation drew Be'naj's attention from her book. She noted that her square of sunlight had slid significantly further down the table and was notably less bright. She rose and walked past the stacks of books to the other side of the library, where Cauzel sat at a desk littered with open tomes. A pair of lit candles dripped wax onto their holders, marking the demise of the afternoon.

"What is it?" she asked when he failed to acknowledge her presence on his own.

"Trigilas was a brilliant Shaper, but even more complicated than I ever assumed."

Be'naj bent to look at the spine of the book he was reading, which was titled, *Father of Spells: a Biography of Trigilas Evermoon.* "I thought you were reading about Tarmuth?"

"Ah, but the heart of Ancient Tarmuth was Trigilas!" Cauzel set down his book and looked briefly toward the ceiling, deciding how to proceed. "Trigilas was the first mortal to learn spellcraft. He discovered that the visiting Avatars of the old gods were infusing the world with magical energy, just by their very presence. What's more, he learned that while this energy was present everywhere, certain natural features were more efficient at storing it than the mere atmosphere."

Be'naj noticed how Cauzel's eyes sparkled as he talked about magic and indulged him, though he once again strayed from the point.

"As I said, Trigilas was a brilliant Shaper. At the birth of mortal magic, however, he had to rely almost exclusively on experimentation, for there was no one who could teach him. After the Revenge of Arkmus, Trigilas established the eladrin kingdom of Ancaoron. He created a spell, now known as the Veil of Trigilas, to hide all the new eladrin realms from outsiders, namely humans, who sought to do them harm. He discovered the Living Fire – the rubies like Saffron's pendant is crafted from – and from them Shaped the Sarnlor: seeing stones to keep the now far-flung, secretive eladrin kingdoms in contact with one another.

"Once he bought the Eladrin some immediate security, he sought a way to banish the Avatars, seeing them as the root of our problems. For this, he needed insight from other planes, such as the one the gods arrived from. Knowing this research might prove perilous, he established Tarmuth in the desert – a place remote to the Eladrin, where they would not be at such risk from his experimentation.

"He began his work on Planar Gateways there, using them to contact species across the cosmos, looking for the knowledge that would allow him to send the Avatars back to where they came from."

Be'naj sank into a chair beside Cauzel, completely dumbfounded. All Eladrin were brought up on stories of the great Trigilas, but they never went this far. Her wings tingled and twitched of their own accord, drawing her attention. If Saffron was right, her father might be one of these creatures Trigilas encountered, and experiments like those at Tarmuth might be how he came to arrive in Elisahd.

"Mmhmm," Cauzel cleared his throat, bringing her eyes back to him. "Although he initially meant to be isolated, Trigilas eventually brought many of his most promising apprentices to Tarmuth to assist in his research. Despite his wishes, a whole community eventually moved in, and the place grew into a thriving desert outpost.

"Supposedly several, if not many, portals were opened to other worlds, and Trigilas had contact with beings from the far planes. His research continued after he died and eventually was successful, as we all know.

"Even after the Banishment, however, experimentation continued, some of which grew dark in nature. Though the gateways were supposed to be closed, a group of fanatics, dubbed the 'Cult of Broken Names,' apparently used them to barter with fiendish denizens of the Lower Planes."

Cauzel briefly halted his narration to pick up and reference another leather-bound book, called *The Mystery of Broken Names*. "According to this, the cult spent more and more time in the Hall of Doors – the partially underground site of Trigilas's original experimentation. The rest of Tarmuth's populace grew fearful as devils of various sorts periodically broke free and escaped to the surface.

"Finally, a group of rivals ventured to end the danger by sealing the laboratory from the outside, blocking the exits with tons of stone, leaving only a single, magically sealed door. To make sure the cultists couldn't escape, they prevented all magic in and around Tarmuth by uncasing one of the Dampening Stones Trigilas supposedly acquired from the Abyss itself. These black spheres are said to be the physical manifestation of chaos and prevent Shaping within a mile at least."

"Do you think such objects exist?" Be'naj asked, thinking how one could prove either tragic or useful, depending on the circumstances. The Eladrin would suffer more than most under such constriction.

Cauzel shrugged. "I see no reason yet to doubt it."

"What was the fate of the cult?" Be'naj inquired.

"Ah, no worse than that of the rest of Tarmuth, it appears. As you might have supposed, Tarmuth was heavily reliant on magic, being founded by the greatest Shaper to ever live and inhabited by his most promising students. Once the Dampening Stone was removed from its own muting chamber, the residents of Tarmuth no longer had a way to accurately predict or protect themselves from the periodic storms unleashed by the desert. Within a year or two of burying the Cult of Broken Names alive in the Hall of Doors, it seems a massive sandstorm blew in and almost completely buried the rest of the city."

Cauzel shook his head at the lack of foresight. "The Dampening Stone was covered but continued to function, so those who were able to get out had no magical means to excavate or save those who ended up starving or suffocating in the storm's wake."

Be'naj could barely fathom the panic of being buried alive. "How horrible."

"But of course," Cauzel straightened in his chair, his voice surprisingly upbeat, "that was centuries ago, and who knows in what condition the desert has left the site since. Perhaps when we find it, Trigilas's laboratory will be uncovered once more!"

"When we find it?" Be'naj asked, drawing to her feet. "You think we should go looking for this cursed place?"

"Well, yes." Cauzel looked confused. "Isn't that what your own prophecy commanded? Go to Ancient Tarmuth?"

Those *were* the words, as Be'naj could not forget. Until that moment, though, she'd assumed they were delivered to her only to be passed on to someone else. She hadn't taken them as personal instruction. And how would taking a trip to a faraway desert help her rescue Saffron from her captors?

Cauzel seemed to read the doubt on her face. "I found a map included in the text, and the site of Ancient Tarmuth lies to the east – the same direction my apprentices are travelling. I would not presume this more than coincidence until we learn otherwise, but a journey toward one is, at least momentarily, a journey toward the other."

How could this man be so confident? Be'naj couldn't deny the desire to learn more about her heritage, as well as uncover the relevance of her dream-vision, but the idea of travelling so far, to such an ill-fated place worried her. Perhaps if they found Saffron on the way, however, her friend would join them. She was certain she'd be able to face this then. "I understand," she voiced at last.

"Good," Cauzel stated simply. He rustled about the books spread on his desk, looking for something. "What we need now is some insight into how we're going to open that door." He finally fished out the book he was looking for. "I'll continue with *The Mystery of Broken Names*, and you can start with *Sites of Magical Influence*." He handed her a thick book with a dark green binding. "Here, let me light another candle for you; it's getting dark outside."

Be'naj lifted her head to confirm that only soft, indirect sunlight was passing through the overhead windows. She accepted the book and took a seat, much more rigid than the one at her table, at the desk opposite Cauzel.

The door to the library squeaked open as soon as she cracked her volume, though the stacks on the main floor blocked any view of who might have entered. She waited expectantly for a moment, but then the door squeaked again as whoever it was chose not to stay.

Be'naj buried herself in the reading, examining the section on Tarmuth for anything about Dampening Stones or a ritual to open the sealed door. As she found out more about the Hall of Doors, she started wondering what the phrase "devilish games" from her prophecy might mean. Could it be literal? It certainly appeared that the portals underneath Tarmuth had been used at some point to enter into communication with fiends fitting such a description.

Finally, she found a promising passage among the detailed portrayal of the city's fall to the elements. It contained speculation that the sandstorm was not natural at all, but somehow an act of retribution toward the inhabitants of Tarmuth who conspired against the Cult of Broken Names. Further on appeared the transcription of a chant that had to be recited in the presence of the door while holding some token of the outer planes, in order to unseal it.

"I think I found it!" Be'naj erupted, speaking much louder than planned, her voice amplified by her surroundings. She rushed the book over to Cauzel, who'd lifted his beak-like nose out of his own tome at her pronouncement.

He read through the passage and beyond, nodding and muttering to himself as he absorbed the information. "Very promising!" he said at last, smiling and raising his bushy black eyebrows in an almost humorous gesture. "Did you get to the part about the Dampening Stone as well?"

Be'naj shook her head. She'd stopped reading in the excitement of her discovery.

"Once outside of their proper casing, cancellation wands were sometimes inserted directly into the Stones to temporarily disrupt the patterns of their chaos."

He'd said it with such promise, Be'naj almost skipped asking if Cauzel had a cancellation wand handy.

"No, I do not," he answered, though the admission hardly seemed to lower his spirits. "I am fully confident, however, that I could attune the Living Fire pendant to act as one." Finally, he frowned. "It would take some time ..."

"How much time?" Be'naj was afraid to hear the answer.

"My best guess ... several weeks."

"A lot can happen in several weeks," Be'naj said, mostly to herself, her thoughts distinctly on Saffron and what she might be going through.

"That is true, but I think we'll have to trust in the others to continue keeping themselves safe in the meanwhile. It would do us little good to travel to Tarmuth if we couldn't counteract the

Dampening Stone." Cauzel stood and lifted what remained of one of his candles by its holder.

"Come, it is late, and we should not have tarried this long. I'm a little surprised the guards didn't shoo us off by now." Cauzel tilted his head back toward the desk. "Would you mind bringing that book along? I'm sure the Keeper wouldn't mind lending it to me for such a cause."

Be'naj obliged and tucked *Sites of Magical Influence* under her arm. Besides the candles Cauzel had lit, the only other illumination in the library was now provided by the starlight globes posted in each corner. Night had fallen.

When she opened the heavy, external door for Cauzel, a rush of cool air extinguished his candle. He took a step outside and peered around.

"That's odd. Those soldiers aren't supposed to leave their post until the doors have been locked for the night."

Be'naj stepped out and confirmed that the guards who greeted them were nowhere to be seen. Crickets chirped in the grass, but though it was dark, enough light escaped from the windows of the library and other buildings of the estate to make walking manageable. "Do you know where the stables are?"

"I do. I also have an acquaintance with less conspicuous quarters in the capital where we can stay the night. We can begin the return trip to Blackfeather Perch in the morning." Cauzel started down the path toward another building, and Be'naj took a second quick look around for any sign of where the posted guards had gone.

Coming up empty, she lifted her gaze to the stars as she fell into step behind Cauzel. Mostly obscured by trees, she could still spot the constellation of the Stallion. Even that bit of familiarity brought some comfort in this unfortunately foreign place.

They were halfway to the stables, in the darkest part of the grounds, when a rustle of leaves to Be'naj's right caught her attention. A pair of cloaked figures dashed from behind a copse of trees, directly at Cauzel and her. She assumed the worst, dropping the book to draw her sword.

The figures must have recognized the introduction of steel for they both veered toward her, one seizing her waist and the other her sword arm, before she could assume a useful stance. As they pulled her to the ground, falling on top of her wings, Be'naj heard Cauzel speaking sharp words she couldn't catch.

A crackling sound from his direction drew the attention of both Be'naj and her attackers, who loosened their holds slightly to determine what was happening.

"Use the dust, quickly," the man trying to wrest the sword from her grip said. He spoke Eladrin, and his slight frame suggested that was his ancestry. The second man released her and stood, darting toward Cauzel, whose face was outlined in the white light of electricity surging around his forearm.

Be'naj used the newfound freedom of her legs to ram her knee hard into the belly of the man still struggling with her. He gasped and relented his grip further, which was enough for her to twist the hilt of her sword and pry her closed fist out of his. She quickly rolled to her feet and extended her blade to keep the attacker at bay. When she spared a glance toward Cauzel, however, it was her turn to be confounded.

The hostile Eladrin who'd approached the Shaper extended his arm and opened his palm, almost as if casting invisible dice. She couldn't see what he threw, but suddenly Cauzel's entire body shimmered and rippled as if its surface was composed of water. The white light surrounding his right arm vanished, and when the rippling stopped, a stranger stood in the spot Cauzel had been occupying. The interposing Eladrin nearly froze in place, perhaps just as bewildered as she.

The other one had gotten off the ground, however, brandishing a long dagger. Be'naj was forced to return her attention to him and watched as he assessed her for weaknesses. From the way he was standing, she didn't imagine he had any formal combat training.

She quickly closed the distance between them, then sliced the wrist of his hand that held the dagger with a slight upward movement of her weapon, causing him to drop it. Removing the element of surprise, he was clearly no match for her. "Be off, or I shall slay you where you stand!" she warned, whirling her sword to display the prowess necessary to back up her words.

The attacker between her and the figure who'd replaced Cauzel swiveled to see she'd disarmed his companion, who was holding his injured wrist.

"It didn't work, let's go!" the injured man hissed through clenched teeth. Drawn hoods still concealing their faces, the second Eladrin nodded.

"The Name of the Beast has marked you!" he yelled as they both darted toward the refuge of the trees they'd emerged from.

Be'naj watched until they'd completely disappeared from sight amidst the foliage, then waited another couple breaths to approach the stranger, who was dusting crushed leaves from his black cloak. She squinted in the starlight to recognize his face, but could not place it. He was full-Eladrin, like her attackers, but obviously not one of them. When he looked up, she saw his wide eyes were solid black, unusual for his kind.

"No need to stare too hard, my dear, it's still me."

"W-who's 'me'?" she asked.

"Cauzel Blackfeather, and this is my true form." He spread his hands, giving her the chance to inspect further. "Well, the one I was born into, at least," he amended. "Very clever of them to use disenchanting dust," he continued. "I must admit to not foreseeing that."

"Yo-you, you're Eladrin?" she stammered, still unsure she could trust her eyes.

"A secret only you, my sister, those fools, and the Keeper of Gilsage share. I would appreciate it not spreading further." Cauzel placed his hands on his hips and pursed his lips.

The voice matched, at least. "But why?" Be'naj asked.

The eladrin Cauzel shrugged. "So I could be a better liaison with the humans, of course. Keeping the peace is easier when I can simply bypass the prejudice against our kind. Now, if you don't mind, it will be some time before this dust wears off, and I'd like to get beyond the range of prying eyes until I can recreate my illusion."

"Of course," Be'naj agreed. She wanted to slip somewhere unnoticed as well, until they could figure out what to do about the cult apparently pursuing them. "Let's find Sheen and be off."

Chapter 17

Transformation

With her eyes still closed, Annoxoria smiled within the cocooned warmth of her bedsheets. After the pleasure Thuvian gave her last night, her body felt like a cat's, vibrating of its own volition. She'd never successfully described it to anyone else and wasn't sure they could ever understand. It was as if making love to him transferred some of his innate power to her. Annoxoria was ready to take on the responsibilities that might otherwise weigh on her. She couldn't imagine what her life would be without Thuvian's love.

Yet when she rolled over in bed, stretching an arm to lay it across his naked, scaled back, she once again found only empty space. Oh yes, she realized as she opened her eyes to confirm his absence, he had mentioned he needed to leave before dawn to make another trek into the Wyrmsmoke Mountains. Her smile receded, slackening her cheeks. She'd had enough of those petty, squabbling orcs depriving her of her Lord. If they didn't submit and join the Skullreaver banner soon, she would murder them herself.

Such a shame, too, that her lover was already gone when her body was so primed. The effects of what he'd done to her last night still hovered like summer morning fog over a cold lake. Her skin tingled, and Annoxoria closed her eyes once again to summon flashes of their recent lovemaking as her hands caressed her ebullient flesh.

She roughly pinched and pulled at her sensitive nipples as she remembered the sting of Thuvian's sharp teeth suckling them. Her hands traversed her firm stomach to her thighs, trying to grasp them with a similar authority as he did before pressing into her, but it wasn't the same. Annoxoria rolled onto her stomach and slid a hand beneath her, thrusting several fingers roughly into herself, trying to recapture the ecstasy of last night's passion.

Her body yearned to ascend that final peak, but satisfaction remained elusive. Beads of sweat blossomed on her temples from her effort, but she finally froze, eyes opening in frustration as she removed her sticky fingers. She rolled across the bed, its delicate sheets entwining her, then sat up to find her reflection staring back at her.

The full-body mirror Thuvian had recently commissioned for her thirtieth birthday was propped against the wall of their bedchamber, positioned a few days ago in a fit of inspiration to capture and enhance their love-making. Annoxoria let the sheets fall from her torso and studied her image.

She poked the burnt sienna skin of her inner thigh, watching as it gave in to the pressure. She was soft. Too soft. She thought of Thuvian's majestic, muscular, rigid form. He was firm, everywhere, from the downward-curved horns abutting his forehead to the glossy-scaled backs of his calves. This current body of hers wasn't worthy of his desire.

Annoxoria stood and walked over to her polished, cherry-wood wardrobe. She pulled on her thigh-length, black scaled boots and horned headband. She grabbed the dark make-up from the matching table and smeared it across the circles underneath her eyes. Lastly, she picked up the newest addition to her accessory collection – a pair of black leather gloves fashioned with real lizardfolk claws at the fingertips.

After fitting them on her hands, she sat back down on the bed across from the mirror and admired her transformation. She turned her head back and forth, taking in the various angles as she put on the fiercest expression she could muster. Far from perfection, she admitted, but certainly an improvement.

She spread her legs and scratched at the spot on her inner thigh she'd poked earlier. Red lines appeared in the wake of the pain that crossed her skin. Much better. That was how it should feel. Her other hand lowered to explore her sex as she once again dragged her claws across the flesh of her upper thighs, harder this time. She gasped as she drew blood, but it only fueled her arousal.

Her thoughts returned once more to her lover and imagined the claws were his, roaming over her body as he bent her in impossible positions, taking her over and over again. She

grasped at her breasts, her stomach, the swell of her buttocks –
all while working herself closer to climax with her spare hand.

At the last moment, she opened her eyes and the sight of her
shredded skin sent her over the edge. Her entire body tightened
and then released its tension, the stinging of her bloody
scratches heightening and mixing with her pleasure to create an
even more intense sensation. She collapsed back onto the bed
after the largest waves had crashed, her body still pulsing with
energy.

Annoxoria lay there until her breathing returned to normal
and all she was left with was the pain. She didn't mind it, given
her current body was only a temporary prison. She would likely
inflict worse on her slaves before the day was through. Now that
they had extracted more of the Seeds of the Avatars, her greed
for them only increased. She needed to make an appearance to
be sure the miners weren't growing complacent.

Gullagion and Izefet were scheduled to arrive by the end of
the afternoon, and she was loathe to part with what she had
promised, especially after what she had learned about the Name
of the Beast since their last meeting. She was going to need
more proof that Izefet could deliver on his part of the bargain –
not that she doubted the abilities of his supposed partner,
Hadrian No More.

No half-fiend was going to help her out of sheer kindness,
and he had never been upfront about what he was getting out of
the transaction. Thuvian's spy-master was the one to bring her
insight on the matter. Still, she wanted to hear it from Izefet, if
only to determine whether he would follow through on his
promise. She had already taken steps to position her Lord

favorably should the cult succeed in sowing discord through the region.

Annoxoria rose and stripped naked again, then rang a small brass bell to summon one of her servants to draw a bath. She needed to wash the blood and clean the wounds before dressing for company.

Prior to meeting with the fiend and his undead associate, Annoxoria had another appointment with the spy-master of Nightwing Castle. The dungeons lay several levels below the throne room, and she used the trip down to mentally prepare for whatever news Pereen Guillory had to deliver. She didn't want to appear as if anything surprised her.

Annoxoria arrived first, which did leave her surprised. She knew of her own reputation around the castle for not taking disappointment well – one she had carefully cultivated. If the spy-master was late, it was likely for good reason. She was leaning against one of the empty restraining racks, watching the door she'd entered, when she heard the swinging of a metal hinge from behind.

She turned to see Pereen entering the dungeon from an ironwork gateway. He wore a travelling cloak and ran a hand quickly over his short brown hair, shaking out leaf and twig debris. The scar running down his left cheek caught the torchlight as he lifted his eyes to meet Annoxoria's.

"Apologies for my tardiness, Lady Nefzen," he offered, peeling off his cloak while navigating around the tables and torture instruments between them. "I ran into some difficulty meeting with one of our agents from Pasaxtree, and I knew you'd want her report."

He looked flustered, almost shaken, which was unheard of for Thuvian's purveyor of intrigues. "Is everything all right?" Annoxoria's curiosity won out over annoyance.

"Oh, I suppose that depends on what you mean." Despite his cryptic response, his eyes steadied and didn't leave hers until she blinked.

Deciding his informality had gone far enough, Annoxoria crossed her arms over her chest, standing firm as she cocked an eyebrow. "Well, don't keep me in suspense. Proceed with your report, Master Guillory."

He nodded and lay his cloak on the nearest table. "Izefet the Damned is certainly well regarded within the Name of the Beast. It is not yet clear to me whether he is the cult's leader or simply a member in high standing. He did come from the east, although stories vary on how far. Some place him as a denizen of the Abyss itself, while others say he sprang full-grown from the depths of Lake Imeel."

"I couldn't give a damn about where he was born," Annoxoria said. "What is he after, and how is he trying to use me to get it?"

"Well, if his goals are the same as the cult's, I've not discovered any coherent plan beyond destabilization of governments and kingdoms. In Pasaxtree, as you know, Lord Skullreaver is already involved in a similar strategy. By orchestrating threats to merchants travelling the Ifelian Corridor, we not only create a hole in the market for our own goods, but will earn gratitude for eventually putting a stop to the attacks."

"Yes, so what is the cult doing differently?" Annoxoria snapped.

Pereen's eyes widened and he paused. "Your pardon," he finally said stiffly, though whether sincere or an objection to her interruption, she could not divine. "We now have an agent posing as an initiate in the Name of the Beast, but the cult already has members in the Merchant Guild. They're petitioning to hire mercenaries to protect the trade route. I have my doubts that is what the troops would actually be used for, since the attacks further the cult's agenda.

"Elwise ambassadors have also been targeted in Pasaxtree, physically and ideologically, creating tension with Gilsage and the possibility of escalating hostility."

Annoxoria remained silent, working through the developments in her mind. They would certainly have to act before a southern force intervened along the Corridor, but a human push against the Eladrin might be just the leverage to force the Keeper of Gilsage in line. Thuvian could promise intercession on their behalf to gain an ally, while lining the pockets of the Pasaxtree merchants to actually end things—

"Is there anything more you need, My Lady?" Pereen was staring at her with a creased brow. "Perhaps a message you'd like to send to our Lord? Or would you like me to write the report?"

"No, I'll do it. I can summon a messenger far swifter than yours." Annoxoria uncrossed her arms and reconsidered the spymaster's tardiness and untidiness upon arrival. "Your agent infiltrating the cult is a *she*, you said?"

The question seemed to surprise Pereen. "Um, well, yes, My Lady."

"Good. Do continue to stay on top of things." She turned without waiting for a response and headed back toward the staircase. The next stop was her laboratory and library. She'd decided to risk probing her fiendish guest when they met, which meant taking a few precautions.

She climbed the stairs and followed the twists and turns to her private rooms. They were her favorite part of the castle, apart from the bedroom she shared with Thuvian. No one else, not even Lord Skullreaver, ever entered this section – not only had she strictly forbidden it, but she'd established magical wards that would prove a danger to anyone but her. Once in her laboratory, she closed the iron-reinforced door behind her.

She'd been coming here regularly for doses of her personal Nightwing venom concoction, but had seen no signs of physical transformation, just annoying muscle seizures in her abdomen. In fact, the vial she'd acquired from the captured Thrall was nearly empty. If anything, the brew was having less effect on her than when she'd started. She would have to remain open to other possibilities.

Wiping disappointment from her thoughts, she sought to focus on the task at hand. The spell she had in mind would last a few hours at most, but would take little out of her, so it was worth the effort for the potential security. She'd had no indications yet that Izefet possessed any special magical power himself, though it would be foolish to presume a creature with fiendish parentage hadn't inherited at least a few tricks.

She poured a small hill of salt from an ornate glass canister into her palm. Sprinkling it in a circle upon the floor around herself, she stilled her blood – for that's how it felt – and drew the power she needed from it as she chanted: "*Gwihir sonothus umbad, gwihir sonothus umbad, gwihir sonothus umbad.*"

After the third utterance, the salt on the floor turned golden and flew upward, vanishing as if nothing more than evaporating water. She didn't feel any different other than the slightest fatigue, but the protection should at least prevent the half-fiend from laying hands on her. The meeting time was near, and after returning to her bed chamber and checking her appearance in the mirror, she headed down to the throne room.

Once seated upon Thuvian's throne, her posture rigid and face composed, she allowed the chamberlain to admit her guests. Not taking any chances, she'd posted a handful of armed guards and Grellock, the ogre, around the perimeter of the room. After opening the door to the antechamber, the chamberlain quickly retreated, covering his nose and mouth with his forearm. The pungent, green vapor surrounding the ghast poured into the room before the lieutenant of the Dread Lich entered.

"Gullagion of the Nether-Court, and Izefet the Damned," her chamberlain announced from behind his sleeve.

"*Ah, I've acquired a new epithet since I visited last. Was it something I said?*" Izefet's telepathy reached Annoxoria's mind before she saw his black-cloaked form enter behind the ghast. He poked his head forward, then craned his neck, taking in the room with his crimson-irised eyes. "*Lost some of your more flavorful decorations, too, I see.*"

Hearing his voice in her mind still felt intrusive, and she wasn't amused by his attempt at humor. Charm, especially demon-charm, wasn't going to dissuade her from her course. She sat tall and still, watching for Izefet's reaction when his eyes finally settled on the black, metallic coffer resting on a marble pedestal near the center of the room. All she got for her patience was the rubbing of his fingertips against one another.

"*Ah, is that what we were summoned for?*"

"Do you need to ask?" Annoxoria responded. "I thought you could read minds."

Izefet jerked his head toward her and she caught the slightest tremble of his lips, but then he had no need to open his mouth to speak. "*I would never presume to know what the Lady Nefzen was thinking.*"

"Bull-dung, you presumed that the first time we met."

This time, Izefet smiled. He walked toward the coffer, leaving Gullagion to stand silently in the corner, thankfully keeping his retch-inducing aura safely away. Without asking for permission, Izefet pried the split-lid open with his ruddy hands, revealing a small collection of uncut rubies. Even with almost no direct torchlight, they glowed brightly in their casing: fire-red jewels more precious than anything fashioned by the hands of men.

"*Excellent. This should be enough for our purposes, don't you think, Gullagion?*" Izefet glanced back toward the ghast, who stepped closer to take a look. His noxious cloud didn't affect the half-fiend in the slightest.

"*I suppose we shall have to reward the Aasimar. They certainly seem to have assisted in expediting the Living Fire's acquisition. If we take possession immediately, you should have your personal payment all the quicker.*"

Annoxoria raised her eyebrows, her hands steady on the arms of Thuvian's throne. Let the games begin. "I have not yet decided to turn them over." This time, both Izefet and Gullagion stared up at her. "I need to be convinced."

Izefet slowly closed the lid of the coffer, as if leaving the Living Fire within view would further her temptation to keep the jewels. *"Convinced of what, exactly?"*

"First of all, I'd like to know precisely what you intend to do with your share of Avatar's Seeds: the ones not being used to bring about my transformation ... you never told me. Secondly, I would like to be convinced that Gullagion actually serves the Dread Lich, so that I know he can deliver on *your* promise. It is, after all, the dweomercraft of Hadrian No More I'm interested in, isn't it?" Neither of the abominations in Annoxoria's court stirred, nor spoke a word, for the passage of several breaths.

"Oh, is that all?" Izefet finally offered, and she couldn't help wondering if the two of them had been concocting a story telepathically during the silence. *"I desire the jewels not for myself, My Lady, but to further the cause of the Name of the Beast. As a servant of the cause, I will only say that they shall be used to transform the world into a better state, not unlike your own portion."*

Of course, that told her nothing. She was going to have to be more direct. "And would the ruins of Rinn-Rhulian have anything to do with this transformation?"

"Ruins? You'll have to forgive me, Lady Nefzen, I am not local to this region and haven't had much time for sight-seeing." Though he didn't miss a beat with his explanation, Annoxoria noticed he bared his canines slightly while projecting his thoughts. *"My orders come from elsewhere, and as a servant, I do what is required of me."*

"Very well," she moved on, confident from his reaction that he at least knew of the place. She could work on determining the nature of his interest later. "Do you have any proof of actual association with Hadrian No More?"

"I believe I can alleviate your concerns in that regard," Gullagion answered in a slow, rattling voice as he stepped closer.

Annoxoria hoped he wouldn't come too close, keeping her eyes on the advance of his noxious cloud more than his person. She intentionally maintained her rigid posture, not wanting to show any sign of unease. Thankfully, he halted his approach at the coffer, atop its pedestal, where he reached a skeletal hand into the folds of his midnight robe.

He withdrew some sort of miniature statuary, the design of which she couldn't make out from her vantage on the throne. The base appeared to be some sort of shimmery, black metal, though the peak was clearly adorned by a polished and cut jewel of the Living Fire. Red light danced around its facets, threatening to leap out into the quiet air of the throne room. Everyone, even her watchful ogre, held their breath as they assessed the superb craftsmanship, leaning in to get a better look.

After a long, hushed moment, Gullagion balanced the piece astride the lid of the coffer and backed away. "That was made by the hands of my master, from the first jewel you delivered. If you inspect it, I am sure you'll conclude that only Hadrian No More could have done so."

Annoxoria couldn't fight the feeling that she was being lured into some sort of trap, but her body had already betrayed her, leaning forward on the throne with a desire to inspect the treasure. With one eye on it and the other on her guests, she stood and descended toward the middle of the room.

Drawing closer, she saw that the jewel was housed in the midst of some sort of surrounding creature – perhaps a kraken – whose folded metallic body projected a set of curled tentacles. It was intricately detailed, smooth and cold to the touch. Lifting it, she found that some of the tentacles fed into a small basin underneath, all part of one, solid piece. "It's beautiful," she said, both eyes now on the statue. The ruby center flickered as she turned the kraken over in her inspection.

"*It has already been enchanted specifically to facilitate permanent transmutation. If you are ready, I shall give you the proof you seek.*"

Izefet's voice could have been the statue itself seducing her, for Annoxoria had yet to take her eyes off it. She thought back to her morning and how much becoming a dragon had meant to her vitality, her arousal – contrived as it was. If she could have that for real, why wait?

"I'm ready," she declared with a hollow tone.

"*Very well.*" Suddenly, Izefet was only a few steps behind her. She turned to face him and found that, even in her boots, he was half a head taller, though not as imposing as her beloved Lord.

"*Since you do not yet have the Nightwing scale, of course I cannot begin your final transformation, but I brought something to help show you what's in store.*" Izefet turned over his palm and, seemingly out of thin air, produced the keratin rattle of a poisonous snake.

Annoxoria eyed it with nervous excitement. "What exactly will that do?"

The half-fiend extended his arm. "*It shall serve as the initial catalyst of your alteration. My form of magic, however, always requires sacrifice.*" He stretched out his other hand, which held the handle of a curved knife. "*You will have to give up a similar part of yourself ... in this case, the tip of a finger should do.*"

"What?!" She wasn't sure she'd heard him correctly.

"*You must always give to get, Lady Nefzen. That is the blood pact required for my magic.*" Izefet took a single step closer, his crimson eyes unreadable. "*Just, part of a finger.*"

Annoxoria hesitated. She looked to Gullagion, but his uncaring, decayed form gave no comfort. She did want proof Izefet could deliver before doing something so foolish as confronting Sepathia to recover a scale.

"*Come,*" he waved his fingers around the handle of the knife, urging her forward. "*You won't even miss it after your full transformation makes you whole.*"

"I suppose," she said, with a final effort to suppress her fear. "I have one more request to prove your good faith." She extended her left hand, then quickly drew it back and wriggled the jade ring from her finger while tucking the kraken in the crook of her right elbow. "Remove the Keeper of Gilsage from his seat of rulership." If her Thuvian could somehow benefit from all this, it may lessen her possible regret. She reached out again, spreading her fingers in an effort to isolate the one she'd resigned to surrender.

"*Perhaps you should set the idol down?*"

"What?" She looked to her right arm, having already forgotten she still nestled the statuary. "Yes, of course." Annoxoria looked to the pair of guards stationed in the open doorway across from the throne. "Clear the pedestal," she ordered.

Izefet smiled. *"Worry not, the Keeper is but one of the mortals in lofty positions the Name of the Beast has decided must embrace a more fitting humility."*

After the guards had lifted the metal coffer from the marble and stowed it on the floor against the wall, Annoxoria set the kraken in its place. With her hands free, she once again extended her left arm. Izefet drew closer and dropped the snake rattle into the tiny basin at the base of the statue. He looked greedily at Annoxoria's hand, and she swore his tongue darted out to lick his lips.

When he reached out to grasp her wrist with his free hand, however, it stopped short as if meeting an invisible barrier. He drew back and stared at her, though projected no thoughts in her direction. Annoxoria let her extended arm fall back to her side, matching his keen gaze with her own. Her spell from earlier that afternoon seemed to be working. She silently dared Izefet to mention it.

Without a word, Izefet stepped up to the pedestal and lay his knife upon it, next to the kraken. Finally, he looked back at Annoxoria and gestured to the blade. *"I suppose you shall have to do the honors yourself."*

Her ogre guard took a couple of thumping steps closer as she picked up the knife, but she stayed him with a raised palm. Slowly, she rubbed the underside of her left ring finger with her thumb, feeling the texture of her skin while reminding herself this wasn't the body she was meant for, anyway. She spared a glance at the half-fiend, then asked. "Do it now?"

"Whenever you're ready." He slid the sleeves of his robe back to his elbows. The reddish skin of his exposed forearms

was covered in dark grey splotches. *"I shall begin the spell when the sacrifice is complete."*

Annoxoria lay her palm flat on the white marble, her darker hue contrasting against the cold stone. She aligned the sharp side of the blade perpendicular to her finger, just below the first knuckle. *Be decisive – you don't want to have to cut twice …*

"Ahhhh!" she cried out through clenched teeth as she sawed off the end of her finger. Blood stained the white surface beneath her hand, and after lifting it, she felt surreal staring at the piece she'd left behind.

"Place it in the basin."

She did as instructed, though couldn't bear to look at Izefet in the moment. Once the fingertip had joined the rattle, she tucked her bleeding hand under her right bicep to apply pressure against her side.

Izefet moved his arms, though if the spell required any words he did not project them in her direction. Annoxoria did see the offerings begin to smoke, and the Living Fire flashed more brightly, its crimson gleam painting the floor beneath the pedestal. She felt her tongue moving of its own accord inside her closed mouth, and when she opened it, a thin, elongated muscle darted out.

When she drew her tongue back into her mouth, she was overwhelmed by all she tasted. She quickly closed her eyes and let her tongue whip out again – even without seeing him, she could sense Izefet standing in front of her.

"Wathisss iss haass—" she clamped her mouth shut. None of her words sounded right. Her eyes widened in shock.

"Speaking will come a bit awkwardly at first, but you'll adapt." Izefet smiled. *"The statue is yours, a gift from the Dread*

Lich. Summon me when you have the scale, and I will return to conclude our bargain."

Chapter 18

The Circle of Twelve

Saffron was anxious about how long she'd have to wait until hearing from Ayez, but only two days after her visit to the Den of Sin, she received a curious visitor. Shortly after Saffron finished her morning meal, Harzhim appeared at the gate of the cage, leading a diminutive man.

"Lady Saffron," he said, "you have a guest."

She did not recognize the man, but figured he must have paid handsomely for the opportunity to visit her within the Wolfspider's pens. If he was wealthy, perhaps he could provide further opportunity. She stood from her bench and approached the bars for a closer look.

"Do I know you, Sir?" she asked in Begnari, knowing full well she didn't. The top of his head only reached the level of her chest, and he wore a brown cloak that seemed much too heavy for the climate. He had a bulbous nose and gemstone rings on several of his fingers.

The little man drank her in with his eyes and, without answering, looked over his shoulder at Harzhim. "I can take it from here, my good man. I'll show myself out when we're finished." The Wolfspider's Consul nodded politely and backed off, disappearing into the labyrinth of tunnels from whence he arrived. Now, Saffron was truly intrigued.

Once Harzhim withdrew, Saffron noticed Phaerim and Thaelios drawing unobtrusively closer in her peripheral vision. The stranger put a hand up to his mouth and coughed to clear his throat.

"It is a pleasure to meet the Crimson Scorpion in person," he began in unpolished Begnari. "My name is Groilen Bonesplinter, and I am here on behalf of Ayez, the Many Colored ... representing our mutual interest."

Saffron's breath caught at mention of the sorcerer and she switched to Illanese, guessing at Groilen's native tongue. "Are you from the Circle of Twelve?"

Groilen looked both ways before answering more confidently in Illanese. "Indeed, Madam, I am. Ayez explained you were open to accepting sponsorship from the Twelve but had concerns regarding your collar." He stepped closer and pushed his fingers through the gaps in the cage, then pulled right up to it and whispered harshly, "Is it true they are magically trapped?"

"So we've been led to believe," Saffron answered, taking a step back.

"But ah," Groilen let out a sour chuckle, "things are certainly not always as they seem. I should know." He winked and relaxed his grip on the cage. "Nevertheless, we shall get to the bottom of it. Sirran will be especially interested ..." he mumbled.

"I've made some special arrangements to convince you our side is the one that will benefit you most." Groilen gave a questioning look to Phaerim and Thaelios, who had inched even closer during the conversation.

Saffron acknowledged them with a glance. "You can speak. I'm not joining anyone's *side* without my team."

Groilen cleared his throat again. "I've got a deal in place with one of the guards. When your evening meal is delivered, your cage will be unlocked and the corridor leading to the exit abandoned. A wagon will be waiting outside to transport you."

"Won't we be missed?" Phaerim interjected. "I'd love some fresh air, but it's not worth my head exploding over."

"As long as you're back by the start of the next shift at dawn, no one will be the wiser. This sort of thing is understood to go on in the Wolfspider's pens, from what I've heard." Groilen waved a hand dismissively. "He sometimes uses his gladiators as extra muscle on certain jobs. Don't worry, we'll have you back in time."

"Where are you taking us?" asked Saffron.

"On a sightseeing trip that will hopefully persuade you. I shouldn't say any more, as the walls tend to have ears." Groilen's eyes wandered in an arc from ceiling to floor. "Just remember, after dinner."

Saffron nodded her understanding, prompting Groilen to wink before scooting off down the darkened hallway.

"What was that all about?" Thaelios asked. He had been silently watching the exchange, but Saffron had no doubt his keen ears had overheard most of it.

Saffron turned her back on the metal crossbars of the cage and rested against it. "Ayez, the man I met in the Den of Sin, belongs to that group Zygrim told me about: the Circle of Twelve. He said they might be able to find a way to safely remove our collars if I agree to their sponsorship. I suppose this is part of their recruitment."

"So, you are going to go?"

"Of course she's going!" Phaerim interrupted, crossing his arms and taking a step closer. "We've got to do whatever we can to find a way out of this predicament, and this is the most promising lead yet, unless you're planning to kill off every single gladiator in the city ..."

Saffron flared her eyebrows when it looked like he was actually considering the possibility. "I was hoping all four of us would go. I don't think we should split up until we get a better sense of whether we can trust them. Speaking of which, where's Dyphina?" Saffron was twisting to peer deeper into the pen when a sudden voice from behind caused her to jump.

"I have an announcement for everyone. Please gather 'round." It was Harzhim, holding a piece of parchment, which meant he was likely announcing fights for the coming week. He waited as Zygrim and his crew wandered over, Dyphina among them. "Everyone now, this concerns you all."

When both teams were in proximity, Harzhim scanned the parchment as if assuring he'd understood it correctly, then let it dangle loosely at his side as he took turns making eye contact with the assembled gladiators. "Last night was the banquet honoring Hizune's Charge, and as the heads of each of the four Houses were present, a wager was made. I am sure wine was not the least to blame, but terms were struck, nevertheless."

Saffron's anxiety heightened as Harzhim cleared his throat. He seemed a well-balanced individual from what she'd seen, though he was clearly shaken by the news he had to deliver –not a good sign.

"This week, there will be a *Battle Royale* to determine House Standing for the coming season. Whichever House wins will earn not only a considerable purse, but the right to first choice in the slave markets. That means the Wolfspider has ordered me to select our top two teams, which happen to be you, to fight in the battle. Eight warriors from each House will participate, and the fight will continue until a dozen have been culled."

Saffron saw Nucril counting on his fingers and quickly did calculations of her own.

"Yes, that means that on average, three of you will not return. We're counting on you to do better than that." Harzhim looked directly at Saffron. "We *demand* you do better than that." He shifted his eyes to Zygrim. "You will have access to extra training sessions this week, should you desire them. I suggest you develop some sort of strategy to play off your strengths and fight together." He rolled up the parchment but stopped mid-turn to offer one last utterance. "Olcuin's Fortune to you."

They waited for Harzhim to leave before collectively exhaling. Saffron translated to her fellows, then immediately sought out Zygrim, curious for his reaction. "Is this unusual?" she asked. "He certainly appeared nervous about telling us."

Zygrim shook his bald head in resignation. "I've not been around for one."

"I remember watching a *Battle Royale* a few years ago," Charilo chimed in, slinking from Zygrim's shadow. "Bloodiest fight I ever saw. The city still speaks of the occasion."

"No doubt it will be difficult accounting for so many bodies," Zygrim said. "And after seeing what you can do," he spoke directly to Saffron, "I'd put a stack of bronze Camelbacks on the other Houses making eliminating you their highest priority."

"Well, let me worry about that," Saffron countered. "I think we should concentrate on keeping everyone alive while the other Houses thin one another's numbers."

They entertained various strategies for the next hour, then started working some of them out in the training room. Saffron was so absorbed in her pursuits, she forgot about their clandestine excursion planned for that evening. Her team was exhausted by the time they broke to clean up for the evening meal, and she was halfway through dinner before Phaerim mentioned it.

"So, are we really doing this?" he asked, staring at the gate of their pen.

When Saffron checked, she could tell the hinged section was not quite flush with the rest of the cage. She looked at the other three, who had naturally separated as a team to eat. Zygrim, Charilo, Nueril, and Wemic were on the other side of the pen, absorbed in consuming their portion of bread and bean paste. "If everyone is ready, we could slip out now," she said. They each nodded at her, and Saffron scooped one last mouthful of her meal before standing.

She tested the gate and it yielded to her, whining as it swung open. The Wolfspider's men allowed the torches to expire on their own in the evening, normally not replacing them until morning. The pens were dimly lit in the best of times and the corridors pitch black when not being walked, but now a singular torch blazed in its sconce along one passageway.

Saffron headed for the light with Phaerim, Thaelios, and finally Dyphina, slinking out after her. Plucking the torch from the wall, she continued down the tunnel. She eschewed two opportunities to deviate before making a final turn that ended in an upward-sloped ramp. After ascending for twenty paces, the corridor was blocked by wooden double doors, barred from their side.

"Phaerim, can you help me with this?" Saffron handed the torch to Thaelios while she and Phaerim pried the beam from its brackets and propped it against the wall. Tentatively, Phaerim pulled on the left side of the portal, which groaned as it swung inward.

A blast of cooler air struck Saffron in the face, and she stepped through to peek at the outside world. She could taste the salt on the wind, and the indigo of the high sky was already chasing pink toward the horizon. White rocks outlined a lane before her, where an open-backed wagon waited. She could still see other buildings in the fading light, but it struck her how much space existed between structures. This was the not the crowded city style she'd seen in the Cradle, or even her home for that matter.

"Well?" came a harshly whispering voice from the front of the wagon. "What are you waiting for?"

"Groilen?" Saffron whispered back as she hustled to the cart. Two sandy-colored horses were harnessed to it, but when she peeked around into the front seat, she saw a slender-shouldered figure. He wore a brown cloak similar to the one worn by their diminutive visitor that morning, but even in the waning light of dusk she could see the face belonged to another. "Pardon me, sir, I thought you might be someone else."

"You're at the right wagon, Lady Saffron." The man winked. "Go on and climb in back – easier to keep a low profile."

Saffron hesitated, but the others were already slipping into the open carriage, so she didn't wait long to join them. It made sense Groilen would send a servant to do the risky work, but the driver's mannerisms sure seemed to echo those from their earlier emissary.

As soon as she sat on the wooden planks of the wagon bed, reins snapped, followed by a sudden lunge forward. Breathing in the coastal air and looking up at the emerging stars made her feel as if their time underground had lasted years, not weeks. Between the mines in the mountains and the Wolfspider's pens, she'd had enough of subterranean existence. The silence and expressions of simple joy on the faces of her companions told her they must have felt the same.

Locating the three bright stars in Hizune's Scimitar, which were nearer to the horizon than she was used to, Saffron oriented herself. When the wagon turned, she knew they were heading west, and then south as they rolled down a wide lane with regularly spaced fig trees. Their squat, thickly rounded boughs blocked some of the scenery, but she could make out the tiny candlelit windows of houses off the lane to the west and the dark shadow of a tall hill, looming to the east. Sounds of far-off haggling and the occasional low bellow from distant horns supplied a backdrop of city life from the lower elevations.

"What is it we're supposed to be doing on this trip?" Dyphina asked, breaking the hopeful enchantment Saffron's heart was casting, desperate to equate being outdoors again with being free.

Saffron's head knew better. "I presume we are being taken to the Twelve. They are trying to convince us to accept their sponsorship."

"You mean they're trying to convince you," Phaerim responded. "They could give two squirts of a goat's teat about the rest of us."

Saffron looked at Dyphina, then Thaelios. "We're in this together. None of us gets out unless we all do."

Phaerim continued. "That's very comforting to hear. I'm sure it will make a good bit of difference to those who survive the *Battle Royale*."

"What's in it for them?" Dyphina asked. "I mean, I can see how we might benefit from a wealthy patron, but why would they need to recruit us? Wouldn't any gladiator be yearning for the chance to secure sponsorship?"

Thaelios finally spoke up. "The Circle of Twelve probably recognized from her last fight how popular Saffron is likely to become." His head leaned back against the rail of the wagon, his solid blue eyes reflecting the stars. "They realize there will soon be competing offers and want to gain her loyalty before those offers manifest."

Dyphina shook her head. "But that doesn't really answer the question. What do *they* receive on their end?"

Phaerim took a stab, not looking up from leisurely threading his fingers around one another, "What does any wealthy bloke get from spending his money on frivolity? A rise in the breeches, I suppose. Not that I'd know – I've never had that kind of gold."

Saffron allowed herself a chuckle. "It's more than that. Success in the Arena is something the wealthy could never achieve on their own. They wouldn't want to, as it's far too risky. By buying an association with someone who does achieve that kind of success, however, they expand their influence in other circles. It's like a form of social currency. They prove that they are powerful by showing off their reach, and the implied threat that comes with it."

Everyone else in the back of the wagon grew silent. "That was impressive," Dyphina finally said. "How do you know so much about it?"

Saffron shook her head and peered over the side of the wagon. "I've spent some time at court." The road led them up an incline as they started to curl east, mounting the hill. "Shifting Dunes of Sesfaran, look at that!" She pointed at an impressive structure coming into view around the hillside.

The base of the building appeared to be octagonal, with three-story towers at the end of each point. The towers were all topped by gilded domes, shining brightly under the light of an orange flame that rose from the opening of a central half-dome. As the wagon drew closer, Saffron saw a number of citizens entering and exiting from three sets of open, bronze portals on what was undoubtedly the face of the building. Above the doors hung a large, golden, eight-pointed star, surrounded by a circle of painted, metallic fire.

"What is that place?" Saffron asked, leaning over the partition between her and the driver.

"Ah," the cloaked man exclaimed, seemingly happy to find his knowledge useful, "that is the recently completed Temple of Hellig-nok, one of the two major competing faiths in Zeblon.

The Hierarch controls not only the church, but one of the four gladiator stables as well."

"Hellig-nok? Is that the name of some god?"

"The god of Fire and the Eternal Stars, my Lady," said the driver.

Saffron sank back into the wagon bed, surprised. She knew of Criesha from Jaiden and the Order of the Rising Moon, and obviously Gholdur the Tyrant, whom the King-priest worshipped. Be'naj had mentioned her devotion to Shecclad. Were there more deities? Had all the old gods now returned to bestow their favor upon humanity? If that was the case, the world was a different place than she'd known her entire life. Even her home in Begnasharan might have drastically changed since she left.

Further eastward along the path and slightly higher up the hill, after passing modest homes, Saffron spotted another grand edifice north of the road. This time she did not have to ask. "To the left is the palace of the Caliph," their driver offered over his shoulder. Everyone in the back of the wagon took a peek over the edge. Carved pillars marked it as an abode of wealth, but at least in the dark, Saffron noted it was markedly less impressive than the cathedral to Hellig-nok.

Once they pulled past the palace and headed south again, the grade of the path grew even steeper and the structures more sparse. At last, they crested a rise onto the flat top of the hill. Night had fully fallen, and the plateau was darker than the rest of the city, with only a score or so of estates spread across its surface. Less noise from the populace carried this high, though the wind was stronger and replaced the sounds of civilization with its own howls.

Saffron looked about with interest as the wagon ambled up a central lane toward a sizable mansion. The path was lined alternately by plants of desert blooms and hollow globes of blown glass, sheltering lit candles. Their small, yellow lights were tinged by the green half-moon hanging large, near the horizon. It almost seemed like she had risen high enough to reach out and touch it.

The driver halted the wagon a dozen paces from a set of thick, stone steps leading up to a wide porch. "We've arrived," he said plainly as he stood and stretched his legs, then hopped down from his seat onto the path of crushed seashells.

Saffron noted three figures standing on the porch, staring out at them by the light of a single torch. As she and the others disembarked the wagon bed, their driver took quick, crunching steps to join the onlookers. Out of the shadows, a pair of stablehands emerged to unharness and tend the horses.

"What are you waiting for?" their driver asked when the four gladiators made no move to leave the vicinity of the wagon. With him standing in proximity to the others, Saffron could see that, though slender, he was still a short man, coming up only to their chests. "I didn't smuggle you all this way to gaze at the moon. You are the guests of honor, after all."

"I suppose we are," said Phaerim, unfolding his arms and gently kicking a round shell with the tip of his boot. "Shall we make the most of our wooing?" He made directly for the gathering on the porch, and Saffron shrugged at the others before following.

Once up the steps and closer to the torchlight, she could better make out the features of their hosts. The one holding the torch immediately drew her attention. Though she'd mistaken him for a man from afar, she saw he was clearly something else. The skin of his brow was rigid and curled back into small, serrated horns. His pupils were slit like a cat's, and the end of his nose was flat and upturned, revealing wide nostrils. When he smiled in greeting, he revealed sharp, jagged teeth.

"Welcome, Saffron and … friends." The voice came from a woman to the torchbearer's left who Saffron quickly recognized as other than human, too. She issued her greeting in Illanese, but then turned and directed something in melodious Eladrin to Thaelios. Her ears were not as elongated as the elwise apprentice's, though, and she was slightly taller – almost Saffron's height. Her hair was black, streaked with silver, and while her skin was the same shade as Saffron's, it possessed the same flecked, iridescent quality as Thaelios's. "I am Ezmina Skysilk," she returned to Illanese, "and this is a fortuitous night."

"You've already met Groilen, I presume." Ezmina gestured to their driver, who gave a short bow and winked.

"But, Groilen is … heavier," Saffron said with mild exasperation.

"He is also an Illusionist," Ezmina added, "and adept at changing appearances."

"A useful talent when you find yourself in need of breaking rules, no?" the slender Groilen said, winking once more.

"The tiefling with the torch is Sirran, our Unseen Seer, and to my left," Ezmina extended a palm, "is Gaeric, Chancellor of the Temple of Life and Blood." The two men nodded. "We are only a few of the Twelve, though we do not wish to overwhelm you with introductions. Suffice to say, you are welcome to the site of our enclave, and we thank you for coming. Shall we go inside?"

Groilen opened the front door, its smooth surface adorned with symbols, with a wave of his hand. Soft, blue light filled the antechamber beyond, and Saffron waited for their hosts to enter before following. Sparing a glance behind, she saw looks of wonderment on the faces of Cauzel's apprentices, and Dyphina didn't fight the wide grin breaking across hers.

Inside the house, the air was dry. The glowing blue light emanated from tinted candle globes on the wall, much like those along the mansion's approach. They passed through to a great hall with stairs rising up to a balcony that lined the far wall. Spacious archways opened to airy chambers on either side, while violet light globes dangled from the ceiling, casting a dreamlike tint upon the room. Once everyone gathered into the hall, the lights brightened of their own accord, and Ezmina addressed them again.

"As you may have noticed, our cabal does not discriminate its membership based on appearances – a rare quality that I see your team shares. A union of our agendas seems utterly natural to me, and we hope you'll agree." Ezmina smiled without showing any teeth, her solid-colored eyes just as difficult to read as Thaelios's.

Saffron recognized she may be hopelessly outclassed if trying anything but a direct approach. "Your home is impressive, but what we really need are answers about neutralizing these deathtraps around our necks." She lifted her chin to show off the metallic collar worn by all the Wolfspider's gladiators.

"Ah, yes," the raspy voice of the tiefling cut in. "Ayez has spoken to us about your predicament. If you will follow me?" Sirran gestured to the adjoining room left of the great hall.

"We shall take our leave now," Ezmina added. She and the other two members of the Twelve stayed rooted in place. "Hopefully you will decide to join us, and we shall see more of one another in the future. Either way, we will be watching your battles in the Arena with interest."

Saffron and her fellows bowed before following Sirran, who was already crossing the threshold into the next room. It appeared to be designed as a formal dining room, but sitting at the oval, mahogany table was the lone figure of Ayez. His robes seemed to consist of all colors at once. While he was still now, Saffron knew from their encounters in the Den of Sin that the pattern shifted hypnotically when he moved.

Curiously, hovering just above the surface of the table in front of him was what looked like a map made of colored light, projected in three-dimensional relief. Ayez had been studying it, and the light seemed to originate from a stone globe mounted in the center of the table, swirling with cloudy patterns of its own.

"Ah, you arrived safely!" Ayez said, smiling as he stood. "Excellent, and welcome." He reached forward, tapped the globe with his fingers, and the map disappeared.

Saffron walked to the edge of the table, which still separated her from their host. "Ayez, these are my companions: Dyphina, Thaelios, and Phaerim."

Ayez raised a hand in greeting and nodded to the lot of them. "I hope no one has scared you off from our potential partnership." He spared a sideways glance in Sirran's direction. The tiefling was still holding his torch, though the room was dimly lit by more candle globes – gold in this location. A body-length mirror rested on a stand at the back of the room. Saffron noted that while she could see the reflections of herself and the other gladiators, Sirran's image was absent, though he stood between her and the mirror.

Her eyes lingered on the oddity for a moment, but she returned her attention toward Ayez to answer. "Of course not. Everyone has been gracious."

"Though a little off-putting, if you ask me," Phaerim added.

Dyphina stared at him and shook her head slowly. "No one did."

"Well, ahem," Ayez coughed, "a full tour of the grounds can wait, but I have something to show you that I hope will sway you in our direction. If you will follow me?" He stepped to the far corner of the room, still on the opposite side of the table. Where the northern and eastern walls met, he stopped. Glass-paned windows revealed the fall of night outside, though the indoor lighting obscured any details other than the darkness.

As Saffron and the others rounded the table to join him, Ayez waved a bare palm across the air, parallel to one of the eastern windows. A panel of the wall clicked ajar on a hinge, moving outward. She had not previously seen a crease or other indicator of a hidden door.

Ayez pushed the wall wide open and continued outside, leading the four gladiators down a pebble-strewn path around the side of the house. Sirran did not follow. Without looking back, Ayez raised his voice to cut through the constant wind. "If I have judged correctly, some of you will enjoy this." The path sloped downward after a dozen yards, where the pebbles ended. They had reached the edge of the plateau the mansion stood upon.

Beyond, Saffron could hear the roar of the sea crashing against rocks far below, though the vantage didn't permit her to see it. What she'd envisioned as a sheer cliff, dropping to the ocean, turned out to be a steeply angled, rocky descent. A smoothed trail, containing several switchbacks, was cut into the weathered stone, dimly lit by enchanted, pole-mounted candle-globes every dozen paces. The trail pushed outward with every turn, eventually leading to a square landing where the edge of the hill finally disappeared downward.

Ayez trudged confidently down the path, and as Saffron followed, the ambient light she had barely noticed drifting up from the city proper vanished behind the hillside, creating an even starker difference between the illumination of the globes and the darkness of night. Luckily, the lamps had been distanced effectively, and she was able to keep sure footing all the way to the landing where Ayez waited. Circular lights were posted at each of its corners – pale green to match the cast of Criesha, when clouds parted enough to show it.

Grasping the eastward stone railing and looking out toward the distant horizon, he didn't speak until Phaerim stepped onto the platform, bringing up the rear. "Quite the view, is it not?"

The wind and surf joined to sing a song of power, and gazing upon the dark expanse of the ocean, Saffron could sense it. It made her feel small, so she gazed up at the sky where swift-moving clouds provided glimpses of the distant stars. She felt even smaller for a moment, then thought of Be'naj looking up at the same sky, somewhere. The flash of a smile was quickly smothered by a pang of intense loneliness and regret. She thought of her sister and Baron Rogan, undoubtedly together, possibly sharing the kind of life she hadn't even known she'd wanted.

"It is breathtaking," Dyphina finally answered, raising her voice to be heard. Saffron turned to find her companions all similarly mesmerized by their surroundings. The incessant wind whipping their hair and the taste of salt helped imprint the moment.

"The scenery is impressive, Ayez. Even more so, I'm sure, when you can see past the end of your own arm. But I'm not sure its memory alone is going to do us much good in the Arena." Phaerim owned the words, but his final sentiment echoed Saffron's thoughts.

"Of course, my friends." Ayez rotated to face each of them in a slow circle. "Another lesson in misdirection. It is not the majesty of the moonlight on the sea I brought you for." He gestured back toward the cliff they had descended, and Saffron could now see another path cutting almost straight back from the landing. It ended in a hollowed archway that would have been invisible in the shadows if not for three, glowing yellow runes placed evenly along its outline.

She waited for Ayez to once again lead the way, for though it was short, no more globes lit this new section of the path. The wind seemed even stronger as she cut across the indented stone trail in the dark, as if it was trying to push her off her feet onto the sharp rocks and down to the sea. She soon caught up with Ayez and watched as the glyphs went dark with another wave of his hand. Once they did, dim light leapt to her starved eyes from inside the tunnel beyond.

Ayez continued forward, taking them into a smooth, worked-stone corridor. After ten paces, it opened into the chamber from whence the light originated. Lamps were mounted on each of three tables within the hexagonal room, as well as a couple on opposite walls. Shelves of leather-bound books, hundreds of volumes in total, lined the four walls not bearing light.

A woman with black hair, tied back and off her shoulders, sat in a high-backed chair, working at one of the tables. She was inspecting an ornate, metal helmet through a monocle set to her left eye socket. Her low-cut, silk vest in sky blue matched her magnified, open eye.

"Myalyssa, our guests have arrived," Ayez announced, halting in front of the table.

The woman glanced over to verify the sorcerer's words, then set down the helmet and plucked the monocle from her socket. "Ah, of course. Welcome, friends." She stood. "Ayez must think highly of you," she said as she gestured to him with her monocle, "to allow entrance to our little subterranean workshop." Myalyssa placed her free hand on her hip as she regarded the newcomers, Saffron in particular. She shrugged. "That's enough for me."

Saffron's eyes flicked over the other tables, which were strewn with various metal instruments, jewels, and a few assorted pieces of clothing, before settling on the stone door across from where they entered. It must lead deeper into the hillside …

Ayez coughed to gain her attention before addressing his partner. "In front is Lady Saffron, the fire-singer I told you about."

"We could be sisters," Myalyssa stated matter-of-factly.

Ayez continued as if uninterrupted, "And, uh, I suppose she should finish up introductions, as I haven't formally met her companions myself."

"Yes, of course," Saffron remembered her manners and turned to her teammates. "Thaelios and Dyphina are apprentices to the Shaper, Cauzel Blackfeather, and behind them is Phaerim of Pasaxtree."

"I see we have added to the already unusual concentration of arcane talent under this roof." Myalyssa smiled, as if the thought pleased her. Her eyes settled on the collars around the gladiators' necks. "And I am Myalyssa Manaar, Artificer of the Twelve."

Ayez broke in, "She will be the one most directly researching a way to overcome your restrictive accessories." He nodded satisfactorily.

"Fascinating contraptions, by first appearances." Myalyssa raised her chin, straining for a better vantage. "May I inspect them more closely?"

"Oh, there will be more time for that," Ayez dismissed with a wave.

Saffron nodded. "Once we've agreed to work together."

"Precisely," Ayez affirmed. "But I wanted you to meet and at least present a glimpse of some benefits of accepting sponsorship from our Circle."

"Well," Phaerim interjected with a rueful smile, "not having to worry about exploding every time I upset the bosses is a good enough reason for me."

Saffron noticed his gaze rested squarely on Myalyssa as he spoke, and she rolled her eyes before addressing the woman herself. "Though without a guarantee of success, we will require something more definite. I've spoken to Ayez on the subject, but to make sure our motives align, I think my companions could benefit from personally hearing why you wish us to represent you in the first place."

Myalyssa glanced sideways at Ayez, then back at Saffron. "Certainly," she smiled. "To state it simply: the Wolfspider is bad for Zeblon. Given your position, I wouldn't assume I'd have to defend that. His underworld dealings are bolstered by an association with the Dread Lich. We oppose the influence of these murderers in our city, and popular support for our cause, won by you in the Arena, would go far in dealing with them."

Phaerim shrugged. "Sure, sounds good to me. How do we start?"

Thaelios followed directly on his heels. "And I suppose the Circle of Twelve would fill the void left by ousting the Wolfspider?"

Saffron watched for their hosts' reactions: Myalyssa's eyes narrowed, and Ayez licked his bottom lip.

The artificer's hand relaxed from her hip. "The future is not spoken for, but I suppose many would stand to benefit from the absence of the Wolfspider's brutality on the streets of Zeblon. Do you not wish our help in the Arena? Yours is a more literal fight for survival, after all."

"What, precisely, could you do to help us there?" Dyphina's voice floated over from the shelves at the edge of the room where she was already inspecting the spines of bound volumes.

"Ah," Ayez said, wandering over to the shelves himself. "I think we have just the thing, here." He scanned the books with a weathered index finger until choosing one. He pulled it off the shelf and handed it to Dyphina.

"Incantations for Close-Quarters Combat," she read.

"As your sponsors, we would be happy to lend you the book to prepare for your upcoming battle. There are several wonderfully useful enchantments within." Ayez looked to each of them with wide, expectant eyes. "So, do we have a partnership?"

Saffron checked with Phaerim first, who shrugged and nodded at the same time, though a little too eagerly to sell his indecision. She caught Thaelios's gaze next. His lips were stretched thin in consideration, but he relented soon enough and nodded as well. Dyphina had completely missed the nonverbal cue and was already flipping through the book with a hungry mind. Saffron took that as a 'yes.'

"We will fight under your sponsorship, though I want these collars removed as soon as possible." She aimed for somewhere between a firm request and a demand, though her heart thumped with a hope she dared not voice.

"Of course," Myalyssa assured her. "I'd be happy to take a closer look now, if you'd like."

Chapter 19

Battle Royale

Not unbravely, Phaerim volunteered to let Myalyssa inspect his collar. She promised to be careful and not allow her examination to drift over the dangerous threshold of tampering. Nevertheless, Saffron saw his relief when the Artificer finished, giving them leave to return to the Wolfspider's Pen. Myalyssa promised to let them know once she had run some experiments and had results to share.

Groilen delivered the gladiators safely back before the arrival of the dawn shift. While Saffron spent the ride searching for familiar patterns among the stars, trying to savor the feel of the outside air on her face, Dyphina strained her eyes trying to read what she could of the Circle's spellbook.

As much as Saffron wanted to dwell on the promise of their excursion and the possibility that freedom was nearly in their grasp, the reality of awakening in the Wolfspider's cage the next morning rendered that impossible.

Zygrim wanted to speak about coordinating practices so each of them could have a better sense of the capabilities of their peers. While she knew that would be beneficial during the fight, Saffron held reservations about giving away too many secrets. Why was it so difficult for her to trust?

Just after their morning meal, before their scheduled training time, Harzhim showed up to give a little extra insight about the conditions of the upcoming event.

"I know every battle in the Arena seems the most important to those involved in combat, but rest assured this battle holds special importance to others as well." The Wolfspider's Consul had dark circles under his eyes, made more severe by the torch he held aloft as he spoke. Saffron once again translated his Begnari for her companions. "In fact, this may well be the most significant event to take place in the Arena since its construction, so you can expect the experience to feel different," Harzhim continued.

"Your owner" – Saffron's muscles tensed when she heard the word – "expects victory and has considerable wealth at stake. He has assured me rewards will be in line for those who acquit themselves well – rewards that shall be realized during your next visit to the Den of Sin. You shall also have your choice of weapons from his stores for the fight, and I am personally overseeing the commission of some finely-crafted additions."

Harzhim lowered his torch as if his arm were suddenly tired, and his inflection dropped with it. "No doubt the other houses will take steps of their own to snatch victory, but I have seen firsthand that this pen boasts some of the finest gladiators in Zeblon. As I stated yesterday, the fighting shall continue until a third of the participants are eliminated; a great horn blast shall be the signal to stay your arms. Those who do not heed it will be punished severely, so take care."

Zygrim took a step closer to the Consul, though the wall of the cage still separated them. "Any chance you can get a word to my sponsor, Harzhim? I have a request I'd like to make before we get too close to the battle."

Harzhim nodded. "Of course." He looked from one side of the gathered gladiator crowd to the other and when no one else spoke, nodded again. "I will leave you to your training, then."

"All right, you soft-bodies," Zygrim bellowed as Harzhim departed, "you heard him. Time to work this crew until you're sharp as knives. If you die this week, you're going to have to answer to me!"

Saffron allowed Zygrim to take the lead, though she noticed that Dyphina and Thaelios buried their noses in their new book when the other wasn't using it. They seemed to develop a system for trading off, and she sincerely hoped whatever they were learning would prove useful.

As for herself, she showed enough prowess with her *ghostwind* fighting style to keep the other gladiators from pressing her about rumors of magical powers. Still, Saffron found time to steal away over the course of the week to practice her singing, making sure she could call upon her inner fire when needed.

Midweek, a courier arrived with slips of parchment, which Harzhim delivered personally to Saffron and Zygrim. She wondered if the Consul read their correspondence, but decided not to dwell on it. Hers was from Ayez, who passed along a word of warning:

"Sirran has learned that the Temple of Hellig-nok plans to make an example out of you for your unsanctioned use of fire-magic. Beware Krygos's gladiators in your upcoming battle."

Saffron was already planning on being careful, but knowing she was being specifically targeted meant less attention going toward the teammates she felt responsible for; keeping them safe was her primary worry. She didn't ask Zygrim what his parchment said, and the bulky brawler didn't offer.

On the final day of practice before the Battle Royale, Saffron took time to gain the measure of each participant from the Wolfspider's pens. Wemic and Nueril sparred against one another and smiled when she asked how they were feeling.

"About as good as can be expected," Wemic responded, showing off with a spinning transfer of his sword from one hand to the other.

Phaerim practiced simultaneous slashes with his twin daggers, making sure his left hand moved just as quickly as his right. "Staying low and unnoticed while you steal all the attention," he responded when she inquired about his strategy. Saffron smiled. She knew she had perhaps been a little overprotective, but it had served them well so far.

Zygrim's large body was wrapped around Charilo, moving his limbs for him in exact measures, instructing on combination moves that would be helpful if he somehow managed to execute them on his own. He made eye contact with Saffron as she passed, and nodded; she responded in kind.

When she got to Thaelios and Dyphina, they were the only ones without weapons within reach. Instead, they sat on a bench beside one another, poring over their book, trying to keep their voices low as they argued.

"What seems to be the problem?" They both looked up at Saffron's interjection. She twirled her shortspear with one hand, then staked it in the ground.

"Dyphina is wasting her time! She's concentrated most of her efforts on an incantation she doesn't have the materials for." Thaelios spoke more animatedly than Saffron could ever remember. Perhaps it took the topic of magic to extract his passion.

Dyphina rolled her eyes. "It's only a few nutshells! Harzhim promised it wouldn't be a problem."

"Then where are they?" Thaelios countered. "You need to let me teach you *Mirrored Image*. You could probably do a decent job if you'd let me show you—"

"Keep your twinkling illusions! Sorry, but that's not the kind of Shaping I'm good at. Ask Saffron, she knows. I do much better with vocal manifestations. Honestly, she would probably be a better teacher than Cauzel."

Thaelios scoffed. "That's ridiculous." He glanced up at Saffron, "No offense," then back to Dyphina, "but Master Blackfeather has forgotten more about Shaping than both of you together remember. You just need to stop daydreaming during lessons."

Saffron frowned at Thaelios, but didn't disagree. "Truthfully, Dyphina, I'm still learning myself – I doubt there's much I could teach you. I don't even understand how some have the knack for this sort of thing while others don't. But if there's anything I can show you regarding fighting, I'd be happy to work with you."

"No, I don't think so. I'd be too far behind everyone we're facing to make a difference with that. I just need Harzhim to show up with those nuts. I'm sure he will, any hour now. Maybe at dinner tonight …" Dyphina stood in the midst of her own thought and wandered back toward Wemic and Nueril, as if they'd stolen her attention.

This left an opening for Zygrim, who appeared out of nowhere to take over Dyphina's abandoned seat. Large as he was, his thick thigh was forced to press against Thaelios's. "Saffron, Thaelios," he nodded. Perspiration formed droplets across his shaved head, collecting along his brow, and his breath was a little ragged. "So, are you both prepared for tomorrow?" He was looking straight down at Thaelios's wide eyes. "I'm guessing you've got a few tricks planned, no? Anything I should be ready for?"

Saffron kept her mouth shut and shrugged, though Zygrim's face remained set in Thaelios's direction, and after a short silence the Eladrin answered.

"I'm certainly going to try and make our opponents feel as uncomfortable as possible."

"Well, I know *that's* something you're blessed at." Zygrim let out an uneasy laugh, followed by a wide grin.

Thaelios looked back at him with a closed mouth and those unreadable eyes, and Saffron decided she could endure no more awkwardness. "I'm going to do some stretches," she said before walking away, though she doubted either of them were paying attention.

As Saffron ate her dinner, Dyphina's squeal of delight drew her attention. She saw one of the guards standing opposite the giddy apprentice on the other side of the cage, and Dyphina looking down into her cupped hands with glee. It appeared Harzhim had come through on his promise.

Falling asleep that night was difficult. Saffron tried to visualize the next day's battle, humming the songs she would use to create different effects of flame, but her thoughts drifted around the continent, wondering what others were up to. Her parents were no doubt missing their daughters, but she was thankful they remained ignorant of her predicament.

Was Dhania still with Baron Rogan? Had her little sister managed to find happiness with the man she'd been unable to commit to? Saffron hoped they were taking care of one another as Rogan searched for his son.

Even though she loathed confinement, Saffron a thousand times preferred this captivity to what Dhania had to survive in the fortress of Hope's End. She at least had the opportunity to defend herself when men sought to injure her.

Shaking off thoughts of her sister's torture brought Be'naj to mind. What she had endured upon reaching adolescence in her homeland was sickening. Why did so many feel the need to strike out at anything different than themselves? That reaction seemed consistent across the various cultures she'd encountered. Be'naj had been so gentle and giving to her, a stranger, and now no doubt thought Saffron a liar who had abandoned her as well. She longed to find her and explain what happened – one of the many wrongs she needed to right.

When she finally fell asleep, Saffron dreamt she flew with angel's wings, but couldn't figure out how to come back down.

She drifted higher and higher, until finally becoming lost in the immeasurable blue sky. She awoke feeling nervous and directionless.

The morning had an entirely new energy to it. During breakfast, the gladiators could hear the occasional, muted blaring of horns from outside. The guards escorted couriers and wealthy patrons back and forth through the tunnels. Saffron noticed nearly all of them stealing glances at the pens' occupants.

At last, Harzhim arrived to lead them to the armament room, adjacent to the tunnel into the Arena. Saffron allowed them to store her armor there after her last fight so she could have it cleaned. She saw new editions of equipment for the gladiators to choose from, and most of her teammates browsed the racks while she separated to a secluded corner to change into her supple, red leather.

"Here," Zygrim said as he approached. He offered a thin strip of black bark, coated in a sticky substance.

"What is this?" she asked.

"I obtained it from my sponsor. Put it under your tongue and let it dissolve. It'll help keep your head clear during the battle."

Saffron peeked around his massive shoulders, now covered by the spiked guards of a chest harness.

"I already handed them out to the others," he stated, following the track of her eyes. "Trust me – you'll be glad once you're out there."

Saffron nodded and took the strip, smelling it before placing it in her mouth. It possessed a scent like sassafras root, and she detected no reason to offend her large partner. Appearing satisfied, Zygrim returned to the racks and Saffron hurried to pick out a round shield and a spear with a nice, flexible shaft. Phaerim had draped a shirt of mail over his torso, adorned a steel cap, and selected a pair of long, polished daggers. Thaelios once again went for a longbow, while Dyphina chanted softly in the corner, her closed fist resting over her breast.

The crowd grew louder as they filled the stands, and Saffron was sure the Arena would be packed. It was almost time. She forced herself to take deep breaths, concentrating on the feel of the wood in her hand, the weight of the shield on her arm. The sound of metal being drawn from a scabbard beside her snatched her attention, and when her eyes went from the scimitar in Dyphina's hand to her friend's face, she blinked hard several times, assuming something was wrong with her vision.

Dyphina's complexion was no longer the bright and smooth, pale brown of an Illanese woman who'd spent many days outdoors. It had transformed into a course, gray-brown covering that looked more akin to tree bark than human skin. Combined with her naturally green hair, she could almost be confused for a walking branch.

"What?" Saffron failed to finish her thought before the question was driven from both of their minds by the opening outer doors. This was it. Sunlight and a burst of warmer air joined the roar of the thousands who had come to see men and women of low rank kill one another for their own survival.

The Caliph's Arena guards strode in to usher the participants out, and Saffron took a quick look around to make sure everyone was accounted for. "Thaelios, your bow!" The silver-skinned Eladrin's head swiveled to locate his weapon, which was leaning on a rack right beside him. She hustled up to Phaerim, who seemed eager to step into the open air, and shouted in his ear to be heard over the cheering, "Stay defensive, protect Dyphina. I'll watch over Thaelios."

He nodded, daggers in hand, then shielded his eyes from the sun as they emerged from the darkened tunnel. All the teams were filing out from four, evenly-spaced openings in the disc-shaped stadium's base.

Once outside, the hollering of the spectators was deafening. The warm, sand floor had been decorated by a dusting of the short, green needles of desert conifers, which mitigated the harsh reflection of the noon-lit sky. Saffron quickly took stock of the other teams, realizing that spacing was going to be even more important with so many combatants.

The fighters of the Caliph's House had all adorned metal armor for the occasion, an expensive but potent advantage. Light shimmered off polished breastplates and greaves, helms and gauntlets. *Your steel won't save you from fire*, Saffron thought as she shifted her observation to the next team.

Gladiators from the House of Life and Blood, Pnemonesis's temple, alternately wielded nets and tridents, which Saffron acknowledged as an interesting tactic. The reach of the tri-pronged spears could certainly cause a problem all their own, and being trapped under the heavy, woven webbing would create a deadly impairment. Fortunately for her and the others sponsored by the Circle of Twelve, Gaeric had given assurances that his temple's warriors would target them last, assuming similar treatment.

That left the members of the House of Eternal Flame. Hierarch Krygos supposedly had a talented band of gladiators, whose leader rivaled Zygrim the Bull in terms of crowd popularity, for good reason. What's more, Saffron had to pay attention to the warning that, as a group, they would specifically be seeking to teach her a lesson today. She briefly wondered if any of them had ever faced an opponent using the *ghostwind*.

Once all the competitors were out on the sand, a moment of heavy uncertainty settled as the doors to the pens were closed behind them. The crowd quieted in anticipation, and Saffron scanned parts of it to see if she recognized any members of the Twelve in attendance. She couldn't pick any out, though many of the audience wore colored sashes according to their favorite House: red, blue, black, and white.

Saffron thought for a moment that perhaps a speech or introduction might precede the battle, but it must have been delivered before they emerged because suddenly a loud horn blew, echoing through the Arena, and the crowd erupted in cheers once again.

The opposing gladiators started moving forward and Saffron instinctively crouched, tucking her shield and spear closer. She looked back for Thaelios, ready to remind him to stay behind her, but he was already fitting an arrow to his bow while the other members of the Wolfspider's House fanned out. With such a crowd, ranged weapons would become a liability soon enough.

Zygrim was far from cautious, screaming a ferocious battle-cry as he surged toward the Caliph's fighters, whirling his spiked chain like a sawing, metallic whirlpool. Thaelios's arrow flew past her into the shield of one of the Caliph's gladiators, and while she had time, Saffron switched her spear to her shield hand and sang, holding out her empty palm to summon a fire-blossom.

She had just blown it from her hand, sending the orb in a fiery trail toward an unsuspecting gladiator, when Phaerim, already engaged with a combatant of his own, called out from a few strides to her left, "Saffron!"

Turning in the direction of her name, she barely had time to lift her shield as a heavy war hammer came crashing down upon it, bruising her arm under its weight and jarring her loosely held spear to the ground. She fell to a knee and desperately reached for her spear as a second attacker joined the first. They were from the Temple of Hellig-nok's stables and must have rushed forward as soon as they saw her begin Shaping.

Saffron grabbed the shaft of her spear, along with a handful of sand and green needles, and rolled over on her right shoulder, eluding a second crushing blow from the hammer slinger. His partner adjusted position to better aim a downward slash of his sword at her head, but doing so opened his stance to a biting stab of her spear-tip. Whatever they may have heard, these men were not prepared for the speed of her reflexes.

An instant later, she had pulled her weapon loose from his belly, retaking her feet as he fell away. The battlefield quickly devolved into chaos. The warrior with the hammer danced sideways in both directions, trying to get her to overcommit one way or the other, not comprehending his heavier weapon was never going to be faster than her reaction.

With his focus upon Saffron, the man was caught completely by surprise as Phaerim plunged his daggers into the base of his neck from behind. His arms slackened and dropped his hammer as he grunted out his painful demise. Phaerim pushed his booted foot against the man's back, kicking him to the ground while creating leverage to unsheathe his twin blades from his victim's flesh.

Saffron nodded her thanks, and as Phaerim responded, her head started to feel funny. Her vision grew more acute, and she was suddenly able to pick out precise movements from the haze of battle-frenzy all around her. She noticed Zygrim, perhaps fifteen paces away, surrounded by a cadre of four of the Caliph's gladiators, swinging his chain to keep them at bay.

Taking a quick look behind her, she saw Thaelios surrounded by four copies of himself, confounding an enemy as the enchanted-skinned Dyphina used the diversion to cast a spell. Judging them in no immediate danger, Saffron yelled "Keep an eye on them," to Phaerim, then charged to Zygrim's aid.

A few steps later, out of nowhere, she felt a snap and yank around her ankles as a whip encircled and took her feet from under her. The next instant she was on the ground, her mouth full of sand and her hip throbbing from taking the brunt of her fall. She held onto her spear, though. Coughing, she rose to her knees, only to be yanked down by another pull.

Although the din of the crowd hovered over her like a raincloud, Saffron could distinctly hear the shuffling of feet around her in the sand, accompanied by derisive laughter. The juxtaposition was an odd sensation, but provided clarity. Lying on her back, she wedged the tip of her spear between the whip and her boot, forcing it away.

A shadow above her gave just enough warning to keep the head of an axe from decapitating her. The force of the downward blow still knocked the rim of her bronze-plated shield into her face, opening a cut above her eye and ringing her head like a bell. Her faculties recovered much faster than normal, however, and noticing the approach of another set of boots to her right, she whipped the butt of her spear outward to sweep the legs of their owner.

Saffron looked back to the axe wielder as she hurriedly tried to sit up, but he already held his weapon over his head for another chop, and she wasn't moving fast enough. She seemed able to taste every one of the dozens of sand grains still on her lips and tongue.

Beyond the scope of imagined good fortune, the man suddenly fumbled with the handle of his weapon and it fell from his grip, landing behind him. As he cursed, Saffron looked beyond him and saw the green-haired Dyphina extending a hand in his direction. Whatever she had cast no doubt saved Saffron's life.

Saffron had just struggled to her feet when the sharp lick of a whip lashed against an exposed strip of her thigh – one of her armor's shortcomings. She immediately sank into a defensive crouch, assessing her position. Ignoring the moving wall and metallic clang of fighting bodies further away, she narrowed her attention to the three individuals encircling her, all members of the House of the Temple of Everlasting Flame.

A short-haired woman with a cruel smile teased her whip back and forth, creating waves along its length that vibrated with potential pain. The man she'd knocked to the ground was back on his feet, aiming a longspear toward her with both hands. The fellow who'd dropped his axe had picked it back up, though he held it near the head with one hand while brushing the other against his leather leggings, as if wiping grease from his palm.

Blood trailed down Saffron's brow, feeling like a spider crawling along her skin, until it reached the outer corner of her left eye. She hummed low at first, spreading her watch among all three gladiators, hoping she threatened enough to keep them beyond reach while her song built in energy. She didn't know if they had seen her fight against the rauggin, but even so, perhaps they wouldn't recognize the effect she was attempting to Shape.

The warrior with the spear lunged forward in a harsh thrust, but she easily shifted sideways and deflected his weapon with the rim of her shield without faltering in her composition. The familiar heat building inside her was reaching a crescendo when doubt suddenly threatened to subvert her intentions.

Would using magic to hurt those she couldn't specifically define as evil forever taint her power? Right on the precipice of release, her inner-flame wavered.

Then, the woman with the whip lashed out again. Though its lick ineffectually struck the strong kank hide of her armor, the cracking sound bolstered Saffron's resolve. More might die if she didn't act quickly. With her brow creased in concentration, she finished her song and a nova of orange fire spread from her in horizontal waves.

Despite all three of her circling adversaries being swept up in its path, they remained as unharmed as if merely a hot desert wind had blown past. Saffron snapped from face to face; they were all smiling, sharing the same jest.

"The Hierarch has gifted us protection from your tricks, flame-witch," the man with the axe bellowed. "And now, you will pay for your heresy." He nodded, and his partner with the spear joined him in closing ranks.

Saffron turned her attention to the one with the longspear – its length would allow him to strike first. As he readied a thrust, however, his limbs started to spasm, shaking uncontrollably and rendering him barely able to grip his weapon. Saffron immediately looked for Dyphina, but she was beside Phaerim, brandishing her scimitar with her back to Saffron.

Taking advantage of the gladiator's confusion, Saffron struck the weapon from his hand with a spinning kick, then turned to her opponent with the axe. Her heightened perception honed in on Thaelios, whose outstretched hands pointed toward the man she had just disarmed. She nodded thanks just as another gladiator cast a heavy net over the eladrin Shaper.

"Thaelios!" she yelled. This shouldn't be happening; the Temple of Life and Blood were supposed to leave her team alone. Saffron moved at the last breath to block the swing of her attacker's axe, though a painful shock from the blow still vibrated through her abused shield-arm. She backed up, putting space between them as she continued keeping an eye on Thaelios. He was too far away to aid, and the feeling of helplessness partially paralyzed her.

Zygrim, however, had heard her cry. Recognizing Thaelios's plight, he dropped his chain and abandoned his teammates who were gathered before a quartet of the Caliph's armored gladiators. Saffron watched as those enemies took quick advantage of the Bull's departure. A vicious sword thrust pierced Charilo's chest and he fell to his knees with a surprised grunt.

Nueril screamed furiously and hacked off the attacker's extended arm before redirecting his blade upward, under the stunned man's ribcage. Blood spurted from his victim's mouth, staining Nueril's face, though his eyes blazed with an uncaring frenzy.

Saffron charged her own attacker, surprising him, and he stumbled backward to avoid her spear thrust, tripping on his own feet. Before she could finish him, though, a lash from her third opponent encircled her weapon.

Her eyes darted back to Thaelios as she tugged her spear, trying to free it from the coiled leather. As a Temple of Life and Blood warrior aimed a trident thrust at the vulnerable apprentice, Zygrim did the only thing he had time to in order to save him. Sliding to his knees in the sun-warmed sand, he placed himself between the tri-pronged, steel point and the ensnared Eladrin.

Saffron jolted at the scream of rage and pain from Zygrim, almost losing her own weapon. Zygrim grabbed the handle of the protruding trident, and after pulling it free, yanked it sideways with such ferocity its wielder stumbled to the ground.

With Thaelios momentarily safe, Saffron attended to her own preservation, spinning to use the rim of her shield to apply pressure onto the whip, tightening it enough to twist her spear's shaft free. A horrible cry from Nueril foretold another likely tragedy, and then suddenly a great horn blew, echoing above even the raucous crowd.

Saffron tensed, then relaxed as she rapidly surveyed the Arena floor. The gladiators, including the nearby woman with the whip, reluctantly lowered their weapons as if unsure whether a trick was being played. Her breath coming in huffs, Saffron let her shield arm hang and turned toward the sound of the horn, which blew for a second time.

The curved instrument was mounted in front of a covered platform, which had more space between its seats than the typical section. There, she locked gazes with a man dressed in a black vest over his grey tunic. His eyes intensely scrutinized her, his black hair and goatee peppered with grey matched his outfit.

A younger woman in brighter, sunshine hues stood beside him, taking his arm as he rose and smiled. He finally redirected his eyes as the crowd around him started shaking his hand and offering congratulations. This must be none other than the Wolfspider, she realized – the man who believed he *owned* her.

Saffron relented to seek out her friends, but not before sparing withering looks for those she'd been fighting. About a dozen figures lay still on the sand, with others kneeling either with injuries or to check on the fallen. Her heart stuck in her throat as she tried to account for everyone, bracing for the inevitable bad news. The clarity she'd possessed only moments ago seemed to be replaced by a cloudy confusion of blood-painted sand, pine needles, and groans of the wounded.

Faces. Find their faces. She located her friends huddled around Zygrim, who grimaced while holding a blood-soaked hand against the wound under his left arm. Dyphina tore the hem of her tunic to use as a bandage, and Thaelios squeezed Zygrim's right hand, which completely enveloped his. Phaerim was watching Wemic, compassion in his eyes, as the man staggered toward the bodies of the fallen Charilo and Nueril.

I have to get us out of here, Saffron thought.

Chapter 20

One Small Scale

As Izefet promised, Annoxoria's new tongue took some getting used to. The way she was able to taste the air filled her with excitement, though learning to speak without a severe lisp was an ongoing trial. She was anxious about Thuvian returning in a few days and how he might judge her incomplete transformation. The fact she had given up part of her finger, no less, worried her that he might dismiss the entire process as madness.

Sitting in her private laboratory, staring at the recently emptied vial of Nightwing venom in her hand, she determined the only course left to maintain dignity in her lover's eyes was to infiltrate his sister's lair and steal a scale. Like most adult dragons, Sepathia had claimed an expansive territory, and Annoxoria didn't have time to seek out another. As dangerous as it sounded, she would rather face death at the hands of a scheming Nightwing than continue indefinitely in her borrowed body or risk Thuvian rejecting her for her recently impetuous decisions.

She also knew he might forbid her to seek out Sepathia's lair when he returned, so she had to leave soon. She set the glass cylinder down and stood, deciding what she needed to bring: ingredients for her shrouding spell as well as a few offensive incantations, should she run into Thralls or the like, and lantam jelly to protect her skin from acid, at the very least.

Annoxoria retrieved the leather satchel she used for field excursions and filled it with spell components and salves as they popped into her head. Thuvian kept a map hidden in a footlocker that she knew he'd marked his sister's lair upon – she would have to borrow that as well.

She threw a skinning knife into the crowded satchel to top it off. Though not likely to overwhelm a larger opponent in hand-to-hand combat, she wanted a means to at least end her own life if she appeared in for a worse fate.

She dressed in scaled, black leather travelling garb, including her taloned gloves. If she was going to take the final step to assume a dragon's body, she felt it important to look the part. Annoxoria looped the satchel over her shoulder, then pinned a black cloak around her with a gold, draconic brooch Thuvian had gifted her. Finally, she retrieved the map from Thuvian's locker.

Catching her reflection in the full-length mirror as she left the bedroom, she let her new tongue flick out of her mouth, watching it with renewed awe and solidifying her resolve. She was doing what had to be done.

Annoxoria told the chamberlain to inform Lord Skullreaver that she was travelling to Rinn-Rhulian and would be returning shortly after him. After exiting Nightwing Castle, she ascended the first hill on foot. Though it was nigh past midday, the outside air had a thin bite of cold to it.

Once she'd crested the rise and was beyond any curious eyes that might be observing from the castle's mighty towers, she used her magic to Shape a steed of shadow and smoke, much like the one she saw the ghast, Gullagion, leave upon. She had to make good speed if she was going to arrive before losing her nerve and return before Thuvian grew suspicious.

Though the day warmed ever so slightly once she'd escaped the elevation of the Wyrmsmoke Mountains, it was clear by the dissipating deciduous foliage that winter would be in full force soon. The summoned steed heeded every adjustment of its reins without objection, and soon her mind was free to wander to what it would feel like to finally become the creature she was born to be.

How her dragon spirit ended up in a human's body was a mystery she might never solve, but she would soon fly like she was supposed to. She would have rows of flexible, glossy scales, and the strength to help Thuvian take what was rightly his.

Annoxoria's surge of elation lasted until night descended. Her mount started evaporating, one wisp of smoke at a time, and she knew she needed to find a place to shelter until morning. She'd travelled parallel to, but west of the Ifelian Corridor, heading north. She wanted to stay clear of eladrin territory for as long as she could, but also remain unseen by nosy human travelers along the road.

If she started early the next morning, she should arrive at the lair by the following nightfall. Drawing closer would demand taking further steps to avoid detection from Sepathia herself, but those could wait for the morrow as well. She selected a spot sheltered by a protruding rock formation on one side to bed down and watched in the little light that reached the clearing as her mount finally dissipated completely on the wind.

She'd grown used to commanding others and, though certainly capable in a number of ways, wasn't sure if she should risk lighting a campfire. The night would be cold for sure, but without a companion to share watch, she didn't want to draw attention to her position. Half an hour of shivering eventually made up her mind.

It took longer than she expected to find and gather fallen wood in the dark. A chill wind had picked up, and her fingers grew numb by the time she returned to her shelter with an ample supply. At least the wood was dry, and she soon had a healthy blaze to thaw out her extremities.

Alone in the dark, with no one to lean on, doubts started to creep in. How was she supposed to trick a demonstrably clever adversary whose existence spanned several of her lifetimes? Sepathia had always hated her half-brother, and Annoxoria could vouch for at least one serious attempt on his life. She had numerous, blindly-loyal followers, not to mention untold others cowed into serving her out of fear. None of them would bat an eyelash at gaining favor by murdering Annoxoria.

The more she thought about it, the more Annoxoria realized she had to hope Sepathia was otherwise occupied when she arrived, or this was going to be a one-way trip. Owls and other night creatures grew more vocal as the night drew on, and she decided to allow her fire to start dying down and get some sleep.

She drew her cloak around her and produced a thin blanket from her satchel, which she used as a pillow. Before long, her dreams all seemed to be punctuated by Thuvian's disappointment in her. Thankfully, dawn came without molestation from other creatures, and her ashy logs still smoldered in morning's first light.

Annoxoria was bone cold and didn't feel rested, but drew enough focus to summon another horse from the shadows. She continued north, and shortly after noon, the day started darkening again as clouds rolled in to reinforce the forest canopy. She dared to head to the road, which had markers every few miles, to verify her position. No other wagons or horses came her way, and when she found the next marker, it confirmed she was getting close.

Crossing over to the eastern side of the Corridor, she headed deeper into the woods, which grew wetter as she went. Another hour found her at the edge of a bog, where she dismounted. Her leather boots sank about an inch into the soft ground when she landed. She pulled the large jar of lantam jelly from her satchel and smeared it across her exposed skin. It would help protect her from acidic spittle, should the Nightwing bite her. After scouring for the correct ingredients, she cast a spell that encased her in a globe of magical shadow.

Leaving her steed behind, she picked her way through the swamps, the dimness following where she went. She was looking for a sloping chasm into the earth, not far from a steep rock face that shouldn't be difficult to spot. Given the uneven ground and the growing pools of water, Annoxoria had to devote most of her attention to where she stepped, though she tested the air every so often with her forked tongue to taste for signs of the dragon's lair.

The swamp was eerily silent beyond the occasional bird flitting within view to watch her. A strange, perpetual gloom settled in, possibly aided by her own spell. She kept one hand near her satchel, ready to draw out spell components if a reason presented itself. The other hand grasped whatever branches or trunks grew within reach, to steady herself as her boots continued to sink in the soft earth.

The pools that had been steadily increasing in size finally coalesced into an actual lake, blocking her progress and diverting her southward along its bank. At last, she heard the unmistakable sound of water moving, and following it, came to the edge of a cliff, over which the lake poured in a tumbling waterfall.

Over the rim, she saw the pooling water carried off by a northward stream. Further south, the cliff wrapped around to cradle a moss-covered, rocky mass, below which the earth sank. Annoxoria's heartbeat quickened – this might be the place! Her first instinct was to check for signs of Sepathia's presence; it wouldn't do to be caught so quickly unawares. Hopefully, if this was the lair, its outside would be littered with enough old scales she could simply pick one to her liking.

Annoxoria crouched, narrowing her eyes as she scanned the cauldron below for telltale signs of a Nightwing's passage. No obvious indentations marked the ground, but the nearby pool would make for a good drinking source. Then, she saw it: what she'd initially discounted from a distance as a cluster of white mushrooms looked more and more like a pile of discarded bones, the longer she stared.

She had to find a way down to check, though peering along the slope of the rock face, it seemed a bit steep. She was probably about ten body-lengths above the water's surface at the bottom of the waterfall, and it didn't look deep enough to absorb a plunge from this height. If only she'd thought to bring a feather, she could use magic to descend ... she suddenly remembered the birds alighting periodically during her journey through the swamp, and turned back to search for any usable feathers.

She broke into a grin when she finally found one stuck to a thorny bramble within reach. Small, black, and puffy, it would serve quite well. *Featherfall* was one of the first cantrips she'd learned as a novice Shaper. After casting it, she confidently stepped over the edge of the cliff, gliding safely to the ground below, her momentum limited by the spell.

Once her feet touched the spongy turf, her smile faded as the sober reality of being mere steps from the opening of a dragon's lair assaulted her. The stench did as well, wafting out from the chasm to hang on the heavy air. She crouched in response, instinctively seeking cover though there was nowhere to hide, even with the sphere of shadow encircling her.

Although she'd hoped Sepathia would be gone when she arrived, the fact that no clear resistance had yet manifested triggered impressions of being lured into a trap. Surely no one could have known she was coming. Remembering why she was there, Annoxoria scanned the area for loose Nightwing scales. If she could find one quickly, she might leave before anyone was the wiser.

She first looked around the periphery of the area devoid of trees. It made sense for the space to be open – Sepathia would need room to take off and land. Perhaps some would have fallen off during that process …

Annoxoria saw nothing from where she stood and realized her feet hadn't moved since she'd descended from the cliff. Fighting to subdue her fear, she finally uprooted them. Creeping around the rock formation, she checked as quickly as possible for scales, expecting to see one at every turn: nothing. She started expecting Thralls of the Nightwing to erupt from the forest at any moment, but the world seemed stuck in a twilight hour where no progress was allowed, for good or ill.

She passed the pile of bones she'd seen from afar. They were gnawed on and picked clean: the remains of deer, lizardfolk, and who knew what else, sitting as a clear indication of a large predator nearby. The smell of the clearing was distinctly dragon as well, yet there was not a single scale on the ground outside the lair. Annoxoria cursed, realizing she would have to go in.

Surely Sepathia wasn't around. Could it be possible she was inside and somehow unaware of Annoxoria? If she was aware, did the Nightwing possess the patience to not expose herself at the first opportunity? These thoughts played off each other, nearly paralyzing Annoxoria with indecision.

Then, without conscious instruction, her tongue snaked out and tasted the pungent air, permeated by the elements seeping up from the gaping sinkhole on the other side of the rock protrusion. The whole place reeked of dragon, but she didn't taste one's presence coming from the chasm. With the reminder of her partial transformation, all the reasons for her excursion bubbled to the fore of her consciousness. They liberated her, and she resolutely made her way toward the lair's entrance.

The rocks sloping into the earth were scored by deep grooves. Slick lichen, green, saturated vines, and colonies of fungi cascaded down their wide surface. The dampness only served to strengthen the smell, and she turned her head to blink tears from her eyes as it hit her full force. Enough grey light filtered through to reach the bottom, but the angle afforded a field of vision accounting for only a tiny slice of the actual lair. What she could see of it, however, was unoccupied. The footing proved immediately difficult as her boot heel slipped on the very first step. She stumbled but regained her balance short of falling. The decline proved steep enough that she realized turning to use her hands for support was the only prudent way to proceed.

Well, not the *only* way. "Brektor's talons," she mumbled, leaping forward far enough to clear the curve of the slope. With her *featherfall* still active, she coasted easily to the bottom of the lair, her only thought during the descent: how am I going to get back up? Perhaps the cave had a second entrance she could utilize.

It was much darker and even cooler upon the floor of the cave. As her eyes struggled to adjust, she used her tongue to see if she could discern Sepathia's presence. The smell of the Nightwing was so ubiquitous she wasn't sure she could differentiate between lair and creature.

Her ears strained to aid her perception, but all she heard was the regular dripping of water onto cold stone, deeper within. The anticipation of danger pricked her skin with gooseflesh. She tiptoed around the floor, hoping to find what she needed within the small section blessed by the weak light from above.

The dripping she'd heard earlier was now completely overmatched by the drumming of her pulse in her eardrums. Still no sign she wasn't alone, though. Unable to locate a single scale among the decaying leaf litter and refuse on the nearby cave floor, she took tentative steps into the deeper darkness.

Annoxoria got on hands and knees and started to crawl, reaching blindly to feel whatever her hands happened to bump against. How could the home of a dragon be so devoid of scales? She was certain from her research that they occasionally shed old ones for new. Finally, after numerous encounters with wet, squishy, formless things, her fingers closed around a promising object.

She lifted it to her face, though the pitch black was beyond the power of her eyes to cut through. Using both hands, she caressed and turned the object over. About the size of her palm, it was slick and smooth on one side, rougher on the other. The edges on one end were frayed like an old garment starting to unwind. Could it be? She smiled from ear to ear in the dark.

She was about to take her feet again when she heard what sounded like a sniff from somewhere behind. She froze. There it was again, this time accompanied by a low groan.

A sinisterly vibrating voice ruptured the stillness around her from above. "You came as he said you would."

Panic flashed through Annoxoria, immediately replaced by enhanced clarity. She rose swiftly, then took wide, fluid paces to her left, hoping to reach the wall quickly without running into it. Her right hand dipped into her satchel as she moved, tucking in the scale and searching for the packed ball of sulfur-coated wax she'd placed inside.

The voice boomed again, closer. "I thought it was too good to be true – my brother's beloved pet seeking me out, trying to steal from me like the *vermin* you are." Sepathia squirreled down the chute into her lair, a raucous, slippery sound announcing her descent.

Annoxoria reached the wall of the cave and put her back to it, then directed her attention toward the cloud-shaped greyness near the entrance as she lifted the wax from her satchel. In an instant, the Nightwing's horned face, all yellow eyes and flashing teeth, darted through the light and back into shadow. Upon actually seeing Sepathia, Annoxoria's heart clenched in her chest and the tiny ball fell out of her frozen hand onto the cluttered floor of the lair. Though she'd read about it, she'd not adequately accounted for such a strong physical reaction to the dragon's aura.

The fear seized up her throat as well, rendering her unable to utter any of the incantations speeding through her mind. She accepted this was the end, after every other thought had fled for safer ground.

Sepathia knew exactly where she was, of course. One bright, amber eye, split down the middle by a black pupil, stared at Annoxoria from the darkness. She imagined the outline of the horn-studded skull, though even from this relative proximity the black was too complete to penetrate. The mass of the dragon's folded wings completely blocked out the shaft of what passed for light in this gods-forsaken cave.

"Why my weakling of a brother cherishes you so is beyond comprehension, but I have no doubt he will come for you." Sepathia's breath was hot, and her voice rattled like the chains of the damned. "Once he is eradicated, our bloodline will be pure again."

The eye closed, and Annoxoria tried to follow the heavy scraping she heard, to no avail. Control over her muscles was returning, though, the fear having passed through her system like a virus. If only she could buy enough time to reach down and find the ball of wax she'd dropped …

"How did you know I would come here?" she asked, not only to delay the otherwise inevitable, but because her own mind was already rushing to conclusions she was eager to confirm.

"You are truly pathetic, placing your trust in one so obviously diabolical as the half-fiend." Sepathia's insult was joined by the reopening of her eyes, now higher and further to Annoxoria's left. "I was skeptical of Izefet when he first promised to deliver you to my very threshold, but at least I didn't offer anything in return that would place me in danger. When he told me you'd be coming for one of my scales I could scarcely believe it – but here you are."

Izefet! So it *was* that conniving demon-spawn ... Sepathia was right; she'd been a fool to believe a promise made by such a creature. Not only was she about to pay the price, but her dear Thuvian as well. She couldn't let that happen.

"…I simply had my thralls pick up every shed scale they could find, and you came right into my lair like a trained animal," Sepathia continued. "No, you're not even that!"

Fairly certain her extremities were back under control, Annoxoria quickly dipped to the ground, using her hands to feel around her feet, hoping she could find—the sticky surface of the ball of wax pressed against her palm. She deftly scooped it up and stood.

As soon as she did, she heard a *whoosh* of air as a stabbing pain pierced her belly. The shock of it stayed with her as she collapsed to the ground in a heap, only then realizing it must have been Sepathia's tail stinger entering her. All the muscles in her body seemed to spasm at once and then lock in place, leaving her paralyzed in a sad, contorted position upon the musty, leaf-littered floor.

"Worry not," Sepathia said, though the Nightwing's harrowing voice brought no comfort. "We have only to wait until Thuvian comes, and your suffering will end. I shall make sure he knows where his soft-flesh doll is."

Annoxoria could feel her nostrils twitching – at least she was still able to breathe.

"All this excitement has made me hungry," the dragon continued. "Don't think me an ill host for leaving you whilst I hunt." The Nightwing's laughter was an unnatural, grating sound, but Annoxoria had only herself to blame for her misery.

Chapter 21

Rewards and Favors

Saffron sat on a plain bench, opposite a stool, in a small, rectangular room with mud-brown walls, waiting. A basin of water sat on the floor in front of her, some of its contents sloshed across the black flagstones from when it was hastily brought in. That seemed like an hour ago. Her forearm throbbed painfully, worse since the rush of the Arena battle had worn off. She clenched her jaw and tried to direct her thoughts elsewhere, knowing others were in more dire condition.

The stinging welt across her thigh from that blasted whip burned as well, but at least she was still breathing. She knew Charilo and Nueril weren't coming back, though she wasn't sure about Zygrim. He'd lost a lot of blood, and the punctures in his side might well have pierced something vital. She guessed it was his injuries keeping the healers occupied.

At last the door opened and a thin, local woman entered with a stern look on her face. Blood was smeared across her tunic though her hands were clean, and she cradled a stack of linens next to the satchel strung over her shoulder.

"And where do you hurt?" she asked in Begnari, not looking up as she set the linens onto the stool. Saffron had changed out of her armor into her plain, grey tunic and lifted its hem to expose her thigh wound.

The healer assessed the gash closely, careful to only touch the skin around it, then finally made eye contact with Saffron. Her lower lip lifted as if she wasn't overly concerned. "I've seen worse." She dipped one of the linens in the water, then added some powder from a canister pulled from her satchel, and placed it over the injury. Saffron winced at the burn.

"Hold that." The woman waited for Saffron to place her hand on top of the cloth, then dug through her satchel. When she had retrieved a jar of yellowish jelly, she looked back at Saffron and sucked air through her clenched teeth. "Shield arm took a beating, didn't it?"

Saffron nodded, looking at the angry red puffiness of her left forearm. The healer set her jar on the stool, took over stabilizing the linen on Saffron's thigh, and held her other hand out vertically toward Saffron's chest.

"Push against my hand as hard as you can," she ordered.

"How is your other patient – the one who lost all the blood?" Saffron asked, half-heartedly pressing against the woman's hand. Even that caused her forearm to ache.

The healer frowned at the effort, then lowered her hand. "I don't think the bone's broken, but it's going to bruise in a day or two and be tender for some time." She retrieved and opened her jar, then dabbed a wad of cotton into it and started smearing the jelly on Saffron's arm.

Saffron blew air from pursed lips as she tried to focus on something besides the discomfort of her treatment and the constant throb of the underlying pain. "Is he still alive?"

The woman glanced at Saffron, then lifted the linen from her thigh and repeated the jelly application on that wound as well. "Yes, he was very lucky. His lung was punctured and a rib or two smashed, but he should recover." Her eyes rolled toward the door as she dabbed. "If *they'll* give him time to."

Saffron sighed with relief. She would mourn for Nueril and Charilo, but losing Zygrim would have been hard. She thanked the healer as the woman cleaned up and gathered her supplies, accepting that she wasn't to touch or otherwise remove the ointment until it had fully dried in a few hours.

Back in the main area of the pens, she offered Wemic her condolences, then embraced her other companions one by one. Their looks of relief at her arrival were touching.

"Good to see you've still got all your fingers and toes," Phaerim jabbed with a hint of a grin. "These two were getting ready to divide your worldly possessions."

Dyphina, who looked like her old self again, shushed him with a gentle shove. "Don't listen to him, Saffron. He's just jealous you're a better fighter."

"I'm not jealous of the bruise that's going to leave," he retorted, gesturing toward Saffron's arm.

Thaelios cut through the banter by solemnly resting a hand on Saffron's shoulder. "I am glad to see you well." Then, with feigned indifference, he added, "Have you any news on the fate of Zygrim?"

Saffron couldn't help cracking a smile at the attempted deception, remembering the attention their bulky neighbor had been paying her thin eladrin co-apprentice. "The healer said she thinks he'll pull through."

They were served an early dinner, finer fare than usual, during which Harzhim appeared in order to congratulate and inform them that part of their reward would constitute a visit to the Den of Sin the following evening. Saffron slept more soundly that night than she had in weeks, and didn't wake the next morning until it was time for their meal.

The ointment on her wounds had dried and crusted, and the pain was lessened. Her left forearm was already turning a deep purple, however, and her thigh had a new texture to its curve.

"When I was getting our rations, I asked about a bath," Dyphina mentioned between spoonfuls of porridge. She stopped for a moment and licked her lips clean. "Looks like we'll get first crack at the warm water again." Dyphina added a wink when sure the others weren't looking, and Saffron nearly choked on her breakfast.

Although a flash of pain presented as she lowered her injuries into the heated water, when she lay back and submerged up to her head, Saffron could have argued that the bath was no less than Nirvana. She closed her eyes, resting her head on the side of the pool as the tension melted from her body. Her eyes shot open when she felt something against her belly but relaxed when she saw Dyphina's face looking down at her and realized it was only a sponge.

"Don't worry, I'll be gentle," she said. Dyphina placed a hand underneath Saffron's back to support her as she made tight circles with the sponge, scrubbing away the dried sweat and dirt of the past few days. Saffron closed her eyes again and dipped her ears underwater as well, blocking out everything but the heat of the water and Dyphina's attention to her skin.

The half-fey's sponge travelled across her body, meticulously avoiding her wounds, and when it came to a stop Saffron sat up, feeling like she was born again. "That was wonderful," Saffron purred, her long, black hair clinging to her back. This woman seemed to possess an inherent knowledge of what felt good.

"Glad you think so," Dyphina answered, handing her the sponge and arching her eyebrows. "My turn?"

"Of course." Saffron lathered up the sponge with soap from one of the overhanging trays and returned the favor. She thought again of her visit to Skywatch Haven and bathing with Be'naj. She paid special attention to the minute reactions of Dyphina's facial muscles as she applied different pressure to different places on her body while she washed. With Dyphina's eyes closed in relaxation, Saffron boldly lingered on places that seemed to feel particularly good: the sides of her belly, insides of her thigh, and the expanse just under her collarbone.

"Mmmm, you should be paid for this," Dyphina murmured at one point, which made Saffron smile.

When they had dried off, applied some of the scented oil to soften their skin, and dressed in the soft, black tunics with gold trim laid out for the occasion, they vacated the bath to make way for the men. In another hour, the group was assembled and ready to leave. Saffron was shocked to see Zygrim join them.

"What are you doing here?!" she asked, smiling unabashedly and rising on her tip-toes to throw her arms around his thick neck. He returned her embrace with his right arm, but kept his left tucked in to protect his side.

"I'm not going to play the hero and then miss out on the victory celebration," he winked. His voice was a little loud for the room, but Saffron felt her spirits rise in his presence. "Besides," he added, "I'd better show my face or my opponents will think they've gotten the best of me."

"Well, we can't allow that," Saffron played along as she sank onto her heels. "Just try not to overdo your celebrating, yes?"

Harzhim appeared in order to guide them once more down the tunnels to the Den of Sin. When they arrived, the Consul gave them each more tokens than before, which he credited to the Wolfspider's generosity and thanks for their performance in the Battle Royale. Then, he took his leave and left the gladiators to enjoy themselves.

"Wine?" Dyphina asked.

Saffron nodded. "Yes, please."

"I'll second that," Zygrim added.

"We could all use a drink," Phaerim put in. "I'll go with you."

"I'll find us a table," Saffron declared as Phaerim and Dyphina cut a path toward the bar. The other men followed her toward the seating area. The place was loud, as usual, and fairly crowded. Musicians were performing on the stage, and Saffron noticed several individuals staring at their group, each looking away when she caught them. "What's going on?"

"You're famous now," Zygrim answered before gingerly lowering into a chair with a groan. "We all are after that fight. Might as well get used to it."

Phaerim showed up with a tray of goblets, which he passed around the table.

"Where's Dyphina?" Saffron craned her neck to look over other patrons, back toward the bar.

"Some wealthy-looking bloke started talking to her on the way over," Phaerim explained.

Saffron spotted her green hair, lending her an unearthly quality in the dim light, as she flipped it over one of her shoulders. Dyphina smiled at whatever the handsome man was saying, and Saffron found herself pushing down a pang of jealousy. Baron Rogan was the last person she'd lain with, and that had been a moment of weakness on her part. Still, it was months ago, which seemed even further after the attention Dyphina had given her during their bath.

She tried to clear her head of such thoughts by taking another sip of wine. Dyphina should do whatever made her happy. Saffron couldn't help considering Wemic, however, who was certainly not unattractive …

"So, what shall we toast to?" Zygrim asked, raising his cup toward the center of the table.

"To still being here," Phaerim responded soberly.

"Nueril and Charilo," Wemic added in his limited Illanese.

"Aye," Zygrim nodded, a somber look flashing across his face. The customary brightness returned to his eyes almost immediately, though. "To the spoils of victory and remembering the fallen!" He nudged his goblet higher.

Saffron joined the others in clinking their cups together, then took another deep swig. "So, Zygrim, how are you holding up? I'm surprised to see you walking around so soon. You lost a lot of blood."

"I can't thank you enough for what you did for me," Thaelios said, prompted out of silence.

Zygrim looked his way and smiled before shaking his head. "I only did what you all would have, given the chance." His eyes went back to Thaelios. "We look after one another; it's that simple."

"Pssh," Phaerim muttered, then took another sip of his drink. "You took a fucking trident to the ribs, my friend. Trust me – we wouldn't have *all* done that." Phaerim patted him on the shoulder and stood. "I guess they don't call you the *Bull* for nothing. Now, if I may be excused, I think I see my courier. Time to check if my special order is in." Phaerim set his empty goblet on the table and waded into the crowd, heading toward the main entrance.

"Would you like to play some Doomsday Dromedary?" Zygrim asked Thaelios. "I hear you're exceptional at it."

Saffron thought she saw whatever passed as a blush rise upon Thaelios's silver cheeks before he nodded. The two of them stood and headed for the gambling tables, leaving her and Wemic momentarily alone. Her mind raced for something clever to say as he took another sip of his wine.

Suddenly, Dyphina clasped her shoulders and leaned into her ear from behind, startling Saffron. "This guy's going to get us a private room," she whispered excitedly.

Saffron turned to respond. "Who is he?"

"I don't really know, some aristocrat? He's definitely got money, and his accent is sooo alluring."

"Really?" Saffron answered dubiously. "Does it sound just like mine?"

"Now that you mention it, it does," Dyphina smiled. "But you're alluring, too." She winked, then puffed her lips out and blew Saffron a quick kiss. "I'll find you afterward," she said, already walking back toward the man who'd been courting her. "Don't do anything I wouldn't!"

Dyphina was gone an instant later, leaving Saffron to eat her response. She wasn't sure she was even capable of anything the half-fey wouldn't do. She was left alone with Wemic once again, still trying to think of something to say.

"So, I thought you fought well in the Arena yesterday," she offered, able to use Begnari now that the others were gone. This seemed to put Wemic much more at ease.

He nodded and scooted forward in his chair to better speak over the din. "You as well. I've seen you in training, of course, but out in the battle, you were even more impressive. Where did you learn to fight like that?"

Saffron mirrored him, moving forward in her seat. "My father allowed me to train with a *ghostwind* master in my home country of Begnasharan."

"That's … unexpected." His eyes narrowed slightly and his tongue wet his lower lip. "How did you end up so far from home?" His hand reached over to take hers, which was tapping absently against her nearly empty goblet.

She felt a sudden rush in the pit of her stomach – or perhaps lower, if she was honest. "I studied music as well, and earned an invitation to play in foreign courts …" Saffron caught sight of

Groilen Bonesplinter standing by the bar, eagerly waving for her to come join him. "Aaaah, my apologies, Wemic. It appears my sponsors would like a word. Can I bring you more wine when I return?"

Wemic withdrew his hand and straightened. "Oh, certainly. I would enjoy that." He forced a smile as she stood.

"I don't think it should take long," she offered. As soon as her back was to Wemic she scowled at Groilen, then made her way over. "What's so immediate I couldn't enjoy a single drink first?"

Groilen, appearing like she'd first met him, raised his eyebrows at the comment. "Oh, are you displeased to see me, Lady Saffron? I thought you'd be in fine spirits after the resounding victory!"

"Slaves still died, Groilen." She placed her empty goblet on the bar top and held up two fingers to the bartender. "Do you have better news for me, then? Has Myalyssa determined how to free us from these collars?"

Groilen's face fell and he burrowed into the rim of his oversized mug, coming away with froth on his lips. "Not yet, though I wouldn't wager against her. I, well, I guess I mean *we*, have a sort of, well, favor to ask."

"Hizune's Scimitar, you want me to do something more for you?"

Groilen huffed, "It's a give-and-take relationship, my dear. We're working hard for you, even if you can't see it. And we all want the same things in the end, right?"

"Oh, I didn't realize the Twelve had lost their freedom as well … I don't need a lecture, Groilen. I need you to hold up your end of our pact." Saffron looked back toward her table to see if Wemic had wandered off yet.

"Now, now, let's simmer down, shall we? I think you'd appreciate the request if you'll hear me out – given how those fellows from Hellig-nok's temple targeted you."

"One of them was a woman," she retorted, tossing a few tokens onto the bar as the bartender placed two more goblets of wine in front of her. Saffron was still salty, but intrigued. She placed her elbows on the bar and leaned forward so Groilen wouldn't have to speak as loudly. "All right, out with it, then."

"Gaeric has ended up in a bit of competition with the Temple of Eternal Flame regarding the recruitment of new members to their respective congregations. As he puts it, Hierarch Krygos isn't above resorting to brutish tactics to assist the growth of his flock." Groilen wiggled his thick mustache as if amused by what he was about to say. "Gaeric would like you to help counter this tide by carrying out a stunt that would surely embarrass their cause."

"What kind of a stunt?"

Groilen lifted his palms. "Nothing violent, I assure you." He ducked in closer again before returning to a whisper, "You see, one of the attractive features of the Eternal Flame's fancy new cathedral is, well, their eternal flame. A magical pillar of fire spurts upward all the way from the base of the floor through the top of the roof. It burns constantly, without any indication of new fuel being introduced."

"Oh, yes, I saw that during the ride to your mansion." Saffron nodded. "Impressive."

"Yes, quite," Groilen frowned. "Anyway, Gaeric is preparing a font of enchanted water he thinks might suppress the Eternal

Flame, if only for a few hours – long enough to be pointed out and capitalized upon by prepared demonstrations."

"That's the job? You want me to sneak into the temple and douse their big fire?" Saffron wasn't sure she could agree with how the Circle of Twelve were prioritizing their efforts.

"There are guards patrolling the floor regularly, so yes, stealth might be necessary," Groilen answered, matter-of-factly. "Or at least persuasion, if the former is lacking."

Saffron took a sip of her new wine. "I don't see what this really accomplishes."

Groilen waved off her concern. "Don't worry so much about that. It's politics – hard for an outsider to understand. Will you do it?"

"You're making it sound as if this is some innocent prank, but I have to assume if it weren't dangerous, you'd be doing it yourselves." Saffron's glare dared Groilen to contradict her. "Tell me I'm wrong." She searched his eyes until he couldn't take it and took a renewed interest in the contents of his mug. Her sponsors' flippant disregard for her safety soured her mood further. They expected her to risk even more on behalf of some religious one-upmanship, merely because they asked?

"I know it may seem petty to you," Groilen started in a contrite tone, "but this is a fight for influence within Zeblon. It's the same reason we're sponsoring you in the first place. When it comes to the real fight ahead, against the Wolfspider and the Dread Lich, we will need the people on our side. They need to believe in us, and feel safe doing so." His eyes finally lifted to meet Saffron's. "I believe this is important, and that's why I'd be going along with you, to help."

"You're coming with me?"

Groilen shrugged. "In disguise, of course."

Saffron regarded the diminutive man for a moment, then looked over to her table, where Phaerim had rejoined Wemic. They sat across from one another, without an interpreter, looking awkwardly at anything but each other. "I've got to get back," she finally said to Groilen, picking up her drinks. "Give me a few more days to heal, then we can pay the temple a visit."

She saw the grin spreading across the illusionist's face before she'd fully turned her back to him. "Did you get what you needed?" Saffron asked Phaerim as she returned to her table and handed a full goblet to the appreciative Wemic.

"That I did." Phaerim winked and patted the belt cinching his tunic. "Red centipede venom – paralyzes the muscles near the wound. Usually not deadly on its own, but it can certainly help you win a fight."

Saffron sat between the two men and took a long sip of her wine. "If that's how you want to win."

"Oh, make no mistake … I want to win in whatever way keeps me the healthiest. Maybe Thaelios can win me enough gold for something really exotic next time." Phaerim looked over his shoulder toward the gambling section, and Saffron followed suit, looking for signs of the obtrusive Eladrin.

She didn't see him immediately, but as she scanned the crowd, she happened to notice Zygrim's large frame leading Thaelios by the hand up the scaffold walkways to one of the private rooms. Her jaw dropped and eyes widened when Zygrim unlocked one of the thick doors and the pair disappeared inside.

Her own inhibitions suddenly seemed silly. "Wemic, come dance with me," she said, grabbing her companion by the hand and leading him closer to the stage where the musicians still performed. He didn't resist, and one dance quickly turned into three.

When they took a break to catch their breaths, strangers started coming forward to introduce themselves, eager for a chance to interact with the victorious gladiators from the Battle Royale. People bought them new drinks, and pretty soon Saffron was having more fun than she could remember: laughing, swapping stories with those she'd just met, drinking, and leaning into the handsome Wemic every so often.

She was quite inebriated by the time Dyphina found her and joined in the revelry. Saffron was fairly sure she'd kissed someone, or perhaps *someones*, though she couldn't remember who, when Phaerim showed up to declare an end to the night.

Despite everyone in the vicinity jeering, Phaerim was insistent, draping Saffron's uninjured arm over his shoulder and practically hauling her toward their special access door. The rest of the Wolfspider's gladiator troop followed. Harzhim waited for them there, looking more serious than she remembered, with an even more serious-looking man in black beside him.

They all stopped laughing and grew quiet as Harzhim regarded them with what seemed to be disappointment – Saffron couldn't be sure. "This is Lodiammon, the Wolfspider's lieutenant," Harzhim said while nodding at the dour man. "He has an offer for you."

Lodiammon appeared middle-aged and local, but without any of the facial hair popular among those Saffron had met during her carousing. Sunken cheeks and deep-set eyes gave him a severe, off-putting quality, compounded by the silver crescent piercing his nasal septum. "I'll get straight to it," he said in a raspy voice that sounded as if it belonged to a creature being strangled.

Saffron straightened and tried to concentrate on what he was saying, though the man seemed to be swaying slightly as she listened.

"...the tunnels connect to all four Houses, as well as the exotic animal pens where beasts for the Arena are kept. A rare sort of bird has just been brought in, nothing to do with the fights, and the Wolfspider would like you to acquire it for his personal collection. Problem is, it's being shipped out in the morning for the paying customer, so you'll have to do it tonight."

Who did this Lodiammon think he was, assigning tasks in the middle of the night? All Saffron wanted was to get back to her mattress and lie down. Although, she wouldn't complain if Wemic decided to help keep her warm ...

"...the key." The far too serious man handed a small piece of metal to Phaerim. "He does not forget those who serve him well," Lodiammon finished before nodding to Harzhim and pushing past them toward the bar.

"Wait, what's happening?" Saffron slurred, confusion winning out despite her attempt at forced clarity.

Chapter 22

A Bird of a
Different Feather

"Maybe you should go back to the pens with Zygrim, and let us handle this, Saffron," Phaerim suggested, shifting her weight against his shoulder. She barely felt her feet on the ground, but was certainly not going to let her friends head into danger without her.

"Not a chance, Phaer, fair, I'm fine," she retorted, taking a step to the side and shoving Phaerim off to prove she could stand on her own. She succeeded, but swayed while doing so.

Zygrim took a turn, holding a torch too close for comfort as he assessed her. "Saffron, I think you should consider listening to your friend. Once you leave the tunnels in the Wolfspider's quadrant, you'd all be fair game. Come with me and I just may share some hooch I keep stashed for special occasions."

Who did these men think they were? They couldn't tell her to sit by while others took risks. Saffron waved both hands at Zygrim, flipping her wrists in an unsynchronized cadence. "You better back that fire up, unless you want it in your face."

Dyphina grunted. "Instead of arguing, why don't we just get this over with as soon as possible? Here, I'll carry the torch." She reached out and waited for Zygrim to hand it to her. He did, but only after letting out a deep sigh.

"I don't think this is a great idea," he said.

"Well, given these collars, we don't really have much of a choice, do we?" Dyphina countered.

"I can go with you," Wemic said in Begnari, directly to Saffron.

He looked so handsome, and Saffron desperately wanted to simply kiss him for the rest of the night, but she wouldn't be able to live with herself if something bad happened to the others and she wasn't there. She also couldn't be the reason anyone else was put in danger.

"That is sooo sweet," Saffron cooed, "but I think you should go with Zygrim. This is something that the three of us, no, five?" She looked around the crowded tunnel.

"Four," Phaerim provided. "All right, then, whoever is coming along, follow me. Dyphina, will you bring the torch closer?"

People started moving. Saffron wanted to give more reassurance to Wemic, who stood beside Zygrim with a hurt look, but if she didn't follow the light it was going to leave her behind. Unsure of the best gesture to use, she half-heartedly waved toward Wemic, then hurried to catch up with Thaelios, who trailed the others by a few steps.

"Be careful!" Zygrim called after them, though she didn't turn back.

"I hope this doesn't become a habit," Phaerim was saying when she drew even with her eladrin friend.

"What's that?" she asked, unsure what he was referring to, and whether she missed anything.

"Running errands in the middle of the night for the Wolfspider," he answered. "It's not like we haven't done enough for him already. How much coin do you think he made off our last victory? The least he could do is hire us like respectable mercenaries."

"But why would he bother when he has such capable slaves?" Thaelios countered.

"Ugh, I was having such a wonderful night, too!" Dyphina added. "I cannot wait to be rid of these blasted collars!"

"No need to yell, Dyphina," Thaelios said in a calm, melodic voice. "We're all within a few paces of you." Everyone grew silent for a moment, and Saffron concentrated on matching her steps to the echoes of the others'.

Thaelios continued just after she'd found the right rhythm. "What we should be discussing, instead of lodging complaints to the air against our undeniably regrettable situation, is how to neutralize this Mystic who oversees the animal pens, should we meet him."

"Oh, well, I have something for that," Phaerim said, holding up the small vial of red centipede venom he'd tucked in his belt earlier that night.

"Mystic? Wait, wait, what are you talking about?" Saffron didn't remember anything about the animal pens being guarded and certainly not by any sort of mystic. There was a period of talking once they ran into Harzhim, though, during which most of her focus was on trying not to vomit when the floor wouldn't stop moving.

"Really, Saffron?" She heard the judgement in Dyphina's voice. "I vouched for you to come along, you know."

"Yes, Saffron, are you sure you're up for this?" Phaerim turned toward her and they all stopped walking. "We're breaking into the Arena animal pens to steal some sort of rainbow-colored squawker the Wolfspider fancies for his own collection. Harzhim warned us the Beast-master is fanatic about his charges, and a powerful shaman to boot. Things could get dangerous."

"Well … fine," was all Saffron could think to say.

"Can you even sing in your condition?" Dyphina asked. "It's not like you have any weapons."

Saffron stood straighter and cleared her throat. Of course she could sing.

"No, not now," Phaerim said, grabbing her upper arm and pulling her along, back up the corridor. She stumbled at the sudden movement, but was pleased she kept her feet. "We're getting closer and don't want to give ourselves away. We should try sneaking in if we can."

Saffron concentrated on being quiet as they navigated a few more turns, but their sandaled footfalls still made their own music against the stone floors. Finally, they reached a shut door at the end of the hallway.

Phaerim lifted a small key and tried lining it up with the keyhole. His hands weren't the steadiest. "Hopefully, this thing works." He inserted the key and turned. A satisfying *click* announced success.

Saffron held her breath as he turned the latch and pushed outward with both hands. She tried peering through the newly formed gap as it widened, but the space beyond was dark. Phaerim peeked through, too, and when he found nothing alarming, he opened the door wide to let Dyphina pass with the torch.

She entered an oval chamber, only a few paces across, where another door waited. As the four of them filed into the room, Saffron noticed a rack of gold-hued robes to one side of the door they'd entered and a pile of purple sashes on an opposite table. When Thaelios carefully closed the door behind them, she saw it was adorned with a fresco depicting a brown spider with menacing fangs.

"Well, this looks like the boundary of the Wolfspider's territory," Phaerim offered, sharing a concerned look with the group. He slipped a dagger from his sleeve and began coating the blade with the poison he'd procured. "Just in case," he said when he noticed Thaelios staring at him. "Who knows what might be down here?"

"There is probably a better way," the Eladrin mentioned. "I do know a bit of magic."

"Is that so?" Phaerim responded, not stopping or looking up from his application.

"And what spell were you thinking of using?" Dyphina asked. "Or were you going to try and charm the Mystic if we run into him? I'm not sure, but I think Zygrim might be jealous," she added, playfully.

"Ha!" Saffron couldn't help herself as Thaelios seemed to be at a loss for words. "Yeah, what was going on in that room you two disappeared into?" Part of her knew she should be minding her own affairs, but it was apparently the part most subdued by the wine.

"Come now, we've got a task to perform," Phaerim butted in, though he brandished a wide grin as well. "We should be ready for anything beyond this next door. Harzhim told us to keep straight after we left the Wolfspider's quarter, but you all know how these tunnels are. Let's not get lost."

Saffron nodded, doing her best to focus her vision in the meager torchlight.

Phaerim used the same key as before to unlock the next door. "Ready?" He looked at each of them.

Saffron nodded again.

He opened the portal slowly, and she saw the dim glow of torches along the wall beyond. Phaerim held a single finger to his lips before slinking into the hallway. Dyphina went next and Saffron trailed her, letting Thaelios keep the rear since he had the sharpest vision.

Phaerim headed toward the light, ignoring an intersecting corridor. Once Saffron passed it, she heard intermittent squeals and mewling coming from ahead. Some of the animals, at least, were awake. She smelled cages in need of cleaning and the combined stench of too many creatures living in a confined space. Phaerim stopped and motioned for Dyphina to put her torch down.

An empty sconce along the wall, slightly behind Saffron, provided a convenient holder, and Dyphina mounted the torch before creeping up to join Phaerim. Saffron soon huddled close behind, looking beyond their shoulders at what lay ahead.

An iron gate of thick, intersecting beams protected what were undoubtedly the animal pens. She saw movement, but it was only the pacing of caged animals. The thought of setting them all free popped into her head, but Saffron shook it out quickly. No way *that* would go unnoticed, and she had no doubt who would end up taking the fall for such an uproar.

"Which one are we supposed to be stealing?" Dyphina whispered.

"I'm sure there's more than we can see," Phaerim whispered back. "Harzhim was quite certain we'd know once we saw it. We're just going to have to get closer."

Dyphina followed as Phaerim crawled ahead, still in a deep crouch. "Won't the animals notice when we enter? What if they get loud?"

"Not much we can do about that," Saffron said, forgetting to whisper.

Phaerim shot her a severe look, then swiveled back to watch the gate. Nothing seemed to change. He waited another moment, stood, and tiptoed the rest of the way while Saffron and the others held behind.

As soon as Phaerim inserted and turned the key, barks and snarls from inside the pens clamored in response. Phaerim winced, then did so again as the iron gate whined at his opening. Dyphina stood to join him and Saffron followed, keeping a hand against her friend's back to stay steady. She looked over her shoulder to make sure Thaelios, who trailed a few steps behind, was still with them.

They all squirmed into the room, none infiltrating more than an arm's length from the gate. The vaulted ceiling was supported by wide beams, and there were enough torches lit along the walls to see clearly, though their smoke added to the dingy feel of the chamber. It was actually a series of chambers, Saffron realized, and recessed spaces contained even more cages. The walls of the main room were lined with pens of various sizes, containing a plethora of creatures, many of which Saffron had never seen before.

Wolves snarled and hyenas mocked them with sinister laughter, making it difficult for Saffron to divert her attention elsewhere. The whole place seemed to be making a horrific ruckus, though she supposed such an environment wouldn't be silent on even the best of occasions.

"Let's find this bird, quickly!" Phaerim ordered, obviously reaching the same conclusion that stealth was no longer a possibility. He and Thaelios each took an alcove, while Saffron and Dyphina pushed further into the main chamber.

"Over here!" Saffron called to her companions, noticing an assortment of birds in hanging cages near the back of the room. She squirmed around the large cage of a disinterested creature that appeared to be half-bear, half … something she couldn't decide. "Which one is it?" she asked as Dyphina joined her.

Five cages held large birds: two appeared to be hawks or eagles of some sort, one was an owl, another was large and white with downy feathers that looked more like fur. The last one … wasn't a bird at all. Though it had brightly colored wings containing every color of the spectrum, the creature's body was serpentine.

Thaelios gasped from the entrance of his alcove, "A couatl!"

"What are you doing in my sanctuary!" boomed a deep voice from behind them.

Saffron jerked her head around. A bearded man, his wild, brown hair matching his cloak and studded leather breastplate, stared at them accusingly from the far side of the room. Everyone froze for a moment, but the armored man bolted into action after taking in Phaerim's dagger.

Turning around, he lifted the pins on a pair of cages, then spun to face Saffron's group again. He clutched a talisman hanging from his neck and began chanting.

She knew whatever was about to happen couldn't be good, and frantically tried to remember how her fire blossom melody began. The howling room full of caged animals kept her from summoning any sliver of concentration, and her mind went completely blank as the doors to the unpinned cages pushed open and a pair of leopards emerged.

The spotted cats looked at the nearby beast-master first, then around the room, trying to acclimate to their newly available options. They considered a number of the other caged animals before focusing on Thaelios, who made the unfortunate decision to grab a wooden pole leaning against the wall in a nearby corner.

Whether they saw him as a threat or food, the leopards pounced on top of cages in route to the eladrin Shaper. They bared their teeth in a challenge, waiting for him to make a move that would increase his vulnerability. Dyphina sprung forward, pushing past the befuddled Saffron, and started humming a tune.

Saffron watched in silent horror as the mystic released his talisman and went through a sudden transformation. Coarse, brown hair sprouted from every inch of his exposed skin, and his hands grew larger until they resembled the clawed paws of a bear. His canines elongated and his eyes expanded, gaining a feral look. He roared and lunged across the room in her direction.

Phaerim exited his alcove, wove around the cage where the leopards stood, transfixed by Dyphina, and interposed himself between Saffron and the transformed beast-master. He took a quick thrust with his dagger, but the mystic seized his arm and flung him atop another cage resting against the wall.

Saffron stumbled backward until her head crashed against the bird cages, her brain cluttered by a fog of alcohol and over-stimulation. The bear-man drew closer, saliva dripping from his open mouth, yet Saffron couldn't help fixating on his talisman. It looked like steel and bore the same emblem she'd seen marked on the door of the farmhouse in Crimsonmoon ... this mystic belonged to the Name of the Beast!

A loud *thwack* accompanied the rap of Thaelios's pole across the skull of the beast-master. He turned and used a paw to gather in the staff, then snapped through it with one bite of his powerful jaws. Thaelios backed away, using the splintered remains of the pole as a stake to keep the mystic at bay.

Saffron started singing, though it wasn't any song in particular. She was just putting together words into a tune in the hopes something would jog her memory. Drawn to the melody, a confused look penetrated the mystic's otherwise feral demeanor as he considered what to make of her.

The distraction allowed Phaerim, who had gathered himself atop the cage of a hysterical hyena, to leap onto the beast-master's back and plunge his tainted dagger into the man's trapezius.

Roaring in pain, the beast-master tried to reach Phaerim with his bear-like paws, but the smaller man leapt to the ground, leaving his dagger embedded.

"Poison shouldn't take long!" Phaerim shouted, and already the mystic had fallen to his knees.

Saffron stopped singing but didn't dare move closer to the beast-master, lest he attempt to grab and trip her. She glanced at Dyphina, who was vocalizing a melody close enough to touch the leopards, though they remained transfixed, staring at her with unblinking eyes.

"What do we do with him now?" Thaelios asked, his demeanor decidedly less calm since his staff broke. "We can't just leave him here with a dagger in his neck, can we?"

"Saffron," Phaerim urged, "can you grab the bird?"

"The couatl," Thaelios corrected.

"Whatever! Can you reach the top of the cage?"

"I, I think so," she answered, turning slowly, reluctant to take her eyes off the beast-master. He was growling continuously on his knees with his face hidden toward the floor. Saffron was not, in fact, able to reach the top of the cage. She grabbed its base with both hands and lifted until its hook came free of the loop that suspended it.

The cage itself was heavier than she anticipated, and she almost dropped it when forced to support its entire weight. The creature inside wrapped itself tightly around the hanging perch, and then, Saffron could have sworn it started *speaking*. She had no idea what it said, but the sounds seemed more like words than just a snake's hissing or a bird's caw.

"Did you hear that?" Saffron asked, turning her head first toward her friends, then back to stare at the couatl.

"Don't drop the cage!" Thaelios responded with a worrisome tone.

"Got it," she replied, moving her arms to cradle the metal prison more snugly.

"Good, now, maybe we can tie him up." Phaerim let his guard down to search for some rope.

Whether the beast-master had eyes in the back of his head or simply sensed the easing of tension, he used that moment to spin and spring forth in a rush of energy. Pouncing upon Phaerim's back, his weight forced them both to the floor. The mystic held Phaerim down and savagely bit him in almost the exact spot he had been stabbed himself.

"Ahh, get him off!" Phaerim screamed.

Saffron, completely occupied trying not to drop the cage, was helpless to do anything but watch, hoping her other friends would act on Phaerim's behalf. She was surprised when Dyphina stopped her singing and pointed toward the mystic, barking a command Saffron couldn't quite make out over the din of restless animals.

To her amazement, the leopards bounded down from the cage and piled onto the back of the beast-master, one of them stretching its sinuous neck to wrap its jaws around the top of the man's spine. He immediately roared and spun to force them off, allowing Phaerim to scramble to his feet and scurry toward the door.

Reaching around to test the bite wound, Phaerim gestured with his free hand for the rest of them to vacate. Saffron didn't need a second invitation. The caged animals grew even louder in the throes of watching their own in the midst of attack.

Dyphina, then Thaelios, followed by an encumbered Saffron, all exited through the iron gate while Phaerim waited to lock it. Saffron glanced back once outside to see the beast-master having a tough time fending off the leopards.

"Someone else will have to sort this mess out," Phaerim declared as he swung the gate shut and locked it. "Let's get out of here!"

Dyphina reclaimed a torch from one of the sconces and led the way back to the oval room, where she asked to look at Phaerim's bite. "It shouldn't be too bad if we clean it out soon. You don't want it getting infected."

Saffron set the cage down on the table of sashes to rest her arms and peered curiously at the creature within. Indeed, this was no normal bird. Its serpentine body was bright green, its underside a vibrant purple. Two feathery wings sprouted from its sides with plumage a blend of yellow, red, orange, and blue.

While considering it at eye-level, the creature again seemed to speak. This time, Saffron wasn't the only one to hear.

"I didn't know you spoke fey," Dyphina said, still inspecting Phaerim's wound.

Saffron lifted her hands and took a step back from the cage. "I didn't say that. The bird did."

"It's a couatl," Thaelios corrected again, taking Saffron's place peering into the cage. "They are said to be highly intelligent."

Her interest piqued, Dyphina walked over to get a clean sash from the table and took a look in the cage as well. The couatl spoke once more.

"What did it say?" Saffron asked.

Dyphina had an expression of awe across her face, and it took a moment for her to respond. "Thank you for rescuing me. Please take me to the surface and set me free." Dyphina looked directly at Saffron, who hoped this would all make more sense once she was sober.

Chapter 23

Doors and Keys

Knowing that Cauzel was actually Eladrin made Be'naj more wary around him. She wasn't sure if that was because she felt deceived or because of her own history with the community she grew up in. They'd made the return trip to Blackfeather Perch without further incident, and Cauzel was back to looking like the human version of himself.

Be'naj was eager to begin tracking down Saffron but agreed to wait until her host had attuned the Living Fire pendant. With correct manipulation, it would act as a counter to the Dampening Stone possibly still buried in the sands near Tarmuth. The weeks until Cauzel was ready were going to be some of the longest of her life, especially if she had to listen to the know-it-all Iliana prattle on about the enchantments she'd mastered or how she would do, whatever Be'naj happened to be doing, better.

She considered getting a head-start on her own since apparently Cauzel could fly, but he was adamant they not separate. Be'naj knew that was the prudent course with the Name of the Beast actively seeking to harm them, but still hated it.

Cauzel sent Aurus home the day after they got back, assigning him some extended reconnaissance in Pasaxtree as an excuse. Be'naj knew Cauzel didn't trust the human to lurk around the tower when he wasn't going to be present. That, and the worry about what Iliana and Aurus might do to one another if asked to continue sharing the same space unsupervised.

The Shaper of Blackfeather Perch spent much of his time sequestered in his private laboratory, but on the fourth day after their return, a visitor showed up at the tower. Cauzel emerged from his workspace to greet the new arrival, whom he introduced as his sister, Lorelei Furthalion.

"But she's Eladrin," Iliana unerringly pointed out. "And beautiful," she murmured out of the side of her mouth. "How can she be your sister?"

"By marriage," Lorelei lied, or at least Be'naj assumed so. She hadn't batted an eye at Be'naj's appearance, and winked after her bending of the truth, so Be'naj gathered Cauzel had already communicated something of their journey to her.

Lorelei approached Be'naj after embracing her brother and offered her hand. They grasped forearms in greeting, and Lorelei placed her other hand gently on top of Be'naj's. "You have a pure spirit and are a true gift from Eriane. It is my pleasure to meet you."

Be'naj's face grew warm at the compliment. "Pleasure to meet you as well."

Lorelei released her grip and sauntered to where Iliana stood with her arms folded. "And you must be the apprentice who was clever enough not to get captured." She offered her hand to Iliana as well.

"The *only* one clever enough," Iliana responded, reluctantly taking Lorelei's wrist, then releasing it almost immediately.

"May I take your cloak, sister?" Cauzel offered, stepping up behind her.

Lorelei nodded and her golden curls bounced in response. She reached up to unclasp her cloak, and when Cauzel peeled the embroidered green cloth back from her shoulders, Iliana gasped and shielded her eyes.

"Spirit of the Spell Father, why aren't you wearing any clothes?" the apprentice asked.

An unabashed smile spread across Lorelei's lips. She wasn't naked, exactly, but her torso was adorned by a garment of crisscrossing silver rods, each about the length of her little finger. The resulting gaps were exceedingly revealing, but Be'naj wasn't embarrassed by Lorelei's brazenness and thought her confidence made her especially beautiful. She'd covered her lower half with a long wrapped skirt of white, with green designs, and practical leather riding boots that rose past her calves.

"Come now, Iliana," Cauzel interceded. "No need to force modesty on Lorelei's behalf. She's a priestess of Eriane and oversees the goddess's fertility rites."

"Well," Iliana gradually uncovered her face, only to stare at Lorelei's exposed chest, "aren't you ... cold?"

"I won't be if we women get to know each other better while sitting around the hearth. Come, both of you. What do you say we go and have a chat while my brother continues his research? You do have work to do, Cauzel?"

"Absolutely," he answered. "That's why I've called you here, after all. I'd be much obliged to get back to it."

"Then off with you," Lorelei said, stepping toward Be'naj to take her by the hand. "I'll make myself at home and find you later to discuss the arrangement." She led Be'naj up the stairs to the second level, where the kitchen hearth blazed with a comfortable heat. Iliana followed like a neglected puppy, hungry for attention.

"How long will you be staying?" Iliana asked once they were all seated with cups of wine in hand.

Lorelei pressed her tongue to the inside of her cheek before responding. "I suppose I'll remain at Blackfeather Perch until Be'naj and Cauzel return." She looked to Be'naj for affirmation, but Be'naj just shrugged; Cauzel hadn't yet elaborated his full intentions to her.

Lorelei attempted to hold a casual conversation between the three of them, but Iliana was short with her answers, and Be'naj didn't feel like sharing much in Iliana's presence. She liked Lorelei and hoped they'd have more opportunities to interact one-on-one.

Be'naj used the need to train as an excuse to exit the uncomfortable situation and left the tower to get some fresh air and engage her muscles. She practiced swordplay on her own quite a lot over the following days, as well as meditated on the meaning of her prophecy, silently hoping to receive more visions. None came.

Cauzel insisted Iliana tutor Be'naj further in Illanese, suggesting they would likely be using it more the further they got from Ifelian. Be'naj also took Sheen for daily rides when it wasn't raining, though never far, promising Cauzel she'd stay within sight of the tower. Every now and then, Lorelei would be tending the animals in the stables when she returned, and the two of them would talk. She had a friendly way that put Be'naj at ease, and eventually their conversation turned toward the long rescue mission ahead.

"So, I know my brother feels responsible for those under his charge," Lorelei said as they brushed the stabled horses. "He made a promise to the families of those he accepted into apprenticeship to teach and care for them. I have no doubt his reasons run deeper – but what about yours? Cauzel mentioned you've lived in seclusion for years."

Be'naj swallowed hard, unsure how to put her feelings into words or whether she should even try. "I met Saffron not long ago. We fought together to defend travelers along the Ifelian Corridor. She, she just saw me as no one ever has: not as a freak or an outcast, but …" Her cheeks did that annoying thing where they heated up all of a sudden. "We've both endured hardship, but she didn't treat me like a victim, either." Be'naj shrugged. "She treated me like a friend, right from the start, and it's been a long time since I've had one."

Lorelei had held still while Be'naj talked, listening intently. She smiled and nodded, like she understood. "I envy you," Lorelei said, returning to her grooming. "It's a special sort of blessing to fall in love."

Be'naj's jaw fell at the presumption, but she couldn't muster the will to deny Lorelei's claim. What did it matter what Cauzel's older sister thought? She'd never even met Saffron.

An excruciatingly long tenday later, as Be'naj and Lorelei were climbing the stairs toward the top of the tower to recover barrels of rain water, Cauzel's laboratory door swung open dramatically.

"I've done it!" he declared, dangling the Living Fire pendant by its platinum chain, a huge smile on his face. "Anti-anti-magic was more complicated than I first thought, but I've done it!" His bushy black hair was in disarray, and it smelled like he hadn't emerged from his rooms in quite some time. "Are you packed for our journey?" he asked.

Be'naj's heart raced, and she shared a glance with a beaming Lorelei. "I've been packed for a week!"

Lorelei threw her arms around Be'naj's neck in an embrace. "Go get her," she said directly in her ear. "You've waited long enough."

Be'naj returned her hug, then nearly flew down the stairs to gather her travelling pack, which had been sitting ready by the door for days on end. "I'll saddle the horses!" she yelled up the stairwell. She didn't bother finding Iliana to share a good-bye and doubted the apprentice would miss her.

Winter had finally crept up on them, and the ground crunched with frost on her way to the stables. The cold air only invigorated her, and she had both horses saddled and dressed for the trek by the time Cauzel showed up.

"I homed in on my apprentices' locations again, and the good news is they're still together and have stopped moving," he said as he tucked burlap-wrapped packages into each of their saddlebags.

"Does that mean there are bad tidings as well?" Be'naj stretched her wings and a single, white feather fell to the ground as she folded them back.

"That depends on how we choose to look at it, Be'naj."

Cauzel sounded upbeat as he mounted his horse, which made her worry more. "And how *should* we look at it?" she asked.

"They are now further away – much further, as it happens: all the way to Zeblon, on the far coast of Elisahd." Be'naj had never studied maps of foreign places, but that sounded far.

"However, now that they seem to be stationary, we can better plan our own route. Since we cannot both fly, it is fortuitous that they ended up near water, for boats will be faster and less labor on our part." Cauzel waited for Be'naj to mount Sheen before leading his horse out of the stables.

"Tarmuth lies closer to Zeblon than here, so that's a boon. Also, I've mulled over what we found in the Keeper's Library quite a bit and have a possible solution to the missing requirement for entering the Crypt of Broken Names, as the Hall of Doors has been renamed."

Be'naj had not considered their research much, assuming her limited experience would not be helpful, anyway. She had been content to let Cauzel stew over the details, and it seemed a fruitful strategy. "I'd almost forgotten. We need a token of the Outer Planes – some other world. From the realm of my possible father, perhaps?"

"Indeed, if we were able to get there, I'm sure it's a nicer place than the home world I was thinking of … but that brings me to my proposed solution. We shouldn't have to travel any further than Lucnere, if I'm correct." Cauzel allowed the horses to take slow, sure-footed steps as they wound down the incline of the hillside from which the Perch protruded.

"My first formal teacher, Embril the Shaper, had a famous encounter with some sort of demon in the jungles of Chelpa, years before we'd even met. After vanquishing the foe, he took the somewhat macabre step of removing the creature's claws and wearing them as a talisman around his neck. He was very fond of that necklace and was buried with it in the catacombs beneath the Chelpian capital. If we can get to his tomb, we may find what we need to enter Tarmuth."

Be'naj recoiled in her saddle. "I'm not going to rob the grave of your mentor!"

"No, no, of course not. I would do it myself," Cauzel assured her.

"Ungh, that's not any better." She wondered what other basic tenets of eladrin culture had been skipped over during his education abroad. "Resting places of the dead are sacred. Neither of us should defile them. We'll have to find another way."

"Another way?" Cauzel scoffed, surprising her. "I suppose you have something easier in mind? Do you really want to spend time trying to track down beings from the Outer Planes and asking if they'll gift you with a token? Just a bit of insight – if they are powerful enough to journey across the cosmos, they are probably more dangerous than some superstitious curse or whatever you believe might befall us for borrowing from the dead. I assure you, Embril is getting no more use from his talisman now than while alive."

"I don't want to make things more difficult, of course, but convenience is *not* a good reason to desecrate tombs!" Why did this man have to be so frustrating? Surely, he could understand her reticence. "Might Embril have kept a second token elsewhere? In a desk drawer, perhaps?"

Cauzel remained silent for a moment. She could only see the back of his head, but imagined he was combing for memories of anything else useful. She sincerely hoped he might think of something.

"While that is an intriguing possibility," he finally said, "Embril died years ago, and all his holdings were claimed by the former King of Chelpa during his rise to power. If anything useful was left in his tower, it has probably either been removed or is held by some unknown party who may or may not still occupy the estate. By most reckonings, the situation there is even more unstable now that the Empire's ruler has been unseated.

"How about this, Be'naj?" Cauzel swiveled in his saddle to look her in the eye. "We have a long journey ahead. If, on our way to Lucnere, another solution presents itself, we shall endeavor to take full advantage. If not, I intend to do what is necessary to avail us of what we need to enter the buried city."

Be'naj wasn't certain if agreeing was truly compromise or defeat, but she nodded and promised to keep an eye out on the way. Cauzel was correct; they did have a long way to go. Never having travelled beyond the boundaries of Ifelian, the journey was sure to be a challenge in itself. She would be exposed to the world, in a sense, and the idea frightened her. She would have to lean on Cauzel, so starting off the trip by digging-in regarding an ethical impasse was probably unwise.

They rode west for some hours, heading for the Ifelian Corridor. Once they'd stopped to share a meal, Be'naj decided to voice an idea that'd been growing since their conversation that morning.

"What about one of my feathers?" she asked, knowing it sounded a little desperate. "Saffron said she thought my father might be from another world."

Cauzel had no immediate retort. "I must admit," he said after a pause, "the possibility intrigues me. It is certainly a premise worth testing." He shifted on the blanket he'd lain upon the frozen ground, in order to more comfortably converse. "However, at this juncture, we're only speculating on the origin of your parentage, and have no guarantee that ancestral other-worldliness is conveyed to progeny born in Elisahd to a native species. Do you want to risk travelling halfway across the continent only to be disappointed in the final hour when a more dependable option is essentially on the way?"

Be'naj's gaze fell to the snowy ground. "No," she admitted. The idea of desecrating his teacher's tomb wasn't the only one bothering her. She raised her eyes to meet his, wondering if the illusion he wore allowed his true emotions to show through. "This forest is all I've ever known. If my own people couldn't accept me, what chance do I have out in the wider world?"

Cauzel nodded sympathetically. "It would be a lie for me to say I think you walk an easy path. If I thought people were beyond such judgements, I wouldn't have chosen to wear a disguise for most of my adult life. Some will accept you, of course. You've seen that already."

Be'naj nodded and a smile crept to her lips as she thought of Saffron.

"Hold close to those who do," Cauzel continued. "For unfortunately, I cannot promise that of most."

At last, he offered to place an illusion spell upon her, similar to the one he wore, which would make her appear human to unsuspecting eyes. It would work best, he said, if he wove in some of her original features, like eye and hair color. Her wings, of course, would have to be hidden. Once the spell was in place, Be'naj checked her reflection in a pool of calm water. She looked like herself … only human. She was curious to find out how walking the world in a normal body might change her interactions and agreed.

Cauzel explained that as an accomplished transmogrifist, he was actually able to shift into several different forms. Yet, none of those provided the same social benefits as the illusion he maintained, and illusions were far less taxing than actual transformation. Given her limitations regarding Illanese, he suggested she still let him do the talking whenever possible. She knew Cauzel liked to talk, and being more reserved, Be'naj had no problems with such an arrangement.

Snow fell, soft and pure, during much of their westward march, creating a fond farewell to the forest. After reaching the road, they turned south. In a matter of days, they passed the human city of Pasaxtree, but didn't bother stopping. Cauzel knew too many people there, he said, and visiting might prove a longer delay than anticipated.

They left the snow behind in the valley between the mountains, and Be'naj got her first glimpse of a land beyond Ifelian. It felt strange to have such an uninterrupted view of the sky overhead, though she reveled in the constant reminder of her revered Shecclad.

Though winter was a slower season, according to Cauzel, they encountered no shortage of wagon traffic on the eastern road toward the River Chelhos. Cauzel explained the lands between their valley and the river were unclaimed by any kingdom, but that wealthy merchants with heavy interests in the route provided a similar dynamic.

Three more days by horse would get them to Lirole Run, assuming they remained unmolested. From there they could catch a ferry across the Chelhos to Talon Barge, where they hoped to secure passage down the river to Lucnere. Cauzel kept their interactions along the way cordial, but brief.

Be'naj thought Lirole Run looked crowded – too many houses packed together along the avenues for her taste – but it was nothing compared to the bustling crowd of Talon Barge. Though she never went further inland than the docks, she got an adequate glimpse of the human city from there. Immense, wooden warehouses for storage, laborers everywhere, gulls swooping down to scavenge; it was overwhelming. Rows and rows of buildings, for as far as she could see, pushed inward from the river like they were fighting for more room to breathe.

Cauzel booked spots on a barge leaving in a few hours. Once underway, Be'naj found that standing on the deck of the river transport introduced another barrage of stimulation. The wind off the water was biting cold and stung tears from her eyes. The sensation of floating, when she closed her eyes and held out her arms, was the closest thing to flying she'd ever experienced.

After indulging for several magical moments, Be'naj accompanied Cauzel below decks to escape the frigid air. Six days later found them docked at the harbor in Lucnere, where the sky was overcast with rippling layers of grey clouds. Cauzel warned Be'naj that this city in particular could be dangerous, and she was not to interact with strangers if it could be avoided.

Not only did Lucnere have a reputation for ruthlessness under the previous despot, but now that he was no longer lording over the populace with an iron fist, Cauzel expressed uncertainty that they could even count on the rigid rule of law to protect them.

Cauzel paid the tax imposed on their horses and another upon Be'naj for carrying a weapon into the city. He suggested they pull up the hoods on their cloaks as they ventured forth, to deter any prying eyes attempting to size them up.

Everyone Be'naj saw along the streets looked miserable. Though less cold than Ifelian, people walked with their heads down and shoulders hunched as if bracing against a chill wind. Despite Cauzel's concern, almost all the locals avoided making eye contact.

As their horses clopped along the stone-paved streets, she did see a surprising number of soldiers standing on the corners of avenues. Unlike the citizens, they had no qualms about staring down anyone who passed. From the shadow provided by her hood, Be'naj had the impression they were looking for an excuse to harass ordinary folk. They wore shirts with rows of small metal plates bound to a backing of black cloth. Leather caps adorned with a crown of steel ridges, also black, gave them a fearsome appearance. Their ash-hafted spears and inky capes didn't help put her at ease.

She didn't see anyone else on horseback as they slowly rode toward the graveyard where an entrance to the catacombs could be accessed – at least, according to Cauzel's memory. If they wanted to blend in, she thought, perhaps they shouldn't be riding.

The soldiers didn't give them any trouble, though Cauzel had made a clicking sound when she stopped to watch a pair roughing up a man who was simply walking down the avenue. He must have sensed how close she was to drawing her sword and intervening.

When they arrived at the graveyard, which was in a run-down section of the city with numerous crumbling buildings and empty lots overrun with weeds, they found it unoccupied. The rusted gate was unlocked and a faded banner, emblazoned with a skull weeping blood and crowned by a wreath of black rosebuds, hung from the iron fence posts near it. The words "Down with Dragnor" were scrawled over it in haphazard, black lettering.

Cauzel dismounted and pulled the reins over his horse's head. "Let's walk them inside," he said, pushing the gate open. It whined on its hinges, loudly enough to make Be'naj wince, but no one else was around to notice.

A distant roll of thunder gave only a breath of warning before a cold rain started to fall. Thankful for her cloak, Be'naj followed Cauzel into the extensive graveyard. An old willow tree near the center of the lot provided enough shelter for them to tie up the horses, though Be'naj wasn't sure what they'd do if someone came along and stole them.

Unencumbered by their mounts, Cauzel picked his way between rows of headstones, heading for an area dominated by larger crypts. Among them, he found what he was looking for: a circular building of sculpted marble and obsidian. Set behind a row of columns that encircled the mausoleum were alcoves populated by the carved busts of severe-looking men.

"This is it," Cauzel said, though when he pushed, the heavy stone door didn't budge. "Wealthy men are buried inside, and even more important, wealthy men lie in the catacombs underneath. I'm sure there are other entrances, but this is the one I know, and it's set far away from scrutiny."

Be'naj was shielded from the rain by the building's overhang, but her cloak was nearly soaked through, and water dripped in front of her face from a crease in her hood. "But how do we get in? That door must weigh a ton."

"That's what Shaping's for, my dear." Cauzel had to raise his voice to be heard over the rain, and his statement was followed by another roll of thunder.

"Do you think we should wait out the storm?" she asked, thinking about the poor horses under the willow.

"I think the storm provides the perfect cover, actually." Cauzel was already searching one of the pouches around his belt for spell ingredients.

"What about the horses?" Be'naj asked flat out. She didn't want to rescue Saffron only to earn her eternal enmity for losing her beloved mare.

"Oh, yes," Cauzel looked up, having retrieved an acorn from the depths of his pouch. "I suppose we should bring them along. We can stable them in the crypt."

Be'naj was about to make an argument about sacred spaces of the dead again but, given her failure to come up with an alternative to this entire expedition over the past weeks, kept her mouth shut and braved the rain to collect their mounts.

With her back turned, she heard a sound like the amplified slap of a bare palm over a hollow reed, coming from where Cauzel stood. When she returned with the horses, the door to the mausoleum stood wide open, and the acorn was smashed to pieces on the stone in front of it.

"After you," Cauzel offered from beside the yawning portal.

The space inside was pitch black, and Be'naj got the shivers thinking about entering a home of the dead in complete darkness. "Not in this life. After you, Cauzel." She nodded toward the bowels of the crypt, her hands occupied holding the reins of their steeds.

"Ah, this would be a bit easier with a little light, wouldn't it?" He wrapped his hand around the pommel of a dagger sheathed at his waist and spoke, "*Lucemi.*" Withdrawing his hand revealed a pleasant glow of white light from the pommel, enough so that Be'naj's half-eladrin eyes could make out the back of the crypt as Cauzel entered.

She followed with the horses, whose hooves clopped loudly on the marble floor. Five sealed, rectangular stone cairns elevated from the floor, their lids carved in relief likenesses of the people laid to rest within. The middle one was adorned with the depiction of a jester, and when Cauzel started groping the sides of the lid, which slightly overhung the base, Be'naj was afraid he was looking for purchase to push the grave open.

"What are you doing?" she gasped.

"Well, I know it's around here somewhere …" he muttered, not looking up from his searching. "Aha!" A brief *click* prefaced the entire lid sliding in the direction of the cairn's head. It stopped moving after half the lid protruded over the side, and Be'naj shut her eyes, imagining a corpse in extreme decay awaited her.

"Well, what are you waiting for?" Cauzel said. "Tie up the horses and come along. They'll be fine – we won't be gone more than an hour. Unless we get lost, of course."

Be'naj opened her eyes and saw he was already waist-deep inside the cairn, the light shining up from his waist creating dramatic shadows on his angular face. "What? What's going on?" She took a few steps forward to find Cauzel standing on a steep staircase that descended into darkness.

"This way to the catacombs," he answered calmly, reading her reticence. "The quicker we're off, the quicker our return."

Relieved that no mummies were involved, Be'naj wound the horses' reins through a crease in some of the stone relief-work decorating the wall of the crypt. "I'm sorry for the gloomy environment," she whispered to them, stroking each of their necks. "Try to rest, and I'll make sure you're well fed when I get back."

Reluctantly, she left them to climb down the steps into a narrow, downward sloping passage of excavated earth. Following Cauzel, whose "getting lost" comment she silently prayed was only in jest, Be'naj kept glancing from wall to ceiling as shadows created by the passing light on uneven surfaces suggested movement of subterranean creatures.

After a straight shot of a hundred paces or so, with her currently unseen wings nevertheless shedding feathers as they dragged along the sides of the tight corridor, Be'naj felt a draft of even cooler air as they reached a cross-passage, which was thankfully much wider and constructed of worked stone.

"Ah, it's coming back to me," Cauzel stated as he peered from left to right before proceeding down the latter. "The original catacombs were expanded years ago, first by a paranoid king who sought secretive ways to spy upon his enemies, then by Ebon Khorel as he obsessively searched for nearby veins of uril-chent. There were none here, of course, but now we have this veritable maze of tunnels to contend with."

Be'naj didn't have a notion what Cauzel was talking about, but she stayed silent to avoid distracting him lest he lose their way. They did come across a number of intersecting passages, though he always made a firm choice after no more than a moment's pause. She started to wonder if they should have brought a spool of yarn to help navigate in case of a wrong turn.

Just as that thought crossed her mind, Cauzel reached back and pushed her toward the wall. He flattened against it as well, trying to cover the light on his dagger's hilt with his hands. She was about to whisper a question when the answer presented itself. The echo of voices in conversation carried from around a bend, further down the tunnel, followed by the flickering orange of torchlight.

Despite his efforts, ribbons of light escaped from between Cauzel's fingers. "Can't you douse that?" Be'naj urged, sure their presence was about to be given away.

"I could, but then what?" he responded, sounding similarly panicked. "Do you want to pick a path through the dark if we have to make a run for it?"

"Who's there?" The question came from the torch-bearer.

Be'naj and Cauzel both fell silent and froze. She could see the silhouettes of two men in the halo of the torch, one of which raised and aimed a crossbow at them.

"Identify yourselves … Fennel's a dead-eye shot." From only twenty paces, Be'naj believed it. "Are you Dragnor's men?"

"I think one of them's a woman," the man called Fennel added.

Cauzel took a risk and fully uncovered the lit pommel. "Indeed, sirs. This is the Lady Be'naj, and I am Cauzel Blackfeather. I can assure you that we are neither Dragnor's, nor anyone else's, men."

The strangers drew nearer, though Fennel did not lower his crossbow. "I don't recognize you," the man with the torch said. "How is it you've ended up down here without us knowing?"

"She's armed," Fennel said, gesturing with the tip of his crossbow toward her sheathed sword.

Be'naj raised her palms. "I have not drawn." She was pleased to find her language lessons with Iliana were not a complete waste of time, for she understood these men well enough.

"We have come to visit the final resting place of an old friend of mine," Cauzel announced. "We certainly do not mean you fine people any harm."

"Hmm, what do think, Dremmond?" Fennel asked his companion.

"I think we had better ask the Baron," he said. "You wouldn't mind coming along with us, would you? Actually, we insist."

"Lead the way," Cauzel said, appearing unnervingly calm.

Dremmond, with the torch, took the forward position, while Fennel covered them from behind with his crossbow. Be'naj walked beside Cauzel, her hand resting on the pommel of her sword, ready to draw. She trusted that Cauzel understood the politics of the city more than she, and his relaxed demeanor gave her hope this might not come to violence.

"How does it do that, with the light?" Fennel asked once they were off.

Be'naj glanced over her shoulder at him but didn't feel much in the mood for accommodating. "Sorry, we don't explain things to people while they've got crossbows aimed at us." She faced forward again and didn't hear another word from Fennel.

Only a few minutes of walking brought them to a large, arched tunnel, which served as a major hub of crossing corridors. Braziers at the corners provided more ample light, and wooden barricades were set up to reduce access down to narrow gaps. A dozen or more individuals occupied the expanse blocked off by the barricades, some wrapped in conversations while others checked through bundles of supplies. A woman, armed with a crossbow, looked out at them from behind the closest barrier.

"Baron, we found a couple strangers wandering the catacombs," Dremmond announced as he reached the barricade. "Don't appear loyal to Dragnor, but perhaps you'd know better than us."

A man with dark hair and a well-groomed beard, younger-looking than Cauzel but well into adulthood, halted a conversation to assess them. He wore black leather armor with slits, much like Saffron's, offset by a scarlet tunic underneath. Be'naj's heart almost stopped when she looked more closely at the woman standing beside him.

"Saffron, you're here!" She broke into a wide smile and darted forward to greet her friend, almost in disbelief at their luck. Clearly she had to reevaluate Cauzel's information if he thought all his apprentices had sailed to the far coast.

The woman looked shocked as well, though a moment later Be'naj realized her error. This wasn't Saffron, though their features were strikingly similar: the same black hair, tanned skin, rounded nose, and plump lips.

"Do you know my sister?" she asked, advancing a step ahead of the man they were calling 'Baron.'

"Sister?" That made more sense, but what were the chances? "You're Dhania?" Be'naj asked.

Dhania smiled at the recognition and reached out in greeting. "How do you know Saffron? Have you seen her lately? It's been some months for me."

"Well, isn't this fortuitous?" the man beside Dhania asked. "I'm Rogan," he tapped his chest, "though most around here refer to me as 'Baron.' Just an old habit. Any friend of Saffron's is a friend of ours. I'm sorry, but I must have missed your names?"

"I am Be'naj, and this is my companion, Cauzel Blackfeather. How we came to be here is a long tale, but you should know that Saffron may be in danger."

"What?" Dhania reacted immediately. "What's wrong, where is she?"

Cauzel flashed Be'naj a sideways glance, followed by an awkward chuckle. "Now, we don't exactly know that she's in any danger—"

"She's been abducted and taken halfway across the world!" Be'naj cut in. Dhania had the right to the truth about her own family.

"Abducted? By whom?" This time it was Rogan cutting in.

"Please, everyone calm yourselves," Cauzel suggested. "No one is served by jumping to conclusions. We don't know who, or if anyone, for that matter, is holding Saffron. She was apprenticing under me and disappeared with a pair of other pupils while I was away on important business."

"When was this?" Dhania asked. "Is that why you're here? Is she near?"

Cauzel sighed, and Be'naj reclaimed the exposition. "Cauzel is a Shaper and has used magic to divine Saffron's location – somewhere called *Zeblon*."

"Zeblon? That's on the southeastern corner of the continent. Pardon, but if you've lost your apprentices, why are you in Lucnere and not on a ship to save them?" Baron Rogan asked.

"Because, Sir, there are possibly more pressing matters." Cauzel sighed again as Saffron's defenders shot him challenging looks. "As her sister and … brother-in law?" – Rogan and Dhania blushed at his presumption – "I assume you know Lady Saffron well. You know how capable she is. I could read it within the first hour of meeting her.

"Given she and my apprentices have survived this long already, I have faith that they've found some sort of equilibrium with whatever situation they're in. We will help them, yes, but it may not be quite the emergency you three assume."

Be'naj didn't want to admit it, but she knew Cauzel's assessment was sound. If she was honest, part of her own distress owed to imagining that Saffron had lost hope, that she thought no one cared for or would come after her. She wished she could send her some sort of comforting message.

They all stood silently for a moment, staring at one another. Be'naj paid particular attention to Dhania, who looked astonishingly like her sister. It made her miss Saffron more.

Finally, Rogan spoke. "So, what can we do to help? Saffron is dear to us both, and I know she would seek a way to assist us if our situations were reversed."

"She would come for me," Dhania said plainly, shaking her head. She looked up at Rogan. "You know she would."

He nodded in agreement. "If you need to go after her, I understand completely. I would join you myself if it wasn't for Dominic …"

Cauzel looked around the crude encampment. "That may not be necessary. Why don't you tell us what *you're* doing in the catacombs first, so we may chart the most fruitful course?"

Rogan shrugged. "We're fighting tyranny, and I'm fighting for my son. If you're not from around here, you may be unaware that the King-priest of Chelpa was defeated in a war to claim the Northern Provinces. Unfortunately, his downfall led to a predictable power struggle over the empire he left behind.

"Dragnor Blacklesh is a cruel warlord, one of the King-priest's lieutenants, who seized control of the capital almost immediately upon news of his king's demise. After years of struggling under the old regime, these people deserve better." Rogan gestured to the men and women around them. Dremmond and Fennel remained a few respectful paces away, listening to the entire conversation.

"And was your son killed by the warlord?" Be'naj asked, unable to hold back. She could see years of pain etched into the lines around Rogan's eyes and felt a stab of sympathy.

Rogan cleared his throat. "I hope not. I only confirmed he was alive a couple weeks ago, after being separated since he was a baby. My sources swear he is being raised as a servant in the palace Dragnor now occupies. I'm fighting to get him back."

"It is a worthy cause," Be'naj offered, wishing she could do more.

Rogan gave a wan smile and looked to Dhania. "Dhania has been with me since my return to Chelpa and has helped immensely." He spoke directly to her. "But your sister needs you, and this is not even your homeland. You should go."

Tears were forming in Dhania's eyes, and she blinked them out. "I'm not leaving you." She looked to Cauzel. "This man is right: Saffron is the toughest woman I know." She gestured to Be'naj. "And she has others fighting for her. Dominic deserves someone fighting for him, too."

Rogan squeezed his arm around Dhania's shoulder, lips trembling, then bent to kiss her eyelids.

Be'naj felt moved and like an intruder at the same time. She looked downward, examining a smudge on the toe of her boot while the moment passed.

"Now, it's your turn to share," Rogan said, looking from Be'naj to Cauzel. "Why Lucnere, if your charges are in Zeblon?"

Cauzel jumped in more quickly than Be'naj would have guessed. "We're looking into a threat that's been on the rise near our homeland, and perhaps elsewhere. My old teacher was buried in these catacombs with something that may prove useful in our getting to the bottom of things, as it were. Therefore, we need to reach his tomb."

"Do you know where it lies?" Rogan asked. "We've been harassing Dragnor for weeks while hiding down here, but he's begun armed patrols to flush us out. You don't want to run into one of them in the dark."

"Embril was buried in a private tomb near the 'Repose of Kings.' I should be able to find it once we reach the area."

Rogan shook his head. "That's nearer to the palace and Dragnor's access to the catacombs. It could be dangerous."

"We'll take you," Dhania offered. "If you're helping Saffron, it's the least we can do to make sure you get out of here safely." Rogan shot her a questioning look but gave in a moment later, nodding his assent.

"We can go now, if you're ready," he said. "I know the way, but we'll want to move quickly. Dremmond, keep an eye on things here. We should have a team returning in the next hour."

"Thank you," Be'naj said. "Trust me, I don't want to be down here any longer than necessary."

Dhania retrieved and fastened a scimitar to her belt, and the four of them set off down one of the wide tunnels extending from the brazier-lit hub. Rogan looked down at Cauzel's dagger, which still provided its aura of white light as they left the encampment.

"So you were teaching Saffron magic, you say? If that's the case, I know you've got to have a trick or two up your sleeves," he grinned.

"One or two, yes." Cauzel responded dryly.

Rogan led the way, with Dhania just behind. Cauzel and Be'naj followed a step after. Once they crossed a channel of foul-smelling water by way of a short, stone bridge, Rogan announced they were drawing near.

"Ah, we are. I recognize the place," Cauzel confirmed. "The 'Repose of Kings' is just a short way off to the right."

Be'naj looked that way, but darkness claimed everything more than a half-dozen paces out. Darting from wall to wall, trying to maintain cover from imagined watchers, Cauzel took over the lead. In a few short turns they stood before a tall archway, decorated near its apex by the carved likeness of a stalking panther.

"This is it," he announced, voice trembling slightly with excitement. He walked to within a step or two of the arch then stopped, holding out an arm to block the others from advancing. "It may be warded. Give me a moment."

Be'naj held her breath while Cauzel chanted in ancient Eladrin, moving his arms like he was tracing the edges of an invisible window. Rogan turned to gaze into the pitch black behind them, probably ingrained to keep watch, though she didn't imagine he'd be able to see danger until it was already upon them.

When Cauzel ceased chanting, the body of the panther above them glowed red. "It's a good thing we stopped," he reported. "I can't say I'm surprised. One of Embril's former students must have trapped the entrance on his behalf. I'll have to go alone from here."

Be'naj opened her mouth, but Cauzel was already shaking his head before she got a word out. "It's not safe for the three of you to pass the ward, but as a fellow Shaper, I should be able to proceed unharmed. I don't think we need to test whether the trap is lethal, do you?"

"You're just going to leave us in the dark, then?" Be'naj asked.

He pointed up toward the glowing panther, which throbbed bright and dim like a feline-shaped heartbeat. "Not completely. I should be back soon." As he started down the corridor beyond, he reiterated his warning, "Remember, do not cross the archway."

Be'naj watched him recede down the tunnel, which possessed a gradual curve, taking him shortly beyond sight. She turned back to the others, but the pulsing red light lent a sinister element to their faces, so she took to gazing out into the catacombs like Rogan.

That wasn't much better, for every time the light weakened she found herself straining into the shadows until it grew brighter again. It was like riding waves of anxiety and relief. The throbbing was so distracting, she thought it just a trick of her imagination when finally the light receded again and distant spots of red remained in the far-off dark. Not until Rogan spoke did she realize they were actually approaching torches.

"Looks like we've got visitors," he said, drawing a saber and dagger. The air instantly dimmed around them, though the panther continued to pulse. Rogan looked down the hallway where Cauzel had disappeared, no doubt fighting the urge to seek refuge there.

Be'naj unsheathed her arming sword, wishing she'd brought her shield, though she hadn't anticipated battle when they'd left the horses. Dhania drew her scimitar and stood between them, also looking into the black.

"There they are!" came a shout from the approaching group. "Whoever it is, they're not ours. No need to take them alive!"

Be'naj heard steel being drawn and tried to assess numbers as their attackers broke into a charge. Two of the black-clad soldiers, similar to those she'd seen above ground, carried torches in their off-hands, swords elsewise. Another two carried spears, and a final pair brandished spiked maces and shields.

She didn't want to get hemmed in, given the length advantage of the spears, so Be'naj took a few, quick steps forward to meet the on-comers, timing her first swing to knock aside the closest shaft. The momentum of the man carrying it caused them to collide, shoulder to shoulder, as they both turned to avoid the impact.

Be'naj stumbled onto her back foot, but as she stabilized and set her front leg down again, she landed an uppercut to the chin of her attacker, then pushed him clear with both fists, creating space to swing her weapon.

Outnumbered, with others to defend, she knew she had to be aggressive. By their own admission, these foes were not granting quarter so she could not afford to either. The man she'd punched was dazed, and after a quick strike to give one of the sword-bearers pause, she turned her blade in a lethal thrust to the staggered man's sternum. Blood gurgled from his throat as she loosened her weapon from his chest cavity, just in time to deflect a mace from her unprotected side.

Rogan and Dhania proved not to be dead weight in battle. Saffron's sister vocalized fierce battle-cries with each swing of her scimitar, and the repeated clangs of metal from behind told Be'naj her new allies were at least holding their own. Be'naj kept on the offensive while working her way around the edge of the melee to flank their opponents. See how they like defending from both sides, she thought. She wondered if these ruffians had any recognition of what they'd gotten themselves into.

Gracefully dropping to a knee to bypass the high-held shield of one of the soldiers, Be'naj nearly severed his leg. She was up again and leaping out of reach of a spear thrust before her enemies could capitalize on her lower position.

Be'naj saw Rogan stabbing one of the torch-bearers in the heart with his dagger, bringing the numbers even. Without that advantage, Dragnor's men had little hope. Be'naj disarmed the last shield-bearer of his mace, and when he put both hands behind his shield to charge, Dhania cut him down from behind.

Beyond the fighting, Be'naj caught a glimpse of Cauzel, his shoulders bent forward, using the wall for support as he neared the archway. Something had gone wrong. She redoubled her efforts against the soldiers, and she and Rogan made short work of their final foes.

As soon as the threat was ended, Be'naj raced toward Cauzel. Careful not to cross the threshold of the arch, which he had yet to reach, she called out, "Cauzel, are you hurt?" His white light mitigated the throbbing red, and she could clearly tell he was having trouble standing straight.

He tried to look up, but doing so caused him to cough roughly. A greenish cloud of mist expelled from his mouth when he did so, though she noticed he was wearing a necklace of gnarly, serrated claws around his neck. He lowered his head and coughed again. "The archway wasn't the only thing trapped."

"What can we do?" she asked, looking desperately at the others for ideas. Perhaps there were healing herbs back at the rebel encampment? But Dhania had not escaped unscathed, either. She was grimacing and holding her sword arm at the elbow, underneath a bleeding cut across her bicep. "Gracious, are you two all right?"

"It's not bad," Dhania declared, though Rogan looked concerned.

Cauzel coughed again, then spoke. "I'll be fine, too, I think. Just need some water and a spot of rest." He finally limped past the panther-guarded arch, which ceased glowing as he did.

"Gods, you don't look good, my friend." Rogan lifted Cauzel's arm over his shoulder to assist him. The hike back to the encampment was slower, but Cauzel was able to resume walking on his own by the time they reached their destination. Once there, he guzzled almost an entire water bladder, then swished and spit a mouthful of green-tinted liquid onto the floor.

"What went on in that tomb?" Dhania asked as another rebel finished bandaging her arm.

"Ah, I'd rather not talk about it," Cauzel got out before coughing again and beating his chest. "I did, however, succeed in procuring what we needed. My thanks to you both for guiding us. And, sorry about the patrol."

Rogan shook his head. "No need. Dragnor's been sending more lately, which tells me he's starting to feel vulnerable. We may be able to plan a successful strike against the palace, soon."

"I wish we could stay and help you find your son, Rogan." Be'naj had considered doing so while on the way back, but realized that might take weeks, if not months, as these people had already been fighting for some time.

Cauzel nodded. "While we may not be able to do that, perhaps I can leave you with some aid …" He rummaged through one of his belt pouches, withdrawing a closed fist. He held his hand out and waved with the other for Rogan to approach.

"I call these, 'Smokestones.' They look like normal rocks, but I've enchanted them to release plumes of dark smoke when they strike a hard surface. Throw one on the ground when you need to mask your movements." Cauzel transferred the rocks into Rogan's open palm.

Rogan looked at one more closely between his finger and thumb. "And you're sure they work?" He looked at Cauzel as if the Shaper might be playing a practical joke. From what Be'naj could see, they looked like ordinary pebbles.

"Absolutely! Very useful. I've got a couple more I'm keeping for myself, actually. They only work once, so don't waste them," Cauzel warned.

Rogan shrugged. "Thank you. I'm sure they will come in handy."

"You're welcome!" Cauzel replied. "And now, we must take our leave. We have a long journey yet, and our horses will be holding a grudge for a week if we don't feed them soon." He shot a look at Be'naj. "Yes, I haven't forgotten them."

Be'naj smiled, then clutched wrists with Rogan and embraced Dhania as they shared farewells.

"Do tell Saffron I miss her," Dhania implored.

"Good fortune in your quest, my friends," Rogan offered.

Cauzel refused to lean on Be'naj as they made their way back to the crypt, but she noticed his cough, though intermittent, stayed with him.

Chapter 24

The Eternal Flame

"If we take the couatl back with us, he's just going to be added to the Wolfspider's collection," Thaelios argued.

"But if we don't," Phaerim said, wincing as he tenderly patted the improvised bandage on his bite wound, "who knows what the Wolfspider will do to us. Need I remind you, we've still got these infernal collars around our necks?"

Saffron closed her eyes, trying to think, but the world spun behind her lids.

"This is an intelligent creature," Dyphina contributed. "It doesn't belong in captivity. Honestly, none of the animals in those cages do."

"So you're saying I just got bit by that rabid fanatic for nothing?" Phaerim countered, the pitch of his voice rising.

Thaelios repeatedly tapped his finger to his chin. "We simply need to figure out a way to release it without being blamed for it."

"So, lie?" Phaerim summarized.

Dyphina shrugged. "I can live with that."

Saffron sighed. "I agree. We can't knowingly consign another to the same situation we've been fighting to rid ourselves of, even if it is a winged snake. I value the truth, but these people deserve to be lied to, given all they've done." She looked from Dyphina, who nodded, to Phaerim, who rolled his eyes but didn't disagree. "Good," she added. "I'll do it."

Dyphina, and even Thaelios, laughed.

"You would be about as convincing as a cat wooing a mouse right now." Dyphina crossed her arms and shook her head as if Saffron was a child who'd just asked to play with knives.

"She's right," Thaelios said. "You are the last person who should be responsible for bluffing at the moment."

"I'll do it," Dyphina declared as she peered into the couatl's cage once more. "I can be quite persuasive when I need to be."

Phaerim shrugged and nodded as she spoke to the winged snake in the fey language. Its sounds were completely unrecognizable as words to Saffron.

"How are we going to free the creature?" Thaelios wondered aloud. "We can't take it back to the pens without risking being seen."

Dyphina straightened and opened the cage. "I'll take care of that, too. Our feathered friend, here, remembers seeing several ventilation shafts on his way in. He can escape on his own through one of those. He says it won't take long."

She extended her arm into the cage and the couatl coiled around it. Its rainbow-hued wings truly were magnificent. Dyphina carried the creature to the door leading back toward the animal pens. "If I don't return soon, it may be because I've gone up the air shaft myself." She winked and slipped out the door.

"Good luck," Saffron called after her, too late. The door was already closed.

As it turned out, not much luck was needed. Dyphina came back in a few moments, which Phaerim had used to sneak into the tunnels to dispose of the cage in a random corridor. No alarm had been raised so far, but he didn't dare go close enough to see what had become of the beast-master.

They walked single-file toward the Wolfspider's pens, Saffron doing her best not to look guilty. Harzhim and Lodiammon must have spotted their torch from an adjacent alcove as they passed, for they startled Saffron from behind when she was tauntingly close to her meager but currently enticing mattress.

"How did it go? Do you have the bird?" Harzhim's voice beckoned in Illanese, which surprised Saffron. Normally, he allowed her to translate from Begnari. She was relieved, however, since they'd all seemed to have forgotten that important detail while deciding who should speak. Maybe she wasn't the only one impaired from a night of carousing …

Lodiammon stood slightly behind Harzhim with his arms folded, looking humorless. Obviously, none of them were carrying a cage. All four turned around silently as if they'd suddenly fallen mute.

"It was a disaster!" Dyphina finally said, lifting her arms dramatically. "We could have all gotten killed for nothing!" She stepped forward and started spilling a story of animals out of their cages and a confrontation with the beast-master, which included him taunting them with the fact that the bird had already been picked up and moved by an agent of its new owner.

Saffron noticed Dyphina flipping her verdant tresses over her shoulder more than once – a bare shoulder, given that she'd allowed her tunic to slip down over it. Imagining the ploy would be more effective with fewer distractions, Saffron quietly shooed the others down the hallway, following until they'd reached their own cage, which had been left unlocked. She glanced further down the pens at the lightly snoring form of Wemic with a pinch of regret before snuggling onto her own sleeping pallet, alone.

Her head throbbed the next morning, but she felt more like herself. Saffron could only remember parts of the previous night and sought out Dyphina before breakfast to ask how their captors had taken the news of their failure.

"I think it went pretty well," her friend assessed. "Harzhim seemed disappointed, but said he'd do his best to explain to the Wolfspider that circumstances were beyond our control. That other fellow was downright sullen, however. I don't know *what* his problem is."

"Do you think we're looking at any sort of punishment?" Saffron asked.

Dyphina gave an uncommitted expression. "Hard to tell with these blokes, isn't it? I wouldn't sit around worrying about it. We did the right thing."

Saffron nodded. That much, she remembered.

She didn't see much of Harzhim for the next few days, actually, until he approached the pen one morning during breakfast to summon her.

"You must have made some wealthy friends, Lady Saffron," he said as he unlocked the cage. "That is good – good for you," he nodded.

She was disturbed by the undercurrent of hostility in his delivery. "What does that mean, exactly?"

"You have been awarded a day pass, it seems." He handed her a small, thin, rectangular sheet of brass with the Wolfspider's emblem stamped into it, threaded by a leather cord. "Transport is waiting for you on the surface. You have a full day of freedom to move about the city. Be sure you return by sunrise."

Saffron furrowed her brow, accepting the pass. Was this the work of the Circle of Twelve, or did she have a new benefactor?

"What is this?" Phaerim asked incredulously, drawn by the conversation. "Just her and not the rest of us?"

Saffron looked back at him and widened her eyes, willing him not to spill any details about their previous hiatus from confinement.

"Honestly," Harzhim shrugged, switching to Illanese again, "it probably means some bored noble has paid a hefty sum to fuck her. Hope for your sake he's got a nice cock."

Saffron flinched at his response, for there was no amusement in it. She couldn't remember the Consul ever speaking so crassly before, and he seemed unusually agitated this morning. "I'll take my chances," she said, then walked straight past Harzhim up the inclined passage she'd already used to smuggle out of the pens.

When she opened the door, guards on the outside twisted to confront her but fell back to their posts when they saw the brass pass shining around her neck. As before, a wagon waited for her. She was relieved to recognize Groilen, albeit in his previous disguise, as the driver. She hoisted onto the seat beside him and reclined, only then peering back toward the Arena tunnel. The guards looked straight ahead, seemingly unconcerned with her departure.

"Good morning, My Lady," Groilen offered in his usual, raspy voice.

"Sir," she replied, deeply breathing in the crisp air. Why did such a simple act feel so different, knowing she was free? Even if the freedom only lasted a day ...

"Where would you like to go first?" he asked, snapping the reins to urge the horses into motion. "Our official engagement isn't until after dark, so you've got most of the day to explore at your leisure. I know you haven't really had the chance to interact with the city we're asking you to help save ..."

"Is there a catch? Can I really do anything I want?" Her eyes narrowed as she considered Groilen, though he broke into a disarming grin that put her at ease.

"Anything within reason, I suppose," he laughed. "I've got a small pouch of silver for the vendors, which you're welcome to make use of if there's something you'd like to try."

Saffron nodded. "Take me to the sea, then. The docks."

Groilen raised an eyebrow. "I've not enough on me to secure passage, if that's what you're thinking. Though, I wouldn't blame you," he added.

"Not that," she answered, though the thought was tempting. "My father took me to the seashore often as a little girl. I'd like to see it again."

"Of course." Groilen steered them the opposite direction from the night he took her to the mansion of the Twelve. Their path led downhill, carrying them around the perimeter of a large, open market. She could see the glimmer of the sun on the ocean in the distance while descending the slope, as well as one or two ships on their approach to port.

The breeze carried the scent of brine and salt, growing thicker as they went, and the sounds of the marketplace – people haggling in Begnari – carried her mind back to her homeland. As they drew nearer to the docks, the wooden hulls of moored ships and even taller masts of curtained sails rose to block her view. Large warehouses full of goods, on an even larger scale than she'd seen at Talon Barge, lined the entire avenue south of the docks.

The wharf formed a right angle, extending east and north, and ships lined it almost to the horizon. A small way back from the boardwalk was a square of sand from the beach, in which children played and dug for shells. Saffron could remember her and Dhania burying their father's feet in the warm sand while he pretended to be asleep. She felt a lump forming in her throat and turned to Groilen, who had brought the wagon to a halt.

"Do you mind if I spend some time alone?" she asked.

His face softened as he stared back. "You won't get lost?" he asked.

Saffron shook her head. "I promise."

Groilen grunted, then started untying the pouch of silver from his belt. He handed it to her, though she hadn't asked. "I will meet you on the benches opposite the temple stairs after dusk."

She nodded, then climbed down from the wagon, patting one of the horses on its rump.

"Don't be surprised when I look different," he added. Groilen waited until she'd stepped well and clear, then snapped his reins and turned the wagon back the way they'd come.

On her own, yet surrounded by hundreds of others as they went about their daily work, Saffron took a moment to decide how to spend the day. With so much of the city unknown, she chose to just see where the morning took her. She tied the pouch of money to her own belt, realizing she probably stuck out in her grey slave tunic and thick, metallic collar. She would have to be cognizant of anyone trying to take advantage of her status.

Those thoughts retreated once she took off her sandals and dipped her toes into the wet sand. Though it was winter, the coast this far south stayed mild, and some of the playing children hadn't bothered wearing shirts. She helped a pair of young siblings build a sand fortress until their mother noticed and scooped them away with a worried look.

After watching the seabirds lazily dive and circle around the wharf, looking either for fish in the water or a free meal out of it, Saffron headed back to the market. She felt a guilty that Dyphina and the others didn't have the chance to share in this taste of freedom, but she could do little about that. No one would be harmed by her enjoying it.

The market was every bit as bustling as those near her home in Sesfaran, and the sheer number of importing ships created a wide range of wares to haggle over. Cloth, foodstuffs, woven and hand-crafted items of every sort were bartered for and sold. She indulged in some honey mead and a small sack of roasted nuts while she walked around the colorful pavilions and carts, taking in the sights.

When the constant noise became bothersome, she drifted on up the hill, leaving the market behind. The walk seemed longer than it appeared when coming downhill on the wagon, and her calves were burning when she reached the next level of the city.

To the south, overlooking the market below, Saffron could make out what was clearly the Temple of Life and Blood. Though the name didn't suggest it, this regal structure was a cathedral to Pnemonesis, god of the open water. Worship of such a deity made sense in a place so dependent on the sea for its way of life, she thought. Massive sculptures of porpoises, ejecting water from their blowholes, formed a large fountain outside the shrine.

Between where she stood and the temple, however, was a park of green fruit trees and a rare swath of grass. Though she was nowhere near the top heights of the city, she could see from her vantage that mostly desert lay inland beyond Zeblon. She decided it might be nice to relax in the arboreal shade and give her feet a chance to rest.

Drawing nearer the park and further from the market, she heard the strains of a flute drifting on the wind, as well as the occasional high-pitched laughter of children. Once she'd infiltrated the outlying circle of trees forming the park's border, Saffron saw a small amphitheater carved into the embankment that formed the far side of the park's boundary.

A Begnari man sat on one of the rows of graduated seating, playing the flute as a sparse collection of people relaxed nearby, basking in his performance. A small cart rested at the heart of the stage, and various instruments sat on or around it. Saffron walked closer and took a seat to listen.

She didn't recognize the composition the man was playing, but he possessed reasonable skill. She guessed that he may be self-taught, for nuances in his performance suggested a lack of formal instruction. Nevertheless, the music moved her and ignited a latent urge to play.

Saffron saw a lyre resting on the cart and crossed the stage to examine it. It had seen its share of use, but was in working condition. She waited for the song he was playing to end, then lifted the instrument and approached, asking if he minded an accompaniment.

The musician gave a warm smile, said it would be his pleasure, and waited for her to make adjustments to the strings before beginning his next song. She listened for a moment to get a feel for the chords, then joined in, providing a sultry harmony to enhance the emotion of his piece.

Others in the park noticed and started coming closer, listening to and watching their duet with heightened interest. They received appreciative applause after their first song, so they played another, and another, and another. Saffron had no idea how long they actually played, but her fingers were red from the strings, and their audience had doubled by the time she realized she should be going.

She couldn't find the sun, for it had already descended below the rise of the hill. The afternoon was late, and she had walking to do before evening. She thanked the musician for allowing her to play, and the audience for listening, then made for the path that continued up the slope.

Passing the foreign houses and trade shops, she knew that days like today were exactly the reason she had to do whatever was necessary to become free once more. Saffron's thoughts turned to Rogan and Jaiden, both of whom she hadn't seen in months, but who she knew would never give up fighting for what they believed in.

As she climbed higher, she could finally see the top of the Eternal Flame burning above the roof of the temple to Hellignok. Before the end of the night, she *would* extinguish it. Hopefully, that would earn enough currency with the Twelve for them to live up to their side of the bargain.

The journey back to Ifelian would be a long one, and she hoped Be'naj, and Cauzel for that matter, could forgive her disappearance. She imagined the surprise on their faces when she showed up, months overdue. Would they be pleased to see her, or angry? She supposed the former, at least on Cauzel's account, given she'd be returning with his other apprentices. She wasn't so sure about Be'naj, but hoped she'd be allowed to make it up to her.

After the things she'd started to feel with Dyphina, she realized she could be aroused just as much by a woman as a man. Did that mean she could fall in love with a woman as well? She'd felt such a quick connection with Be'naj that she wondered if that's what was starting to happen before she left. Was it possible she could convince Be'naj to be open to such things?

Saffron shook her head. Entertaining such thoughts was silly. She'd only spent a couple days with Be'naj – now she was spinning hopes in her head of them falling in love? Captivity had made her lonely.

Maybe she should visit her sister first and talk it out. They'd always been able to share about boys. Well, at least until Rogan came along. She missed Dhania and needed to be free of her damned collar!

She'd finally wound around the bend of the hill, and the sky was purpling as the Temple of Eternal Flame came fully into view – an impressive structure, to be sure. She couldn't deny that Hierarch Krygos of Hellig-nok possessed style. That didn't mean he hadn't specifically tried to eliminate her in the Arena.

She could look at tonight as a little spoonful of revenge on that front. Taking a seat on a bench across the pebbled path from the temple, Saffron looked around, wondering what Groilen's disguise would be for the evening. She anticipated nearly everyone walking past as a possible imposter, and almost embarrassed herself by starting conversations with a couple of likely subjects.

When she caught a middle-aged man in the red and orange robes of the temple staring at her from the steps of the cathedral, she thought she'd been recognized. Her stomach clenched as he descended and stalked purposefully across the lawn toward her. Where was Groilen? Should she try to run away and circle back later?

The priest carried a swollen, worn-in rucksack on his back, which slowed him enough that she was certain she could outpace him if she bolted straight away. Something about the look on his scraggly-bearded face kept her from moving, though. Was it the eyes? Perhaps he didn't mean her any harm.

Stopping in front of the unoccupied half of the bench, the priest struggled to remove the pack from his back, not making eye contact with Saffron. He set his load on the ground at his feet, then plopped down wearily beside her. He wiped sweat from his brow. "Whew, I regret not asking Gaeric to at least shrink the cauldron first." The man spoke while still facing the gilded temple, and Saffron briefly wondered if he was touched in the head.

Leaning slightly in his direction, she raised an eyebrow and risked a whispered, "Groilen?"

"Mmmhmm," he hummed, still not addressing her overtly. "I've got an extra set of supplicant robes in the pack for you, courtesy of Gaeric."

"We're pretending to be priests?" The idea left Saffron conflicted.

"It's the best way to penetrate the Inner Sanctum where the Flame is kept," he answered.

"So, you've got a plan?" she asked, finding the concept refreshing.

Groilen chuckled, still appearing to ignore her. "For what it's worth. I can even share it with you, if you like. And further, I'll throw in a bit of good news."

"Well, I can't argue with that." Saffron turned her head to look at the drooping branches of a nearby tree to keep up the guise that they were strangers.

"We've got some time before the late crowd heads home, so first, why not a bit of a lesson?"

Saffron chewed lightly on the end of her tongue before speaking. "What makes you presume I need lessons?"

"Oh, don't get offended," Groilen huffed. "You seem like you have considerable wild talent, yet I'd wager not much formal arcane instruction. Am I right?"

Saffron considered her observations of the musician in the park, earlier. While the untrained crowd might not have been able to tell the difference between his playing and hers, or the reason for it if they could, she could spot his limitations straight away. Perhaps this was the same for Groilen. She relaxed her shoulders back on the bench and nodded.

"The major competing faiths of Zeblon, as you undoubtedly know after your recent Arena battle, are those of Hellig-nok, God of Fire and the Innumerable Stars, and Pnemonesis, Lord of the Unforgiving Waves." Groilen the priest stroked his mustache. "They are both chaotic and terrible in their own right, but it is the church's business to present their gods in a positive manner.

"I wonder; do you know the difference between Shaping, like the magic you do, and what is referred to as Channeling?"

Saffron slid a little closer on the bench so they could both continue looking forward, yet hear one another without raising voices. "I had a friend who told me Channeling was the magic of the gods."

"Yes, well, it is power bestowed by the gods on those they favor. Now, which do you think is greater?" Groilen asked.

The question had never occurred to Saffron. "Well, I suppose the gods are more powerful than any mortal …"

"And yet," Groilen cut in, "they are limited in how much of that power they can grant to other beings. My colleague, Resasha, has studied this topic extensively, using Gaeric as something of a test subject, though she doesn't let on as much. The reverence received, the worship, and for reasons of simplification, the followers any of the gods have on Elisahd plays into the relative power they are able to manifest on this world through the acts of surrogates – often their priests.

"A singular relationship, a bond stronger than all others, can exist between a god and only one mortal conduit at a time. This 'Champion,' as they're known, can receive benefits and powers beyond other Channellers, though this connection is also ultimately limited by the Veil of Nessus – the force separating the Outer Planes from ours."

Saffron felt a prick in her chest that may have been pride. Was that the relationship Jaiden had been contending with when he rejected her? "As fascinating as this all is, Groilen, what does any of it have to do with our current mission?"

Groilen pushed on, undaunted. "Krygos, Hierarch of the Temple of Eternal Flame, is supposedly the Champion of Hellig-nok. As such, we should not underestimate his connection with his god. He was the one who conjured the fire that burns within the temple, apparently without need for new fuel. The feud between the temples, Lady Saffron, is for more than just an increase in tithing. It influences the very real, manifested magical power of their deities, and so should not be taken lightly. The task we seek to perform is of consequence because in temporarily stealing the flame from this temple, we could very possibly be stealing power from Krygos, and he's not going to like that at all."

Saffron nodded. "Understood." She watched as a large swath of people exited the brass doors of the temple, ambling down the stairs to head home. Stars were starting to peek out from behind the darkening curtain of the evening sky, and most of the devout would likely be bedding down soon, after a late meal. "You said you had some good news for me?"

"First, change into this robe." Groilen pulled a red-orange bundle of cloth from his pack and set it on the bench between them. "You can pull it on over your tunic; just, go behind a tree or something so the whole city doesn't notice."

Saffron snorted, then grabbed the robe. "Give me a moment." She disappeared behind a pair of close growing poplars, shielding herself from view of the main avenue as best she could. The robe was rough on her skin, but fit fairly well. Gaeric must have guessed her size.

"Pull the hood up to hide that collar," Groilen suggested as she rejoined him on the bench.

"So what are we, a pair of priests?" Saffron postulated. "Aren't you worried what will happen when people ask us questions we can't answer? Other clergy, for instance?"

"These robes are slightly different than those worn by the priests inside," Groilen explained. "I am Verigo, an ambassador from the shrine to Hellig-nok in Zarway, and you are a supplicant prodigy. I've brought you so that you may offer yourself to Hellig-nok more fully after being purified by the Eternal Flame. If anyone asks, we'll say you've shown signs of being chosen by the fire god, which hopefully you can prove to them through some of your Shaping tricks. That's your way into the Inner Sanctum where the source of the flame lies."

"Well, that's simple enough," Saffron mocked. "All I have to do is convince the zealot worshipers of a fire god that he likes me better than them. You do know my songs take time and concentration before showing an effect, don't you?"

Groilen shrugged, "We'll improvise. Nothing we haven't both done before, and we're still here to talk about it, no?" He stood and waved an arm toward the temple. "Shall we to it, then? Oh, one more thing." He reached into his pack again and withdrew a sheathed dagger with a short, buckled strap attached to it. Handing it to Saffron, he added, "Just in case."

She took it, huffing as she seemed to be the one taking most of the risk. She was glad, at least, that she was not expected to pull this off all on her own. If it came to it, Groilen's legs were shorter than hers, and they would probably catch him first. She smiled at that mental picture while buckling the dagger around her forearm so it could be hidden by her sleeve. Groilen seemed to interpret the smile as good favor and smiled back.

He took her gently by the waist and urged her forward, toward the temple. "You should walk a pace or two ahead of me for the sake of deference. Don't worry, I'll tell you where to go."

By the time they reached the base of the steps, the building appeared huge. The eight golden domes of the roof each looked like a small sun, reflecting the light of the Eternal Flame at their center. Acolytes in white robes bowed their heads and opened the heavy doors as they approached, and Saffron bowed hers in return, unsure of what else to do.

Inside, the temple was just as spectacular. The air was warm, even at the entrance, from the cast-off heat of the pillar of fire at the cathedral's center. Partial, curved walls created the impression of tower-like segments at each of the outer reaches of an eight-pointed star, though each cylinder was incomplete, remaining open to the rest of the space.

The cathedral consisted predominantly of three levels, all constructed like rings focusing attention to the inner, open shaft where flame met sky. Interspersed worshippers still knelt in silent prayer within a block of cushioned stations, but the first floor was mostly empty. Here and there, pairs of white-robed acolytes stood in reflective discussion or walked from one place to another, but Saffron couldn't identify any higher-level priests. That calmed her nerves, slightly.

"When you gain entrance to the Inner Sanctum, I'll switch the pack over to you. You can claim it holds requirements for your ritual, if necessary. Inside it is the Bottomless Cauldron – an artifact Gaeric and his superior enchanted for just this purpose. Place it at the base of the fire and then get out of there, quickly. It may not take effect immediately, but you want to be out of sight by the time it does. I'll create a distraction to keep the priests from catching on to what you're up to." Groilen continued steering her toward the central shaft. When she drew nearer, she saw that it sank below the level they were occupying.

Two sets of stairs, on opposite sides of the shaft, led down to the Inner Sanctum, though both were roped off and guarded by a pair of men. One of the men standing in front of the nearest stairs wore red priest's robes and the other a steel breastplate, painted red, bearing the insignia of the eight-pointed star inside a ring of fire. He had a ridged helmet that left his mouth exposed, but covered his eyes, and stood stiffly, grasping the hilt of a two-handed greatsword, its point nestled in the red carpet under his feet.

Saffron felt the heat of the fire more intensely at the sight of these obstacles, and perspiration broke out along her forehead. She noticed a number of what she took for ordinary citizens, gathered around the rim of the inner circle facing the fire, marveling at its magnificence. She understood why they might be swayed to this church after viewing such a miracle.

"What was the good news you had?" she murmured to Groilen as their approach caught the eye of the red-robed priest. "You never told me."

"Oh, I saw Myalyssa this afternoon. She's created a Lodestone with properties she thinks will neutralize the enchantment in your collars."

"What? That's great news!" Saffron's mind immediately swam with thoughts of returning to Ifelian.

"We can visit the mansion as soon as we're done here, if you like," Groilen replied.

"Of course." Saffron stopped talking as they drew close enough to the stairs for the warrior and priest of Hellig-nok to hear. She needed to reclaim focus and work through the present situation.

The red-robed priest took a step forward to greet them. "Welcome to the Temple of the Eternal Flame, brother and sister. My superiors did not inform me we'd be receiving guests of the cloth. Please, let me take your travelling gear that you might relax. What temple are you visiting from?" He reached out to accept Groilen's pack, but Saffron's companion made no move to comply.

"Thank you for your welcome, brother. I am Verigo, from the Temple of the Desert Wind in Zarway, but ours is not an official church visit. I found Tuphelia, here, at an oasis during my own pilgrimage to your Temple, where I longed to behold the wonder of our Lord's Eternal Flame with my own eyes."

The priest folded his arms, placing his hands back into the sleeves of his robes, and bowed at Groilen's indirect flattery. Then he shifted his gaze to Saffron, assessing as he awaited her story.

"Tuphelia is something of a prodigy, it seems. Hellig-nok has spoken to her directly and touched her with a gift of power over that most wondrous element of fire. I invited her along on my pilgrimage and request that she be allowed to commune directly with the Flame, in accordance with the will of the Fire Lord."

The priest's brow furrowed, though Saffron thought his disappointment looked feigned. "Unfortunately, Brother Verigo, the Hierarch has set restrictions upon which of the devout are permitted to enter our Inner Sanctum. I do not hold that privilege myself, so cannot therefore bestow it upon another without definitive proof that the Fire Lord wills it. You understand, of course, that as you are from another temple and not on an official visit, I cannot simply take your word."

Saffron felt the eyes of both the priest and the silent warrior beside him boring into her. She was fairly certain what would be asked of her next and started quietly humming a tune, allowing the heat inside her to simmer.

"But of course," Groilen transitioned smoothly, "I would not presume to be let inside, for I am no one of consequence. Truth be told, I don't think I could sustain proximity to that fire for very long indeed. But Tuphelia, here, is truly the chosen of our Lord – as surely as the Hierarch himself."

The red-robed priest's shoulders lifted while his mouth drooped. "Is there any sign she might be able to deliver to convince us? I would be happy to allow entrance if she could, let's say, cause that bush to combust?" He lowered his head sideways in an attempt to see Saffron's face more clearly under her hood. "What do you say, dear? Has Hellig-nok granted you such ability?"

Saffron responded by whipping her hands out to her sides, fingers spread. Her sudden movement caused the doubting priest to take a step back and his armored companion to lift the point of his blade slightly from the floor. She didn't answer his request directly with words but began singing louder, drawing looks of bewilderment from the true servants of the fire god. She briefly wondered if such a deity would have feelings about an outsider utilizing fire magic in his temple. Should she expect a smiting for being so brazen?

She had ignited tinder for a campfire by magic before, but that was dry and directly in front of her. The potted plant the priest had indicated was still living and several body lengths away. Still, she had selected the appropriate song, and Cauzel had given her some direction on the general amplification of effects. It was time to apply what she'd learned.

Saffron brought her hands slowly inward, focusing the friction of her intent on the creosote bush across the floor. She modulated her voice and interjected new words of power into her song. A quick flash of fire burst into existence on one of the outer stalks, followed abruptly by the heart of the plant igniting in a bright yellow fireball.

Saffron quieted her voice and relaxed her hands, which had grown tight from the strain, while the bush continued to burn, absent of her concentration. Looking to the others, she read disbelief in the expression of the priest even as a grin spread across Groilen's.

"Is that proof enough?" he asked, already slipping the heavy pack from his back to hand over to Saffron.

The priest didn't say anything immediately, but maintained a slack-jawed appearance until Saffron had slung the leather straps of the pack over her shoulders. Its weight dug the material into the creases of her flesh, and she gained a new respect for Groilen having hefted the thing this far without complaint.

"You – you're sure she's not already been ordained into the priesthood?" the priest finally spit out, looking at Groilen.

"I can answer for myself," Saffron interjected.

"Ah," Groilen laughed nervously, "no, she is but a supplicant, with much to learn about decorum as you can see. But, the Fire Lord did speak to her directly and insist she join with the Eternal Flame to commune with him. Who are we, his servants, to stand in the way of such a decree, hmm?"

The red-robed priest's eyes darted to the armored man beside him, then across the chasm of the open shaft to the other set of stairs. He looked decidedly nervous, no longer sure of himself. "Well, perhaps I should contact the Hierarch first. He may wish to be present, and of course, meet this untrained prodigy."

Saffron could scarcely believe he was calling her *untrained* after what she just did. Although, that was the crux of their ploy …

Groilen shook his head noncommittally. "I would not presume to weigh in on questions of authority within your own temple, brother. Perhaps, though, Tuphelia could wait down with the flame for your Hierarch? We have come a long way, after all, and she's no doubt eager to fulfill our Lord's desires for her."

The priest considered the request for a moment, then shut his eyes as if channeling a reclamation of certainty. "No, I don't think so," he said, opening them again. "She can wait here until I return with the Hierarch." Saffron noticed he was delivering this as an order to the warrior beside him. "Worry not, I shan't be long. You can have a seat along those benches while you wait." He gestured to a row beside the still crackling creosote bush.

Groilen smiled while glancing sideways at Saffron. She was unsure how to interpret his look. "Very well," he said. "As you instruct." He lightly gripped Saffron's upper arm and moved with her toward the benches. They sat down while the priest murmured something to the warrior. He then made for one of the nearby tower-like sections of the temple, which had stairs climbing upward.

As soon as he had passed beyond a wall, Groilen whispered to Saffron, "We don't have much time – we need to do this before the Hierarch shows up. Get up and walk away from me. That dotard with the sword will no doubt keep his eyes on you, allowing me to create a diversion. When he vacates his post, head down those stairs and use the cauldron. Do it, now!"

Saffron responded to his insistence, standing up with the cumbersome pack still strapped to her and ambling in the direction opposite of where the priest had gone. She had no idea what she was waiting for but felt her stomach spinning in anticipation, nevertheless. She glanced over her shoulder at the warrior, who was indeed watching her cross the floor.

From a fair distance away, where people had been kneeling in prayer closer to the entrance, unmistakable screams of panic suddenly carried across the temple. Saffron looked back to Groilen, who was pointing in that direction.

"By the innumerable stars, what is that?" he shouted, pointing at what looked like a gargantuan cobra, sleek and black and several times longer than a person, rearing back with its hood expanded in a threatening posture. Groilen shook his hands at the warrior who still guarded the stairs. "It's going to strike those worshipers dead. Quickly, do something!"

The man lifted his greatsword but was obviously torn between acting the hero and obeying his superior. He glanced back at Saffron who stood as still as possible, keeping her head turned in the direction of the giant snake.

"What are you waiting for, man?" Groilen continued his pressure. "Your Hierarch will be arriving any moment. Are you going to allow him to be put in danger?"

Saffron could hear the man groan before yelling, "Wait here!" and charging off to engage the monstrous cobra.

"Go, now!" Groilen hissed at Saffron once their previous obstacle was in a dead run. "I've got to get closer to manipulate the illusion," he said, following in the warrior's wake.

Glancing around and finding no eyes on her, Saffron stole down the stairs to the bottom level. The heat was intense. Perhaps one reason only chosen priests were allowed was that they needed magical protection from the fire, like the gladiators from this House had been given, in order to survive. She pressed against the outside wall, but was already drenched in sweat as she set down and unbuckled the lid of her pack.

Inside was a pewter cauldron, sealed with a circular cover. Images of porpoises decorated its surface, and Saffron could feel the contents sloshing as she removed the cauldron from the pack. Groilen had said it was magic, but she didn't know exactly what to do with it. She had no desire to step closer to the Eternal Flame, whose surging roar blocked out any commotion from the higher levels.

With no clear idea how to proceed, she unsheathed the dagger from her arm and used it to pry open the cauldron's lid.

As soon as she did, the water inside started to bubble as if possessing a life of its own. Or, perhaps, it was instantaneously brought to a boil. The cauldron itself didn't seem hot, however, so Saffron replaced her dagger and tentatively dipped a finger into the surface of the liquid.

Thankfully, it remained cool. What's more, she immediately felt less of the heat from the fire herself, so long as her hand was in contact with the water. Saffron looked over at the pillar of fire, which was huge – she surmised it might take a dozen people joining hands to encircle it. How was this cauldron, which she could lift with two arms, going to have any chance of putting it out?

Shaking her head, she knew she had to try something fast. Saffron carried the cauldron, one deliberate step at a time, closer to the fire to test her resistance to its blistering heat. Careful to keep the fingers of at least one hand dipped into its effervescent waters, she found she could approach without immolating herself.

Unsure of what else to do, when she got within a couple steps of the Eternal Flame, she tipped the Bottomless Cauldron toward it, spilling its contents upon the floor at the base of the fire. A surge of steam hissed and began filling the air. Saffron closed her eyes and continued to pour. As she did so, she noticed that the cauldron failed to grow any lighter in her arms.

After what seemed like a ridiculous amount of pouring, she opened her eyes again. Water was still dumping from the mouth of the cauldron, and the fire was all but extinguished. The hissing steam was less intense, though a fog of evaporated water hung about the entire chamber. From above, she heard shouts of alarm and decided she'd stayed long enough. She set the cauldron down on its side, still pouring, and darted for the stairs.

Halfway up, she saw the red-robed priest pointing and shouting at her from the railing of the central shaft. She sprinted upward, and upon reaching the top of the stairs, saw the armored warrior charging straight for her, sword raised. She had no idea where Groilen was but couldn't take the time to look.

Saffron took off running away from the temple's front entrance, barely staying ahead of the man's swinging radius. Figuring he'd have a tougher time climbing stairs in his armor, she bolted toward the next of the eight, tower-like formations, where steps led up to the higher levels.

Saffron grabbed the rim of a lit brazier at the base of the stairs and tipped it over behind her, hoping to slow down her pursuers. Glancing back, she saw she'd gained three or four acolytes and priests in addition to the warrior. When she reached the second floor, she saw a group with spears and shields pounding down the steps from the floor above, and immediately darted for the next tower.

She'd just gotten back to the open section of floor nearer to the central shaft when, out of thin air, a wall of red fire leapt into existence in front of her. Saffron pivoted quickly to avoid rushing into it, but even so, its heat caused the right side of her robe to smoke. The sheet of flame extended ten long strides in either direction, but she never stopped moving, sprinting parallel to the wall while keeping far enough away to avoid ignition.

Sweat poured down Saffron's face again, and as soon as she reached the end of the fire wall, she cut toward the next tower section of the eight-pointed star. She hoped no soldiers were already there and that she may be able to climb to the next floor to somehow hide. Still, she had a dagger and was ready to make a stand if need be.

Breathing hard, she was elated to see no one else occupying the partially enclosed space when she reached it, yet shifted into panic once she realized this section had no stairways; it must only be every-other-one! Her legs were shaking, but she had to keep moving or be trapped in the tower.

As she was about to press on, the movement of cloth against the outside wall caught her eye. It was a golden curtain, blowing in the wind over an open doorway. Saffron made the snap decision to head for it, hoping it may provide a way out. She heard yells approaching from behind as she ran to the doorway. It led to a shallow balcony, from which she could see the lights of the Caliph's palace in the distance, and dimmer candles in the windows of houses in between.

An iron railing with pointed bars protected view-seekers from an accidental fall, but left her quickly calculating the likeliness of surviving a second-story jump versus the wrath of a dozen armed fanatics and perhaps the Fire Lord himself. Saffron grabbed the bars and hoisted herself over the top, though the hem of her disguise caught on one of the tips, nearly ripping the red robe completely off as she dangled from the other side.

"Saffron!"

She heard the shouted whisper from below, though couldn't see a thing as she struggled to slip out of the ensnared robe without losing her grip on the bars. Suddenly, a hand grasped her wrist from above. Without thinking twice, she released the iron enclosure, her falling weight enough to slip the grip of whoever had grabbed her.

The red robe stayed behind, and Saffron caught a flash of wall passing her field of vision before her feet hit the ground. They erupted in pain at the shock of landing and her knees buckled, dropping her in a heap. Luckily, the landscaping contrived to leave a gentle slope of palm tree bark leading out from the cathedral, absorbing some of the impact that assaulted her throbbing feet.

After a brief allotment for moaning, Saffron felt hands grasping her shoulders, helping to bring her upright. She slapped away the intruding hands but then saw it was Groilen, no longer in the disguise of Verigo, the visiting priest.

"Are you alright? We've got to get moving," he said, not waiting for her to answer.

Saffron shifted her tunic back into position to cover herself and half-ran, half-limped after Groilen, who cut toward the houses of a nearby neighborhood. Though her steps were a little painful, she thought she'd avoided serious injury.

"Hopefully, we'll lose them between these houses," Groilen whispered as she caught up. He hugged the corner of a building, briefly looking onto the next street before striking out to cross it. "I've got the wagon stowed not far from here."

A few more moments of weaving between houses in the dark brought them to a paved path, which wound its way up to the palace. True to his word, they reached Groilen's wagon parked just off the road and climbed into the front seat.

Groilen spared a laugh once he'd snapped the horses into forward movement. "Well, you certainly did it," he said, looking back over his shoulder.

Saffron followed his eyes to the rooftop of the Temple of Eternal Flame, which looked much less impressive now that its fire had been extinguished. She expelled a cross between a laugh and a snort herself, though it was more a release of the tension she'd been holding for the last hour or so than actual amusement. "I suppose I did. Though I wouldn't want to be in the Temple of Life and Blood tomorrow when Hierarch Krygos shows up, hurling accusations."

"Agreed," Groilen nodded. "Well, that's not *our* problem." He gave a long look across the seat at her, and Saffron thought she saw empathy, or at least appreciation, in his eyes, though it was hard to tell in the dark. "Let's go get you out of that collar, no?" he finally said.

"Sounds like a great idea to me," she responded, relaxing her shoulders against the back of the seat.

Chapter 25

Alone in the Dark

Time became difficult to gauge in the dark stillness of Sepathia's lair, especially with Annoxoria unable to move. Her mind remained restless, cycling between despair and the urgent need to think of a way out of this predicament so she could warn her lover about his sister's trap.

She'd already condemned herself for being such a fool as to trust anything a fiend like Izefet had to say. Annoxoria had never anticipated his making a pact with the Nightwing because she hadn't imagined they might have anything to give one another. It must be Rinn-Rhulian, she thought. He needs unfettered access to whatever's in the ruins and decided it would be much easier without her and Thuvian around. Sepathia's and

Izefet's needs would align when it came to eliminating the Lord of Drachenmark.

Annoxoria knew from her research that Nightwing poison could incapacitate a human victim for a day or more, though getting stung almost always meant a quicker death at the hands of the dragon dealing such a blow. The light that had penetrated the shaft to the bottom of the lair was all but faded, suggesting night was near. How long would Thuvian have, she wondered. How long would it take Sepathia's messenger to tell him of her plight?

Of course, that depended on who she used. If she already had someone in place at the castle, it would only take the few hours for her to fly close enough to give a signal. If she had to send someone from further, Annoxoria's Lord might have more time.

As powerful as Sepathia was, she held a respectful fear of her brother and the many loyal followers who would defend him to their own death. This much, Annoxoria was sure of. It was the reason she'd never attacked the castle directly. Thuvian had wounded her during a previous attempt on his life, and was immune to her acidic spittle. But if she lured him into the open somewhere, alone, Sepathia might try her luck with an ambush.

Annoxoria struggled again, commanding her arms and legs to move, but they simply wouldn't respond. She couldn't shape if she couldn't speak or move her hands, either. It was no use. Sepathia had gotten the better of her and would probably be returning soon to devour her, slowly.

She relaxed her mind, giving in to the blackness that had almost completely enveloped the cave. Perhaps if she relented altogether, her heart would stop beating and she might drift away peacefully.

Annoxoria returned to consciousness suddenly as if she'd been shaken awake. She was still surrounded by complete darkness, uncertain how or when she had fallen asleep. She felt a twitch in her right arm, though, and this time when she struggled, found she was able to move it. By the level of pitch blackness, she presumed the night had not yet fully passed.

A burst of hope sprang forth when she realized she could move her neck and other arm as well. Perhaps her experimentation with the Nightwing poison had transferred some level of resistance to it? If Sepathia presumed she would remain immobile at least into the next day, Annoxoria might have the time she needed to escape. Assuming she was able to.

That task loomed before her as a formidable obstacle, for she remembered how steep and slippery the shaft leading down was, and she was still a fair distance from its base. Now that she had a chance, she had to try. With an unreasonable amount of effort, like she was learning to use someone else's body, she stretched her arms upward and rolled onto her stomach.

From that position, she grasped at the cave floor until she found good handholds, then pulled, bending her elbows and thrusting the rest of her body forward. She repeated the process, moving one body length at a time, cracking her fingernails and dragging herself over the uneven rock. The leather she wore protected most of her body as she slid, but her stomach ached terribly with every shift. One positive thing about the dark was that she couldn't see how bad the wound from Sepathia's stinger was. Another was that she didn't have to see what any of the squishy objects she kept touching were.

After what seemed like an hour of sweaty, grueling toil, she reached the base of the entrance shaft. She could lift her head just high enough to distinguish the starlit opening high above. It looked so much further than the bottom had appeared when she was outside. Annoxoria gave her arms a few moments to rest and tried moving her legs again, though they had yet to recover.

Hopeful she might be able to use them soon, she reached up the rocky slope and used her raw fingers to grip a fracture in its surface. She proceeded slowly up the slanting wall, which was wet and mossy. Her wrists, forearms, and biceps were all on fire from exertion, with the top still so far away. There was no way her muscles had enough strength to get her there, but she continued on.

A fraction from the point of giving up, she felt a twitch in her left leg. She painstakingly raised her foot to rest on a lumpy outcrop of stone, giving her arms a brief respite. She tasted the salt of tears that streamed down her cheeks from her effort, but with a renewed surge of energy she fought on, her legs working their way back into usefulness.

More than halfway up, the grade of the slope increased for perhaps two body-lengths. She paused to rest her arms again while trying to gauge if there was an easier route. So little light was available from overhead, it was nearly impossible to differentiate between various depths of shadow.

Annoxoria spotted a long string of green moss dangling from the slope above, near a rivulet of reflective water dripping past. Perhaps the moss was clinging to a vine – something she could hold onto. Stretching as far as she could with her left hand, she took hold of the bottom of the moss and tugged lightly. Whether root or vine, the underlying structure held fast, and she decided to use it to lift herself high enough to gain purchase with her other hand.

As soon as she released the slope with her right hand, however, the extra burden of her full body weight caused the moss to give way, and Annoxoria started sliding back down the incline. She scrambled with both hands and feet to find purchase, and one of her fingernails tore loose as she tried to claw her way into the solid rock.

After a depressingly far slide, her leg, stuck out at an awkward angle, managed to catch along a thin ledge, stopping her descent. She held still for a while, in disbelief of the ground she had lost. When she looked up and saw how far it was to the top, allowing herself to feel the pain of her worn out muscles and abused hands, she rested her head against the cold, wet stone and wept.

"Nox!" A snarlish call came from the night air above.

She stifled herself in mid-gasp, listening hard, sure that her ears and mind had just played a trick on her.

"Nox, is that you?"

It was Thuvian's voice, but how was that possible? She looked upward, yet all she saw through the darkness and tears were vague, black shapes. No one was around to judge her if she was crazy, so she dared to believe.

"It's me. I'm stuck," she yelled back into the night.

"Hold where you are, I'm coming for you," Thuvian replied, his voice the most welcome sound Annoxoria could imagine.

He had draconic sight, and she knew Thuvian's vision was almost as keen by night as by day, though perhaps not as far-reaching. She heard indistinguishable sounds from above, then a short moment later the slap of what she guessed was rope hitting the wet surface of the rock nearby. He must have had his two-bladed sword strapped to his back, for suddenly she saw the bluish glow of each enchanted end lowering toward her.

She watched their twin lights approach as he rappelled the rock face, and they may as well have been the hands of a god reaching down to scoop her up. Annoxoria held fast until the outline of Thuvian's lean body reached her.

"My sister isn't home?" he asked as he wound cords of rope around her waist and tied them off.

Annoxoria shook her head. "Out on the hunt."

"I don't know what could have possibly driven you here, Nox."

She heard disappointment in the tone of his voice, but also concern, and love. The fact that he was using the nickname normally reserved for their most tender moments warmed her insides.

Thuvian lifted and cradled her with one arm once his knots were secure, and she wrapped her arms around his back to give him more freedom to climb. They made slow, steady progress up the slope with the aid of the rope, though she no longer took notice of the distance. She simply closed her eyes and listened to the strong heartbeat in her lover's chest. They reached the top, where Thuvian set her on the ground and unfastened the rope from each of them, then the rock he'd used to anchor. Annoxoria welcomed the starlight like an old friend.

"We're not safe anywhere in Sepathia's territory," Thuvian declared. "Are you fit to travel?"

She nodded, unsure that was at all true. He reached a hand down to her, which she took and rose to her feet. Upon standing, she immediately doubled over in pain, clutching her abdomen.

"What's wrong?" Thuvian asked, crouching and placing a hand upon her back.

Annoxoria winced, "I got stung."

"By Sepathia? Let me see." He gently lifted her torso, then pulled back her anxious, still raw hand, exposing the wound.

She didn't dare look, though probably couldn't have made a useful assessment in the dimness, anyway. Instead, she raised her head skyward and concentrated on taking regular, deep breaths. He pawed at her stomach experimentally, and each touch brought a new spasm of pain. Annoxoria bore it, knowing she was to blame for her predicament.

"How are you even standing now?" he asked after his evaluation. "That much poison should have left you shriveled in a ball at the bottom of her lair. The good news is that it's also congealed the blood around the injection, so you haven't lost nearly as much as you would have from a nonpoisonous bite. We should get this bandaged before moving on."

Thuvian didn't wait for agreement, rummaging through a pack he'd already set aside. Annoxoria stood still while he wrapped clean cloth several times around her waist, trying not to grunt too loudly at the constriction. He worked quickly, no doubt concerned about the return of his nefarious half-sister. "How does that feel?" he asked once finished.

She simply nodded, refusing to complain, and took a few steps on her weary legs to show she was able. Annoxoria wasn't keen on the idea of another ascent, frowning when confronted with the height of the cliff she'd dropped down so many hours ago. Yet, Thuvian had come this far to rescue her, and she wasn't giving up now. She steeled her resolve and headed for the shadow-painted wall of earth.

"This way," Thuvian called from behind her. The long shaft of his two-bladed sword was gripped by both his hands; his pack had taken its place on his back. His body faced the eastern woods, opposite the direction of Nightwing Castle, but Thuvian Skullreaver was one of the most accomplished hunters living in view of the Wyrmsmoke Mountains. She wasn't going to question his trail knowledge.

"Ignite," he commanded, and the already glowing blades hissed further to life, extending the reach of their light and adding a green tint. Annoxoria appreciated the gesture, allowing her to see where she was stepping much easier. She smiled with pride as well, for she had enchanted Viper's Kiss in the first place.

Thuvian led the way, weaving a path through the edges of swamp and woodland as if he'd blazed it countless times before. Annoxoria did her best to keep pace, and they'd passed a few miles in silence before he broke it.

"When Pereen told me you'd headed north after announcing a westward journey, I knew something was wrong. I didn't believe until I found your tracks, however, that you'd be foolish enough to visit Sepathia's lair."

"The spymaster betrayed me?" she said aloud, instantly regretting she had.

"And isn't it well he did?" Thuvian's voice rumbled, unwisely loud. He spun to face her and all his earlier tenderness was gone, replaced by hard, practical authority. "Why did you do it, Annoxoria? She could have killed you a thousand different ways, you know. I could have found you draped from the ceiling of her lair, skinned alive."

Annoxoria knew what he said was true and that she'd acted foolishly, but her bottom lip trembled as she fought hard not to give in to the idea that what she was after was foolish as well. Becoming what she was meant to be was worth risking a painful death.

She'd never shared this need with anyone else – at least not out loud. Her thoughts slipped to Izefet and how he'd either guessed or somehow stolen the secret from her mind. It wasn't right or fair that such a damned, sinister individual should know while her own lover did not. The thought of Thuvian laughing at her or rejecting her altogether were worse fates than the Nightwing's stinger piercing her stomach.

"I, I came to get a scale," she finally blurted, unsure of how to transition from that thought to what she really wanted to say.

"A scale?" She didn't know what he'd been imagining as her reason, but Thuvian seemed utterly surprised at the simplicity of the truth.

Annoxoria nodded and pulled the shed piece of dragon skin she'd collected from her pouch.

Thuvian's horned chin dropped to his chest and his shoulders sagged as he let out his breath. "Nox, I don't understand." He looked up into her eyes, the magical acid from his blade lighting the exquisite contours of his jagged face.

She swallowed hard and nodded, hoping she could find a way to make him. "You know how I sometimes collect ingredients for my magic? Sometimes they're as simple as acorns or feathers, but this magic is more complex, and it requires one of your sister's scales. Or, so I thought." She realized while speaking that Izefet's betrayal could mean that the entire transformation process was part of a ruse. She needed to find out at what point he'd made his offer to Sepathia.

"What magic was so necessary that you would risk dealing with my sister?" Thuvian asked. "And why wouldn't you come to me for help if you were determined to try something this dangerous?"

Tears started streaming down Annoxoria's cheeks. "I should have," she nodded. "You've always known me as the woman standing before you now. I know you love me as I am, but this body isn't truly mine, and I've been afraid you wouldn't continue loving me in the body I'm supposed to have. So I haven't shared that part of myself with you, and I know that was wrong."

Thuvian was shaking his head slowly. "Nox," he said, dissolving the space between them with a few strides and embracing her, "you're not making any sense."

His touch felt good, comforting, but she forced herself to push him away. "It does make sense. You know your mother was a Nightwing and your father human. You feel both parts of yourself; they each have a place in your soul. You've expressed as much to me. And you got the body that matches your identity.

"But I have the soul of a dragon – I know I do – and yet for whatever reason, the gods or the cosmos or some power I don't even understand, put my soul into this body … this *human* body. And it doesn't belong." A mere step from Thuvian, she purposefully allowed her snake-like tongue to dart forth, right in front of his face.

"What trickery is this? I know your tongue well, Annoxoria Nefzen, and that was not it!"

They stood in silence for too many heartbeats, staring at one another's faces. Annoxoria decided not to speak again until he did, calculating that Thuvian would calm if she didn't press her argument. His features softened in the lingering silence.

"Show me again," he finally said.

She kept the rest of her body stiff, but complied.

"When did you do that? How did you do that?"

She shrugged. "Magic."

"And now that you have one of Sepathia's scales, you're going to become a full-sized Nightwing? Through magic?" Thuvian crossed his arms as he waited for her response.

She lowered her face. "I don't know. It may have all been a lie."

His fingers tucked under her chin and lifted her gaze to meet his. "I had no idea you were so unhappy, my love," he said.

"I'm not, when I'm with you. You make me forget. But every time you leave and I'm alone, it's hard to think of anything else. I wish you didn't have to travel so much." She embraced him again, tucking her head underneath his chin.

His clawed hand wrapped itself into her tight curls. "We'll sort this out, Nox. Don't forget that you're my queen. We have to trust one another – there's no one else."

She nodded but didn't say another word. Perhaps she did need to share more, but she also knew some things could only be experienced alone.

Chapter 26

The Lodestone Solution

Τ he wagon couldn't get back up the hill fast enough for Saffron, though her body wouldn't have argued with more rest. As they approached the mansion belonging to the Circle of Twelve, it was all she could do not to jump out and sprint down to Myalyssa's laboratory. Between the bandaged cut on her thigh from the Arena, the enormous bruise blooming on her shield arm, her aching feet and knees languishing after her drop from the balcony, and the heat she still feel on her skin from her recent proximity to magical flame, Saffron was more than ready to retire from gladiator life.

If they were rid of the collars, it would be a small thing to manage an escape from the slave pens. She somehow subdued her impulses long enough for Groilen to park the wagon, but rushed ahead up the pebbled path to the open front door.

Ezmina crossed the threshold as Saffron cleared the steps onto the front porch, with Groilen trailing at a more leisurely pace. The half-Eladrin turned her head back into the house. "Ah, wonderful. Lady Saffron has returned."

Saffron caught movement beyond in the parlor, and when she followed Ezmina inside, she was greeted by another half-dozen of what she assumed to be members of the Twelve, sipping on brandy underneath purple lights.

"Is it done?" Gaeric inquired with a hint of urgency, stepping to Saffron as soon as she entered the larger room. At least he had the consideration to hand her a chilled glass of amber liquid.

She took a sip to calm her nerves before answering, and Groilen stepped in to speak on her behalf. "It is," he said, a trace of joviality in his voice. "The Eternal Flame is doused. Our confidence was well placed. Lady Saffron was extraordinary."

Gaeric smiled broadly and abruptly clinked his glass to Saffron's, which she'd just brought away from her lips. "Wonderful news! Oh, I just may have to borrow the wagon and go see for myself before morning. Well done." He peeled away back toward the heart of the room, allowing space for others to approach.

Ayez was next, wearing his customary colorful robes and carrying a slender, grey walking staff, capped by a fist-sized crystal sphere. "I'm glad you've returned to us safely, my dear. I thought that stunt with the cauldron was a little much to ask. If it reaches the populace that you were somehow involved, and I have no doubt such rumors are bound to crop up," he looked over each shoulder to check who else was in earshot, "your personal notoriety will reach full bloom."

Saffron's hand tightened on her glass. "You don't think Groilen would tell anyone it was me, do you?"

Ayez raised his eyebrows and took her by the arm to walk a little distance from the rest of the hovering coven. "It's not Groilen, specifically, I would be wary of. Mind you, this is exactly the sort of thing that my Circle could play upon to win over many in the city. While I can't lament that, I hope you do not end up paying the cost. Hierarch Krygos will be furious, and he has gladiators of his own who can reach you."

Another sip of the brandy was necessary to cool her temper. This was all a game to them, wasn't it? Yet, if Myalyssa the Artificer came through, she and her friends might be away from this den of snakes before her enemies were the wiser.

"The good news," continued Ayez, as if reading her mind, "is that Myalyssa is ready to try her solution to your collar problem. That's why so many of my fellows are here tonight – hanging around to see whether your head will explode, I suppose." He winked.

If Ayez thought she could find any humor in the moment, he was mistaken. She blanched at his words. She took another drink to recover, and then responded, "Perhaps we can just get on with it, then?"

"Ah, of course. You shouldn't have to wait on our accounts." Ayez turned to address the rest of the room. "Time to discover whether the fruits of Myalyssa's work have ripened enough to successfully overcome the craft of Hadrian No More!" He took Saffron's drained glass and nodded in the direction of the Map Room. "Shall we?"

Saffron felt like a mother goose leading her goslings to the pond; at a respectful distance, Ezmina, Groilen, Gaeric, Sirran, and a couple more members of the Twelve she hadn't been introduced to, followed her in a neat line. She, in turn, followed Ayez, the Many Colored, out through the hidden door of the Map Room and down the winding stone path.

The crystal on the end of his staff lit up in the dark, swirling its way through the colors of the rainbow, which was distracting but provided enough radiance to maintain safe footing along the path. When they reached the archway into the rock face, Ayez waved his hand to deactivate the glyphs, and they proceeded into the smooth tunnel.

Myalyssa waited for them in the workroom, which seemed overfull once all ten people had packed in. The Artificer was smiling triumphantly, dressed in blue with her dark hair worn up off her shoulders. Her hands were cupped together in front of her as if she cradled a delicate baby bird. "Have a seat," Myalyssa instructed Saffron. A chair was already set up in the middle of the chamber for her.

Saffron wondered if they realized all the fanfare only served to increase her nervousness. They probably didn't care as long as they got to witness some new magical achievement. She wanted to get the collar off as soon as possible, however, so she acquiesced and sat in the chair.

Myalyssa stood in front of Saffron and uncovered her lower hand to reveal a thin, black, rectangular stone. "Rune magic is particularly powerful, but used sparingly because it takes time and often rare materials to craft," she explained. "The Dread Lich has placed such a rune inside the slave collar you wear. When active, either a command word or too much tampering with the protected surface can trigger the magic, which in this case we believe to be an explosive trap."

Saffron was fairly sure a speech was unnecessary and wished Myalyssa would get on with it. But her palms were sweaty and her mouth dry, and she couldn't find the words to interrupt. Instead, she watched the Artificer's lips move and tried to follow along with what she was saying.

"Based on the rune used, I've specially attuned this lodestone with a counter-rune to neutralize its effects, once attached." Myalyssa leaned forward and gathered Saffron's hair in one hand to fully expose the collar.

"Is it going to work?" Saffron was barely able to whisper, her mouth was so parched.

"We'll know in a moment," Myalyssa answered, unconcerned. "It should emit a low hum temporarily if the runes are synchronized." She dipped closer, and Saffron could tell she was trying to align the lodestone precisely.

Saffron sat still while eight other faces leaned in, as if doing so would help them determine success.

The tiefling, Sirran, decided to add to her stress. "Hadrian No More is an accomplished sorcerer. It would be quite a triumph to magically overcome something he has personally created."

Saffron swallowed and moved her tongue, trying to introduce some moisture into her mouth. Staring at the Unseen Seer's jagged teeth as he talked didn't make her feel more relaxed. She heard the click of the stone adhering to her metal collar, followed by Myalyssa straightening to her full height.

At nearly the same time, a slight hum started right beneath Saffron's ear, followed by a huge grin from Myalyssa and boisterous congratulations from her peers. Saffron continued sitting still, amazed at just how insignificant her personal stature seemed to be at the moment.

"Alright, alright," Myalyssa pushed the crowd back, though not very convincingly. "Let's not get ahead of ourselves. There's still the lock." She selected a pair of slender, steel implements from the table beside Saffron and once again bent over her, attempting to pick the collar's catch.

Sirran and one of the unfamiliar Shapers got even closer, craning their necks to watch their colleague ply her skill with the lock-picks. Saffron felt like an attraction on display at the village fair. Over the hum of the lodestone, she heard mumbling and shifted her eyes to the side while keeping her neck still.

She could barely make out Ayez, standing a little ways back, moving his staff in tight circles as he recited something, appearing to concentrate in her direction.

"Almost there …" Myalyssa said, her cold hand brushing against Saffron's cheek.

"Wait!" Ayez yelled, startling everyone in the room.

Saffron jerked her head in his direction, knocking one of the tools from the Artificer's hand. "What is it?" she asked.

Myalyssa cursed under her breath and knelt to retrieve her tool. "Yes, Ayez, what is it?"

"The explosive rune is not the only enchantment upon the collar," he replied. "I just performed a divination to be sure, and there is still powerful necromancy upon it."

"Negative energy?" Ezmina contributed from the far side of the room.

"What does that mean?" Saffron asked, her eyes travelling from Ezmina, to Myalyssa, to Ayez.

Ayez's face fell, and she felt her stomach plummeting with it. "It means, my dear, you could still be in grave danger if we attempt to remove that collar."

Myalyssa was still on her knees, staring at the floor. "I, I didn't, I hadn't even considered ..."

Gaeric lay his hand upon her shoulder. "It's not your fault. You did well to isolate and neutralize the rune."

Saffron blinked twice in amazement at what she was hearing. "Pardon me! I'm sorry if you're all disappointed with tonight's entertainment, but I'm the person who nearly got killed performing one of your petty stunts earlier this evening. My friends and I are the ones still wearing these contraptions that could kill us any time an undead Shaper or our unscrupulous owner gets struck by a sadistic whim!"

She bolted upright, knocking over the chair beneath her, and clenched her fists. "Yes, I said 'owner.' Because right now I'm a slave. Do any of you have a sliver of insight into what that feels like? Waking up every sunrise without the freedom to walk more than ten paces in any direction? To be put in front of a crowd almost every week so they can enjoy an afternoon of watching someone else try to murder you?

"So I'm sorry if your little experiment didn't work out the way you wanted, but you've got bigger problems to worry about if that's what concerns you most." She immediately headed for the door, pushing aside the bodies in her way, uncaring who they belonged to or what their response to her eruption might be. Saffron was most of the way down the tunnel toward the outside air when Groilen came hustling after her.

"Saffron, wait!"

She spun on her heels and delivered a scalding gaze, silently challenging him to defy her.

He seemed to wilt under the pressure and his chest deflated. "Can I at least give you a ride back to the Arena?"

"Thank you, but I'll walk," she replied icily, her anger and disappointment banishing all memory of her aching limbs. She continued toward the exit with long strides until she tasted the salt on the sea wind. Groilen didn't follow.

Saffron paused momentarily at the overlook platform to take in the vista, briefly wondering if a dive off the cliff into the ocean could carry her beyond the range of what seemed to be her fate. She disregarded the impulse and picked her way slowly up the hill to the mansion, where better lighting made walking easier.

As she started down the path toward the edge of the estate, she wondered how she was going to pass along the news to Dyphina, Phaerim, and Thaelios that the hopes they'd placed in the Circle of Twelve had been premature. Saffron knew she had to keep fighting and looking for another way, but she was growing weary.

Saffron's mind harkened back to the women she left behind in the harem at Hope's End, to the countless prisoners toiling in the mines of that witch, Annoxoria, to the men and women dying every week in the Arena – some at her own hand. So much unfairness existed in the world, so many with power using it to take advantage of those without. The thought made it difficult to breathe.

She had to find a solution to her own hardships in order to fight for people like those she'd already let down. She had to help make things right. Consumed by regrets, Saffron found herself already a fair way down the hill by the time she reconsidered her surroundings. She could already see the Caliph's palace and decided it would be wise to cut down the hill behind it rather than continue on past the Temple of Eternal Flame, which was still dark.

Cauzel was a powerful Shaper, she mused once she'd adjusted her course, and for that matter so was Willem in Selamus. She had a number of influential acquaintances already – even Jaiden Luminere, who was now Grand-Master of the Order of the Rising Moon. She was disillusioned with the Circle of Twelve, but maybe Ayez would be able to get a message to those others, who might intercede on her behalf.

Saffron took a break from her strategizing to negotiate an unfamiliar part of the city. Somewhere between the mansion of the Twelve and the palace, the humming of the lodestone had ceased. Behind the edge of the Caliph's estate was a sharp cliff, which had a public ramp descending in a series of switchbacks. Though the hour was late, several people moved along the ramp in either direction, and it seemed a popular spot to gaze over the lower part of the city as well. She used the opportunity to gain her bearings and was able to pick out the Arena in the distance, though she guessed she still had at least another hour's walk.

She worried one of the occasional watchmen she passed might give her trouble, but the brass pass around her neck seemed to dissuade harassment from the city's authorities. During her descent to the lower wards, she happened across the same park she'd played the lyre in earlier that day. It looked even more peaceful at night, and she sat down on the amphitheater stage to rest her tired muscles.

The opportunity to play music for the sheer enjoyment of it had been a welcome and unexpected gift, and she took a moment to cherish it. That was something she had to do more of as well. Though she couldn't cease her battle against the cruelty of slavers, she needed to remember to pay homage to the parts of her that existed prior to her discovery of that struggle.

When she decided it was time to continue, she took a different way out of the park than she'd entered that afternoon, for the sake of exploration. How long would it be until she had another chance to wander freely? She stumbled upon a botanical garden, which in the blue and green moonlight, looked like it belonged in the world of the fey.

Unfamiliar but beautiful blossoms flecked a number of bushes along the garden's border, as well as some of Saffron's favorites from her homeland. Memories of picking flowers with her mother in their garden in Begnasharan flooded her and brought on sudden tears. She caressed a few of the unopened buds, then decided to leave quickly, lest she spend the rest of the night lost in memory and not return in time.

She hoped she'd find an opportunity to visit the garden again, during daylight, with adequate time to take in all the smells and textures of the cultivated plant life. For now, though, she needed to pick up her pace. The moons were getting low and she was so exhausted she was in danger of falling asleep on her feet.

Finally coming within sight of the rows of palms that flanked the main avenue into the Arena, Saffron looked for a place to hide her dagger in case she was ever out on her own again. She stashed it under a hedge that wove through the spaces between the trees, mentally marking the location for later. She would wait to tell the others about the failed attempt with the collar until after she'd gotten some sleep. None of them knew when she left that Myalyssa was ready to implement a solution, so the disappointment could wait until she at least had the strength to deliver it.

The guard seemed to be expecting her and opened the door without a word. He followed her inside and unlocked the gate to the pens, then held out his hand and stated, "Your pass."

It took Saffron a moment to comprehend he was asking her to hand over the brass rectangle around her neck, but she complied and slid into the pen, tiptoeing to her mattress while he locked the gate behind her.

"How was your day of freedom?" Dyphina whispered drowsily in the dark as Saffron unstrapped her sandals.

"Exhausting," Saffron answered, sliding onto her back. "I'll tell you all about it tomorrow." Before long, Dyphina's breathing became deep and regular, and she wished she could drift off just as easily. She lay awake for another hour at least, but when she opened her eyes again morning had come, and everyone else was stirring or already up, starting another day in captivity.

"Welcome back, Princess," Phaerim greeted as he squatted beside her before handing over a bowl of porridge. "Sleeping in today? Must be nice to be so special."

She frowned but accepted the warm bowl, not yet ready to engage with Phaerim's teasing.

"Ouch," he said, directing his spoon at the bruise on her arm. "That one's coming along nicely, then?"

"That's how my entire body feels after yesterday," she complained.

"So it went that well?"

Saffron took a scoop of porridge into her mouth and didn't wait to swallow before continuing. "You realize they got me out yesterday to do a job for them? As it turned out, a dangerous job. I think I've had enough of the Twelve."

"Well, you can give them the rub-off as soon as they've come through on these collars, no?" Phaerim settled in beside her on the mattress as they continued with breakfast. "Although, that one lass was not difficult to look at. The one with the blue eyes."

"Myalyssa," Saffron provided, but not without a dash of vinegar.

"Yeah, that's right. Did you see her again last night, then?"

"See who?" asked Dyphina as she sat cross-legged on her own nearby mattress and balanced a bowl in her lap.

Now was just as good a time as any, Saffron decided, given they were practically on the subject. "Look, I have something to tell you all. Thaelios, could you join us? This concerns you as well." She waited until he drew nearer to continue.

"I have no desire to relive my entire day outside the confines of our temporary home, but I did end up on the Circle of Twelve's estate last night after a close escape from the Temple of Eternal Flame. I didn't know it starting off, but Myalyssa was ready to implement her solution to our collar problem. Actually, this is it ..." Saffron felt along the cold metal around her neck until she reached the lodestone, still attached. She moved her fingers across it, but didn't dare manipulate it further.

"What is that?" Thaelios asked.

Saffron tried to remember exactly how Myalyssa explained things back in the laboratory. "This, supposedly, has cancelled out the rune-magic placed on the collar that makes it explode."

"But ..." Phaerim provided, "you're still wearing it."

"So it doesn't work?" Thaelios tried to follow along.

"Not well enough," Saffron answered. "Ayez says there's a second spell on the collar that could kill us if we tamper with it."

"So, how long do we have to wait for them to work through it?" Phaerim asked.

"Unless …" Thaelios interjected, the index fingers of both hands aligned to a point directly in front of his lips. "You said the Twelve had you perform some service to them earlier?"

"Yes," Saffron answered, "and I don't think I'll be welcome in that cathedral any time soon."

"So what if the Twelve aren't trying to actually provide a solution to our collar problem?" Thaelios continued, "What is their motivation to solve the issue? If they fix it, we leave. As long as we're around, they can string us along to do their dirty work all over the city."

Dyphina's head whipped around to look at Saffron. "You don't think they'd do that, do you?"

"No, no," Phaerim waved his spoon in the air, "Big Eyes makes a lot of sense. Everyone else seems to be trying to benefit from our apparent knack for causing trouble. And if there's any heat for things going awry, or we get caught, the blame falls on us."

Saffron bit her lower lip, considering their words. The possibility hadn't entered her mind before now. Would Groilen play her for a fool? Would Ayez? Admittedly, she hadn't known them that long, and their coven only stood to gain by prolonging her captivity. Regardless, she wasn't going to wait. "I think we should start looking for other options," she said, taking another spoonful of porridge.

Dyphina's cheeks bulged from her own mouthful, but Saffron saw her eyes open wide while gazing beyond Saffron's shoulder. Twisting around, she noticed Harzhim and Lodiammon, the one who'd assigned them the job of stealing the couatl, approaching.

When he was directly outside of the gate, Harzhim spoke. "You four. Finish your breakfast and come with me." He seemed just as cold as yesterday, and Saffron wondered how long she would be out of favor. It couldn't hurt to smooth things over if she got the chance, though she still had no idea how she'd offended the Consul.

All four of them set their bowls down without delay and stood, swapping glances. Saffron had the feeling they were sharing the same thought after spotting Lodiammon: the Wolfspider had decided on a punishment for not bringing him the "bird."

She was a little surprised when Harzhim took them down the tunnel to the ramp leading outside, and couldn't decide if it was a good or ill omen. Regardless, the fresh air was welcome. Without asking or receiving any questions, they followed in single file down the tree-lined avenue, flanked by a pair of guards who'd joined them at the outer door.

Saffron had been out a couple times but had never gone the way they were heading – further north down the wide thoroughfare, away from the Arena. They walked for perhaps a quarter of an hour before turning toward an unimpressive, medium-sized warehouse. She wondered what was stored inside and if they were only going to be put to another kind of labor. That wouldn't be so bad, would it?

Harzhim opened a door on the side of the building and finally addressed them. "Inside," he said without emotion, meeting Saffron's eyes and then quickly looking away. She walked past him into the midst of a mostly shaded, open space with wooden scaffolding lining the wall furthest from her. Beams of slanted light came in from high slits near the ceiling, cutting across the outlines of nearly a dozen men who stood in front of the scaffolding.

Saffron looked behind her as she heard the door close. Dyphina stayed close, with Phaerim and Thaelios spreading out. Harzhim remained just inside the door with the escort guards, though Lodiammon pushed past her on his way to the group of men already occupying the warehouse.

Saffron got the distinct impression that this was not going to be merely a work reassignment. The men were all dressed in dark cloth and leather – almost exclusively browns and black. No weapons were drawn or held, but she did see harnesses holding bows and sheathed blades – daggers mostly – on arms, backs, hips, and legs.

One man in the center of the group was seated on a plank of the scaffold while all the rest stood, angled slightly toward him. She looked closer, and though the intermittent beams of light made such discernment difficult, she had a feeling she'd seen him before. Where was it? Ah, in the stands after the Battle Royale! He had been with a younger woman, then. This had to be their "owner," the Wolfspider himself.

Saffron straightened once she realized his identity, and felt stronger somehow for interacting face-to-face. She'd finally be able to gain his measure, even if they were about to be punished for failing at some foolish errand.

"I've watched each of you in the Arena," the seated man said after Lodiammon finished whispering in his ear. "Not the most conventional gladiators, but effective. I realize we've not met in person – do you know who I am?"

Saffron answered quickly, "You're the Wolfspider, whatever your real name is."

The man's gloved hands pressed against the plank he was sitting on to prop himself up. He had a slender build, with dead eyes that Saffron could well imagine overseeing boundless cruelty. His demeanor, however, suggested calculated restraint. This was not a madman.

"The *Crimson Scorpion* herself! You're the talker of the group, then? *Saffron*, I believe it is. What a fabulous name, it almost sizzles like the fire you conjure. Yes, 'the Wolfspider' is all you need call me." He stood and paced in front of his men, hands holding one another behind his back.

"I've made a good deal of profit off you four already, especially our little fire-singer. Imagine, I acquired you for *free*, which I must admit made me immediately suspicious. But, no longer. I'm fairly sure I've figured you out."

Saffron couldn't hide scoffing at his presumption. The man had never met them, but was arrogant enough to think he understood them?

"You disagree? Well, no matter." He shrugged. "We shall see by the end of this conversation."

"A conversation requires two participants," Saffron interjected, crossing her arms. "So far, it sounds like you're doing most of the talking."

The Wolfspider smiled as the rest of his crew murmured disapprovingly at her interruption. "True enough, Saffron. Do you have anything to add at the moment? I haven't even gotten to my proposal."

"Proposal?" Saffron was genuinely surprised. She also wanted to buy time to figure out how to turn this situation to her advantage, if they weren't here to receive judgement. "That word suggests we have the option to decline."

"Indeed," the Wolfspider continued. "Any situation comes with multiple outcomes – some are just less attractive than others. That's truer when you're the party with less power." His last statement didn't seem directed at her, more a general acceptance of truth.

"I know your troupe is capable. You wouldn't have received an escort to my city from the Dread Lich's favorite minion if that weren't the case. And I know you'd probably like nothing better than to stick a spear straight through my heart right now, but that's not going to happen." He stopped pacing and faced Saffron directly.

"You're in a unique position. You four may actually be able to deliver something I need that I cannot simply take for myself."

Saffron's first impulse was to mention the bird as another example of this, but she quelled it just in time.

"I, obviously," said the Wolfspider, pressing one hand against his chest, "can give you something you crave in return – your freedom." He looked up to gauge their reactions at the mention of this reward. Saffron tried to keep her expression unchanged, but felt Dyphina gently squeeze her right forearm from behind.

"You may have heard rumors or been informed directly, for all I know, of a partnership between my empire and Hadrian No

More. Of course, you may have extrapolated as much from the fact that an undead abomination brought you into my service in the first place. I won't go into details about all he does or doesn't do for me – the fact that people are aware of this association, real or not, gives me quite an advantage. It reminds my adversaries that there are, in fact, fates worse than death."

Saffron sensed movement from her left and glanced over to see Harzhim, now leaning upon the door for support, his face gaunt. She turned back to the Wolfspider as he stroked the well-groomed facial hair on his chin. "And what could you possibly give the Dread Lich in return?"

The Wolfspider turned without answering and lifted his arms to grasp pipes that supported the scaffolding above his head. He arched his back, which bore a sheathed short sword angled across it. "Souls," he finally said. Saffron wasn't sure she'd heard him right, but then he expounded. "I deliver him souls of the innocent."

His statement hung in the unmoving air of the warehouse as Saffron tried to process what he meant. No one else dared speak.

"A few times a year I clean the streets, taking unfortunates who usually have no protection to speak of, no homes to seek refuge in. Beggars, orphans, mostly. Much of the populace is actually pleased to find them gone, though they don't know what's become of their daily annoyance." He laughed ironically at his narrative. "They consider it a service."

Saffron felt a wave of disgust pass through her, leaving her legs shaky. This man was actually standing here, admitting he culled the city's population of the poor by handing them over to the Dread Lich?

The Wolfspider released the scaffold and turned back around. There was no joy in his face, which, if anything, looked tired after his revelation. "The latest batch has already been rounded up, only this time Hadrian No More had a specific request: my daughter."

Saffron's attention once again switched to Harzhim, whose head had banged into the door as he sank to the floor in obvious distress. What was going on? This was not at all what she thought the morning's expedition would yield. "Why would he want a specific individual?" she couldn't help asking aloud as she tried to think of a reason herself. Of course, she was only guessing what a creature like that might want innocent people for in the first place.

"Because he's a deranged lunatic!" the Wolfspider howled. "Because he's mad, and immortal, and acts beyond the confines of logic! He said she was *special*, that she was born on the bicentennial of his transformation, under the same phases of the moon … that their nursemaids were raised in the same village. None of it makes sense!" He closed his eyes, breathed deeply to return his composure, then opened them and nodded to Lodiammon.

His lieutenant and about half of the men in the warehouse started moving. Saffron tensed, anticipating a physical confrontation, but they simply walked past her and her companions, gathering Harzhim from the floor before departing. Once they were out the door, the Wolfspider drew a dagger from a sheath around his thigh and started playing with it.

"I cannot refuse Hadrian No More's request without risking dire consequences – such is the drawback of aligning oneself with the most powerful madman in Elisahd. However, that does not mean you four cannot rescue my daughter once the caravan is far from my jurisdiction. If you care to end the existence of that Gullagion creature in addition, you will not find many mourners."

"And *that's* your proposal?" Saffron clarified. "We procure your daughter's safety and you remove our collars?"

"Precisely," the Wolfspider answered, pricking a finger against the tip of his dagger before meeting her stare. "If you agree, you will leave after sunset tonight. I will provide an escort, provisions, and map of the route Gullagion will be taking toward the Shadow Gate. The escort will unlock your collars and part ways at an oasis near the route. From there you are free. I am wagering on you to protect the innocent, including my daughter."

Saffron turned to her friends. "What do you think?"

"I think what they're doing to the children is horrible," Dyphina responded.

"Of course, but do we risk our necks again to save strangers?" Phaerim whispered harshly.

"We were all strangers not that long ago," Saffron noted. "And it might be a way out."

Thaelios shook his head, "Do we really think we can trust the Wolfspider any more than the Circle of Twelve?"

"At least he's not pretending to be our ally," Dyphina countered.

The Wolfspider raised his voice to be heard over their semi-private conversation. "If you refuse, I can always make your remaining stretch as gladiators more unpleasant. I'm sure I could even make a nice profit betting against you, given your current popularity and the resulting odds. I have much more control over the health of my own fighters, you see."

Saffron rolled her eyes, but knew he was right. "The sooner we're beyond his influence, the better." She looked to each of her companions, and they all nodded in turn. "All right," she said, turning back to the Wolfspider, "we'll do it."

"Never doubted it." He forced a smile. "Lodiammon will take you back to the pens and make sure the preparations are in order for tonight. Say your goodbyes or whatever else you have to do, but do *not* mention this undertaking to anyone else or there will be consequences. Remember, there are fates worse than death."

They all stood motionless for a moment, and though Saffron wasn't sure what he meant by his threat, she was certain she didn't need to find out.

"You may go," the Wolfspider said as if it was obvious, gesturing toward the door they came in. Lodiammon and a quartet of guards waited outside to escort them, though Harzhim was nowhere in sight.

Back in the pens, Saffron informed Zygrim and Wemic that they were being sent to an owner in another city. She didn't like lying to them, but couldn't think of a way to say farewell without sacrificing either the truth or their safety.

Zygrim frowned at the news. "Are you sure you'll be alright? This smells of political underhandedness to me."

"It'll be fine," Saffron assured him. "We're survivors – you know that."

"Aye," he answered, then looked to Thaelios. He took the Eladrin by the hand and led him a ways off to exchange a more private good-bye.

She met Wemic's eyes and tilted her head toward a bare corner of their cage to do the same. "I wish you the best," she said in Begnari once they were alone. She gestured to the interlocking steel bars that formed the boundary of their environment. "You deserve better than this."

He shrugged. "We all do."

"Take care of the big guy." She looked over at Zygrim who was bent forward, resting his forehead against Thaelios's crown as his lips moved.

Wemic nodded, leaning in a bit as well. "Take care of yourself."

She considered kissing him farewell for a moment but realized … she didn't really want to.

Chapter 27

A Step Behind

Be'naj noticed the cough Cauzel had dismissed so easily was growing worse. They had been at sea for four days, which took a great deal of getting used to on its own. Floating along the Chelhos River was one thing – strange and exhilarating in its own way – but they had always remained within sight of the shore. The rocking movement once they'd reached the open ocean was terrifying.

Be'naj knew a storm could blow in and shipwreck them at any moment; there was no way she could swim all the way back to land when it happened, even if she could tell what direction to go. She stayed below decks much of the time, but between her constant queasiness and Cauzel's lung-rattling, she felt very much like they were on the cusp of disaster.

Unsure when it would end, she continued practicing her Illanese by interacting with a young passenger who had been so bored that he welcomed even an unfamiliar play partner. His parents seemed to be glad for an interruption to his whining, so Be'naj and the boy explored the whole of the ship's interior while pretending it was a castle among the clouds, their shifting from side to side a result of the wind.

They exhausted their game after at least two trips around every nook of the hull, including several violations of what turned out to be private quarters. On their sixth day at sea, Be'naj was heading up to the foredeck for some fresh air during an unusually calm moment, when she heard the clear ringing of bells from above.

Emerging onto the deck under a startling blue sky, she was pleasantly surprised to see a looming cliff of coastline passing portside. The bells were sounding their final approach toward blessèd land, and Be'naj immediately spun around to find Cauzel.

Her seasickness abated with the nearing terrestrial horizon, and Be'naj was ready to disembark as soon as the gang plank was laid steady. Cauzel followed more slowly, his movement labored by a shortness of breath, and he sat on the edge of a dockside crate while they waited for their horses.

"Where now?" Be'naj asked as she saddled Sheen amidst the bustle of port activity. "Can you use your spell to tell us where Saffron and your apprentices are?" Excited to finally be nearing her reunion with Saffron, she was desperate for some detail to focus on – the congested population and noise surrounding them put Be'naj on the verge of being overwhelmed. She hadn't ventured past the docks when they reached Talon Barge, and the thought of wading into the vast ocean of people beyond had her hands shaking.

"Unfortunately," Cauzel coughed before continuing, "it would not be of great service to us at the moment. I could establish a general heading, perhaps, but without my enchanted map, a precise location is impossible. More practical would be asking a local where we can find the nearest magical authority. I'd wager if three young Shapers were brought across the continent, it was either at the behest of, or at least not unknown to, whatever arcane talent resides here. In a city this large," he coughed again, "there is bound to be one."

Be'naj nodded, then mounted her horse. "We should also find a healer to look you over. Your condition is getting worse."

Cauzel waved her suggestion off. "It's this damp air. Once we get further inland, the drier climate will clear it right up." He led his horse by the reins, walking over to a man who was helping unload cargo from the ship they'd disembarked. "Pardon me, friend, but would you happen to know where I could find a Shaper in this fair city?"

The man stared at Cauzel with a blank look, a drop of sweat running down his nose, which he wiped away with the back of his hand. Displaying his palms, he started speaking in a language Be'naj didn't understand but thought she recognized from Saffron's singing.

"Ah, he speaks Begnari. Wonderful," Cauzel added sarcastically. He patted the man's shoulder while nodding. "Thank you, thank you," he said in Illanese.

"Looks like you've been having me learn the wrong language," Be'naj observed.

"That could be the case," Cauzel answered while surveying the docks. "What we need is a human with paler skin … there's bound to be someone who speaks Illanese in a port city of this size. Let's try further in from the docks."

Be'naj nudged Sheen forward to follow Cauzel. The crowd seemed to ignore yet part for them as the horses' hooves clicked along the planks of the boardwalk. The ground sloped upward to her left, carrying the city right along with it, as they penetrated inland. A break in the hill offered a relatively flat area, where billowing banners, colorful pavilions, and boisterous haggling signaled a marketplace, though vastly more animated than what Be'naj remembered from her childhood in Gilsage.

"Ah, there we are!" Cauzel exclaimed, pointing to a woman standing behind a small wooden cart displaying silver trinkets. She had a dark cloth wrapped around her forehead and hair, masking its likely lighter color.

Be'naj recognized that, even with Cauzel's spell disguising her, she stood out amongst the natives here. Her brass-colored hair and almost pearlescent skin were noticeably fairer than the coal locks and deeply tanned tones of the surrounding populace. Cauzel's chosen illusion fit in somewhat better, with his olive-tinted skin and bushy black tendrils of curling hair.

He cut through a swath of loitering, would-be customers, taking as direct a path as possible to reach the woman behind the cart. "Greetings! Do you, perchance, speak Illanese?"

The vendor glanced to the side as if unsure Cauzel was speaking to her and not someone else nearby. As he got closer, though, she nodded and gestured toward her wares. "I speak your tongue, yes. What kind of goods are you interested in? Something for the lady, perhaps?" Her lids raised to acknowledge the trailing Be'naj, seated on her horse. "All my pieces are crafted to be a unique enhancement to your personal beauty. She is quite stunning – I'm sure we could find something to suit her."

Cauzel dipped his hand into his money pouch and came out with a silver coin. "I am not currently in search of adornments, but I would happily pay you for useful information. Are there any Shapers in Zeblon, and if so, do you know where I might find them?"

The woman looked from Cauzel to Be'naj, then back to him and held out her palm. He placed the coin in it and, fast as a viper strike, she tucked it into a hidden pocket behind her belt.

"Of course," she stated, as if he could have gotten the same information from anyone else. "Everyone knows of the Circle of Twelve. They live on a grand estate at the topmost level of the city." She pointed up the southern hill.

"Pardon me, did you say Circle of *Twelve*?" Cauzel asked.

The trinket vendor shrugged. "That's what they call themselves."

"As in, there are twelve Shapers in Zeblon, all working cooperatively?"

"I suppose," she answered. "I've never personally counted them."

Cauzel looked at the height of the upcoming climb and mounted his steed. "It's a good thing we've got the horses," he said to Be'naj, "or this would take until next week." He looked back toward the vendor. "My thanks," he said before pulling his horse out of the thickest path of foot traffic. "Twelve Shapers," he repeated to himself, shaking his head as he prodded his horse along the path that wound up the hill.

Everything about Zeblon was foreign to Be'naj: the smells of the sea and spices she couldn't place, the yelling of people engaging in commerce or talking in clusters beside the streets, the draped clothes and odd fashions of the citizens – the effect on her senses was nearly debilitating as she struggled to decide where to allot her attention.

They passed a huge, round building at the top of the first hill, but it wasn't a castle or palace. It had no roof, in fact, though banners on long poles bearing varied insignia blew in the wind all around its circumference.

Further along came smaller dwellings, then up another hill they went, passing what had to be the grandest shrine she'd ever seen. The roof was punctuated with golden, teardrop-shaped bulbs, like the caps of priceless mushrooms left behind by the gods. "Humans built all this?" she asked, awestruck as they continued following the road.

"That's one thing I've found they excel at," Cauzel remarked. "Instead of honoring the natural world with their shelters, they seem inclined to challenge even the mountain's grandeur."

After another stately manor and a host of more reasonably-sized homes, they started climbing the final slope. When it plateaued, Be'naj found another collection of immense houses, each estate as large as the Keeper of Gilsage's back in Ifelian.

"Ah, this looks like the right place," Cauzel said, standing in his stirrups to stretch his legs. "It makes sense an arcane collective would desire separation from the untrained population, for safety and privacy. I wouldn't be surprised if they owned all of the buildings on this plateau."

Be'naj looked from one impressive structure to the next with no real clue as to the most likely residences for a group of sorcerers. A boy and a girl were struggling to get a kite off the ground on a flat stretch of yard in front of one house. Further ahead, a stable-hand carried an armful of hay toward a barn. An older woman tended a half-dormant garden off to their right. "Shall we ask one of the laborers, then?"

"A sound course, I should think," Cauzel replied, making a clicking sound with his cheek to entice his steed to continue moving. Be'naj followed on Sheen.

"Do you think any of them speak Illanese?" she asked.

"We can only hope, as it's more likely than Eladrin, no?" Cauzel allowed his horse to drift toward the barn, which it did of its own accord. The nearest house, right of the barn, was sizable, with two, pointy-topped towers, numerous windows, and several stone gargoyles poised where the roof changed angles.

"Are you lost?" came a voice from the direction of the mansion. A short man, who must have been previously sitting on a bench on the covered front porch, looked out at them with a hand shading his eyes. He had a beard, but not much other hair on his head. He did, at least, speak Illanese.

Be'naj and Cauzel halted at his question, and she was relieved when Cauzel took the initiative to answer.

"Good Sir, not so much lost as trying to find something," he yelled to cover the distance between them. "I am Cauzel Blackfeather from Ifelian, far to the west. A local in the marketplace told me there were practitioners of the arcane arts living at the top of this hill. Do you know this to be true?"

"I fancy there is truth in that, for you are speaking to one, Cauzel Blackfeather. Might I ask what brings you such a distance? A problem with only a magical solution, perhaps?" the man asked, staring at them even harder.

"It may prove to be so," Cauzel answered casually, coughing as he dismounted. He walked his horse toward the house to limit the amount of yelling. Be'naj dismounted with a frown and followed his lead, worried anew about his condition.

"Greetings, friend. I am a fellow Shaper, and this is my companion, Be'naj." Cauzel gestured to her with the hand not holding his horse's reins.

"A Shaper? From Ifelian, you say? Is that … Pasaxtree?" the man questioned, finally lowering his hand.

"Near there," Cauzel answered.

Be'naj felt more comfortable now that she could see the man's eyes. They were deep brown, much the same as his beard and outer garments. With his work-worn trousers and threadbare shirt, she thought he dressed more like a farmer than a powerful mage.

"So, this is a little embarrassing," Cauzel almost chuckled, giving an extremely good impression of someone not at all concerned, "but I appear to have lost a few of my apprentices while conducting other business. I was wondering if you were aware of any other foreign arcanists arriving within the last month?"

"Misplaced apprentices?" The man stroked his bearded chin. "My, my, that does sound embarrassing. Uh, I don't suppose they went missing on purpose, did they? Perhaps not too keen on your teaching techniques?" He laughed and Cauzel followed suit. Be'naj thought they were both acting strangely and didn't have the patience for it.

"My friend, Saffron min Furasi, was supposed to meet me and didn't show up," she blurted. "I'm afraid she was taken against her will."

Cauzel's jaw dropped and his hand opened and closed again, as if the gesture's purpose was forgotten. "Well, there you have it." He afforded another brief laugh, which quickly turned into a cough.

"Saffron, you say?" The man looked at her intently, perhaps weighing her trustworthiness. Be'naj tried to let the feelings in her heart show in her expression, hoping she would pass the test. After a moment, he held his arm out to her, and she responded by clasping his wrist. "I'm Groilen Bonesplinter, and perhaps you two should follow me inside."

Cauzel raised his bushy eyebrows at Be'naj, who silently accepted Groilen's invitation. They walked through a slim antechamber into a great room with sand-colored walls, gilded appointments, and a wide staircase leading up to a balcony. Ample light flowed in through large windows facing the front of the house. She barely had time to look at all four walls before hurrying through another doorway to keep up with their host.

When she did, she found a taller man in gaudy, multi-colored robes leaning down to listen as Groilen whispered to him. They both stood in front of an oval table of polished wood, which took up most of the new room. Another row of wide windows gave the space an open feeling, though the sunlight was indirect in this late-morning hour.

Be'naj patiently allowed their host to finish his private dissemination while Cauzel, who had taken more time to look around in the great room, joined them.

"Allow me to introduce Ayez." Groilen lifted a palm toward the man he'd been whispering to. We are both members of the Circle of Twelve, a cooperative of magical talents who hold Zeblon's best interests as our common priority."

"My Lady," Ayez gave an abbreviated bow. "I approached Lady Saffron a number of weeks ago about accepting sponsorship from the Twelve. I believed we could be of mutual service to one another, but I'm afraid she left here a little disappointed two nights past. You say you knew her before she became a gladiator?"

"She was here the other night?" Be'naj could scarcely believe they were so close after all this time. "And she was in good health?"

Groilen shrugged, avoiding her eyes. "Uh, more or less. Perhaps she had a few minor ailments, bruises and the like. Nothing abnormal, given her time fighting in the Arena."

"Excuse me, what did you say?" Cauzel butted in. "Saffron has been forced to fight as a gladiator? There is organized slave-fighting in Zeblon?"

Ayez shrugged. "A barbaric tradition that fell by the wayside long ago, recently revived by the rivalry between the guilds and the current Caliph. It is one of the practices the Circle of Twelve is working to end."

"So, where did Saffron go from here?" Be'naj insisted. The civics lesson could wait for another time.

"Were my other apprentices with her?" Cauzel added.

The answer to their questions came from a new, sinister-sounding voice, approaching from the great room behind them. "Alas, though they are together, they left the city under cover of darkness."

"What are you speaking of, Sirran?" Ayez inquired from behind Be'naj as she spun to face the newcomer.

He was a lanky, strange-looking fellow, wearing unusual garb colored like rust and coal, consisting of a multitude of extraneous straps and buckles. Be'naj immediately started to itch as he drew nearer. Tight, ruddy skin stretched across his face, and curved horns protruded from the crown of his head. His appearance was disconcerting, and she felt an instant distrust as he spoke.

"I have been looking in on our investment since the previous night's development," he answered in a thin, hollow voice. "They met with the Wolfspider in person and were subsequently taken into the desert. They left late last night."

"Why didn't you inform the Circle?" Groilen asked sharply.

Sirran returned an innocent look. "I am informing you now. The development is an ill omen for them, I'd wager." He shifted his gaze to Be'naj, then Cauzel. "My skin crawls," he said, looking down at his arms, though they were completely shrouded by sleeves, "and you are both wearing disguises. Why? Are you ashamed of how you look?" Sirran followed his question with a mocking smile that showed off pointed teeth.

Be'naj tried to push past his inquiry and keep to the subject of rescuing Saffron. "Who is the Wolfspider, and where is he taking them?" she asked, turning back to Ayez.

"The Wolfspider, My Lady," he answered while circling to the far side of the table, "is the head of a nefarious guild of cutthroats and thugs. He controls much of the merchant traffic in and out of Zeblon, and oversees the criminal element in our city as well."

Ayez reached out and placed his hand on a crystal orb set in the center of the table. It came alive with swirling colors at his touch. "As for where Saffron and her fellow gladiators are now, allow me a moment ..."

He closed his eyes in concentration and, a breath later, the colors exploded horizontally from the orb, forming a full-relief map of the city over the surface of the table. Rendered in astonishing detail, Be'naj looked closer at the map and saw it even included tiny people, moving up and down the streets about their business.

"Sir ... Blackfeather, was it?" Ayez asked, opening his eyes.

"Yes," Cauzel answered after a delay, his attention focused on the intricate map as well. "This is extraordinary." He bent to examine the thin gap between the table and the map, confirming its leviatation. "My own enchanted map is much more mundane."

"Having tracked them this far, I presume you brought trinkets of your apprentices for a location spell?" Ayez inquired.

"Oh, yes, of course," Cauzel said, standing erect. He peeled off his pack and fished through it until coming up with an ivy wrist cuff and a small, metallic disc Be'naj couldn't decipher. "Shall I, then?" Cauzel asked, holding one implement in each hand.

"Of course," Ayez responded, taking a step back from the table.

While Cauzel concentrated on casting his spell, Be'naj snuck a hand down to feel the map. Her fingers passed straight through it as if it was no different than the surrounding air.

The scenery of the map began shifting in ripples, outward from the sphere in its center. When it stilled, the cityscape had been replaced by barren ground and stretches of sand. A dozen camels travelled along a dusty trail, their riders too small to identify.

"That's the Path of Bones," Sirran explained. "They're heading west."

Ayez's brow creased. "There is an oasis with a small outpost the Wolfspider uses along the trade route. They will likely head there to refill water stores. Whether your friends make it that far alive is another matter. You can see they are not alone."

"We have to leave now, then!" Be'naj pleaded to Cauzel.

"Yes, yes of course. We shall have need of speed, but also more water if we're heading into the desert. Cauzel looked at Ayez and asked, "Do you have a well we might draw from?"

Chapter 28

Ambush

L odiammon had pushed them hard. As a result, late on their second full day out from the city, Saffron saw the green of the oasis looming ahead as the sun dipped its toes into the line of the eastern horizon. The journey had been terribly dull, with the land flat, brown, and dry. Her back ached from trying to maintain posture atop the unfamiliar angles of her camel.

She did have plenty of time to think, however, and had already bent her mind toward planning the ambush. The Wolfspider's lieutenant informed them that delivery of the tribute – a horrible term applied to parentless children and those unfortunate enough to be stricken with poverty – would take place in the desert just outside the confines of Zeblon. From there, Gullagion would oversee the transport on wagons. The Wolfspider was providing some of his collared slaves to assist as guards, but Lodiammon warned that the right-hand of Hadrian No More would also bring his own entourage, including other undead and bound servants of the Dread Lich.

During the trip, Phaerim whispered the possibility of taking Lodiammon and the other five members of their escort by surprise, then searching for the key to their collars in the aftermath. Saffron and the others put down the suggestion as too risky since any of the Wolfspider's crew might know how to set the devices off, and they were hopefully about to be set free anyway.

"Keep it moving," Lodiammon called as he dropped back to the end of the camel cluster. "We're making that oasis by nightfall, or I'll be dragging your bleeding corpses there."

Saffron couldn't wait to be rid of him; the man was extremely unpleasant to be around. She gritted her teeth and choked down her response, knowing it wasn't worth the breath with their freedom so close.

Stars peeked out and only a dim glow from the setting sun remained when their camels trudged under the ring of palms circling a sad-looking watering hole. Several clay buildings had been constructed nearby, including barracks housing a small retinue of the Wolfspider's soldiers. Even a hundred miles from Zeblon they had still not escaped the reach of his influence. Controlling the oasis no doubt gave him the ability to manage land-driven trade to the capital.

After the camels were unpacked and tied up, Lodiammon showed Saffron's company a flat, cleared plot where they could camp. The Wolfspider's men would be sleeping indoors. When she asked if he was willing to remove their collars so they might sleep more comfortably, he laughed.

"You can have your freedom in the morning, when we're ready to leave. Just so you know, there are a few conditions my employer wants to make sure you're clear on. First off, none of you are to ever return to Zeblon. He needs to disassociate with you, and if you show up, you will be shown no mercy."

The encroaching night made it difficult for Saffron to assess his face, with deep shadows obscuring his features. She was almost certain that he was looking forward to being rid of them as well.

"Secondly," Lodiammon's raspy voice continued, "when you have rescued his daughter, you are to lead her back to this oasis, unharmed. If that's not possible, take her to some other town, but she is not to return to Zeblon, either. Can't have the Dread Lich demanding her again if she shows up at her father's house. One of my men will wait here for a few days to take her somewhere safe, or she can pass along a message to her daddy – she will know how. He'll make sure she's taken care of once she reaches her new home. Understood?"

Saffron nodded, though she wasn't going to bother wasting time tonight on what to do *after* they somehow freed the hostages from Gullagion. She had yet to work out how they were going to accomplish the hard part.

"Good," he responded. "And now, sleepy time." He laughed to himself as he turned toward the barracks, leaving them to make sleeping arrangements for themselves. Saffron had noticed Lodiammon purposefully spoke to her only in Begnari so the others couldn't understand, though she was fairly certain he comprehended Illanese. She'd guarded against talking openly while he was around, just in case.

Now that they were alone, however, she didn't have to worry. At least they had been gifted a bevy of supplies as a parting concession. Apparently, the Wolfspider was wise enough to know they'd be much more motivated the likelier they were to make it out of the desert alive.

They had padded sleeping rolls to keep them warm during the desert nights, a pair of water bladders each, several flasks of oil, plenty of food, and their choice of weapons from the gladiator armory. Phaerim even talked their outfitter into handing over a dose of expensive Nightwing poison, which was legendary for its crippling potency.

Saffron didn't see any harm in building a fire and thought it would be easier to discuss their final preparations if they could see one another's faces. After she started a blaze and everyone had set up their bedrolls, they turned to making what she realized might be their final meal together. She reflected, while heating a small pot of broth, that many of their meals over the past month could have been viewed that way, given they were asked to fight to the death almost every week. This felt different, though, being out under the open sky. She certainly felt that Yune hadn't spun a destiny for her that ended tomorrow, but she'd already experienced the loss of others. She was not naïve – battle always found ways to inflict cost.

The plan so far was to backtrack and hit the enemy caravan before they reached the oasis. She'd picked out a likely spot during their ride the day before, one with rocky hills and a few dunes elevated over the trail. They had a large canister of dragon jelly she planned to use to great effect, and the element of surprise would be crucial. Thaelios and Dyphina both prepared spells out of the book they'd borrowed from the Circle of Twelve's library and never returned.

The four of them talked around the fire until Saffron felt there was nothing more to be gained. She thought she'd feel more anxious, but lying down on her bedroll, covered by a blanket and looking up at the stars, Saffron felt strangely at ease. She'd been fighting for a while now. Tomorrow's conflict was nothing new, it wasn't unexpected, and at least she'd have some control over the circumstances. The resulting confidence allowed her to fall asleep rather quickly.

She was loathe to rise in the morning, for she had been dreaming of Be'naj. They'd been bathing together in the springs at Skywatch Haven and playing in the water without any reservations or awkwardness. Saffron felt like they both understood one another and wanted the same thing. In the dream, they were in the midst of building a life together, and it seemed so natural when they kissed.

Coming from the image of Be'naj's angelic face, to the sight of Lodiammon's sullen features staring down at her when she opened her eyes, was abrasive.

"Do you want this collar off or not?" he asked, holding up a glowing, green key.

She snapped upright on her bedroll, almost colliding heads with the Wolfspider's lieutenant in her haste. "Of course," she spouted, her senses working to catch up to her wakened state. The head of the key was shaped like a skull, and it shone with a sickly green light.

Saffron held still while Lodiammon inserted it. She heard the sound of metal on metal, then with a satisfying *click*, the weight of the iron slid the opened collar from her neck into her lap. She immediately rolled her shoulders, which seemed oddly light. Now that the collar was no longer there, she felt like she'd been carrying an extra hundred pounds.

Whether already awake before her or not, Saffron's mates were all sitting up and waiting their turns when she swiveled her head. Lodiammon went from one to the next, and with no need for exchanging words, slid the green skull key into each of their collars, unlocking them.

Another member of their escort came around to gather the devices, though Saffron had just enough awareness to pluck and pocket the Circle of Twelve's lodestone from hers before handing it over.

"Well, this is where we part," Lodiammon stated. "Your crew had best not tarry long, or you'll be the ones ambushed." He didn't wish them well, though Saffron imagined their success or failure would likely hold repercussions for him as their overseer. He simply walked over to where the camels were tied, leaving Saffron and her friends to do as he suggested.

As Saffron stood, she noticed the green key slide to the ground from her lap. Had Lodiammon dropped it on purpose, or had it merely slipped from his grasp? Either way, she decided it would make a nice keepsake and palmed it before anyone noticed.

By the time she'd changed into her red leather armor and pulled her boots on, Lodiammon and his fellows were already headed west, further down the Path of Bones. She surmised they had a secondary mission to accomplish, given how far along they'd already come. The garrison stationed at the oasis remained, but didn't seem interested in interacting. Saffron figured it was just as well.

Phaerim, dressed in the same black studded leather popular among the Wolfspider's crew, approached her while they packed the camels for the day's journey. "So, in case today goes the way I think it might, I just wanted to give you my thanks for all the times you've looked out for us. I know it was only chance that we happened to be chained together in those blasted mines, but I've noticed how you take on extra burdens to keep us safe."

Saffron was speechless. She'd never made choices with the expectation of thanks, but receiving it moved her. Apparently, the look on her face and her lack of response was making Phaerim uncomfortable, because he started stammering.

"Anyway, just, uh, don't be too proud to let us return the favor. If you need help, we'd all do whatever we can to give it." Finished, he circled the camels to check the security of the saddle straps.

She thought about what he said while trying to swallow, which had suddenly become difficult. Pride was something she had in ample supply and she'd have to be vigilant that it didn't lead to more trouble.

Once all four were mounted, Saffron led the way back east, keeping an eye out for the spot she'd selected yesterday. Starting only a few miles out, they arrived within the hour and immediately set to work. They unpacked the camels first so Dyphina could tie them north of the road, a healthy distance from where the ambush would take place.

Saffron painstakingly created a design in dragon jelly that culminated in the center of the road. Timing its ignition correctly would be vital, lest she risk burning the very people they were hoping to rescue. While she was busy, Phaerim selected multiple defensible positions from where they could either strike or fall back, and divvy the supplies between them.

Thaelios, whose eyes were keenest, kept watch from atop a rise a little further east to give them as much warning as he could while still having time to withdraw himself. Not knowing how swiftly the slave caravan was travelling, Saffron could only guess how much time they had to prepare. According to Lodiammon, Gullagion's wagons left the morning after their own party had departed.

When she was satisfied with the placement of the dragon jelly, Saffron rolled the empty barrel behind a rock outcropping and joined Phaerim to wait in one of his dug-out, sandy shelters, south of the road. "Dyphina shouldn't be much longer, should she?" she asked, looking north for signs of the half-fey. "She didn't need to go that far …"

"She'll be back in time," Phaerim stated calmly. "The gods wouldn't miss a chance like this to get us all at once."

Saffron watched as he coated the blades of two daggers with the poison bestowed by the Wolfspider. "How do you know that stuff even works?" she asked, raising one eyebrow.

"Because nothing could smell this bad and not work," he answered, eyes not leaving his task.

She was about to move to another spot to keep them from being targeted together when they saw Thaelios, crossing and uncrossing his arms above his head as he ran toward them. That was the signal. Where was Dyphina?

"Stay here, I'm crossing the road to look for Dyphina." Saffron placed both hands on Phaerim's shoulders, lingering for the space of a deep breath, realizing this might be their final moment together.

He stayed put, offering no words as she picked up her spear and shield. After popping out from their hiding place, she careened down the sandy slope to the road. Thaelios drew ever nearer as she started climbing the embankment on the northern side. This was her fault – she should have woken sooner to allow an earlier start. When she crested the rise, she saw Dyphina picking her way up the opposite side of the hill, obviously unaware their ambush was imminent.

"Where have you been?" Saffron couldn't help scolding in her anxiousness, though she tried hushing her voice.

"What? I couldn't find anything good to tie them to."

"Get ready," Saffron urged. "Thaelios already gave the signal." That was enough to spur Dyphina to a quicker pace. Saffron ducked behind the crumbling rock of the hilltop and peered over to watch, exposing as little of herself as possible.

Thaelios was just disappearing into position over the hill on Phaerim's side; he was responsible for sowing confusion from a distance with spells and arrows. It was imperative to give their enemy every impression of facing greater numbers than they actually were.

Saffron's mind ticked through the list of necessary actions for once the caravan pulled into position. Every shallow breath seemed a short lifetime as she waited for the foremost wagon to appear around the bend. The first thing she saw was the green fog descending from Gullagion on horseback.

Memories of their journey through the back country from Nightwing Castle to Talon Barge flashed through her head and turned her stomach. His noxious aura would complicate direct attacks; she would have to be careful not to get too close. A safe distance behind him, the first wagon, pulled by a chained creature that looked like a cross between a large, leathery grey iguana and a muskox, came into view. More disconcerting than the massive draft kank was the armor-skinned rock troll beside it, easily half-as-tall again as Saffron.

Two more wagons appeared in succession, the last coming with another troll. The wagons had barred sides, covered with canvas tops for protection from the overhead sun. They were full of prisoners, nearly a dozen each, and another handful of weary tribute slaves walked beside each one, chained to its bars.

A half-dozen collared guards had been conscripted for added protection, and Saffron could sympathize with their position, unable to decline the loathsome duty. Sprinkled throughout the caravan, she saw the sun reflecting off bright bone – a dozen or so animated skeletons, carrying spears, added to the profane presence of the Dread Lich's lieutenant.

Saffron realized she'd already tensed up, her body preparing for what her mind knew was coming, and forced her muscles to relax. She steadied her breath, which she'd also been holding, and closed her eyes to visualize what a successful ambush might look like. When she opened them again, she calmly waited for Thaelios to make the first move.

Once Gullagion had advanced past his position on the trail, the Eladrin obliged by rising up and taking aim at the rear rock troll with his bow. The arrow zipped downward into the monster's belly, and Saffron watched the entire caravan halt and turn at the bellowing sound of the troll's howl.

She turned to Dyphina, crouched in a depression several paces away. "It's begun." Dyphina nodded and started casting a spell as Saffron inhaled deeply one last time before singing. Swinging her legs over the crest of her ridge, she descended the slope diagonally, encouraged by the attention her enemies were giving the opposite hillside. She never ceased her tune, and as she reached level ground, the tip of her spear burst into flame.

On the far side of the road, one of the trolls and a small team of skeletons had been dispatched to deal with Thaelios, who was visible just over the ridge, lining up a second shot with his bow.

Saffron took the opportunity to blindside a quartet of skeleton guards on the near side of the wagons. Her spear rattled against the ribcage of the closest one when she thrust, causing them to turn in unison. Her fire blackened the bones around it, but her strike was not sound enough to visibly do harm. Battling the undead was going to be tricky.

She assumed a defensive stance and concentrated on avoiding their spears, which were an arm longer than hers. She let them strike, swatting away two of the shafts with her own while deflecting the others with her shield, gaining a sense of her opponents' prowess and recovery time. Saffron backed up slowly, luring them away from the rest of the caravan as they continued to strike.

Beyond the skeletons, she spied a cluster of the human thralls approaching to reinforce them; becoming overwhelmed by sheer numbers was her greatest concern. Halfway to her, however, they all turned to chase one of the kanks as it tore off the road behind them, suddenly spooked, dragging one of the wagons with it. Saffron acknowledged Dyphina's handiwork with a smile.

She feinted toward the skeletons to give them pause, then took another few steps back as a roar snatched her attention. Up the hill where the rock troll had been sent, Phaerim had slipped behind it and delivered his dose of Nightwing poison with a plunge of his dagger. Saffron hoped it would be potent enough to affect such a massive creature. Thaelios had added to the confusion with his mirror image spell – a slew of identical Eladrin surrounded the actual Shaper.

Saffron refocused as a skeleton's spear vibrated against her shield. Luckily she did, for her peripheral vision caught just enough of the green bolt zooming toward her for her to block it. Even that was not without cost. The projectile turned out to be a corrosive dart, conjured by Gullagion. Her shield sizzled as the acid ate away at its surface.

She once again backed out of reach of the skeleton's weapons, locked in a stare with the Dread Lich's lieutenant as she retreated. Gullagion's eyes burned fiercely underneath his black hood as he directed his unearthly mount forward.

"I remember you," the ghost hissed in an echoing tone that sounded like a snake calling up from the bottom of a well. "I see you have not suffered enough yet to quell your rebellious nature, slave!"

Saffron continued falling back, biding her time, keeping both her spear and melting shield raised. "I am a slave no longer, unholy one!" she retorted. She glanced down at the dragon jelly lining the ground as she passed over, then slowed her pace to allow the skeletons to fall in behind their commander. "You and your Lord have no power over me!"

"You have yet to see the extent of our power, fleshling!" Gullagion's mount came to a halt as he raised an emaciated hand to cast another spell.

Close enough, Saffron hoped. She quickly touched the burning tip of her spear to the earth where she'd drawn out a design in the oily mixture. A rush of heat blasted her as the jelly ignited, and Saffron leapt backwards to the ground to escape it. Fire surged skyward in front of her as the snaking sigil exploded to life, obscuring her view of Gullagion and whatever spell he'd been in the midst of casting.

Some of the jelly had stuck to her boot as well, and she tried not to panic as she released her spear to scamper to her feet. She recalled one of Palomar's first lessons on elemental magic, a reminder that fire needed air to thrive. With a wall of flame and black smoke temporarily shielding her from her enemies, she heeded the lesson and ran to the side of the path where there was more loose sand. Saffron buried her burning boot in the fine powder, quenching the flame.

The initial surge of the dragon jelly didn't last long, and she could already see over the weakening blaze by the time she reclaimed her spear. The skeletons consumed by the inferno had fallen apart, the magic binding them shattered. Gullagion's shadowy steed had likewise evaporated, but the ghast sorcerer still stood, having retreated to the far side of the flames.

His robes had burned away, and singed, decayed flesh clung to a frame of bones and atrophied muscles. The green, noxious vapor that surrounded him like an aura continued to replenish itself.

Saffron's eyes danced across the battlefield, looking for her friends, though everyone else seemed mesmerized by the conflagration. Phaerim and Thaelios stood over the fallen form of the rock troll sent to attack them on the southern slope, the poison having done its work. Dyphina was beyond view, though sounds of chaos rose from among the distant wagons.

"You want to play with fire?!" Gullagion screamed from across the burning sigil before lifting his palms skyward and chattering toward the heavens.

Fearing another spell, Saffron raised her shield, though the ghast's acid dart had reduced it to a crescent. With Gullagion immersed in his complex casting, Saffron watched Phaerim bounding down the hill to take Hadrian No More's lieutenant from behind. She held her breath, worrying what was to come, but hoping she might be wrong. Phaerim dashed toward Gullagion's exposed back, dagger raised, but keeled over a step short, his spasming stomach pouring vomit from his mouth.

The ghast paid him no mind, and as he completed his spell, a pair of pony-sized hounds appeared within the flames, accompanied by a thunderous crack. They cared not about the heat, for their eye sockets and mouth poured forth fire of their own, and their cinder-black coats were streaked with cracked lines of sulfur yellow.

The hounds snapped and barked menacingly as they sprinted toward Saffron, who immediately turned to bolt toward higher ground. She could hear the pads of many feet slapping against the ground behind her but didn't spare any time to look back. She charged toward the northern slope, hoping the incline would keep the beasts from encircling her.

As if there was no limit to the strangeness of the moment, Saffron caught sight of a giant, black bird diving in her direction out of the fathomless, blue sky. She immediately thought of Noki, Cauzel's raven familiar, but this specimen was three times larger. She never stopped running, though, and used the butt of her spear to push into the ground as her climb up the hillside began.

A quarter-way up the slope, knowing the hounds had to be nearly upon her, she spun to face them, whipping her spear in an arc before her. Her turn coincided with a chorus of roars, and Saffron's weapon nearly slipped from her grip when she saw the infernal hounds had been cut off by what looked like a dragon with metallic, copper-colored scales.

She looked to the sky but the bird was nowhere to be seen. The dragon, however, was the size of both the fiery beasts combined, and they clearly feared it. Its sinewy neck moved fluidly, and it snapped at the hounds with razor-toothed jaws.

The hounds responded by shooting jets of flame from their maws, but the fire seemed inconsequential to the dragon. Ignoring their attacks, it lunged forward to grab one of the beasts with its fore claws. Holding the hound by its flank, the dragon crushed its neck with a mighty snap of its jaws. The beast crumpled into a heap while its partner seized the dragon's front leg in its mouth and shook. The dragon merely growled and tossed it away like a toy.

"Look out!" Saffron yelled in warning to the dragon without even thinking. The shimmering-scaled creature heeded her, snapping its head up in time to see the remaining rock troll bearing down on him with its club. Flapping its wings, the dragon whipped up sand and glided backward to avoid a wild swing.

The dragon jelly had nearly burned itself out, and Saffron realized she'd become a spectator since the dragon's arrival. She clenched her teeth and descended toward level ground to rejoin the fight.

The dismayed hounds suddenly disappeared in clouds of green smoke, their borrowed time run out, no doubt returned to whatever infernal realm they'd been summoned from. Saffron wondered if the same would soon happen to her mysterious ally, which spurred her to strike quickly.

The troll and dragon danced in a wide circle, swinging and lunging as they tested one another. With the rock troll entirely focused on the metallic menace threatening him, Saffron was able to approach undetected from the side. She thrust her spear at the troll's exposed ribcage as he raised his arm to strike a blow with his club. Her aim true, the monster howled at the injury and drew back instinctively to cover the wound. The motion snapped the shaft of her spear in two, but granted the dragon the opening it needed. With a snap of its jaws it grabbed hold of the troll's other arm and yanked the giant toward it, causing the troll to stumble.

Saffron heard faint notes of song coming from the direction of the caravan and was glad to know Dyphina must still be fighting. Bereft of her weapon, Saffron began humming a tune of her own, conjuring a bloom of fire to hurl at her enemy.

The dragon had not yet relinquished its hold and, having dragged the troll to the ground by its arm, continued pulling it across the road to keep it from regaining its feet. An arrow, launched from the southern side of the road, suddenly pierced the leg of the prone troll, who had not ceased yelling in whatever crudeness passed for its language.

Saffron was nearly finished with her spell, but Gullagion completed one first. Tendrils of solid shadow sprung up around the dragon and seized it, tightening until it had no choice but to release the troll. Saffron shifted her aim to the ghast sorcerer before blowing the blazing bloom from her palm.

The blossom zoomed across the field, past the rock troll who was pushing up from the ground, but scattered into impotent sparks a mere hand from the ghast. Like the gladiators from the House of Eternal Flame, Gullagion must have warded himself from fire after she ignited the dragon jelly!

A twinge of panic took hold in her mind, spreading as she watched the rock troll wind up and beat the ensnared dragon across the head with his spiked club. The reptilian body went limp within its shadowy prison, then started shrinking and changing shape.

Saffron steeled her nerves and continued singing, trying to conjure another fire blossom while the troll looked confused. Gullagion was staring at her and had begun chanting as well. She quickly realized her magic was no match for the Dread Lich's lieutenant. She was going to have to endure whatever spell was coming, because she needed more time to build power behind her own if she was going to subdue something as large as that rock troll.

With one eye on the troll and the other on Gullagion, she saw a timely arrow zip downward and strike the ghast in his shoulder. He turned his attention toward the source of the shot, leaving Saffron free to release her fire bloom at the still bewildered troll. Launched from her palm by a blow of her pursed lips, it streaked toward her enemy like a burning comet.

The troll never saw what was coming. The incendiary cluster struck him square in the side of the face and exploded with such heat that it scorched both eyes to uselessness and ignited the course, shaggy grey hair on top of its head. It dropped its club and raised its palms to smother the flames but mercifully fell to its knees a moment later, then forward onto its stomach, dead.

By the time Saffron looked back to Gullagion, he was releasing another magical green dart in Thaelios's direction.

"No!" she called out as the projectile surged toward the eladrin shaper. He turned just before impact but fell onto his back, screaming in pain as the acid began dissolving the flesh of his left side and arm.

Saffron's cry drew Gullagion's attention. Phaerim had crawled away on his knees but was still spitting into the sand. Wherever Dyphina was, dealing with the other wagons no doubt, it was too far for Saffron to see. She was out of friends and didn't know how she was going to defeat the ghast – he was protected from fire, and she couldn't draw near without nausea claiming her, too.

Gullagion looked truly horrid. Devoid of his robe, with one of Thaelios's arrows protruding from his shoulder, parts of the bluish skin of his decrepit body were singed black from the surge of the dragon jelly and did an inadequate job of covering all his bones. He looked even worse cracking what Saffron supposed passed for a grin, no doubt aware of the situation he had her in.

"Too bad you never learned another trick, fire-starter," he said, walking closer. "I think I'm going to let you live for all the trouble you've given me – at least long enough to serve as a sacrifice for my master."

Saffron wasn't sure what she was going to do but held her ground, trying to think of something. Had Palomar taught her anything else that would be useful?

"You can injure me, but I feel no pain," the ghast continued. "I sometimes forget what it felt like to suffer, but I'm reminded every time I hear the screams of agony as Hadrian No More peels the skin off the living or slowly impales them with their own weight."

Saffron suddenly heard the unmistakable cadence of a galloping horse approaching from the east. Her mind recognized it, yet told her she had seen only kanks in the caravan, save Gullagion's smoky mount.

"But I can't have you interfering with that meddlesome singing, so perhaps I'll just cut out your tongue before binding you against the wag—"

Apparently, Gullagion heard it, too. He stopped moving toward Saffron and turned to face the oncoming steed. She peered that direction as well to find the glare of the sun playing tricks on her eyes: the thundering hooves belonged to a winged horse! As it drew closer, stretching its neck forward with each stride, Saffron spotted the brilliant mane of hair belonging to its rider and realized the wings belonged to her as well. Be'naj!

Somehow, beyond any reasonable hope, Be'naj had not only come for her but found her. The two of them locked eyes for the briefest moment – or was it a lifetime – and Be'naj, who had freed her boots from the stirrups, lifted her knees to push off the saddle and launch into the air. She extended her glorious white wings, their ends dipped in liquid brass, drew her sword, and extended her shield arm as she glided to the ground.

Remembering Phaerim's mistake, Saffron called out a warning. "Not too close, Be'naj! He's—"

Her blessèd friend moved too quickly, however. She had already engaged the sorcerer, who had conjured a black staff of solid shadow to parry Be'naj's fierce blows. Amazed that Be'naj showed no effects from the green vapor surrounding Gullagion, Saffron's thoughts went to securing another weapon. Perhaps she might have the same luck … or perhaps she needed a bow!

She ran to Thaelios on the southern slope, who had at least moved to a sitting position. His face was stuck in a perpetual wince as he tried to tear the sleeve off his tunic with his right hand to bandage the sizzling skin of his left arm. "Are you all right?" she asked reflexively, knowing the answer but unable to help as she picked up his discarded bow.

Thaelios didn't bother responding but obligingly bent forward to make it easier for Saffron to draw from the quiver on his back. She appreciated the gesture and his lack of complaint, though she could tell he was suffering. Triage would have to wait.

Saffron lined up a shot, noting the steady barrage of incoming strikes from Be'naj's sword. Gullagion's staff seemed to be changing shape of its own accord to block Be'naj's weapon. The woman was a determined and skilled warrior, but that didn't mean she couldn't use some help.

Aiming for the middle of the ghast's back, Saffron released her arrow. The force of the impact was enough to distract Gullagion, who glanced over his shoulder before realizing his mistake.

With the shadowstaff out of position, Be'naj arced a swing level with the ghast's un-beating heart. The blade cut straight through his atrophic left arm and halfway into his chest cavity before stopping. Gullagion's legs gave way and he toppled to the ground, forcing Be'naj to release her weapon as he fell.

Watching from above, Saffron dipped her hand into Thaelios's quiver again … just in case. Gullagion didn't move, however, and Be'naj kicked his body over while removing her sword. Thaelios's gasp stole Saffron's attention. He was attempting to tie off his makeshift bandage with one hand.

"Let me help," she said, dropping to one knee and laying down his bow. She took hold of the torn sleeve and cinched it for him. His wound looked painful, and she could see the white of an exposed rib where the acid had eaten furthest. She wished Palomar had taught her his Song of Soothing. "Is there anything else I can do?"

"Water?" Thaelios answered, his lips quivering. "If you can find some."

All their water was with the camels, of course, which Dyphina had tied up who-knew-where before the battle. The caravan must have some, Saffron reasoned, and as she stood, Phaerim and Be'naj approached, the former regarding the angel-winged woman with awe.

"Saffron, we found you!" Be'naj nearly assaulted her with her embrace. Saffron slowly put her arms around Be'naj as well, returning the gesture tenderly, wishing the moment could stretch on forever.

"Where's Dyphina?" Phaerim finally interrupted, and Saffron forced herself to break contact.

Time for reunions and gratitude would come. They still hadn't accounted for the half-fey, let alone the fate of the thralls who guarded the wagons. "I heard her singing down by the caravan," Saffron responded. Phaerim nodded and turned. "I'll come with you," she added. "We need to find Thaelios some water. This is Be'naj, everyone. She's a friend."

Be'naj cast her eyes downward at the introduction.

Saffron quickly took her hand and squeezed. "Will you watch over Thaelios until we get back?" Be'naj raised her eyes and nodded. Saffron patted her hand and offered a smile, which Be'naj returned.

"Have you seen Cauzel?" she called out when Saffron started down the hill.

"You know my master?" Thaelios asked, the pain still stretching his voice.

Be'naj nodded. "We travelled together from Ifelian. He was scouting from above while I rode in on Sheen."

"Sheen?" Thaelios inquired.

"You brought my horse?" Saffron couldn't help herself when she heard her mare's name. Then, her mind started connecting information and her heart dropped into her stomach. "That was Cauzel?"

She turned and bolted down the hill toward the fallen troll and the body lying beside it on the scorched earth. Phaerim chased after, pulling up short when she stopped. She gasped and covered her mouth at what she saw. Indeed, it was Cauzel's broken body lying twisted on the ground, his dark, bushy hair and signature black robe instantly identifying him despite his contorted pose. The truth crashed over her like a tidal wave, dropping Saffron to her knees.

"Saffron, who is that?" Phaerim asked.

She could hear the fear for her in his voice, but her own lips trembled and she couldn't speak. When she tried giving an answer, she wept instead. Cauzel had given his life protecting her.

Pyre in the Desert

An immeasurable moment later, Saffron heard Be'naj gasp. A rush of feathers brushed her face as Be'naj sped to Cauzel's side. And still, Saffron couldn't seem to move.

"Cauzel, no!" Be'naj exclaimed, her hands firmly but gently turning him so she could look upon his face. The damage made it unrecognizable. She was checking to see if he might yet live, hoping perhaps that he was only unconscious, but Saffron knew better. She saw the blow from the troll that felled him, even though she hadn't realized it was Cauzel at the time.

He was gone, and though she hadn't known him long, Saffron knew he possessed a kind soul. He could have taught her so much. Forcing herself to stand and step closer, she rested a hand on Be'naj's shoulder as her friend's wings expanded and contracted ever so slightly, the feathers rolling hypnotically as if riding the incoming tide.

"He … he can't be dead," Be'naj whispered. "How will we …?"

Saffron looked around for additional enemies, aware they still might not be safe. Thaelios was occupied with his wound, still waiting for water, and Phaerim had wandered off, probably to find Dyphina. She had so many questions, but they would have to wait. Losing Cauzel hurt, but made it even more important she didn't allow any other casualties.

"Stay with him," she said, squeezing Be'naj's shoulder, the mail rough against her fingers. She sniffed to clear her nostrils. "I have to make sure the others are safe." Saffron picked her way around the heaps of previously animated bones, steering well clear of Gullagion's marred body, and headed for the wagons. She glanced over her shoulder at Be'naj, half-expecting her to have disappeared like a figment of her imagination.

Pleas, in desperate strains of Begnari, erupted from the back of the nearest wagon as she approached. "You've got to let us out of here!" "Set us free!" "Please help us!" The kanks shifted anxiously in their harness but showed no desire to resume pulling their load.

"I will," she responded without turning to look directly at them, lest she become distracted, "as soon as I know we're safe." This didn't stop their attempts at convincing her, but she blocked out their appeals as she crept around the wagon, searching for danger.

The second wagon was perpendicular to the road, some dozen paces east. Saffron froze when she spotted four skeletons clustered in front of it, spears clutched in their hands. She hummed the opening to her *Fire Blossom* song, but maintained the distance between them. As the swelling fire built within her, she noticed they didn't seem aware of her presence, nor to be moving at all.

Suddenly, Phaerim appeared from behind the furthest wagon. Its occupants followed him with their eyes, though they made no vocalizations. Jogging toward her, he completely ignored the skeletons and they did the same. Saffron broke off her tune, deciding the undead were no longer a threat.

"Saffron, over here," he called, waving her toward him.

She approached, shifting her uneasy gaze from the skeletons to the prisoners, who watched things playing out in an unnerving silence. Saffron could hear Dyphina's softly singing voice as she reached Phaerim, and relief flooded her at the sound.

When they rounded the second wagon, Saffron better understood the prisoners' restraint. Dyphina's skin and tunic had changed hue to match the thirst-cracked ground she stood upon. If not for her still-green hair and the sound of her singing, Saffron would have completely looked past her. Standing across from her, eyes glazed over in a trance, were a handful of humans dressed in padded armor and armed with an assortment of blades. From their collars, Saffron deduced they were fellow slaves of the Wolfspider.

"I think she's ensorcelled them, but I don't know what will happen if she stops singing," Phaerim said. "I could slit their throats ..."

Saffron shook her head. "They're not our enemies."

"Who's going to convince them of that?"

Dyphina shifted her eyes toward Saffron, though she continued facing the conscripts while humming her mesmerizing tune. Walking to her side, Saffron decided diplomacy was worth a try. She placed a hand on Dyphina's shoulder for reassurance. "You can bring them out of it." Turning to Phaerim, she quickly added, "But stay ready just in case."

The half-fey apprentice ceased her harmonics, shoulders slumping as she exhaled. Her camouflaged appearance shifted back to normal as well. Within a few breaths, the collared guards all began blinking and stretching their faces.

Saffron raised her hands, palms out, demonstrating she was unarmed. "The undead lieutenant is slain, and we mean you no harm," she said in Begnari. "You are free men." She leaned over her shoulder and raised her voice so those in the wagons could hear. "You are all free, now."

The guards considered her and her companions for a moment, then seemed to pick up on the absence of the rock-troll enforcers. "What has happened?" one of them asked. He was Begnari, lean with sunken eyes, and armed with a scimitar.

"We have come to emancipate you. We were gladiators in the Wolfspider's pens not long ago." Saffron pointed to her own neck, referencing their collars. "No one should live in cages."

The man nodded, looking at Dyphina once more before turning to the nearest wagon.

"Will you help us free them?" Saffron continued, hoping she'd read him correctly.

"Aye," he responded. "But one of the trolls kept the keys around his neck."

"One of the trolls has the keys," she relayed to Phaerim in Illanese.

"On it," Phaerim offered instantly, cutting back toward the southern slope where he had brought the first one down. The guards split up to carry explanations between the different wagons.

Saffron turned to check on Dyphina. "Are you unharmed?"

Dyphina blew a stray strand of hair from her face. "I am," she smiled. "Still a little impressed that spell worked on so many at once."

"I'm glad it did." After a pause, Saffron added, "I'm afraid not all the news is good." Watching Dyphina's expression of satisfaction crumble, she wasn't sure where to find the words to tell her about their mentor.

"Did Thaelios fall?" Dyphina guessed.

Saffron shook her head. "He took a spell from Gullagion and is badly injured, but still alive."

Relief and sober understanding swirled across Dyphina's features before she nodded. "What can I do to help?"

"We need to find some water to treat his wound, and some actual bandages wouldn't hurt, either. But that's not all ..." Saffron found it difficult to swallow. "Be'naj and Cauzel found us, somehow. Came to our aid. Cauzel didn't ... couldn't ..." She didn't have to say any more. A frown corrupted the inherent beauty of Dyphina's countenance and she rushed past Saffron to verify the truth.

Saffron remained rooted to the spot, attempting to master her own emotions until Phaerim showed up with a large ring of keys.

"I found them," he stated plainly.

She exhaled deeply. *Move to the next task.* She joined Phaerim at the nearest wagon. In addition to their cages, each held a covered compartment for supplies in its rear, which Phaerim discovered and unlocked as well.

Saffron found a cache of water bladders under a spare saddle blanket and handed one to Phaerim. "Take this to Thaelios, will you? I'm going to talk with the prisoners, then we can plan our next move. I don't think it's best to stay here too long."

"Agreed." Phaerim took the full waterskin and left Saffron to figure out how she was going to tell the two dozen citizens of Zeblon that they couldn't return home. They'd already spilled out from the confines of their respective cages.

Some milled about taking in the scene of battle, some chatted with their neighbors about what would happen next, while others bemoaned their empty stomachs and began sifting through the wagons' storage compartments for nourishment. A good many stood silently, likely in disbelief that this wasn't just another cruel trick unfolding in the desert.

"Can everyone hear me?" Saffron called out in Begnari, making her way into the thickest swath of gathered prisoners. "For your own safety, I need you to listen." Most of their heads turned toward her, and the pockets of conversation evaporated like sweat in the desert sun.

"Good," she said, once satisfied with their attention. "I am Saffron min-Furasi. Some of you may recognize me from my appearances in the Arena of Zeblon. Like you, I was taken against my will by those in league with the Dread Lich. But also like you, I am now free." She paused while looking over the crowd and was pleased to hear a majority of them murmuring agreement.

"That does not mean that any of us are yet beyond the reach of danger!" Just as quickly, the voices died and Saffron reclaimed their full attention. "We all need to reach a place this evil will never touch us, but for now, survival means heading to the oasis as quickly as possible. From there, you will receive options on where to go next. Unfortunately, back to Zeblon is not one of them."

She allowed the crowd to react without interruption, some of them obviously upset at the prospect of not returning home. Better to deal with the reality now than draw things out to when the immediacy of gratitude had faded. The slave-guards stepped in and calmed the protestations in short order, pointing out that had it not been for their rescuers' intervention, they would all be following on the heels of the kanks toward their deaths.

When the noise receded, Saffron spoke again. "Is there one named 'Rhazine' among you? If so, I would speak with her privately ..."

Some of the freed prisoners looked over their shoulders, and amidst more muttering, a young woman finally advanced from the back of the crowd. Saffron guessed she was perhaps her sister's age, maybe a summer or two younger.

"I am Rhazine," she said, eyes kept low, one arm across her middle as its hand clasped her opposite elbow.

"Come," Saffron gestured for Rhazine to join her. "I have news for you. I will not bite," she added, seeing the girl's reluctance. Once Rhazine stepped forward, Saffron placed an arm around her back and led her around the corner of the nearest wagon.

"I hold no loyalty toward your father, but he did send us to rescue you. That was the price of our freedom, though I don't hold his faults against you." Saffron watched the girl's face closely for her reaction.

"My father?" Her brown eyes looked up at Saffron, giving nothing away.

Saffron sighed. "You are the daughter of the Wolfspider, are you not?" Under her hard stare, Rhazine looked away, confirming the truth of it. "Your father has placed a man at the oasis who will recognize you. He will lead you to a secret location where your needs will be met. I wouldn't let the others know who your father is, if they don't already know, for your own safety. What I said to the others stands for you as well – you will not be able to return to Zeblon."

Rhazine brought her eyes back to meet Saffron's. "Is it Harzhim?"

"What?"

"Waiting for me at the oasis … he said he'd find a way for us to be together, even after I told him it was too risky and sent him away." After her declaration, Rhazine struggled to maintain eye contact.

A wave of understanding for Harzhim's odd behavior crashed over Saffron, and she felt stabs of sympathy for both of them, but it was nothing she was going to dwell on. "No." She decided to keep it simple. "Harzhim is not there."

Rhazine tucked her chin in response but almost instantly perked up again. "Where are you going?"

The question surprised Saffron. She had been striving to return to Ifelian and Blackfeather Perch to continue her studies with Cauzel, but that part of her dream had shattered with his death. She wasn't sure she had an answer, yet. "My home is far away," was all she said.

"Can I come with you? If I'm to be exiled, I at least deserve a new life."

Saffron found herself shaking her head before she could articulate any objections. "You don't know me, and I don't know you. Why would you even want to come with me?"

Rhazine shrugged. "I saw you fight in the Arena," she mumbled. "You can do magic."

That wasn't a good reason, was it? Saffron had already started calculating the difficulties of taking along another refugee before shaking her head again and striking the idea altogether. "I'm sorry," she said. "My path is too dangerous, and I've got enough responsibility as it is."

Saffron abandoned the conversation and walked back to where the collared warriors had congregated. She decided to put them in charge of the caravan, but wanted to gift them further safety before parting ways. "Do you think you can manage to drive the kanks?" she asked the lot of them. Several nodded. "Good. We need to leave as soon as possible. Get the others loaded up, and I'll return with the key to your collars."

With heavy steps, she finally joined her friends around the fallen Cauzel. Be'naj was helping clean Thaelios's wounds. Phaerim sat with Dyphina, cross-legged on the blackened earth, staring across at Be'naj's wings. Cauzel had been moved into a more restful pose, and the satchel carrying his belongings rested beside Dyphina.

What were they going to do now? Saffron certainly didn't have an answer, and she wished someone else would just make all the decisions so she could give in to the weariness that threatened to overwhelm her.

Staring at the unmoving Shaper, she realized his marred face wasn't the only part she didn't recognize. He seemed smaller, shorter than she remembered, and his hands were iridescent gray, like granite-flecked steel. This imposter wasn't Cauzel, he was an Eladrin! She opened her mouth to announce her discovery but looked again at Dyphina, who was seated directly beside him. She'd known him longer; how could she have not noticed?

Saffron didn't want to upset anyone further but had to address what was now obvious. "Be'naj, you said you travelled all the way here with Cauzel, no?"

Be'naj momentarily looked over her shoulder at the question. "Yes. Overland and then by ship."

"And this is the same person you travelled with?" Saffron gestured to the black-robed body. While she waited for a response, something cold and wet pushed up against her cheek, causing her to jump. "Sheen!" A spring of joy welled up inside her at the sight of her steed, momentarily drowning the doubt and pain. She clasped both arms around the horse's neck, who lowered her forehead to meet Saffron's.

Thaelios must have pieced together what she was after, despite the distraction, and responded first. "Cauzel was apparently Eladrin, Saffron. He lied to all of us." His voice sounded hollow, like there were no feelings behind it at all.

Be'naj nodded, though her attention stayed with her hands as they wrapped Thaelios's torso with a bolt of fresh cloth. "He revealed it to me, though only after I saw the truth," she said.

The hope that had momentarily emerged within Saffron crawled back into its deep, black pit. *Move to the next task.* "I need to retrieve the key to unlock the slave collars," she said, mustering her best semblance of normalcy and patting Sheen's neck. "Dyphina, would you come along to direct me to the camels?"

Dyphina nodded and rose.

"We'll be back, shortly," Saffron announced, mounting her horse and assisting Dyphina in climbing behind her. Saffron knew the general direction, and they'd passed beyond the hill to the north of the road before either of them spoke.

"Be'naj is exquisite," Dyphina finally said. "I can see why you'd want her."

"What?" Such thoughts were the furthest thing from Saffron's mind at the moment.

"I saw how you looked at her back there," Dyphina added. "I'm just saying I understand." She squeezed Saffron's waist a little tighter.

Saffron couldn't even contemplate a response, though her friend's words brought back how much she'd missed Be'naj during their months of separation. She shook the thoughts away. "Which way to the camels?"

Dyphina rode one of the pack animals back while Saffron tethered the other to Sheen. By the time they returned, most of the Zeblon refugees had boarded the wagons, though a few refused to do so in favor of walking, Rhazine among them.

When Saffron used the glowing green skull key to remove the collars from the conscripted guards, they universally embraced her and thanked her for their freedom. She reminded them she hadn't done it alone, but they didn't seem any less appreciative.

"Good speed on your way to the oasis," she offered, "and may fair fortune follow you after!"

Phaerim and Be'naj had raided the wagons for a few additional supplies, mostly water, and Saffron claimed one of the skeleton's spears as the final packing of their camels commenced. Like bone statues, the animated dead stood inert in the middle of the thoroughfare, still bound together by dark magic.

Given their eerie presence and the reminder of undeath, the living agreed to burn Cauzel's body rather than bury it in the sand. They stripped wood from one of the wagons, and Dyphina wrapped his corpse in a shroud of the same cloth Be'naj had used to bandage Thaelios.

Saffron took charge of the body upon one camel, allowing the injured Thaelios to ride Sheen, who was easier to manage. Be'naj insisted on walking until they'd finished the funeral rites, leaving Phaerim and Dyphina to take the second camel. They headed north of the road until the first stars shown above, though a band of blue persisted closer to the horizon.

Finally feeling clear of anything to do with the Wolfspider and Hadrian No More, Saffron proposed they set up camp and prepare to pay their last respects. They ate a quick meal in relative silence. Saffron imagined the others were also reflecting on personal memories with the Shaper, save Phaerim. He'd never met Cauzel, though he seemed to understand the man had meant something to the rest of them and refrained from asking questions. She appreciated that.

As the indigo sky deepened toward the horizon, marked by distant dunes, Dyphina and Be'naj prepared the body upon a simple pyre of the planks they'd pried from the wagon. They doused the shroud in oil, then the five of them formed a circle around Cauzel, with Saffron holding a burning brand from the campfire.

Dyphina was first to break the silence. "As great a Shaper as Cauzel Blackfeather was, I don't think any of us really knew him. That's easier to realize now, of course, knowing he hid his heritage from us, but that was only one secret amongst a sea of arcane secrets we never got to glimpse. I truly believe, given time, he would have revealed more, for that's what he did. He enjoyed sharing his knowledge, and we all benefited from knowing him."

When it became clear she was done speaking, Thaelios took over. "Master Blackfeather shared my language – I knew that much. Apparently, he shared my culture as well. It is challenging me, coming to terms with the inherent deceit, but everything I experienced with him as my teacher suggests he must have had good reason to hide who he was. I will mourn his passing and the lost opportunity to learn more from him."

"I did not interact with Cauzel long enough to feel betrayal," Saffron began. "He did not owe me anything. Yet, he still gifted me a greater understanding of myself and of the magic that is undeniably part of me. For that generosity, he has my gratitude." She looked across the circle to Be'naj, who stood nearest Cauzel's shrouded head. The half-Eladrin, half-Aasimar looked truly otherworldly, her wings outstretched in the waning light, the bright hair of her bowed head whipping in a sudden swirl of desert wind. Saffron waited a moment, unsure if Be'naj had any words of her own to share. She didn't want to ignite Cauzel's body if there were still goodbyes to be said.

Just as Saffron took a step forward and lowered the brand, Be'naj raised her head, the dimmed jade of her shadowed eyes peering straight at her. Saffron held still, then straightened as Be'naj finally spoke.

"I have not known Cauzel long, either, but we travelled across the world together. I found that he usually had answers while my heart only poses questions. When I told him I needed to find you, he helped. He gave me guidance. And eventually," she lifted a palm toward Saffron, who realized Be'naj was speaking to her directly, "we did."

Saffron could just make out the glisten of wetness on Be'naj's cheek. No one else had shed a tear.

"He was already sick," Be'naj continued, shaking her head, "though he wouldn't admit it. Something in the tomb infected him," she sniffed sharply, composing herself, "but he never complained. I suppose we should not now." She dropped to one knee, bent forward, and kissed Cauzel's wrapped forehead. "You will be missed, *ashenn jolech nabari*."

"*Ashenn javar*," Thaelios answered.

As Be'naj stood, Phaerim unexpectedly cleared his throat, clasping his hands together. "I, uh, never knew this man, but I can only hope that when I die there will be people who care enough to remember me like this. May his gods give him rest."

Saffron nodded, pausing to make sure no one had anything to add. With silence winning out, she knelt and reached out her burning brand, touching it to the oil-soaked cloth. The flame instantly licked across the surface of the shroud, and Saffron retook her stance in the circle.

Knowing the fire lacked the fuel to adequately burn the Shaper's body, Saffron began singing. She thought of the lesson Cauzel had given her on amplification and concentrated on harnessing magical essence into the flame. The fire grew taller, changed to blueish-green, and Saffron could feel its intensity rise as well. Everyone took a few steps backward and shielded their eyes from the brightness. Ignoring the smell of cooking flesh, she sang on, even as her throat grew dry and more stars came out to greet her, until nothing remained to burn.

Sitting around their small campfire afterward, Saffron felt exhausted, yet unable to sleep. Be'naj had taken a seat directly beside her, and she badly wished for some privacy so they could share everything that had happened to one another since parting.

As usual, wishing didn't yield results, and eventually Phaerim brought up the question Saffron guessed was on the other apprentices' minds as well.

"So, where do we go from here? We're not just going to become hermits and crawl into holes in the sand or something, arc wc?"

"It seems strange to return to Ifelian with Cauzel gone," Dyphina mused. "I was considering going home to Hithannon from here, though it's a long journey, either way."

"Someone needs to let Iliana and Aurus know what became of Master Blackfeather," Thaelios added. "I intend to make my way back to the Perch. There is no doubt something yet to learn from the research still present in the tower ..."

"I don't think any of us should go home quite yet," Be'naj interjected, startling Saffron with her insistence. "Cauzel and I crossed the continent to find you, yes, but not only to set you free, I'm afraid."

Saffron shifted to look directly at Be'naj. She'd certainly grown more confident in her Illanese since they'd parted. "What else did you have in mind?" she asked.

"Cauzel was working with me to unravel the meaning of a dire prophecy I believe came from Shecclad. After ensuring you were all safe, we were headed to the ancient eladrin city of Tarmuth." Following Be'naj's statement, the crackling of their meager fire was the only sound for a few moments.

"What exactly does that mean: dire prophecy?" Thaelios asked.

"I've received trance-visions since I was a girl," Be'naj explained, her voice calm. "Shortly after meeting Saffron, I had one with words, as well. It warned of danger to the Eladrin, and suggested acquiring the means to prevent disaster started with a trip to the buried city."

"*Buried* city?" Saffron repeated.

Be'naj nodded. "We found a book in the Keeper's Library explaining the significance of Tarmuth, of how it was the experimentation ground of Trigilas himself."

"The Father of Spells?" Thaelios chimed in, obviously intrigued.

Be'naj affirmed again, feeding off his interest. "The 'Hall of Doors' was magically sealed and buried in a sandstorm, but we stopped in Lucnere along the way to get a key from Cauzel's deceased teacher. That's when he fell ill.

"I intend to continue the quest, but don't know if I can succeed without help." She turned to Saffron and lay a hand upon her protruding knee. "I hoped you'd come with me, once I found you."

A part of Saffron yearned to scream "*Yes!*" But there was more to consider than the urging of her heart. Words of any kind resisted escaping her mouth at the moment. "I, I don't know." She turned to Dyphina for support of the weakening voice of her conscience. "What about all the slaves still working in the mines? What about the rest of the gladiators in Zeblon? What about … Phaerim?" she asked, turning to the odd man out.

He shrugged. "I think a buried city sounds exciting. I figure I'd have died back in those mines by now if I hadn't met the three of you. So, any time I have left is not really mine. If this 'Cauzel' fellow died fighting for you, seems right to try and finish what he was doing, eh?"

"You can't save the world all at once, Saffron," Dyphina offered with a note of sympathy. "There are wrongs everywhere you look. That's the way of things. If Cauzel was trying to save the Eladrin, his own people as it turns out, that seems as noble a cause as any." The half-fey played with the braided locks by her ear while appearing in momentary consideration. "I'll come with you, Be'naj," she finally said.

"Aye," Thaelios added.

Phaerim grinned. "Aye."

They all looked at Saffron.

She sighed deeply and shook her head, but was smiling also. "Aye."

Chapter 30

The Sands of Tarmuth

When morning came, they looked through Cauzel's satchel for the map on which he'd marked the location of Ancient Tarmuth. Thaelios pointed out it was almost a week's travel north, through what they had to assume was more desert.

Saffron was experienced in such terrain, having grown up in Begnasharan, and bluntly explained that while the camels would be fine, they were going to need more water. Sheen, especially, would have need of an oasis along the way in order to survive.

None of them had any idea what lay ahead, however, and if Cauzel had a plan as to how to proceed beyond that point, he hadn't shared it with Be'naj.

Be'naj took Saffron's hand and softened her with one gaze of her large, green eyes. "The fact Cauzel never brought it to attention suggests it may not be too serious," she argued.

"Yes, but Cauzel could apparently fly," Saffron interjected. "A great number of things may not have been concerning to him."

"We'll be careful with what we have, and I'm sure a solution will present itself."

Given their current abundance of water, no one else seemed to take Saffron's reservations to heart, but she knew a change of attitude would come as soon as they spent a few days sweating under the hot sun. She exchanged her leather armor for a lighter tunic and convinced Be'naj to change out of her protective mail into one of her spare outfits as well.

After looking at the map, Thaelios extracted Cauzel's personal spellbook from the satchel with trembling hands. He leafed through a few pages as a wide-eyed grin stretched across his face. Saffron had to prod him twice to put it away because everyone wanted to begin the journey.

At least it was winter, Saffron reasoned, though the sun was still a danger with so much exposure. Once they stopped for the night, she took stock of their supplies and guessed they had two more days before Sheen would start to suffer from their water rationing. She silently prayed to Hizune that he would provide for them among the dunes, for she didn't want to contemplate losing her horse to the desert.

After the sun set, the cold became a larger issue than the heat had been. They bundled up as best they could and huddled to sleep, but without shelter or anything left to burn, the wind and nearly freezing temperatures sucked much of that warmth from them. Saffron woke to the sound of chattering teeth more than once and couldn't always be sure they weren't hers.

During their downtime, Thaelios seemed to be cycling between Cauzel's spellbook and another text, *Sites of Magical Influence*, which Be'naj explained they had borrowed from the Keeper's Library in Gilsage. With his left arm bound to his side to aid in its healing, he enlisted Dyphina to help turn the pages, and she followed along nearly as eagerly.

Be'naj showed them the passage outlining the steps to open the Crypt of Broken Names, including the chant that would have to be recited. She even brought out the macabre talisman of demon claws Cauzel had liberated from the tomb of Embril the Shaper. While the others seemed fascinated, Saffron's worry grew. She guessed they would end up missing Cauzel more than they knew.

Be'naj also returned the pendant of Living Fire to Saffron, but explained how Cauzel had attuned it to counter the Dampening Stone, so she shouldn't use it until they'd overcome that obstacle.

The desert shifted between loping hills of sand and patches of dry, cracked earth, from one day to the next. Saffron kept an eye out for any signs of water but vegetation was sparse, and she grew more concerned as they made camp on the fourth night. They'd been extremely careful but would run out of water the next day while travelling, unless they denied Sheen her share.

After changing back into her kank-leather armor to serve as another layer against the nightly cold, Saffron casually asked Dyphina if Cauzel's spellbook contained any incantations for their predicament. She'd already skimmed through it for a solution and come up empty.

While everyone else was bedding down for the night, Saffron went to do a final check on the animals. The camels were already lying down next to one another, legs tucked beneath them. She hadn't bothered untying their packs, since their load rested on the ground while they slept. One of them groaned when she came near, but they seemed content enough.

"You'll get more water when we find it, I promise," Saffron whispered before moving on toward Sheen. The moons were down to just green and blue slivers, but the stars were out in force, and the silhouette of her still-standing horse was highlighted by their soft, yellow light.

Sheen's saddle sat beside her on the ground, along with her saddle bags. She whinnied at Saffron's hand running along her rump. "I know, girl, it's getting cold again. How about another blanket?" As she retrieved a second, thick cloth from one of the packs to unfold over Sheen's back, the red glow of the Living Fire drew her attention. "You might keep me from tripping over myself in the dark," she said, withdrawing the pendant and fastening it around her neck.

She felt a little uncomfortable wearing jewelry the King-priest had forged, but realized that was silly. Jaiden had assured her all his enchantments had broken upon his death. She finished tucking Sheen in, rubbed the spot between her horse's ears, and started back toward the others, using the pendant as a candle.

Only a few paces from her horse, she spotted something sticking up out of the sand. "Oh, Be'naj must have lost this," she said aloud as if Sheen were still listening, then bent to pick up a thin feather. It looked almost violet in the red light of the Living Fire, but Saffron didn't think much of it, rolling the plume between her fingers as she returned to her spot beside the winged warrior.

Dyphina and Phaerim were pressed close and sharing a blanket, appearing to already be asleep. Thaelios had entered his trance with Cauzel's spellbook still open, spilling halfway off his lap. Be'naj sat cross-legged, prepared to trance as well, though waiting for Saffron to return.

"I think you may be shedding," Saffron said lightly, holding out the feather to her friend.

Be'naj considered it with a momentary turn of her head, but resumed her meditative position almost immediately. "That's not one of mine," she said matter-of-factly. "Should I be jealous?" she added, the left side of her lips starting to curl.

Saffron held the feather up to the closest of Be'naj's wings and immediately saw the difference. She tucked the pendant under her outer tunic to get a clearer look under the starlight. The feather, much thinner than the half-Aasimar's, was most definitely some sort of bluish hue. "That's odd." It was the first sign of animal life they'd had, beyond reptiles and scorpions, since entering the desert. "Perhaps that means there's water near," she allowed herself to hope aloud.

"Hmm," Be'naj hummed in mild interest. "Maybe we should fan out tomorrow to cover more territory?"

"Yes," Saffron said, sliding down into a more restful pose and throwing her own blanket over her legs. "We should do that." She held the feather in front of her face and blew on it a few times, watching its fibers bend to her breath. She knew falling asleep was the quickest way to escape the cold already numbing her fingers, and was soon blissfully ignorant.

Saffron's nightmare of dozens of insects biting her face all at once was interrupted by Be'naj seizing and lifting her upright by the shoulders. "We need to find shelter, now!" she roared above the wind, which whipped sand through the air all around them.

The night had grown heavier, the stars all obscured by the dust cloud that was thickening with each moment. Saffron jolted to her feet, though her mind was somewhat slower in its transition to wakefulness. She could see the broad, white shape of Be'naj's wings nearby, but little else. Bowing her head to keep the sand from her eyes, she stumbled in the direction she imagined Sheen to be, but had only gone a few steps before Be'naj seized her hand and yanked her away.

The wind had grown deafening, and Saffron's heart beat a hundred times with every breath. Where was her horse? Where were the others? She knew nothing outside the confusion of wind and sand, but for the hand pulling her along and the mass of feathers brushing against her arm and face.

They were trying to run, but even that was becoming more difficult. Sand was deepening around her feet, and soon Saffron was trudging through a calf-high layer of silt. They continued on and Saffron had to close her eyes, the stinging was so bad. Another few moments and the sand was up past her knees. Her legs burned with the effort, the cold of sleep a distant memory. Where was Be'naj leading her?

Her hand slipped from Be'naj's grasp and Saffron stopped moving, terrified she'd lost the one, familiar thing she had left. Her heart had beat another thousand times before she felt something against her arm and fingers once again clasped her wrist. Cracking her lids for a peek, she saw the sky was gone entirely. She was inside a cloud of stinging dust, and waves of sand crashed into her like she was wading in a perverse ocean sucked dry of its own moisture.

Running was no longer possible. She was now shifting her entire body to move inch-by-inch as the sand reached her hips, then her waist, climbing ever higher. Be'naj's hand left her again, and Saffron felt the despair of knowing it was for the last time. She was paralyzed from her chest down and possessed just enough cognizance to realize the inevitability of being buried alive.

How had fighting through so many hardships come to this? Caught in a desert storm on the wrong side of the world, her prayers to Hizune had obviously been meaningless. As the sand rose to her neck, Saffron struggled to stay calm, cupping her hands around her mouth and breathing normally for as long as she could, trying to think of a solution. She was wearing the Living Fire – surely that had to count for something. How could she use her own fire to escape her rising tomb? *Foolish woman, you can't breathe, let alone sing!*

Suddenly, the crashing of the wind went quiet. The sand had risen past her ears. At least it was easier to think. She'd saved a bubble of air to breathe within her hands, but that wouldn't last long with no fresh air to replace it. What could she do? What could she do? No ideas sprang forth, only the intruding thought that she'd run out of time.

Then, she heard something. It wasn't the wind or the sound of Be'naj calling her name, but a low, sliding sound, like the sand being disturbed somehow underneath the surface. The disturbance grew closer, though Saffron wasn't sure how she could tell until she absolutely felt movement and an investigatory prod against her cupped hands.

She inhaled sharply at the bump, which she immediately regretted as sand infiltrated her mouth. Whatever it was moved away, until the disturbance ceased altogether, to Saffron's relief. The only thing she could think of at the moment that was worse than being buried alive was being eaten alive while buried.

But the silence didn't persist. A whirring sound suddenly filled her existence, followed by the realization that the sand above her head was definitely moving, and quickly. A few dozen heartbeats and Saffron could breathe, though she once again felt the blast of wind upon her face.

She dared to open her eyes but was greeted by a backwards reality that insisted she may have been dreaming the whole time. Caught within a vortex that bore into the sand around her, expelling it outward, she had the impression of being in a huge tub of sand as it drained. At the same time, rain fell from above, and she stuck out her tongue to confirm that the drops were indeed water.

Looking around, she saw her companions were all accounted for, strung out in a line but separated by only an arms-length or two between them. They wriggled to get free and gasped for breath, so she knew they were all still alive. Once the sand was down to about their waists, the whirlwind instantly dissipated, leaving behind the sound of coughing and the pounding of rain.

The rain came down so hard it pooled on the surface of the sand, with ever more liquid sliding down from the bowl-like incline around them. Saffron joined the others in digging the rest of their bodies out as quickly as they could, the wonder of their freedom suspended by a new spurt of panic.

Be'naj was free first and helped lift Saffron from the sand, though they were already knee-deep in rising water. Thaelios needed the most help, given his injury, but once they were all unburied, they crawled to higher ground.

Momentarily safe, Saffron lay on her back in exhaustion, the cold rain soaking her completely. She opened her eyes at a crack of thunder. Tilting her head up and wiping the water from her eyes, she spied a flutter of color in the air. It came to a hovering stop, several body-lengths above, and the origin of the blue feather suddenly made sense.

The couatl they had set free from beneath the Arena had found them! It seemed to consider her, its tongue occasionally darting out to taste the air. Its wings moved amazingly fast, allowing it to dart through the air like a hummingbird. Moving closer to Dyphina, it spoke and she responded, though Saffron couldn't make anything out above the rain. Suddenly, it plunged down into the sand, burrowing beyond view.

"We should wait out the rain here!" Dyphina yelled with her hands beside her mouth. Saffron was so exhausted, she accepted the instruction without challenge, and it turned out they didn't need much patience. The downpour slowed to a slight shower shortly after, then vanished altogether as a predawn glow reclaimed the western horizon.

The couatl emerged erelong and hovered near Dyphina as it spoke to her in the mysterious tongue of the fey. When their conversation was over, the creature landed upon the sand and coiled upon itself as if resting.

"Did you thank it?" Saffron asked. "How did it know we were in trouble?"

Dyphina bowed her head, then took a few steps closer and relayed, "I did. He's been watching over us since we arrived at the oasis. He could not find the camels or Sheen, I'm afraid."

Be'naj turned to Saffron and laid a hand softly upon her shoulder. "They had already run off by the time I became aware of the storm," she offered. "Sheen might have outrun it, or found shelter …"

Saffron accepted the news and steeled herself. Her horse was exceptionally perceptive, after all, and had survived other dangers. Just as well they were parted now, for there was likely no place for her where they were headed. Except … "What about our food? What about the talisman to unlock the door?" She went from person to person with a questioning look.

"I've got my water bladder," Phaerim announced proudly.

"I have Cauzel's spellbook, but no food," Thaelios admitted.

"I have … nothing," Be'naj acknowledged with a sigh.

"Nor I," said Dyphina, who still looked radiant despite her wet hair and clothes.

Saffron pushed back the frustration that threatened to consume her like the desert almost had. They were alive, when they shouldn't be. That would get her through the day. It had to. "Well, the last I saw the map, the fastest way out of the desert was north anyway, so we might as well continue on."

The winged snake rose up and spoke again, causing Dyphina to announce, "The couatl says he will guide us to our destination if we'll tell him where we're going."

Saffron was out of ideas and shrugged in return. As Dyphina continued her conversation in fey, the rest took drinks from Phaerim's bladder until it was empty, then he refilled it with rainwater.

Soon they were on the move once more, though now on foot. That first day seemed the longest, as Saffron couldn't help looking back for Sheen, hoping to see her outline somewhere along the horizon. The rain brought a remarkable transformation in the affected land, as numerous plants sprang into bloom with the sudden nourishment.

The next day brought a return to sterilization as they progressed, and the day after that was the same, with no outward signs of danger or their lost animals. Hunger overtook thirst among their concerns, for the couatl at least found them another drinking hole along the way.

As they waited out the midday heat around the murky pool, Be'naj called out Thaelios for staring incessantly at her wings.

"My apologies, Be'naj. I was just considering our problem regarding the loss of Cauzel's claw talisman. If your father truly was not born of this world, then such a trait might be inheritable. Even if you're a native of Elisahd, the magic involved may not make a distinction."

Be'naj languidly flapped her wings. "That's what I said to Cauzel, but he wasn't sure." She seemed excited to have someone else take up her idea.

Thaelios raised the palm of his still mobile hand. "Nor am I," he said. "But it's certainly worth a try. Of course, we won't be able to test the idea until we reach the door."

Saffron wasn't holding out hope for such things. She simply wanted to find some semblance of civilization before they all starved or dried into dust.

Late in the afternoon on the third day since the storm, the couatl announced to Dyphina that it'd spotted something notable ahead. Soon, they reached a spot where stone ruins protruded from the sand, revealing the tops of mostly buried buildings. A deep, throbbing hum caught their attention as they drew closer, and following it to the source, they reached the exposed stone of a large pedestal.

Upon the pedestal was a black sphere, the origin of the hum, which was obviously magical. The sphere was taller than Saffron and looked somewhat like black marble, though the discolored swirls of lighter pigment moved as if its core was spinning.

Thaelios approached, mouth agape, his right hand upon his bottom lip. "This must be the Dampening Stone mentioned in the book … it's bigger than I expected." He drew even closer, extending his right hand as if to touch its surface.

"I wouldn't, Thaelios!" Be'naj admonished. "It's from the Abyss, and Cauzel worked for weeks attuning the Living Fire to affect it, so I'm sure it's powerful."

"Of course," he said, lowering his hand and taking a step back.

"Well," Be'naj continued, turning to Saffron, "it's up to you, if you're ready."

"What's that?" Saffron asked – she'd turned her attention back to the swirling darkness of the Stone.

"The Dampening Stone prevents all magic. In order for us to complete the incantation to open the door to the Crypt of Broken Names, you'll have to disable it with your pendant." Be'naj nodded toward the jewel around Saffron's neck.

Saffron unclasped its chain before looking at the other apprentices. "Does anyone know how?"

Dyphina shook her head. Thaelios answered meekly, "I suppose you just … bring them into contact."

Saffron swallowed and looked to Be'naj, who gave an encouraging nod. Climbing the mound of sand that brought her within reach of the Stone, she held the back of the pendant's platinum setting and gently pressed the ruby against the spinning heart of chaos.

The ruby sank into the blackness as if it was liquid, and the Dampening Stone's hum immediately changed frequency. Saffron had to let go of the pendant before it was completely consumed or risk touching the Stone herself. She wasn't sure what she'd expected, but losing the Living Fire completely certainly hadn't been it.

"Did it work?" Phaerim asked.

"Why don't you sing something, Saffron?" Dyphina asked.

"Why don't you?" she snapped. Saffron felt that, whatever this magic was, it was far beyond her capabilities, and that made it dangerous.

Thaelios sighed. "*Aperon ishti falak.*" He flicked his right wrist upward and a slew of crackling sparks jumped from his fingertips. "It worked. Now, we have to find the door."

They fanned out and searched the ruins, though Saffron felt fairly useless as she couldn't read Eladrin, and therefore couldn't interpret any of the runes that marked the exposed portions of buildings. She wondered how much of the city was buried under the sand and how many had been caught unaware when the storm had come.

After over an hour of looking, Be'naj announced victory. The top of a damaged archway bore writing that pronounced it the "Hall of Doors," as the location in question had originally been named. Problem was, the doorway itself was still buried.

Dyphina whistled, and the couatl came streaking down from the sky. She spoke with it briefly, nodded, and then told the rest of them to stand back. The winged snake flew higher and the air started spinning beneath it until a funnel cloud appeared and began excavating the sand.

Saffron backed further away and shielded herself from the spraying granules. "How does it do that?" she asked the nearby Thaelios.

"Couatl's are said to be masters of Air," he explained. "They have magic that gives them power over the element."

Within minutes, the cyclone had cleared out enough of the sand for the five of them to slide down to the building's base, at least two body-lengths below. Its door was metallic and marked with runes. In place of a handle, a molded hand reached out from the door, palm up and fingers spread.

"Shall we?" Thaelios asked Be'naj. When she nodded, he plucked one of the brass-colored feathers from the end of her wing. He placed the feather onto the hand and began reciting the chant he'd thankfully memorized from *Sites of Magical Influence.*

Be'naj reached over and slid her hand into Saffron's. They looked into one another's eyes, and Be'naj smiled as her fingers squeezed.

Saffron couldn't help smiling too, though she wasn't sure why she felt particularly hopeful – they were still starving with very little water between them.

When the chant was completed, a loud *snap* announced the magical seal on the door had broken. The metal panel swung open an arm's length or so on its own. No fanfare, no ostentatious display accompanied their violation of the centuries-old, protective magic. The door to the Crypt of Broken Names was simply open, and they had but to step through.

PHILLIP M. LOCEY

Phillip studied Creative Writing at the University of
North Carolina at Chapel Hill and earned a Master's in
Library and Information Science from the
University of South Florida.
Weaned on the fantasy genre from a young age,
he spent decades creating the imagined world of Elisahd,
where the majority of his tales are now set.

Visit elisahdbooks.com for more stories,
artwork, and news about books to come!

Check out "The Hall of Doors,"
Book 3 in The Chain of Living Fire